DOCTOR WHO

RECKLESS ENGINEERING
NICK WALTERS

CW00550485

BBC

DOCTOR WHO: RECKLESS ENGINEERING

Commissioning Editor: Ben Dunn
Editor & Creative Consultant:
Justin Richards
Project Editor: Jacqueline Rayner

Published by BBC Worldwide Ltd
Woodlands, 80 Wood Lane
London W12 0TT

First published 2003

ISBN 0 563 48603 1
Cover imaging by Black Sheep, copyright © BBC 2003

Printed and bound in Great Britain by
Mackays of Chatham
Cover printed by Belmont Press Ltd, Northampton

For IKB and Bristol

Bristol, 1 November 1831

It was like the aftermath of a battle. Fires still smouldered within the ruined buildings, sending columns of smoke up into the autumn sky. The square was littered with rubble and wreckage. The red uniforms of the Dragoon Guards were the sole points of colour in the dismal scene. Some stood or sat, fatigue evident in their soot-streaked faces. Others were still busy, moving people on, searching the burned buildings for valuables, or for bodies. People passed through the square, some daring to call out at the soldiers, others hurrying on, not wishing to tarry in the arena of destruction.

In the centre of the square, a statue of William III on horseback stood as it had for almost a century, supported on a mighty block of stone. A man was leaning against the plinth. A nondescript young man with thinning blond hair, wearing a long overcoat and a scarf wrapped up under his chin. He had a pale, studious face with wide, sensitive blue eyes.

His name was Jared Malahyde, and he was a poet.

The conflagration had stirred up an unusual number of gulls. They wheeled across the sky, seeming to slalom between the drifting pillars of smoke. Malahyde watched the birds whilst he tried to take in the devastation before him, tried to quell the sense of dread and foreboding rising in his heart.

Queen Square had been set afire, on its North and West sides. Not a building had escaped – not even the mansion house, or the Custom House; none of the merchants' houses.

Soot coated every surface, and the neat short-cut grass of the square had been churned into a slurry of ash and mud by countless footsteps and soldiers on horseback. The air had a smoky, infernal taint. Malahyde's throat itched and his eyes wouldn't stop watering.

The riots had lasted for three days. Malahyde had only been tangentially aware of them, hearing reports from fellow customers in his usual coffee-shop. Alarming reports of looting, prison break-outs, destruction of property. Something to do with the rejection of Lord Grey's Reform Bill, he had heard. He had never cared for politics. Whatever their cause, the mere occurrence of these disturbances was enough to worry Malahyde. They could be a symptom of a far greater malaise.

Could this be the beginning of the Fall?

Poets are the unacknowledged legislators of the world, or so Shelley had written – a phrase which Malahyde had seized upon with youthful vigour, as though living in lodgings in south Bristol, scratching out verses on cheap paper by candle-light, straining his eyesight and his imagination, was anything like wielding the sword of truth of which Shelley spoke. But Shelley had also said that poets were the mirrors of the gigantic shadows which futurity casts upon the present. That phrase had always stood out to Malahyde as incongruous and melodramatic. But remembering Shelley's words now, he shivered. *Could he have known?* he wondered. For he, Jared Malahyde, had been touched by the biggest shadow of all. His calling now was not to merely reflect the shadow of the future in verse, but to prevent its ever being cast.

He coughed and rubbed his eyes, looking around the devastated square. He couldn't help feeling that these riots were the very finger-edges of the shadow, clawing its way into the chilly November day.

Malahyde looked up at the statue. From this angle, William III's horse, depicted in mid canter, seemed demonic, its iron nostrils flared and its hoof raised as if to strike down and crush Malahyde's skull. By a quirk of fate, the statue King's gaze – imperious, unseeing – looked over towards the smouldering rooftops of the ruined buildings. Malahyde fancied he could detect a cast of sadness in the burnished metal.

He stepped away from the plinth, began thinking of a stanza

about the King's statue, then banished the thought. He strode across
the square, kicking up the ash.

*Why? Why was I chosen for this? Why not someone more fitting
– why not an engineer, like –*

Like the man he was going to see.

An hour later, Jared Malahyde arrived in Clifton. It was an area he
had never visited before, though he had heard of it from his friends
and his father's business acquaintances. Here the wealthy and
eminent merchants of Bristol had taken up residence on the
limestone heights above the city. It was a fashionable, genteel area –
wide streets of elegant, tall buildings, untainted by the smoke and
bustle of commerce. Or civil disturbances, reflected Malahyde as he
traipsed from street to street. It had been a long walk and he was
feeling tired. His head seemed to throb in time with his heartbeat.
The cold November wind caressing his face soothed him, a little.

Malahyde stopped at the end of a curving terrace of impeccable
three-storey town houses. Even on this dull autumn day their
stonework seemed to shine with an inner golden light. He set off
along the street. There was no one about, but he could imagine
every window hid suspicious, judging eyes. He quickened his pace,
scanning the row of imposing doors for the number he sought. At
last, he came to the right one. Despite the cold, he was sweating, a
hot prickling under his arms and down his back, so intense it was
almost painful.

He reached out a trembling hand, knocked. And waited.

And began to doubt – what if no one was in?

Then the door opened abruptly, to reveal a man in black breeches
and a white shirt, casually unbuttoned at the neck. A short man, he
nonetheless suggested through his birdlike, almost pugnacious
stance, great power and self-confidence. Strength of character shone
from his piercing brown eyes, and his high brows indicated great
intelligence.

'Who the devil are you, and what do you want?'

Malahyde's nerve almost failed him. Then he remembered he
needed this man's help, if he were to succeed.

If he were to save Mankind.

'M–Mr Brunel?' he stammered. 'I – I have a proposal for you. A business proposal.'

Isambard Kingdom Brunel stared at him.

Bristol, 19 July 1843

Emily ran along the pavement, laughing, her skirts streaming out around her. *Pigeons!*

The silly grey birds scattered at her approach, their wings making an awful clatter. One flew right at her, and Emily ducked, shrieking in delight.

She turned round to watch the pigeons fly up. They spread out across the sky like spilt peppercorns on a white table-cloth. Some settled in the eaves of the houses towering like cliffs above her. Others descended to the flagstones.

She grinned and hoisted up her skirts, preparing for another attack.

'Emily! Come here this *instant*!'

Emily froze. Nana had caught up with her!

She drew her lips into her sweetest smile and raised her eyebrows to make her eyes as wide as possible. This usually worked on grown-ups. Not Nana. But it was all Emily had.

She stayed put and let Nana walk up to her. Nana's cheeks were red and she was panting. Dressed all in black with her thin face and nose, Nana looked like a big crow.

'You wicked girl!' wheezed Nana. 'Trying to get away from me like that.'

'I'm sorry, Nana.' The sound of her own voice made Emily want to laugh.

'And you can wipe that look off your face at once!'

The things grown-ups said! How can you wipe a look from your

5

face? Your lips and nose and eyes, they wouldn't be wiped away for anything.

'I'm *sorry.*'

'So you say. But I can see in your eyes that you are not. I shall have words with your father.'

Emily looked down at her shoes, hiding her smile. She knew Daddy didn't like Nana.

'Come along.' Nana held out a black-gloved hand, and, grimacing, Emily took it.

They walked in silence, Emily looking at the horses and carriages clattering by in the road. She could feel Nana's disapproval in the tightness of her grip.

Then Emily began to feel funny.

It started in her legs – a big ache, like she sometimes got in bed.

And then it went through her whole body.

She heard Nana scream – and let go.

But she was scared and even Nana's hand –

Suddenly she was falling, falling down. Everything was whirling around her and a wind was tearing at her, battering her from all directions.

And she *hurt* so!

Her bones felt like they were breaking out of her body.

And then –

Emily woke up. Above her, a pale, white sky. Pigeons! But there were none.

Where was she? Was she dreaming?

No dream. She was lying on the pavement. It was cold against her back. This was real.

She sat up. 'Nana?'

Nana was lying down too, on her back with her hands… Emily gasped. Nana was old – but now she was –

Her face was like a dried fruit, the toothless mouth open wide, the eyes sunk deep into her head. Nana's hair, once black, was now white and *long*.

Emily crawled away from Nana, shivering. She realised her own hair was now also long, coiled around her.

She looked down at her fingernails. They were like twisting claws. Horrible. Horrible.

Tears blurred her vision. Emily began to shudder and shake. The hurting was still there, in her arms and legs.

Her mouth hurt too. She leaned forwards, and spat out a sticky mouthful of blood. She gasped in horror to see, in the crimson puddle, a dozen or so gleaming white objects. Teeth? She put her hands to her mouth, and found that she still had her teeth. Only they felt big and rough, like pegs.

Shivering, Emily looked down at herself. Her clothes had burst and torn, and hung in shreds from her shoulders and hips. And she was – *big*. Her legs were great long things, with pale, flabby skin. Her feet had busted out of her shoes, and were – *horrible*. Her chest had grown into two pale, sagging balloons. And there was hair, where there wasn't before.

She tried to stand up but couldn't.

Everywhere was quiet. Almost – she could hear cries in the distance that sounded like seagulls. In the road ahead of her, a horse and cart had stopped – but the horse was dead, its flesh withered away to nothing, white bones sticking through the skin. The driver was a skeleton. Like Nana.

Emily crawled past Nana towards the railings which ran along the front of the town houses. Her only thought was to find somewhere to hide, to curl up and cry, to wait for Daddy to find her and make everything all right again.

She found a gap in the railings and crawled down the steps, her long toe-nails scratching at the stone.

There she stayed, shivering and naked, aching and alone.

After what seemed like hours, she heard footsteps approaching along the pavement above.

She moaned.

The footsteps came closer, stopped. She could see two pairs of reassuringly normal shoes.

A man's head peered over the railings.

Emily gasped. A stranger! With the bluest eyes she had *ever* seen.

Chapter 1
Across The Bridge

Aboetta danced.

She let the see-sawing notes of the violin take control of her body. Let her feet skip and pirouette across the parquet floor, let her arms sway and rise with the melody. She loved the sensation of her dress whirling around her, loved the almost dizzying sensation that gripped her as she danced. She felt as though she was being taken to places of which she could only dream.

She knew she was smiling and wondered if he was watching her. Or perhaps he was keeping his eyes down, as usual, intent on the bow and strings.

Then the music stopped.

In its place, a jarring sound. A discordance. An intrusion. A high-pitched, agitated ringing.

Aboetta twirled to a halt, wondering how she'd managed to avoid colliding with the furniture that lined the edges of the room. She was facing the cavernous fireplace at the narrow end of the hall. Tiny flames danced, dwarfed by the hulking stone mantel. To her left, tall windows, framed by heavy curtains, allowed swathes of light into the room, golden motes of dust caught within them. The opposite wall was completely taken up with book-cases, their shelves stacked with Mr Malahyde's treasured volumes.

Mr Malahyde's chair, to the left of the fireplace, was empty. His violin lay on the occasional table beside the chair, its curved wooden body reflecting the firelight. The bow was neatly laid by its side. Of Malahyde himself there was no sign, but the heavy door clicked shut the moment Aboetta turned her gaze towards it.

As Aboetta moved towards the door, stepping into a warm rectangle of sunlight, the tinny, harsh ringing stopped.

The silence it left felt accusatory. Aboetta bit her lip. She should have been the one rushing to answer the summons, not her employer. But she had been too wrapped up in the music.

Just as she decided that she ought to follow him, Mr Malahyde came back into the room. He closed the door gently and stood facing her, hands clasped in front of him.

His face was serious, unsmiling. The day's dancing was definitely over.

Malahyde sighed, rubbed his hands together, looked at Aboetta, looked away.

'Whatever's the matter, sir?'

His eyes met hers. They were blue, under a prominent brow made youthful by blond-white eyebrows.

'It is bad news, I am very much afraid.'

He spoke softly, but Aboetta felt a chill despite the ray of sunlight she stood within. 'What do you mean, sir?'

'My Bridge Guards have received a message from Totterdown.' He paused. 'Your father has been taken ill.' A pained look crossed his face. 'He asks to see you.'

Her father was a strong man, tall and broad-shouldered, working seemingly without effort and certainly without complaint. For a moment Aboetta couldn't connect the fact of illness with him.

Malahyde walked towards her, his eyes searching her face. 'Aboetta.' His gentlemanly voice was a whisper. 'Of course, you must go to him.'

'What's wrong with him?'

'A fever.'

Working on the river was dangerous and infections were an occupational hazard. 'How advanced?'

'That's all the message conveyed. I am sorry.'

Aboetta bunched her fists in frustration. For someone to come all the way from Totterdown, braving the ruins of Bristol – surely there was more news! 'Can I not see the messenger?'

Malahyde shook his head. 'The guards on the Clifton side took the message. The bearer will already be back in Totterdown by now, God willing.'

Aboetta closed her eyes. Images of home filled her mind. Her father's house, the church, the Wall, the safe and ordered community. Coming here had seemed like a betrayal at first, and news of her father's illness came like a reminder of such disloyalty.

She felt Malahyde's hand on her arm, and opened her eyes.

'I understand that you must go. It will be dangerous. I will send my best men with you. You had better go and prepare.'

Aboetta's mind began to whirl around what she now had to do: travel across Bristol, avoiding all the dangers, and then return to Totterdown, see everyone again. See her father.

See Robin.

'You will return, Aboetta?' His voice was soft, yet imploring.

Surprised at the question, Aboetta shook her head. 'I don't know.'

He smiled, but his gaze flickered up and down her body. 'It's just that I've – grown accustomed to having you here.'

'That's all very well, sir. But I must attend to my father.'

'Very well. You had better go quickly. Two of my men…' He hesitated, as if working out a complicated sum in his head, '…will be waiting at the Lodge.'

They shook hands slowly and solemnly.

'Goodbye, Mr Malahyde. If I choose not to return, I will be sure to send one of the other girls from the settlement. And even if I don't come back for good, I'll come and see you again.'

Malahyde nodded, but something in his eyes told her that he didn't believe her. 'Thank you, Aboetta. Until we meet again.' He walked to his violin, picked it up, but didn't play. Just stood staring into the fire.

Aboetta hurried from the room, her thoughts turning to the dangers ahead.

Aboetta closed the door to the mansion house behind her and

walked along the narrow path – she always took care to trim the grass back from the edges of the paving-stones – towards the only exit in the perimeter wall which marked the boundary of her day-to-day world. It rose ten feet high, cutting off the view of the wider estate. Yellow spots of lichen marred its stones. All she could see above it was the pale grey sky, like a ghostly barrier extending up from the coping.

The door was tall and thin, wide enough for one person to fit through, and set in a plain, undecorated archway. It had been constructed long after the house and its design was purely functional. The only keys belonged to Mr Malahyde. He rarely let her borrow one, so she could only leave the grounds at his say-so. This effectively made her a prisoner, but somehow it didn't feel like that. She was in his employ, after all. She had to do his bidding.

Aboetta paused and looked back at the house. It had been built well before Year Nought and unlike other buildings from that unknowable time, it had been well maintained. Its architecture was ostentatious, gaudy, compared to the simple cottages and huts of Totterdown. The main doorway was set into a turreted portico, fronted by a Gothic arch which yawned like a stone mouth. On either side, the vast mansion house sprawled asymmetrically. There were two wings, of differing sizes – the south wing was enormous, looming above her and casting a shadow across the face of the house, and stretching back across the gardens. Amongst many rooms it contained the hall and dining room, with their bedchambers on the first floor. There were so many windows, fussily decorated in stone, staring down at her.

Then Aboetta remembered why she was leaving. There was no time to waste. She turned back hurriedly to the thin door, drawing the key from a pocket in her overcoat.

She unlocked the door, heaved it open with both hands and went outside. Something seemed to pass through her mind as she stepped under the arch, a stray thought or an elusive memory. But it was gone in an instant and Aboetta forgot about it as she drank in the vista before her. The rolling fields and woodlands of the Estate greeted her, looking unusually green for February. The sky also seemed different, less bleak, once she was outside the confines of the house.

She closed the door behind her, making sure to lock it. She saw a groundskeeper in the distance and waved, then set off at a tangent, up a steep hill towards the woods. Aboetta took a winding path through the trees, enjoying the tranquillity. The leaves were all golden-brown and yellow, there was a thick carpet of them underfoot. Strange for the time of year. She began to regret wearing her overcoat – it was thick, rough cotton dyed dark blue, and she was already beginning to feel hot. It really was most unseasonable weather.

She emerged from the trees and was soon walking down a long tree-lined colonnade. At the end, framed by golden-brown branches, was Clifton Lodge – the only way in or out of Ashton Court. This small building looked to Aboetta as if it were a piece sliced from the mansion house and set down at the edge of the estate. A substantial archway framed a formidable iron gate. Two castellated pillars rose either side of the arch, and the building had two small 'wings' which held the guards' quarters. The same fussy windows, the same old grey stone which evoked the time before the Cleansing.

As she neared, a green-painted door in the south wing opened and two Estate Guards emerged. She recognised them as Captain Bryant and Lieutenant Collins. She smiled, glad that two people she knew would be accompanying her.

Collins grinned widely as she approached, his gaze roving from her boots to the top of her head. 'Well, Miss! You look as lovely as the day you arrived!'

Captain Bryant silenced his subordinate with a look and walked out to greet her, saluting smartly.

Bryant was tall and dark-haired with a tired, weather-beaten face. As he approached, smiling at her, Aboetta noticed how old he looked. His face was more lined, his black hair showing streaks of grey.

'Captain Bryant.' Aboetta felt like saluting, but resisted the urge. 'Has Mr Malahyde briefed you?'

'We're to take you back to Totterdown, quick as possible.' He suddenly looked concerned. 'I'm sorry about your father.'

'We'd better get a move on,' said Collins, hefting a pack. 'We don't want to be in the town when it's getting dark.' He was younger than Bryant, thin and wiry with beady eyes and a strangely swaggering way of walking. He looked different too – his face was more lined, there were bags under his eyes. She could only assume that the two soldiers had been on duty a lot recently, and felt a twinge of concern for them.

'Right. Take this, Aboetta.' Captain Bryant handed her something.

She looked down at what she was now holding. It was a pistol, its handle fashioned of polished wood which contrasted pleasingly with the metal of the barrel and mechanism.

'You know how to load and fire one of these?'

Aboetta nodded. 'Yes, we use the same sort of weapon in Totterdown.' Though the basic mechanism was the same, this was a thing of beauty, unlike the crude rifles of the Watchkeepers of Totterdown. She looked questioningly at the Captain. 'It's from before Year Nought, isn't it?'

'Over a century and a half old, and still in perfect working order,' said Bryant with a smile. 'Here's some shot and a bag of gunpowder.' He handed her a canvas pouch which also contained some rags for cleaning and a metal spike for loading.

She handed Bryant the pistol whilst she attached the pouch to her belt.

'Maybe we won't have cause to use 'em,' said Bryant, handing her back the gun. 'But it pays to be prepared.'

The gun felt heavy and deadly in her hands, the wood smooth against her palm, yet when gripped tight in her fingers it didn't slip at all. The mechanism was well oiled and gleaming. She checked over the hammer and flint approvingly. Its curves held a mystery. Who had wielded this pistol? What had their lives been like?

She shook her head. None of that mattered now. It was a new world. A dangerous world.

She slid the gun between her belt and her dress. 'Let's go.'

It was a short walk from Clifton Lodge to the Suspension Bridge, and Aboetta and the two soldiers proceeded in silence, apprehensive about leaving the safety of Ashton Court. Soon they were at the bridge, and whilst Captain Bryant and Lieutenant Collins jogged up to the barrier, Aboetta held back, gazing up in wonder. The grey stone suspension tower was a sturdy yet graceful 'A' shape, its 'legs' thick and powerful, like the battlements of a fortress. These days, it was – a Bridge Guard was leaning on a parapet on the cross-beam, keeping watch over the river. Below, a sturdy wooden winch-operated gate barred the way on to the bridge.

The deck of the bridge stretched effortlessly away to the far side of the Gorge, its surface impeccably maintained. The graceful curve of the suspension cables, sweeping in a shining arc between the towers, and the supporting rods running in parallel lines down to the deck, made the bridge look like a giant harp stretched out over the river.

Aboetta walked to the parapet and leaned over. The view was giddying. The massive brick buttress plunged down into the side of the Gorge, stunted trees clustering around the base.

Below that, rocks sloped sharply down to the muddy river. The other side of the Gorge was a great jagged cliff of stone, topped with grassland and shrubs. The river curved round to the south until it was swallowed up by the ruins of the city.

A burst of laughter from the men. Aboetta suddenly felt angry – her father was ill, and here they were wasting time!

She hoisted her pack, slung it over one shoulder and went over to them.

Captain Bryant saw her approach and nudged Collins. They saluted the Bridge Guards and began to pick up their packs and rifles, suddenly efficient.

Bryant smiled as she walked over. 'Sorry, Madam, we were just discussing the best way to Totterdown.'

'By boat, surely?' said Aboetta. Mr Malahyde kept a small fleet of rowing boats moored beneath the bridge. 'We'll follow the river round.'

Collins shook his head. 'Low tide. Nowt but mud from here to Hotwells.'

'Then we'll have to walk,' said Aboetta, settling her pack more comfortably. 'It's the only way.'

'Right,' said Captain Bryant, trying to keep his tone light. 'Off we go.'

The three of them stepped on to the deck of the bridge. Aboetta heard the barrier mechanism give a protracted creak as it closed behind them.

It was eerie walking across the bridge. A cold, hard wind blew up from nowhere, moaning through the suspension rods, whipping Aboetta's long black hair around her face. The deck swayed slightly as they crossed, not enough to see, but certainly enough to feel. The bridge always seemed a delicate thing to Aboetta, despite all Mr Malahyde's assurances that it was perfectly safe. She kept her gaze firmly on the far side, not daring to look down.

Soon enough they had crossed the bridge and passed through the Clifton barrier. Ahead and on either side of the road, the twin arms of the bridge's suspension cables ran into the ground, showing no sign of the enormous strain under which they operated.

The land immediately beyond the Clifton end of the bridge was barren and wild, a sharp contrast to the cultivated acres of Ashton Court. Aboetta was glad to see Bryant and Collins exchange only a nod and a salute with the Bridge Guards on this side, and so they were quickly on their way. To the left, thorny scrubland rose up, following the edge of the Gorge. To the right, to the south, it fell sharply down towards ruined hulks of hotels and town houses. Between, the cobbled road quickly deteriorated, becoming over-run with weeds and riddled with cracks and potholes. The road led into Clifton, once a genteel neighbourhood above Bristol, but now, all those houses of golden stone were mere shells, crumbling and decaying.

They came to the edge of the scrubland, where the road ran parallel to a row of town houses. Hardly any stood with all four walls intact. They reminded Aboetta of skulls, unable to speak of the life they had once possessed. To the left the grass grew long over what once must have been a park. On the far side was a church, the main building collapsed, but the spire somehow still standing. The sight of it made Aboetta shudder. It wasn't God's house any more.

Forsaken. Desecrated.

Aboetta muttered a prayer and looked back to see the Bridge Guards alert, one standing in silhouette in the cross-beam of the suspension tower. They had cover for as long as they were in his line of sight. Which wouldn't be long. Until the end of this street.

Collins started humming a tune, his nervousness obvious. Bryant hissed an order at him and he fell silent. The younger soldier shot a rueful grin at Aboetta, but she frowned back at him. They had to keep quiet, keep on the alert. The only sound she could hear, now that Collins had shut up, was the scuff of their boots on the road.

Once round a pile of rubble from a collapsed building they were out of sight of the Bridge Guards. No wind stirred. The sky above was pale, a blank sheet. They came to the end of the road, near to the ruined church, and turned right, into a wide street lined with once-palatial homes which stood like gravestones behind the bent and rusted remains of ornamental fences. Their gardens, untended for decades, managed to look at once overgrown and threadbare, the plants that had overtaken them spindly and starved-looking. Despite having studied the pictures in Mr Malahyde's books, it was impossible for Aboetta to see the town as anything other than a hostile wasteland, something to be got through as quickly as possible. Behind her, the serenity and security of Ashton Court. Ahead, the stout yet civilised fortress of Totterdown. Both safe enough within their boundary walls. Both worlds she knew well.

'We'll cut along down to the river by Canon's Marsh,' whispered Bryant. 'We should be able to pick up a boat there.'

Collins agreed and Aboetta shrugged, wishing she'd had more time to plan this journey.

Suddenly, a stone skittered on to the cobbles directly in front of them. The two soldiers were instantly on the alert, rifles drawn.

Aboetta slid the pistol out of her belt and scanned the rows of houses for movement.

'There!' hissed Collins, pointing with his rifle to an upstairs window to their left. Aboetta caught a glimpse of a pale face drawn quickly back from the light.

Another stone hit the tarmac, coming to rest against Bryant's boot. Another flew in an arc from the other side of the street, hitting a lamp-post with a sound as clear as a ringing bell. Suddenly there was a hail of missiles – stones, half-bricks, chunks of masonry – hurtling down from the windows on either side of the street.

The men fired – two cracks like breaking stone, the sound echoing away down the street. There was no let-up in the deluge.

'Run!' yelled Bryant. 'We can't re-load under these conditions!'

Aboetta was already running, shielding her head with her arms, aiming for the open end of the street. Collins was ahead of her, crouched against a wall, busy re-loading his rifle. As she drew level with him, a stone as large as a fist hit the back of his head, sending his cap flying, and he slumped against the wall, rifle clattering to the ground.

Bryant grabbed Aboetta and they stumbled into cover behind a crumbling wall. He was bleeding from a cut on his forehead.

'Wildren!' spat Bryant as he poured gunpowder down the barrel of his rifle. Most of it went down the outside. 'Bastards must have seen us coming. Never seen them so organised!'

He quickly dropped a piece of shot down the barrel and rammed a rag tightly down after it using a long metal stick he carried attached to his belt.

'I'm going back for Collins. Stay hidden!'

He darted out from cover. Aboetta loaded her pistol, knowing that their weapons would be useless against a mass attack. The time it took to re-load after each shot made them too vulnerable. And they needed to conserve their ammunition – they had hardly even started their journey! The Bridge Guards would be able to hear the gunshots – but had orders never to leave the bridge under any circumstances. They had only one hope – flight.

She peered over the top of the wall, and gasped as a ragged, pale-skinned figure darted out from hiding. Another followed it. Then another. Aboetta shrank back behind the wall, trembling. She had one shot, and then she was going to run for it.

The Wildren were making for Collins, some distance back on the other side of the wall she was sheltering behind. She couldn't see Captain Bryant – but the crack of a rifle from farther up the street told her where he was.

She stood. One of the creatures had been hit, was lying sprawled in the road. Others fell upon it, shrieking, their rags flapping around them. They began to drag the body over to the far side of the street. Aboetta's lip curled in disgust. *They even eat their own.*

Then she saw Collins' body, being dragged through the dust and rubble.

And then she saw that one of the Wildren was wielding the Lieutenant's rifle with ugly glee. Did the creatures know how to use guns? Could they have learned? Another shot from farther up the road – and the Wildren with the rifle fell. Another picked it up, and aimed it at the source of the shot – Captain Bryant.

He'd have no time to re-load before he was shot.

It was up to her to save him.

Aboetta gripped her pistol with both hands, took aim and pulled the trigger. There was a metallic click as the flint hit the frizzen, a flash of igniting powder and a whiplike crack.

The recoil made her stagger backwards and she gasped.

The two Wildren stood unhurt, glaring in her direction.

She'd missed. And now they'd seen her. The one with the rifle swung the weapon towards her. Thoughts tumbled madly through Aboetta's mind: *Collins had re-loaded – it had one shot – it would kill her but Captain Bryant would be safe – where was Captain Bryant?*

Suddenly, a shot rang out, off to her right, and the Wildren dragging Collins away fell, a red spout of blood pumping forcefully from its shattered head.

'Captain Bryant!' yelled Aboetta.

Almost before the words were out of her mouth the beast with the rifle turned on the spot and fired.

She heard a shout – the sound of a falling body. A howl of triumph from the Wildren – from *many* Wildren. More of the creatures came scampering out of the houses, hooting, shrieking.

No time to re-load. No time to check if Captain Bryant was alive.

She turned and ran, not caring where she was going, intent only on escape. She could hear the shrieks and howls of the Wildren, horribly close behind.

Aboetta saw a gap between the houses and ran in, fumbling for more ammunition. It was a canyon of rubble, formerly a narrow service road. And it was a dead end.

She skidded to a halt, breath tearing in and out of her. She whirled round. A dozen Wildren blocked her way. Rags, made from the skin of their own dead, barely covered their undernourished bodies. A foul stench preceded them.

They revolted her.

She re-loaded and fired. One of the Wildren fell with a piercing shriek. The others just shoved the body aside.

She was as good as dead.

'Sorry, Father,' she moaned. 'Sorry, Mr Malahyde.'

And then from behind her came a low, distant-sounding boom, like far-off thunder, followed immediately by a roaring, tearing tumult. It sounded like the breath of the Devil himself.

The Wildren stopped in their tracks, their pallid features frozen in almost comical grimaces of fear.

The hellish noise went on. Aboetta opened her mouth and yelled, a roar of fear which tore at her throat, and screwed up her face into a snarling feral mask.

The devil-roaring behind her reached a crescendo and Aboetta's voice rose to match it, her yell breaking into a scream.

The Wildren turned and fled.

Aboetta was still screaming when the sound stopped.

She fell to her knees, muttering a prayer and scrabbling for her pistol, which she'd only just realised she had dropped. She grabbed it, re-loaded quickly. In one lunging movement she stood upright and whirled round, bringing the gun to bear on –

A blue box.

In front of the rubble, where there had been nothing but empty air, stood a strange, tall blue box with panelled doors and square windows.

Aboetta ducked into hiding just as the doors began to open.

Her finger closed around the trigger.

Chapter 2
The Ruined City

Aboetta stared in amazement as three people stepped out of the blue box.

They weren't Wildren. They weren't outlaws. If anything, they looked like the people in Mr Malahyde's books – people from before Year Nought. The woman caught Aboetta's attention first – her skin was light brown, her hair glossy and black. She was dressed in fine clothes, but strange: a short, dark green jacket and dark trousers. The two men were similar – both had long brown hair which reached to their shoulders. But one was scruffy-looking and unshaven, a bit like an outlaw, with a long brown jacket that looked like (but couldn't be, surely?) *leather*. The other was dressed in the kind of clothes that Mr Malahyde would wear. A long, elegant coat, a waistcoat and a cravat. All three were looking around with interest.

They could have no idea of the danger they were in! The Wildren would soon re-group, their hunger overcoming their fear.

Pistol held in both hands, Aboetta stepped out of hiding.

All three strangers noticed her at the same time. The scruffy man raised his hands, the dark-skinned woman just stared, but the well-dressed man stepped forwards.

He was smiling.

'Hello! I'm the Doctor, these are my friends Fitz and Anji.'

He seemed oblivious to the pistol aimed at his chest.

'We mean you no harm,' said the man – the Doctor.

'Really, we don't,' added the scruffy man from over the Doctor's shoulder.

'Trust me.' The Doctor indicated his companions. 'Trust *us*. You look like you've been running and you're carrying the gun for a reason, yes? You're in danger. Someone's after you.'

Aboetta's heart was hammering away in her chest. The Wildren might return at any moment. Whoever these people were, they seemed harmless, if strange. But she had the gun. And if the Wildren attacked again, she'd have more chance of escape if she was with others.

'It's not safe here,' she said. 'We have to move – now. Either come with me – or stay, and die.'

They went with Aboetta.

She led them out of the dead end and into the ruined street. There was no sign of Captain Bryant or Lieutenant Collins. Aboetta tried not to think about what had happened to them and led the strangers on at a pace. The road led down, becoming more overgrown, until they broke into a patch of open countryside. This was just as ruined as Clifton had been: great thorny bushes rose on every side, and ivy sprawled in massive banks.

Soon they emerged on to the side of a grassy hill. Aboetta swished through the long stems, beckoning to the strangers to follow her. At the top, a copse of half a dozen twisted trees provided cover. Once there, Aboetta felt safe enough – she could see for miles around, no Wildren could ambush them here.

She ushered the strangers into the copse. The scruffy one, Fitz, sat on a log with a sigh of relief. The dark-skinned woman stood staring out over the ruins of Bristol with a stunned look on her face.

And the Doctor turned to face Aboetta.

She instinctively went for her pistol again, but something in the Doctor's gaze made her hesitate.

'What's your name?'

'Aboetta.' Somehow, she felt she had to answer him, and this annoyed her. 'Now you answer me. What was that blue box – and who are you?'

'That isn't important now and if there is time, I will explain. All I ask is that you trust us,' the Doctor entreated.

It was a lot to ask. 'I trust no one I do not know well.'

'What about your pursuers?' said Fitz. 'Someone was after you, right? They had you cornered, and the TARDIS – the blue box – appeared, and they legged it. We saved your life. You owe us that.'

'This is true,' said Aboetta slowly. 'If that box had not appeared, the Wildren would have overcome me.'

The Doctor looked at Fitz, then back at Aboetta. 'Wildren? What are they – wild children?' He said this with an amused laugh.

'They are nothing to laugh about. If they catch us, they will eat us.'

Fitz sat up and began to look around.

'We're safe enough here,' said Aboetta. 'But we must move on – we won't be safe until we're in Totterdown.'

'Totterdown?' said Fitz. 'Never heard of it. Often felt like it.'

'It's my home. My father's ill. I need to be there.'

The woman, Anji, spoke up 'So – we're coming with you now?'

Aboetta nodded. 'You saved my life. And there is safety in numbers...'

'All right, you've convinced me. We'll help you.' The Doctor smiled at Aboetta. 'I always hate asking this, but – can you tell me what the date is? Including the year?'

Stranger still! 'It is the second of February, in the year 151. Why do you ask such a thing?'

The smiled vanished from the Doctor's face and he turned away. 'I've lost my calendar.'

Aboetta frowned, but decided to ignore the remark. 'There isn't time to stand around talking. We must be in Totterdown before nightfall.'

With that she walked out of the copse and down the far side of the hill, towards the river.

Anji glared after Aboetta. She couldn't help noticing the way the girl had been staring at her. She sighed. 'We're clearly in some other reality where people like me are freaks. Again.'

'It *is* odd,' mused the Doctor as they set off after Aboetta, 'that a white denizen of twenty-first century Bristol should be fazed by the sight of someone from a different ethnic background.'

Fitz shoved his hands into his coat pockets. 'So, we're in another alternative reality?'

'Obviously.' The Doctor gestured at the ruins of the city. 'Bristol 2003 isn't – wasn't – *shouldn't* be like this.'

'It certainly shouldn't.' Anji had been to Bristol a few times on business trips. 'So what's happened?'

'I'm not sure. One thing I've noticed,' said the Doctor, 'is that the buildings are all Georgian or pre-Georgian. There's nothing beyond.' He frowned. 'And there are a few features and structures which look as if they shouldn't be there at all.'

Aboetta led them down the hill, and along a curving crescent of once-respectable houses which overlooked a shining ribbon of water. It looked wide and deep, its banks shaggy and overgrown.

'We follow it round,' called Aboetta from ahead. 'Wildren can't swim. They stay away from the river.'

A beaten path ran along the bank, but it was so crowded with thorns and nettles that they sometimes had to walk in single file. Aboetta was already some distance ahead.

'Year 151,' said Fitz. 'Can we really be sure this is a different version of 2003?'

'Yes,' said the Doctor. 'The yearometer is one of the few TARDIS instruments I can rely upon. Something must have happened a century and a half ago that was drastic enough to not just change history but initiate a new calendar.'

'What do you think happened?' asked Anji.

'I wouldn't like to hazard a guess until I've seen more,' said the Doctor.

Typical. 'We should question her,' said Anji, squeezing past a clump of thorns.

'Maybe we'll get some answers once we're in Totterdown.'

Fitz held up his hands. 'Hold on – how many alternate realities are there? I mean – are we going to spend the rest of our lives going from place to place, "restoring" the right version of history?'

'I sincerely hope not. Could be one or two, could be hundreds. Or an infinite number.' The Doctor grimaced. 'If it's just the one or two, then we're more or less OK, we can go back and fix things, but if it's a great number the Time Vortex will collapse and, well.' He sighed. 'It's the end.'

There was something about the simplicity of his words that chilled Anji.

'The end. Wonder what it'll be like?' There was an edge of breezy hysteria in Fitz's voice. 'Will we feel anything? Will it hurt? Or will there be a moment of blissful nirvana, then – nothing?'

'You're babbling, Fitz,' said Anji.

'I know,' Fitz snapped. 'I tend to when I'm worried.'

'So I've noticed.'

Fitz shoved past her. 'I'm gonna have a word with our gun-toting gypsy friend.' He grinned. 'Turn on the good old Kreiner charm. Might get a few clues.'

Anji stared at the Doctor, and the Doctor stared back at her.

'He seems a bit – manic,' said Anji.

'Hmm.' The Doctor looked thoughtfully at Fitz's back.

Aboetta looked round as Fitz approached, squinting slightly.

Fitz smiled at her, but she didn't smile back. He fell into step, sussing her out. She had slightly gawky features – wide mouth, nose rather too big, eyes widely spaced under untended eyebrows which were a bit too beetling for his tastes. Her teeth were yellow, there were visible gaps between them, and the gums were receding. But her eyes were a sparkling golden-brown, her skin was pale olive flecked with freckles, and her hair was thick and black, falling in glossy curls around her neck. Not a conventional beauty by any means, but there was something about her, something wild and untamed, which fascinated Fitz.

After a minute or so she turned her head to stare suspiciously at him. 'What do you want?' Her voice was low and husky, with a slight lilt that wasn't anything like the Bristol accent Fitz knew.

'Nothing,' said Fitz. 'Just wondering how far it is to…'

His voice tailed off as she stopped, reached out a hand and

fondled the lapel of his leather jacket, a look of amazement breaking over her face. She looked into his eyes, shaking her head in admiration.

Wha-hey! thought Fitz.

'Your coat. It's leather!'

Fitz sighed. 'Of course, what else?'

'Where did you get it?'

Fitz hesitated. 'London.' Probably a safe bet.

'So – you are from one of the London settlements?'

'Ah. We get around a lot.'

'What did you barter for it?'

'Guns?'

Aboetta shook her head slowly. 'You strange people. You arrive in a blue box which appears out of nowhere, and you barter weapons for clothes.' She snorted. 'I must be mad for taking you with me.'

'But we did save your life,' said the Doctor. He and Anji had caught up with them.

Aboetta put her hand on the gun again. 'And for that I am thankful. But I feel that you did not save my life on purpose, it was an accident of your arrival.' She sniffed and walked on. 'You're going to have to prove to me that you're worthy of my trust.'

'I wonder if they're all as friendly here as she is,' muttered Anji.

'Oh, I should imagine not,' said the Doctor blithely. 'We'll probably be locked up and interrogated the moment we arrive in Totterdown.'

'Great,' said Fitz. 'I could do with a few more sessions of torture, you know. I'm getting a taste for it.'

'That's the spirit,' said the Doctor, patting Fitz on the back and walking off after Aboetta.

'Find out anything?' asked Anji.

'Nope,' said Fitz. 'She seems impervious to my charms.'

From his vantage point in the Three Lamps Tower, Head Watchkeeper Robin Larkspar could see the ruins of Bristol spread out before him, a wasteland of crumbling buildings through whose streets mist crept. Mist, and other things he didn't like to think about. On the nearest structures – the old station and warehouses on the other side of the river – ivy had taken hold, as if wanting to haul the stone back into the ground. Beyond, a few church spires still stood, though no worship went on beneath them. From his elevated position, Robin could make out the contours of the hills beyond the ruined city.

A sudden cold wind blew up, sighing through the gaps in the wooden parapet of the Watchtower, sharp against Robin's bared teeth. He turned away from the breeze and gazed westwards. Here, within the settlement, a grassy hill rose, bare but for a few wooden buildings and half-a-dozen windmills, their sails turning serenely. Around this hill, and down towards the Three Lamps Tower, ran the Wall, which stretched in a rust-coloured line all around Totterdown settlement. Above everything, the sky was golden-white, a perfect October day.

But this vista did nothing to stir Robin. He turned again, facing back towards the main settlement, looking up the road which ran from Three Lamps between the cottages, up the bigger hill which led to the church. Next to that he could see the stout shape of the Henry, and imagined himself there later with beer inside him and more in front of him. He needed to drink. Because Aboetta hadn't returned, even now.

He turned back and looked in the direction of the Suspension Bridge, though its towers were hidden from view by a line of decaying town houses which crested the Bristol side of the Avon Gorge. Why was she taking so long? The messenger had returned two days ago. What had happened to her?

Robin didn't want to think of the possibilities. Of any possibility other than Aboetta appearing from the ruins of the city. He cursed Malahyde under his breath. If anything had happened to Aboetta, Robin would make sure the recluse would pay.

He drew his rifle, checking over its mechanism and ensuring the powder was dry. Then he bent and checked the crossbow leaning against the inner wall of the Watchtower. All in perfect working order. He gazed out again across the town, toying with the idea of taking a squad of the Watch out to search for Aboetta. But he was

Head Watchkeeper. He couldn't abandon his post. Damn them! People rarely left the settlement these days. Aboetta had been the last to leave permanently and that had been so long ago now.

A shout from his fellow Watchkeeper in the lesser tower on the other side of the gate made him jump. Thomas Cope was pointing towards the river. Robin looked.

Four figures were crossing the bridge.

Chapter 3
Totterdown

The path eventually rose up to meet a wide, cobbled road running from north to south. To the left, the road ran northwards into the outer tendrils of the ruins of Bristol.

Anji shuddered. Whatever those buildings had once been, they were now unrecognisable, hulking ghosts being teased apart by ivy. It was amazing how quiet everything was. No traffic, no birdsong, none of the hurly-burly of the city as it should be. Only the sound of their own footsteps and conversation, and the wind sighing through the trees.

To the right, the road ran southwards over a bridge which led across the river. Aboetta was already half-way across, clearly anxious to be home.

'We don't have to go with her,' said Anji. She suddenly felt apprehensive. They knew nothing about this world. Aboetta might be leading them into danger. 'Can't we go back to the TARDIS?'

'We need to find out what happened that changed the course of history,' said the Doctor. 'And you're forgetting the Wildren. Come on.'

He set off across the bridge.

Anji looked at Fitz. He seemed more composed now, the manic gleam had gone from his eyes. But he looked worried, preoccupied.

On the other side of the bridge, the road rose steadily up across a bare, muddy hillside. To the east the land sloped sharply down to the river, beyond which Anji could make out grassy marshland disappearing into the misty distance. Ahead, at the top of the incline where the land met the sky, was a wooden, rust-coloured wall. As they got nearer Anji could see that it was built of tree trunks sharpened to points and was at least thirty feet high. It blocked the way ahead, and continued on up the hill to the right, and down to the river to the left. Evening was falling. The sun was just above the horizon, and the sky was streaked with blue-grey cloud.

Aboetta was making for the point where the road met the wall, between two towers set either side of a pair of enormous wooden gates.

'A hill fort – in the twenty-first century.' The Doctor's eyes were alight with curiosity.

'Civilisation, I hope,' said Anji.

'Come on,' said the Doctor.

The gates had opened a little, and through the gap Anji could see people milling about, simple stone and wooden houses, and the road continuing up a grassy slope. Only when they were at the wall itself did Anji realise that running along its base was a deep, steep-sided V-shaped ditch with evilly sharp-looking wooden spikes at the bottom. The only crossing-point was an embankment which carried the road through the gates.

Aboetta had already stepped through the opening and had disappeared into the crowd.

The Doctor hesitated at the edge of the embankment, staring up at the smaller wooden tower to the left of the gates. It looked like a prison-camp watchtower, with a square turret topped off by a sloping roof which came to a sharp point. There was a guard standing braced on the platform, pointing a rifle down at them.

Anji felt a qualm of fear.

'What a welcoming place this looks,' muttered Fitz.

'Just do as I do and don't say anything.' The Doctor smiled at the guard, and then walked through the gates.

Anji followed. She tried not to look down at the spikes in the ditch.

As soon as they were through, the gates rumbled shut behind

them and they suddenly found themselves in the middle of a jostling, shouting throng. Anji saw pale, drawn faces, ragged clothes of every shade of brown, weathered hands gripping daggers and cudgels. Grubby children ran about switching the air with thin sticks, shrieking, the sound seeming to pierce Anji's eardrums. Everyone looked thin, malnourished, with bad teeth and sunken eyes.

Anji backed away, grabbing on to Fitz for support. The Doctor was shouting, his voice hoarse with urgency, but he couldn't be heard above the din. Fitz began to yell too, calling for Aboetta. The horizon was a bobbing mass of heads, waving arms and nasty spikes. As she stumbled about Anji caught a glimpse of a squat red-brick tower on top of a hill some distance beyond the crowd.

Anji felt something rough and hard against her back. They were right up against the wooden poles of the gate. Trapped.

Stubbly faces thrust themselves at her, gawping and jeering. She caught a whiff of alcohol fumes and bad breath. The Doctor had manoeuvred himself in front of her and was holding up his hands in a pacificatory gesture. Or maybe he was just surrendering.

No one paid him any attention. Many had noticed Anji and were pointing at her and laughing. Some of the children darted out from the crowd, and hit her about the legs with switches of long grass until Fitz shooed them away.

Above the crowd Anji glimpsed curves of shining metal which reflected the setting sun. When they were near enough she saw that they were helmets, worn by big men in chain-mail tunics. They forced their way through the crowd, shoving people roughly out of the way. Once clear of the rabble, they pointed their rifles straight at the Doctor, Fitz and Anji.

The crowd fell silent.

Anji nudged the Doctor. 'Say something that will make them like us. Now!'

'What sort of welcome is this for the man who has come to sort out all your problems?' cried the Doctor.

Anji groaned and Fitz put a hand over his eyes.

The tallest of the three rifle-bearers spoke. 'We ain't got any problems. Apart from you.'

There was a hubbub somewhere at the back. A large man with silver hair was surging through the crowd.

'Ah, someone of authority,' said the Doctor. 'Let's hope they're reasonable.'

Anji looked at the hostile faces leering at her with open curiosity and contempt. *Reasonable?* No hope.

Aboetta knew that the Watchkeeper in the Three Lamps Tower was Robin, even before she was close enough to make out his features. Somehow, she had known all along that he would be waiting for her.

As soon as she was sure it was him, she stopped and called out.

He called back, his voice thick with emotion. 'Aboetta!'

Then he was gone – she could hear his footsteps as he almost fell down the stairs. Seconds later, the gates began to grind open and Aboetta ran towards the gap. Her heart felt as if, in one beat, it was soaring within her at the prospect of seeing him again. And then in the next, being dragged down with worry about her father.

Aboetta slipped through the gate. The sounds, sights and smells of her home assailed her with such force it was like being physically struck. A crowd had gathered but she ignored them, pushing past the questioning faces, looking for –

– There he was.

He had emerged from the door at the base of the Three Lamps Tower and was marching across the square, rifle stowed in its back-holster. Aboetta stepped towards him, lips parted to cry his name, arms ready to seize him with a passion which made her dizzy.

Then she stopped. Something was wrong.

'Aboetta!' cried Robin breathlessly, coming to a halt before her. 'Aboetta, at last!' His arms, clad in stormcloud-hued chain mail, reached out towards her, but Aboetta drew back, staring into his face, a feeling of horror dragging her heart down lower than ever before.

This was not Robin – and yet it was. The young man she had loved had been tall and handsome, with thick black hair and skin as pale and smooth as river-washed pebbles. His body had been lithe and strong, his eyes clear and blue like jewels made of pure sky.

But this man, though tall, was stooped, as if his chain mail was hanging heavy on him. His hair – what she could see of it beneath his spiked metal Watchkeeper's helmet – hung limp around his face. His skin was as pale as before, but puffy and unhealthy looking. He had a paunch and a double chin. His eyes had lost their blue fire, and had bags beneath them, the lines etched deeply in the flesh.

'Robin?' she said at last.

'What's the matter, love?' he said. There was a worn-out gruffness in his voice she hadn't heard before. 'Where have you been? We sent for you *days* ago!'

Aboetta was still trying to take in the changes in Robin, still trying to find some explanation. With a pang in her heart, she felt her passion for him curl up and die like a leaf in a fire. Concern overrode it. 'Robin, what's happened to you? Have you been ill?'

He frowned at her – she noticed his eyebrows, thick and ugly. 'No.'

Then she realised what he had said. 'What do you mean, *days* ago? Where's my father?'

Robin began to speak again, but Aboetta wasn't listening. Fearing the worst, she turned and fled up the hill towards her father's house.

The silver-haired man ignored the Doctor, Fitz and Anji, and addressed the tallest of the guards. 'Who let these people in?'

'Head Watchkeeper, sir.' The man had a recognisable West Country accent, soft and deep with languid vowels. 'He was lettin' Aboetta Cigetrais in, sir. She's come back!'

Several voices shouted out in support of the guard's story.

The silver-haired man looked around. There was an anxious cast to his expression. 'Where is she now?'

'Gone off to her father, sir.' The guard hung his head.

'Well, I'll speak to Larkspar later. He shouldn't have let these three in, though they don't look like outlaws.'

The man walked towards them. He was an impressive figure and, as she was standing behind the Doctor, Anji saw the Doctor's back straighten as he squared up.

The man was large and dressed in a close-fitting tunic and trousers of what looked like brown leather. He wore a heavy black cloak fastened at the neck with a hefty looking golden clasp in the shape of a sideways letter 'S'. Unlike the guards his head was bare, with long hair tied back from his face. He had a beard of spiky grey and a great slab of a nose which had clearly been broken at least once. Around his forehead was a circlet, the same gold colour as the clasp.

Though powerful in appearance, his movements were languid and his voice was gentle.

'I am Morgan Foster, Chief Elder of Totterdown Settlement. What is your business here?'

The Doctor spoke loudly and commandingly. 'We are travellers, we have no specific business here – but we have done you a great service. We rescued Aboetta from the, er, Wildren.'

A murmur of comment ran through the crowd. Some laughter.

'Did you now? Well, we'll have to ask Aboetta about that.' Morgan Foster's eyes darted from the Doctor to Fitz and then Anji. 'Travellers, eh?' He smiled, revealing widely spaced yellowing teeth. 'Well one of you at least seems to have travelled very far indeed.'

Anji steeled herself and stared right back at the Chief Elder. This time, in this reality, she was determined that they wouldn't get the better of her. 'You wouldn't believe how far.'

'We have indeed come a very long way,' said the Doctor, frowning at Anji. 'We'd be grateful for some food and lodging.'

'We'll see what Aboetta has to say first.' Morgan Foster said something to the guards, and then called for the crowd to disperse.

The three guards then herded the Doctor, Fitz and Anji out of the square and up the hill after the massive figure of their leader.

Aboetta stood in front of the house she had grown up in. She had spent all of her life here, apart from the last four months. It was part of a terrace with grand views over Bristol, houses built a few years before the Cleansing, like many of the houses in Totterdown. Father had been the chief river-worker and the house was one of the privileges which came with the position.

The paint on the door had long worn away, the naked wood beneath bare and warped, like something dragged from the sea. But it was a strong door – Father had reinforced it with steel braces both inside and out. Crime within Totterdown itself was virtually non-existent, limited to the occasional drunken brawl, adultery and petty theft, but Father had wanted to make the house into a stronghold for his family, should the walls of Totterdown ever be breached by outlaws or Wildren.

Father had travelled far and wide, to barter in settlements around Gloucester, and south as far as Exeter. He had even once made the perilous trip to London. He had been gone for two months. Aboetta remembered sitting wedged into the sill of her bedroom window, anxiously watching the river for signs of his return, getting excited at each flurry of activity around the river-gate. She'd missed his return – she had been at school – but she remembered the sheer joyous relief she had felt when she arrived home and he was there, weary and weathered but smiling to see her. She remembering hugging him so hard she thought she would never let go.

Aboetta reached out and pushed the door. The wood was warmed by the evening sun – the grey stones of the house were bathed orange in its setting glow – and the door opened without a creak. The house was empty, she could already tell. It had always been a noisy house, its wooden beams creaking with every movement. Now, though, it was silent. Aboetta knew then that her father wasn't inside.

A cold, hard feeling gripped her heart.

The door opened straight into the kitchen and Aboetta stepped in, her boots echoing dully on the stone floor it shared with the other two downstairs rooms, the parlour and Father's workshop. Pots and pans still hung on the walls, and there were dirty plates on the wooden table which took up most of the room – but there were ashes in the range, and the water-butt was empty. The place looked like it had been deserted for days.

Although she knew the house was empty, she still called out. 'Father?' Her own voice sounded weak, wavering. She gritted her teeth.

Though the kitchen and into the parlour. Barren. Her father's chair empty in front of the cold fireplace. His boots beside his footstool. Aboetta couldn't take any more. 'Father!' she cried, her voice breaking, the tears coming, her feet taking her out of the parlour, up the steep wooden stairs, across the landing and into the master bedroom.

Empty. The sheets on the bed were folded neatly back, the curtains closed, the room in near darkness. The furniture – all of it made by her father – loomed like grey ghosts. Aboetta made herself stop crying. The warm dusty air smelt of nothing. Not even decay and death. Just a dusty nothingness. Where was her father? A glimmer of hope – perhaps he'd been moved to the infirmary.

The sound of boots on the stairs made Aboetta jump. She wiped her face with her sleeve and turned round.

Robin.

He'd taken off his helmet and was carrying it under his arm. She could see that his hair was receding, and his face looked even more pallid in the half-light of the empty house. Aboetta reached out and held on to the door frame. It was as if everything she had known had been knocked out of true, like a botched pot.

'Aboetta,' he said, gently and with clear concern.

He didn't have to say the words, she could read it from the look on his face. 'My father is dead.'

Robin looked down at his feet, a grimace of anguish distorting his face. When he looked back up at her, his eyes were gleaming with tears.

Another shock. The Robin she knew had never cried, not even at their parting.

'He died three days ago, Aboetta,' said Robin suddenly. 'The funeral was yesterday.' The glimmer of tears seemed to refract a flash of anger, and his voice became accusatory. 'Why didn't you come?'

'What are you talking about? I left this morning!'

He shook his head angrily. 'Then you left it too late. You were gone for so long! Couldn't you have sent word?'

A pang of guilt. But getting messages across Bristol was dangerous and often needlessly risked the life of the messenger. 'I didn't think it worth it. Anyway I've only been gone four months.'

'Four *months*?' Robin stepped towards her. His eyes, with their bags and wrinkles, were screwed up in a snarl of anger and disbelief. 'Aboetta, you've been gone *ten years*!'

Chapter 4
The Lost Decade

Aboetta backed away. 'Robin, I've been away since last October. That's only four months.'

Robin's eyes widened in disbelief. 'What has that hermit *done* to you?' He walked up to her, reached out his hands, rested them on her shoulders. 'It's been ten years since I last saw your beautiful face,' he whispered. 'A decade I've waited for this kiss.'

Before Aboetta could protest, his arms slid around her waist and his lips touched hers. She closed her eyes, felt his stubble against her cheek, the hardness of his chain mail pressing against her breasts. She allowed her arms to snake around his body, pull him towards her.

But her heart seemed to curl up in revulsion at his clumsiness, her mind to reel at what was happening. Whoever this man was, though he looked like Robin – as maybe an older brother would – he wasn't the man she'd fallen in love with.

Aboetta squirmed against him, put her hands against his stomach, on the cold chain mail. He resisted at first, but eventually he released her and stepped back.

He stood there, his eyes scared-looking. 'What's wrong, Aboetta?'

She hardly knew what to say. The sense of his words permeated to her brain, and the evidence was there: he looked older, looked like he was in his mid-thirties, not his mid-twenties which was how she'd left him. But that was impossible. 'I don't know,' said Aboetta at last. 'But something is wrong.'

'What? What's wrong?'

The sound of footsteps on the stairs. More than one person – a crowd. Aboetta felt a flood of relief.

Robin turned round to face the door as Morgan Foster entered, followed by the three strangers and a guard bearing a crossbow.

Robin saluted and made room for Morgan.

'Aboetta,' said Morgan Foster, his voice at once grave and concerned. 'These strangers say they rescued you from a Wildren attack.' He raised his iron-grey eyebrows. 'Is this true?'

Aboetta saw no reason to lie. 'If it wasn't for them, I wouldn't be here now.'

Fitz and Anji visibly relaxed and the Doctor smiled at Aboetta.

Morgan turned the Doctor. 'Then you are welcome in Totterdown. You'll be expected to put your shoulder to the wheel, mind, in payment for your lodgings.'

'Thank you,' said the Doctor. 'I don't yet know how long we'll need to stay, but we'll do anything we can to help.'

Morgan dismissed the guard. 'Luckily for you, Larkspar, they seem harmless.'

This might be true, thought Aboetta, but they were still strangers. And strangers were never to be trusted.

Morgan Foster turned to her. His eyes were full of compassion. She noticed how much older he looked; his face more wrinkled, his grey hair now almost white. Older. Ten years older. Aboetta felt weak, unsure of anything. His words floated by her, useless words of concern. 'Are you all right?'

Suddenly Robin spoke up. 'No, she's not. She thinks she's only been gone four months!'

'Really?' said the Doctor.

'Well?' said Morgan Foster.

'I *have* only been away four months,' said Aboetta, trying to keep her voice calm. She wanted to get out of here, be in the fresh air, be by herself, not to hear any more of this madness. She moved towards the door.

But the Doctor barred her way. His eyes were clear, like Robin's had once been, but there was something else about them, a depth which unsettled Aboetta, a slightly skeletal quality to his features adding to her unease.

'What date did you say it was?'

Aboetta looked defiantly around the group, settling her gaze on Robin. 'It is the second of February, Year 151.' It was a fact. They couldn't argue with that.

Morgan and Robin stared at each other.

'See what I mean?' said Robin, his voice breaking with exasperation.

'This could be serious,' said the Doctor. 'Tell her what the date really is.'

'Second of October 160,' said Robin.

The Doctor nodded. 'This *is* serious. Fitz, Anji – come with me.'

The three strangers went to leave, but Morgan barred their way. 'Be in the Henry at eight bells tonight. I want to talk to you some more. Then I'll decide whether or not to let you stay. Don't try to leave – my Watchkeepers will be observing, wherever you go.'

The Doctor nodded. Then he addressed Aboetta. 'I'll want to speak to you later.'

Robin stepped towards the Doctor. 'You leave her alone!'

'Steady on, lad, they did save her life.' Morgan gestured at the door. 'You'd better go. But remember – eight bells.'

The Doctor nodded again, and then he and his companions were gone.

Aboetta was alone with Morgan and Robin.

'Now, what's all this confusion about the date?' said Morgan.

'There is no confusion,' said Aboetta. 'Look at me, Morgan! I'm barely twenty.' She thrust her face towards his. 'According to you I should be thirty; does this look like the face of a thirty-year-old?'

Morgan stepped backwards, shaking his head, clearly searching his mind for an explanation. 'I'll admit you look well, girl, but it must be soft living on Malahyde's estate.'

'It's Malahyde – he's messed with her head!' exclaimed Robin.

Aboetta hated being talked about as if she were not there. And blaming Mr Malahyde for this! With a sneer of contempt she shoved past Robin. Ignoring his protestations she stormed down the stairs and out of the house. She walked, not caring where she was going, hating Robin, her mind in turmoil. She hurried along the wide road which ran along the spine of the settlement from Three Lamps Gate to Knowle End, ignoring the people calling out to her, keeping to the shadows of the trees.

The trees. If it were February, the trees should be bare. But they bore leaves of rust red and bright yellow. And she was swishing her feet through wet piles of them which had built up on the road. She remembered the trees in Ashton Court – they wore their autumn colours too. The weather was mild, with none of the chill of winter. That was odd too, but again, it hadn't registered. Because time couldn't just 'jump' like that, could it?

Aboetta strove to calm herself. If time couldn't change, climate could. Perhaps this was some new effect of the Cleansing, only coming to light now, a century and a half on from Year Nought. But that wouldn't make sense of what Robin had said. Or how he looked.

Aboetta hurried on, past the rows of stone houses, up the hill towards the church at the centre of Totterdown. The effort she was putting into walking calmed her down a little. At the brow of the hill she turned round. There, above the misty ruins of Bristol, she could see the suspension towers of the Bridge, distant enough to look like a toy. The sun had sunk down below the hills beyond the bridge; there was a line of bright gold light against the horizon. The sky was pale blue with banks of purplish cloud like great cliffs in the air.

Below, she could see the roofs of the houses by the side of the road stretching down, and the open land beyond leading to the Wall. Over to the west she could see the windmills against the sky, still now after the day's work, as were most of the people in the quiet of the early evening.

Aboetta turned and walked towards the church. It was built like a fortress, the original red-brick building reinforced over the decades since Year Nought. Its bell-tower doubled as a Watchtower as it was the highest point in Totterdown and for miles around.

Next door to it and farther down the slope was the inn, a stout L-shaped building with a thatched roof. It had been an inn before Year

Nought, called the George after the last King before the Cleansing. Now it was called the Henry, in honour of Henry Foster, the Citizen Elder who had founded Totterdown Settlement. Its windows were unlit as yet, though she knew there would be workers inside, quenching their thirst after the work of the day.

She hesitated before the entrance of the church. Just as it was said that the Cleansing had been God's will, perhaps this dislocation in time was also His doing. But why? Aboetta was suddenly consumed with the need for prayer, the need for answers, and hurried towards the church doors. It would be some time before evening worship, hopefully she would be alone.

But as soon as she was upon them the doors swung open and two figures emerged, dressed in the black robes of the Church. The one on the left she recognised as Father Cluny, a short man with thinning red hair and a pinched-looking face (but older-looking now, deeper wrinkles, the flesh on his face sagging). The other one was a stranger who she at first took to be the Doctor, but as he emerged from the shadows she saw this was not so. He was tall, and seemed about the same age, and his hair hung around his shoulders, but his features were darker than those of the Doctor. Whilst the Doctor was skeletal and pale, this man was swarthy, almost feral.

They stopped in front of her. 'Aboetta,' said Father Cluny, his voice quavering with pity.

Aboetta was tired of hearing her name spoken in such tones. 'Father Cluny. Father...?'

'Gottlieb,' said the other priest. His voice was strong and clear in contrast to the older man's.

'Father Gottlieb is from the Odd Down settlement near Bath. He's come to pay his respects to your father.'

Father Cluny began to speak of her father, of how sad it was that he had to die without seeing his daughter again.

Whilst he spoke something struck Aboetta. She had heard about her father's illness only that morning – but according to Robin, he had died yesterday!

Time out of joint. God testing her.

'I need to see his grave,' she said, cutting across the old priest's

42

flow of sympathy.

'Of course, of course,' said Father Cluny. He put an arm around Aboetta and led her around the side of the church, down a narrow path between bushes towards the cemetery.

'What are your plans now, Miss Cigetrais?' said Father Gottlieb, bending to avoid a low branch.

Aboetta looked sideways at him. Another stranger. But he was a priest, and Father Cluny seemed at ease with him. Didn't mean Aboetta had to trust him. 'I have no plans.'

'Will you return to Ashton Court?'

It was a possibility. What was left for her here? 'I may. I may not.'

Father Cluny was struggling down the slope, his breath coming in annoyed-sounding wheezes. 'Stop questioning the girl, can't you see she's grieving?'

'I am sorry. Please forgive me. I am merely curious about the estate, and its inhabitants.'

Aboetta was instantly on her guard. Was this man really a priest? He could be the leader of a band of outlaws, planning to attack Ashton Court.

She gently removed Father Cluny's arm from hers and said, 'I would rather be alone at my father's graveside. You had better return to the church – it can't be long until evensong.'

Father Cluny looked shocked as if he'd just remembered, and Father Gottlieb bowed.

'Of course,' he said. 'We will talk later?'

'Yes. Later,' said Aboetta, mentally urging them to go. And at last they did, one hobbling and bent, the other tall and striding, walking slowly to keep pace with the older man.

When she was sure they had gone Aboetta turned and ran down the hill towards the graveyard.

Anji stuck close to Fitz as they walked up the hill towards the church. It was now full evening, the sky was a deep blue, and it had grown quite chilly.

'So. Not only are we in another alternative reality,' said Fitz, 'but someone appears to be dicking around with time as well.'

'Either that, or Aboetta's mad,' said Anji.

'If she isn't, and this is Year 160, that means history changed in 1843,' said Fitz. 'At least we know that now.'

'Much good that knowledge does us – we can't do anything without the TARDIS.'

They reached the top of the hill, where a red-brick church stood, commanding a view over the whole settlement. As they drew level with it, a bell rang out. Anji counted seven tolls. From here, she could see torches blazing in the towers spaced along the wooden wall which surrounded the settlement. The land beyond was in complete darkness. In contrast, Anji could see soft yellow firelight from behind the windows of the cottages lining the road. It all seemed very cosy, very civilised.

'Things seems to have stuck at a nineteenth-century level,' said Anji. 'There doesn't seem to have been an Industrial Revolution.'

Fitz grinned down at her. 'Hey, maybe that's a good thing! No pollution, no exploitation of the working classes...'

His voice tailed off. Two men approached them, barring their way.

This was it, thought Anji.

Fitz squared up to them. 'Evening.'

The two men said nothing. They glared at Anji, and then shoved past.

Despite herself, Anji was shaking.

'We'd better get to the inn,' said Fitz. 'We'll be safer there.'

But Anji didn't want to show that the encounter had rattled her. 'We've got an hour. Shouldn't we look for the Doctor?'

'Huh!' said Fitz. 'In a place this size? It's as big as a small town! He could be anywhere.'

After leaving Aboetta's house they'd had a brief conference. The Doctor had seemed agitated, as though the apparent time discrepancy had really got to him. He'd assured them the settlement was safe, said he was going for a recce, and advised them to do the same. Look for clues.

But they hadn't found any.

'We could at least try to talk to some of the locals,' said Anji. 'Try to find out something.'

'After what just happened?' said Fitz. 'And – look.' He pointed to the far side of the street.

The two men had stopped in the shadow of a long, low stone building. They were speaking to another man, and pointing at Fitz and Anji.

'It's not worth it,' reasoned Fitz. 'Come on, we'll be safer in the inn.'

'You mean, you fancy a pint,' said Anji, but she allowed Fitz to lead her back down the hill.

'That too,' said Fitz, licking his lips.

Aboetta knelt before her father's grave. It was just a mound of mud, speckled with stones like stars. It smelled of fresh, wet earth, like the flowerbeds in her garden at Ashton Court. Hard to believe her father – tall and strong, always full of jokes and stories and love – was underneath. No tears, not even a feeling of sadness, nothing: her heart floating on an empty sea.

There was no headstone, not yet. It was probably still being engraved. She remembered the engraver, an old stonemason with hair and eyes as grey as the materials he worked with, always coughing, but hands always steady. Would he still be alive, after ten years?

The church bell rang out, making her jump. She waited for the ringing to die away. Seven bells. Aboetta raised her gaze from the mound, and stared at the torches in the distant Watchtowers, suddenly realising that she was beginning to accept it. Beginning to accept, however mad and impossible, that ten years had passed whilst she had been with Mr Malahyde.

Footsteps behind her. Aboetta sighed, almost swore under her breath but remembered where she was. Why was it so hard to be alone when there were so few people in the world? The black humour of the thought made her smile in spite of herself.

She turned round, expecting to see Robin, but it was Morgan Foster. She relaxed. The Chief Elder had been a personal friend of her father's, she'd known him since she was a child.

'Aboetta, I am glad that you have come back.' He held up a massive hand. 'Now I am not going to talk of how long you have been gone, or about Robin, or the attack from which these strangers rescued you. I am simply glad that you are safe.'

He held out his arms, and, after a moment's hesitation, Aboetta allowed herself to be hugged. And found herself hugging him back, and crying, face buried in the rough folds of his cape. A part of her hoped no one would see her like this – probably couldn't in the dusk of the wooded cemetery – but another part was glad of the release.

After a while they stood apart and looked at each other. Then Morgan said, 'You don't have to stay in your father's house. Come and stay with me, at least for a few days.'

Aboetta wiped her tears away with her sleeve. 'I don't know.'

'You must be hungry, after such a journey, such a day.'

Aboetta realised that she was, ravenously so. Her stomach gave a low grumble as if reminding her it still existed. 'Yes, I am.'

They began to walk back up the hill through the wrought-iron cemetery gates to Morgan Foster's house.

'Has Malahyde been treating you well?' asked Morgan after a while.

'Yes, of course,' said Aboetta, heart sinking a little at the prospect of more questioning.

'He had to let you come here, of course,' mused the Chief Elder. 'But did he say if he expected you to return?'

Aboetta remembered her last conversation with Malahyde. 'I think he would like me to.'

'You know why he wants you back.' A pause. Then it came: 'He has no heir.'

Aboetta stopped and stared at Morgan Foster.

The old man looked uncomfortable. 'Surely, you must know? He has mentioned this?'

Aboetta stared. Mr Malahyde never mentioned his parents. But they must have lived in the mansion house, and their parents, and so on all the way back to Year Nought. 'No. He never talks of his family.'

Morgan shrugged, his cape lifting in a slight breeze. 'Well, that's my theory.' He pointed at her. 'But I rather think I am right.'

They walked on in silence. The thought of Mr Malahyde, and

herself... He was so unlike Robin in every way.

'You'll stay here now, of course,' said Morgan. 'Your place is here.'

The hug had worn off completely now and Aboetta felt that she had never known Morgan Foster. 'I shall decide where my place is.'

Morgan Foster said nothing. They walked in silence to the Chief Elder's house.

Fitz lifted the metal pint pot to his lips and took a big draught. He swallowed the beer, feeling it slosh down into his stomach. He plonked the pot back on the table, smacked his lips and grinned at Anji. 'This is good stuff!'

'Any idea how we're going to pay for it?'

'Nope. Haven't seen any evidence of money in this place.' He shrugged. 'Perhaps they use a barter system?'

Anji smiled wickedly. 'You could trade in your jacket – how many pints do you reckon it's worth?'

Fitz hunched over the table. 'From the attention it's been getting, infinity. How's the wine?'

Anji had a little metal tumbler of pale golden liquid. 'Foul beyond belief.' She picked up a slice of bread which looked like a hunk of wood.

Fitz mouthed a 'may I?' and took a sip. Then he grimaced and put it back down on the trestle table in front of Anji. 'Never mix the grape and the grain,' he said hoarsely.

They were sitting at a corner table in the main room of the Henry. Fires blazed in stone-lined pits along the middle. People were roasting things in them. At one end was the 'bar' – really a collection of barrels and a bench across the width of the inn – and at the other end was a balcony reached by a set of wooden steps against the wall. This balcony was empty at the moment. Fitz wondered if it was for the local band. Minstrels. Mummers. Whatever.

The air was laced with smoke from the fires and fumes from the stuff the locals were smoking. The atmosphere was raucous and ribald, but in a laid-back way. Fitz and Anji had caused a stir when they'd entered half an hour ago, people were naturally curious about them. Blaney the landlord had ushered them to their table and given them drinks 'on the house' in thanks for saving Aboetta. And food: rough chunks of bread, and a steaming stew, very oniony, with dumplings that looked disconcertingly like little grey brains.

Now Fitz was on his second pint and, as Anji had pointed out, it wasn't clear if it was on the house.

'Why are they so interested in my jacket?' muttered Fitz.

'Seems to be a rarity,' said Anji through a mouthful of bread. 'The only other leather I've seen is on that Chief Elder chap.'

Fitz thought about this. 'Come to think of it I haven't seen any animals.' He looked around the smoky interior of the inn. 'And this is the sort of place where they'd be roasting a pig if they could find one.'

'No animals,' said Anji, gazing into a nearby fire. 'Or birds!' She grabbed Fitz's arm.

This was true. Fitz couldn't remember seeing a single bird either. 'Well, it's autumn – don't they all fly south?'

Anji grimaced. 'You're asking me, the city girl?'

Fitz remembered the bird table in the garden from when he was a kid. Remembered his mother putting out bits of suet for the winter birds. She attached great importance to it, always making Fitz watch, and gazing up into the autumn sky as if she expected birds to flutter down and alight upon her as if she were some kind of saint. The memory seemed horribly distant, stretched across multitudes of realities. Fitz suddenly wondered if there were any Kreiners in this version of Earth.

He picked up his pint and took a deep draught. 'There should be some birds around, anyway. Sparrows, robins, those sorts of things.'

'The only Robin I've seen is that miserable bloke who fancies Aboetta,' said Anji.

'No ducks on the river, either,' said Fitz. 'Or geese. So you're saying, whatever happened to create this version of Earth wiped out all the animals, but let humans survive?'

'I'm not saying anything,' said Anji. 'Just keeping my eyes open, and so on.' She frowned. 'Where is the Doctor, anyway?'

'Dunno. Maybe he's collared Aboetta.'

'He'd better be here.' Anji glared at some locals who were pointing at her and laughing. 'The sooner we sort this out and get to somewhere properly civilised, the better.'

She was – what was the word? – bridling, thought Fitz. Like a police horse on a hot summer day. He wished he could do something to help her relax. 'Seems civilised enough.'

'Not very observant, are you?' said Anji. She pointed to a corner of the bar. Fitz had to turn round to look.

Two of the chain-mailed guards – Watchkeepers – were leaning on barrels, chatting to the landlord. Pistols, similar to Aboetta's, were laid across the top of the barrels. Every now and then the Watchkeepers looked across at Fitz and Anji.

Fitz turned round and shrugged. 'So what? Look at it from their point of view. We're outsiders. We have no idea what dangers we could represent to these people. I'd say we're lucky being treated so well. At least they haven't locked us up.'

'That's only because we saved Aboetta,' said Anji. She grimaced. 'God help us when we have to explain where we're from.'

Fitz took another gulp of beer. 'Oh, the Doctor will see us all right. He always does.'

Anji coughed into her hand.

'Well, all right. He usually does.'

Chapter 5
A Forbidden Subject

There was a stone seat outside the church, tucked into the corner between the bell-tower and the main building, hidden under the branches of an ancient yew tree. It was one of Aboetta's favourite places, and there she sat now, staring into the night. It was fully dark, the sky as black as tar. Bright beacons of fire marked the boundary of Totterdown as the Watchkeepers kept their endless vigil. Inside the settlement, soft yellow lights burned at the windows of the houses, and off to the left she could hear sounds of drunken merriment at the Henry.

Aboetta watched the dancing flames of the braziers on the Watchtowers and munched on an apple. She had gone back to Morgan Foster's house, where he had served her a plain but welcome meal of bread and a delicious turnip and swede stew which brought back in an instant memories of the past. She had been saddened to discover that Morgan's wife Anne had died some years ago, and the Chief Elder now lived alone. He hadn't yet taken a new wife, but Aboetta knew that he must do so soon, to produce an heir. The Fosters had been rulers ever since Year 3 and if Morgan didn't produce a son, the Citizens' Council would call for the election of a new Chief Elder and the family's unbroken rule of Totterdown would be at an end.

Things had moved on so much.

Aboetta threw the apple core out over the churchyard, where it vanished into the shadows between the gravestones.

Footsteps approached, from around the front of the church. Aboetta stood. Probably Robin, come to plead with her again. A part of her hoped it was him, as she had known him, tall and strong and handsome. If only she could roll back time.

A figure resolved itself out of the darkness. A man. The Doctor.

He nodded politely when he noticed her, then sighed and stared out towards the beacons on the Watchtowers.

Aboetta stayed on her guard, not yet ready to trust these strangers. The method of their arrival still bothered her. She hadn't told anyone about it yet, mainly because she didn't know what to say. That blue box arriving out of nowhere – an impossibility. Another impossibility.

'I came out here to talk with you, Aboetta,' said the Doctor at last.

'You did?' Perhaps he was going to explain himself.

He turned his face towards her. He had something of the bearing of Mr Malahyde, a gentlemanly way about him, and his voice was cultured and accent-less, almost clipped. The voice of a man who knew what he was about. 'Something's happened to you which you can't even begin to rationalise.'

She never liked talking about her feelings to anyone, but with a shock she realised that something about the way this Doctor spoke, the look in his eyes, made her trust his words. 'Yes.'

'Something to do with time.' The Doctor kept his eyes fixed on hers, watching her carefully.

'Yes,' said Aboetta again. 'I don't understand it. It's impossible, surely? Unless I've been asleep for ten years.'

'There could be a number of explanations. You could as you say have been asleep or in some form of suspended animation – but no, you'd know about that. Or you could have been caught up in a temporal anomaly.'

The sound of breaking glass from the Henry. A raucous chorus of cheers.

'So you believe me? That I have only been gone as long as I say, not what others believe?'

The Doctor sat beside her on the stone bench. To her surprise, this didn't annoy her. 'Where were you for those four months?'

So he believed her – or seemed to. 'In the employment of Mr Jared Malahyde.'

'Who is?'

Aboetta gaped in astonishment. 'You must have heard of him!'

'Sorry, I'm new to this, er, area.'

'He lives in the mansion house in Ashton Court, on the other side of Avon Gorge. No one knows much about him. Not even me.'

'Jared Malahyde,' said the Doctor slowly, as if trying to fetch up a memory. 'Malahyde, Malahyde, Malahyde.' Then he shook his head. 'Never heard of him. In your time there, did you notice anything odd about him? Or the house?'

Aboetta smiled. 'Everything about him is a little odd, I suppose. He is a hermit, after all. And the house…' Aboetta shrugged.

'It's big, isn't it? Rather big for just the two of you. Any places that he doesn't let you see, forbidden rooms, that sort of thing?'

'The cellar,' said Aboetta. 'Mr Malahyde says it's not safe, there's dangerous equipment down there.'

'The cellar.' The Doctor began shaking, and Aboetta was alarmed until she realised he was laughing. 'The obvious place for secrets. Well, I wonder if you could arrange it for me to have an audience with this mysterious Malahyde?'

Aboetta shook her head. 'He sees no one, Doctor, except for me and his staff.'

'Staff?'

'Gardeners, estate workers. Guards. Like Captain Bryant and Lieutenant Collins. And me. If I go back.'

'We'll see about that,' said the Doctor. Suddenly the silence was split with the sound of a tolling bell. Eight chimes rang out, clear and resonant. The echoing cadences rolled away into the night.

'Eight bells,' said the Doctor. 'Time for my little chat with Morgan Foster.'

He made to walk off.

'Doctor,' called Aboetta.

He turned back to her. 'Yes?'

'Who are you?'

The Doctor walked round so he was standing in front of her, his silhouette outlined by stars. 'Who am I, where am I am from? That doesn't matter. What matters is that you trust me. I am here to help. So, for that matter, are Fitz and Anji.'

Aboetta felt a surge of emotion – she wanted to trust the Doctor, it would make things so much easier. But there was something about him, something wrong, an aura of danger. She knew somehow that he represented a threat. How, and to whom or what, she didn't yet know.

His voice was an urgent whisper. 'Do you trust me?'

Perhaps it would be best to say that she did. Humour him. 'Yes.'

The Doctor smiled. 'That is all I ask. Thank you.' He turned to look up at the stars again. After a minute or so he said good-night and slipped away into the darkness.

Aboetta watched him from the shadows of the church. Then she stared out over the city, in the direction of the bridge and Ashton Court.

Fitz was beginning to feel nicely sloshed when eight bells clearly sounded from the church tower next door to the Henry. He couldn't help but smile at Anji's worried 'where the hell is the Doctor?' expression.

As soon as the final chimes were swallowed up in the general hubbub, the door swung open and Morgan Foster stepped through.

A hush fell over the rowdy ensemble. Several low, respectful salutations were heard, gleaming metal tankards were raised. Morgan nodded at Blaney, at which signal the level of noise returned to normal.

Anji nudged Fitz. 'Trust the Doctor not to be on time.'

The Chief Elder strode over to their table. He stood above them, hands on hips, his face red in the firelight. 'Where is the Doctor?'

Fitz felt a sudden, strange urge to stand up and say, 'Don't know, Sir.'

'We don't know,' said Anji.

Fitz frowned. Why had he felt the need to respond to Morgan as an authority figure? He may be top dog of some rain-sodden hill fort but that should mean zip. Suddenly there was a commotion at the doorway and the Doctor appeared, a little out of breath. He caught sight of Fitz and Anji and beamed. Then he saw Morgan Foster and his smile vanished. 'Not *too* late, I hope?'

The Chief Elder shook his head, a quick, curt gesture, and bellowed, 'Blaney! Pint pot for our guest!'

Blaney the landlord hurried over. He was a small man, wiry and watchful, and he seemed to be perpetually sweating. He held out a frothing tankard to the Doctor, who was looking around himself with interest and a vague smile on his lips. He took the pot from Blaney without looking at it, and, to Fitz's open-mouthed astonishment, raised it to his lips and downed it in one go.

This hadn't gone unnoticed, and the inn swelled with a ragged chorus of cheers.

Morgan laughed. 'Thirsty work, rescuing young maids, is it, Doctor?'

The Doctor nodded and wiped his lips. He was glaring at Morgan, watching him like a hawk watches its prey. 'Very.'

Then Morgan grew serious. 'Follow me. Bring your friends.' He turned and made off along the length of the inn towards the balcony.

Fitz drained the rest of his pint and stood. Anji had already leapt up with alacrity, clearly pleased to see the Doctor again.

They followed Morgan up the steps. Fitz wasn't surprised to hear the two Watchkeepers who had been, well, keeping watch on them, clump up after.

The balcony was dominated by a table which ran along its length. At the far end of this was a wooden chair with a high back. An oil-lamp burned in the centre of the table.

Fitz was surprised to see two people already sitting down, on the side away from the balcony: a young man with dark hair and an older man with receding red hair. Both had black robes which seemed to merge into the gloom. The younger man had a hefty silver cross around his neck, which glinted in the murky yellow light. Priests?

Morgan motioned for them all to sit. The wooden boards creaked alarmingly as they did so. Morgan sat in the large chair, as Fitz had expected, the two priests to his right, the Doctor, Fitz and Anji to his left with their backs to the railing. The Doctor sat nearest the Chief Elder, Fitz nearest the exit, as was his policy in situations where a quick leg-it might be needed.

'I'm the Doctor, this is Fitz and Anji.'

'Father Franz Gottlieb,' said the younger man.

'Father Cluny,' said the red-haired priest curtly.

They all reached over the table and shook hands with each other, an awkward manoeuvre as they had to avoid the oil-lamp.

Morgan shrugged his cape on to the back of the chair. 'Doctor,' he began. 'You are clearly a civilised man, maybe even a Citizen, as are your companions.' He nodded to Fitz and Anji. 'Such people as ourselves are rare. The world is full of outlaws and Wildren.'

The old priest nodded at this and clasped his hands on the table in front of him.

'So you will understand,' continued Morgan, 'that I need a full and frank account of yourselves. I cannot risk the security of this settlement. It would be far easier, from my point of view, to have you thrown out, than to risk any danger.'

He leaned back, the chair creaking as it took his full weight.

Fitz's mouth was dry. What the hell was the Doctor going to say? They knew nothing of this world, *nothing*. Fitz wished he had another beer.

'We are travellers, that much you already know,' said the Doctor. 'We are from the north. Six months ago, our settlement was overrun by outlaws and burned down. Ever since then we have been nomads, moving from place to place, staying for a while, helping out, then moving on.'

Morgan Foster seemed to consider this. 'Your clothes', he rumbled, 'are very fine, for nomads.'

There was the briefest of pauses. Fitz could almost hear the whirling of the Doctor's thoughts. 'We like to take good care of them. They are all we have, being nomads.'

Morgan looked like he didn't believe a word of this.

'And what of you, girl?' said the priest with dark hair. 'You are certainly not, originally at least, from the north of *this* country.'

'How perceptive of you.' Anji looked daggers at the young priest.

Father Gottlieb smiled. 'Forgive my curiosity but it is rare to see someone from the Indian sub-continent. Where are you from, Hindustan?'

Anji glanced at the Doctor, who gave a slight nod. 'Well, my grandparents were,' she said slowly. 'I was born here. I am a native of this country.'

Fitz wondered how many – if any – other non-whites lived in England in this reality. From the silence that followed Anji's explanation it seemed as though no one believed her.

But at last Morgan Foster said, 'It is plausible, I suppose.'

Then the Doctor, who had been silent for a minute or so, drummed his fingers on the table. 'What do you know about Aboetta's employer, this Malahyde chap?'

Everyone seemed a bit thrown by this non sequitur but Fitz was glad the Doctor was changing the subject away from themselves.

Morgan shrugged. 'Not much at all. He keeps himself to himself. We don't have much to do with him.'

'Why do you want to know?' asked Father Gottlieb.

'Because of what Aboetta said. She thinks she's only been gone for four months, yet according to you she's been away for a decade.'

Morgan shook his head. 'The girl is disturbed. The death of her father must have shaken her up.'

'I've spoken to her and I don't think she's "disturbed",' said the Doctor.

'What other explanation can there be?' said Morgan.

'That something has gone wrong with time.'

There was a silence. Then the younger priest spoke. 'You mean, like the Cleansing?'

The older priest glared at him. 'Father Gottlieb!'

Gottlieb sighed. 'It's all right to talk about it amongst ourselves, surely?'

This produced quite a reaction. Morgan Foster took a sharp intake of breath.

'Discussing the Cleansing is forbidden,' said Morgan gravely. 'It is not spoken about among the common Citizenry. Most believe it to be God's doing.'

'For there is no other explanation,' said Father Cluny with passion.

The Doctor was doing a great job of covering up the burning curiosity Fitz knew he must be feeling. 'Well, I'd like to hear what you think caused it.'

The old priest stood, watery blue eyes blazing as much as they could. 'The Cleansing was God's purpose! His will! The human race was reborn in full innocence at Year Nought!'

The Cleansing? Fitz couldn't help but notice that Anji was staring down at the table top, blinking furiously. He suddenly had a pretty horrible idea of what it could mean.

'That's interesting!' said the Doctor. 'Are there any secular explanations?'

'Lock them up!' snarled Father Cluny. 'They are questioning God's will!'

Father Gottlieb put a hand on the old man's shoulder, a look of irritation on his swarthy features. 'No, don't lock them up, they haven't done anything wrong.'

Father Cluny swung round to face him. 'How dare you question my authority? Remember you are a visitor here too – do you want to join them in their cell?'

'Morgan,' said the Doctor, hands spread in a conciliatory gesture. 'Surely you are not going to have us locked up?'

Morgan looked undecided for a moment, but then nodded. 'I'm sorry. The security of the settlement is paramount.'

Fitz could hardly believe it. 'Bloody hell. We rescued Aboetta! Brought her back safe and sound!'

'You could have influenced her, made her lie for you.'

Fitz sprang to his feet, ready to run, hoisting Anji up by the arm. But the two Watchkeepers were barring the only exit from the balcony.

'What's the matter, Morgan?' said the Doctor. 'Have you no mind of your own? Are you going to let the clergy determine your every decision?'

Father Cluny began bleating again but his words were cut off by Morgan's roar.

'Enough! Take them away. We'll decide their fate in the morning.'

The Watchkeepers advanced.

'Well done, Doctor,' said Anji, her voice a tired lilt of sarcasm. 'You took your time, but you got us locked up eventually.'

There was complete silence in the inn as they were marched out into the October night.

Chapter 6
No Going Back

It was with trepidation that Aboetta knocked on Evelyn's door. From her point of view, four months ago Evelyn had been married to Adam Rebouteux for just over a year. But if ten years *had* passed, what could have happened? Anything – children, disease, even death.

But when the door opened Aboetta knew it was the first of these. A tousled head poked out. Big eyes in a pale face peered up at her.

Aboetta was lost for words. The child – a boy – was a miniature Evelyn, the same button eyes and black hair.

'Is your mother there?'

The child turned and bawled, 'Ma!'

Aboetta stood on the threshold, feeling at once thrilled and saddened. A woman appeared, tucking the boy inside with one hand and holding the door with the other. Evelyn, but older, more worn-looking. Her thick black hair was cut close to her head, and her face, once as smooth as water, was now showing lines across her forehead and under her eyes. Which still sparkled, but, Aboetta fancied, less than they used to.

'Ab!' cried Evelyn. 'God, so it's true!'

They hugged, and went inside to the parlour.

A fire blazed in the hearth, a long wooden table in front of it, the small square room a mess of wooden children's toys.

Evelyn dodged around the room, her angular frame bending and unbending as she tidied up, talking all the time. Aboetta remembered how upset Evelyn had been when she had left. She had cried, hugged Aboetta so hard she thought her ribs might crack.

'I'd heard you come back! I would have sought you out earlier but I've been so busy – Jake! to bed, now! – my God, you don't look a day over twenty, girl!' Evelyn stopped and stood before her. 'What's that Malahyde got? The fountain of youth?'

Suddenly it seemed to Aboetta that there was a barrier between herself and her friend. Ten years between them, and a child – probably more, from the thumping and bumping she could hear coming from upstairs. And worse – to Evelyn, Aboetta was now part of the enigma that was Malahyde and his estate.

'You're looking good too, Evelyn,' said Aboetta awkwardly. 'How's Adam?'

Evelyn sneered. 'Ah, he's in the Henry getting pot-valiant with all the others. Won't see him till gone midnight.' Evelyn reached out and stroked Aboetta's arm. 'Your skin, so smooth,' she whispered. 'Easy life for you, eh?'

There was an undertone of resentment in the remark. 'Not really.' She did enough work – the reason her skin looked so young was because she was, somehow, still only twenty.

'Hey, seen Robin yet? He's been moping after you this full ten year!'

'No,' lied Aboetta, not wanting to talk or even think about Robin. 'Look, Evelyn, this might seem a bit sudden, but can I stay here tonight?'

'Course you can!' said Evelyn. 'I'll make up the spare room.'

Evelyn poured some wine and they talked about events in Totterdown over the last decade. Nothing much seemed to have changed. People had died, like Anne Foster – like her father – others had been born. Evelyn had four children aged from eight – Jake, the boy who had answered the door – down to one born just this year. Life went on. It reassured Aboetta that there were places like Totterdown. It gave her hope for the future of the people left in the world.

After several goblets of wine, Aboetta was beginning to feel relaxed and sleepy. She was just drifting off when there was a knock at the door.

Evelyn, who had also been dozing, leapt up, muttering dark things about Adam.

But Aboetta was surprised to see not Evelyn's husband enter the parlour, but Robin.

'I'll leave you two alone for a while,' said Evelyn, flashing a meaningful glance at Aboetta and retreating upstairs.

Aboetta stood to confront Robin. 'How did you know I was here?'

Robin wasn't wearing his chain mail. Instead, he wore a coarse coat with a high collar. He'd brought in the cool sharp smell of the autumn night. 'You had to be somewhere.'

'You mean you've been knocking at every house where you thought I might be? Aren't you supposed to be keeping watch?'

Robin's eyes flashed, reflecting the firelight. 'I'm Head of the Watch now, Aboetta. I don't work this late at night.'

Aboetta wished Evelyn would come back down. 'What do you want?'

He stepped towards her. 'Those strangers, the ones that say they saved you?'

'What about them?'

Robin smiled broadly. 'Morgan's had them locked up.'

Aboetta took her hand away from his, alarmed. 'Why? What have they done?'

'Asked questions,' said Robin gravely. 'About the Cleansing.'

'Oh. Shocking. Surprised he's only locked them up.'

'You know we never speak of it!'

'Why not?' said Aboetta, feeling suddenly rebellious. 'It shaped our world. Made us who we are.'

'It was the will of God and shouldn't be questioned!' He shook his head. 'That Malahyde's been filling your head with ideas! God-fearing, is he?' He stepped towards her. 'Are you?'

Aboetta was suddenly scared. Robin was Head Watchkeeper, after all. He could report her to Morgan, get her locked up with the others. 'You've come looking for me, only to threaten me?'

There was a pause, filled by the gentle crackling of the fire.

'I'm sorry,' he said at last. Then he looked at her, a pleading expression in his eyes. 'I had to see you.'

'Robin, we're strangers to each other now. Something has happened I don't understand, which has changed everything.' He began to speak, but she held up a hand. 'I don't want to talk about it. All I want to do is go to bed and sleep and maybe in the morning…' She tailed off. She didn't really believe things would be any different in the morning.

'Aboetta,' he said softly. 'I don't understand it either. So I'm older, so what? We all get older. I'm still me, still Robin.'

She looked at him then, allowed her eyes to meet his. And in the soft orange glow of the fire, she believed him. Maybe it was a trick of the light, but he looked like the handsome young man who had courted her.

'I know,' she said. 'I'm just scared. Confused.'

'I'm glad to see you again. You're so beautiful.' His voice was level, calm. No confusion there.

They were standing almost toe-to-toe now. Aboetta leaned forwards and kissed him gently on the lips.

She let herself fall.

Robin's was the largest of the Watchkeepers' cottages, set aside from the rest, at the foot of the hill near to the Three Lamps Tower. It was a simple, one-storey affair, with three rooms: a kitchen-washroom, a parlour and a bedroom. Robin got the fire going, making a play of fumbling the logs and dropping the firelighters as he always used to, and poured out some wine.

They sat next to each other at the large kitchen table.

Soon they were embracing, then kissing passionately. All of her confusion seemed to vanish as his strong arms held her to him. Yes, said her heart, this is where I am meant to be. I am home.

She allowed him to lead her through to the bedroom. They undressed, and embraced again. In the candle-light, his body looked bulkier than she had known before, and felt softer, but his passion was as strong as it had ever been.

They fell on to the bed and made love. Aboetta gave herself fully, feeling her pleasure beginning to soar towards a distant, heady peak.

But before that peak was within reach, it was over. All too soon, he was beside her on the bed, his breath surging in great wheezes, his thinning hair plastered to his head with sweat.

Aboetta lay unfulfilled, wanting to forgive him – it had been his first time with her for ten years – but too angry with herself for sleeping with him in the first place to feel any sense of forgiveness. And there was something else – in ten years, could she really believe he had found no one else? Surely, he would have said. Or would he? In his silence, was he lying to her?

Aboetta turned away from him.

'Aboetta. Why did you leave?'

The question was like a cold shock. 'You know why. My mother died.' She felt tears prickle her eyes. 'And now father's gone and I didn't even have the chance to say goodbye.'

'That wasn't the only reason, was it?' His voice was gentle, but reproachful.

'No. You know it wasn't.' She sat up, needled. 'Why ask questions to which you already know the answer?'

He turned to look up at her. 'Because, Aboetta, you're still young! There's still a chance you – we – can have children.'

'I don't know.' It was rare for a girl of her age not to have produced at least one child. Part of the reason she'd left was to get away from the constant pressure on her – mostly from Robin, but also from the other women of Totterdown.

And now she'd returned, it was exactly the same! Robin still expected her to bear his child!

No – not the same. Worse: now, her father wasn't there to take her side.

Robin mumbled something and rolled over. Soon he was asleep.

Aboetta realised, finally and utterly, that she didn't love him. Wine and nostalgia and lust had led to this moment, this mistake. And what a mistake! What if, now, Robin's seed was growing within her? She'd be trapped in Totterdown forever.

She thought of the mansion house, the calm serenity of its rooms, the shelves of books, the gentle companionship and kindness of Mr Malahyde.

Robin began to snore.

Aboetta couldn't even cry.

As she lay there in the gloom, she made up her mind. And a plan began to form. When she was sure nothing would wake Robin, she slipped from the bed and dressed as quickly as she could. Then, picking up her pack and pistol, she slipped out into the night.

Anji sat in darkness, her back against the rough stone wall, her knees drawn up under her chin. Despite the cold, damp air, she was drowsy. How long had they been here? Seemed like hours now. An irregular metallic clicking prevented her from falling fully asleep.

'How are you getting on?' Fitz's voice jolted Anji wide awake.

'Not very well.' The annoying noise suddenly stopped. 'Are you sure you haven't got anything sturdier than this paper-clip?'

'Nope,' said Fitz, sitting down on the bed.

'You, Anji?'

'No.' Anji yawned. 'Face it, Doctor, we're here until morning.' She shivered. 'And then we'll probably be chucked out into the wilderness.' She thought longingly of the TARDIS, somewhere in the ruins of the city.

'Oh well,' said the Doctor, and set to work on the lock again.

Their cell was part of Totterdown's small gaol, a slab of grey stone in the middle of an overgrown area at the edge of the river. Stone walls, floor, and ceiling, one tiny window. A big wooden door braced with metal, completely immovable, with an apparently unpickable lock. Three wooden pallets which passed for beds, rough mattresses and pillows stuffed with straw. Anji's arms and legs itched, so probably fleas as well. The only light came from the window, a shaft of pale moonlight making a square on the opposite wall.

Anji thought back to what had got them locked up. They seemed to have broken a pretty major taboo. 'I wonder what this Cleansing business is?'

'I don't know, but I've got a few nasty ideas,' said the Doctor.

'So have I,' said Anji. 'Have you seen anyone who isn't white? It's the twenty-first century and I'm the only person of Indian extraction in Bristol.'

There was an uncomfortable silence. 'If that's your theory,' he said gently, 'then wouldn't their reaction to you have been more, well, violent?'

'I suppose,' said Anji. But she wasn't convinced.

'I wonder what Father Cluny meant, "reborn in full innocence at Year Nought"?' came the Doctor's voice out of the darkness.

Anji's closed her eyes. It didn't make much difference. 'A massive epiphany of some sort? An alternative reality of born-again Christians?'

'That's the trouble with religion, it's very hard to separate the facts from the myths. If, indeed, there are any facts to begin with – aha!'

Anji opened her eyes and sat up.

'I've picked the lock!' The Doctor grunted as he pushed the door. 'Oh dear.'

'What?' asked Anji.

The Doctor sighed. 'They must have barred the door from the outside as well. Taking no chances.'

Suddenly there was a scraping sound and then the door opened, with a jolt at first, then more slowly.

'How in Lennon's name did you do that?' marvelled Fitz.

The Doctor shrugged. 'I don't know.' He moved to the door, ready to clobber whoever it was.

The door opened fully, and someone stepped in.

'Aboetta?' said the Doctor. 'What are you doing here?'

Aboetta raised a finger to her lips. 'The guard sleeps. Come with me.'

'Why are you doing this?'

She moved towards the Doctor, the ray of moonlight falling across her face. Her eyes were red and puffy as though she had been crying. 'I need your help, Doctor. I want to go back to Ashton Court.'

Anji saw the Doctor's smile caught in the moonbeam. 'You've got my help, Aboetta.'

Aboetta smiled, and grabbed Fitz. 'Help me with the Watchkeeper.'

They crept outside into the guard room – really just a flagstoned corridor at the front of the cells. At the far end, a Watchkeeper was slumped over a wooden table, his bulky figure picked out in a sphere of yellow light from the oil-lamp on the table next to him. Beside the lamp was a bottle. Empty. Anji could smell the alcohol fumes hanging in a cloud around the guard.

Anji watched as Fitz and the Doctor picked up the guard – chair and all – and manoeuvred him down the corridor and into the cell. The Doctor closed and locked the door.

Suddenly they were plunged into darkness. Anji realised that Aboetta had walked back up to the guard table and snuffed out the light.

'Well, what do we do now?' said Anji. 'We're out of the cell, but…'

She didn't need to finish her sentence. The wall – and its spiked ditch – and the watchtowers – loomed large and impassable in her mind.

Aboetta was a shape in the darkness. 'We go out through the river-gate.'

There was a scraping noise, as of boot against stone. 'Someone's coming!' said Anji.

The door to the gaol opened and a cloaked figure strode through. Something glinted in the scant light.

'Father Gottlieb?' said the Doctor, incredulously. 'What, come to read us our last rites?'

Anji realised what the glinting object was – the cross around the priest's neck.

Gottlieb stood in the door, barring their way. 'No. I have come to help you.'

'Why?' said the Doctor.

Gottlieb smiled. 'I find this place – confining.'

Anji followed Fitz in a crouching run to where two rowing boats were tethered to a small jetty. As Fitz fumbled with the mooring ropes, Anji glanced along the river.

The water-course had been artificially narrowed, the banks shouldering inwards to create a bottle-neck. On either shoulder stood two winch-towers which between them supported a portcullis-like gate: the river-gate. The Wall ran right up to the winch-towers, and a simple wooden bridge had been constructed across the bottle-neck. A torch blazed atop each winch-tower, and a Watchkeeper stood on the bridge.

Apart from the torches on the winch-towers, all was darkness – a bank of cloud hid the moon.

The mooring ropes untangled, Fitz helped Anji into the nearest boat. It was just like a pleasure-boat at a seaside resort: wide at the back, narrow at the front, with two crosswise planks for seats. Oars were stowed against the side, and once Anji was sitting, she fitted them into the – what were they called? – rowlocks.

'You OK?' whispered Fitz.

'Yes,' answered Anji.

'Good.' Fitz gave her boat a shove and it moved out from the jetty towards the centre of the river. Struggling with the oars, Anji brought the small vessel round to face the river-gate.

She looked up anxiously at the Watchkeeper – but he was facing away from her, looking outwards rather than inwards.

She heard a bump and the splash of oar on water from behind her, and then Fitz drew level with her, his eyes fixed on the solitary figure of the Watchkeeper.

Everything was picked out in black and orange. The river was so dark it looked like it wasn't there. The river-gate loomed like a giant metal mouth, and Anji could already feel the current speeding up as they approached the bottle-neck. She relaxed a bit and let the boat drift.

'Where are they?' hissed Fitz. 'We're too exposed here – all that bloke has to do is turn round – ah!'

Aboetta had appeared on the bridge. She began talking to the Watchkeeper – they were too far away to hear her words. Suddenly, she drew her pistol.

'Oh, cripes. Here it comes,' muttered Fitz.

The Watchkeeper was backing away, hands in the air.

Then Anji noticed that the right-hand winch-tower had a big, brass-coloured bell inside it.

A movement from the bank. From the bushes where they had been hiding, the Doctor and Gottlieb scuttled towards the bridge.

'Row, Anji!' whispered Fitz.

Anji gripped the oars and heaved, pulling the boat through the night-dark water. She was aware of Fitz's boat surging ahead of her, but her attention was mainly fixed on the drama playing out on the bridge above the river-gate.

The guard was almost at the bell-rope now. Aboetta still had the pistol aimed at him – but could hardly fire, as the noise would bring the whole settlement down upon them.

The Doctor and Gottlieb had reached the bridge. Anji gasped as the priest pushed past Aboetta and piled into the Watchkeeper. There was a muffled cry, a scuffle. The Watchkeeper fell into the river, there was a splash, then he was gone.

Anji gasped and stopped rowing. The chain mail he was wearing – he'd sink like a stone...

'Try not to think about it, Anji,' said Fitz in a shaky voice.

On the bridge, the Doctor had grabbed Gottlieb by the shoulders, was remonstrating with him. Gottlieb shoved him away, pointing to the left-hand winch-tower. The Doctor ran to it and began hauling on the winch-handle.

Anji grimaced, expecting the screech of badly oiled metal or at least the telltale clanking of chains which would bring Watchkeepers running from all over Totterdown. But the river-gate opened with only a low, throaty rasp.

Fitz pulled into the bank, indicating to Anji that she should do the same. With difficulty she tucked in her boat behind his. Once the gate was open enough for them to pass through, the Doctor, Aboetta and Gottlieb ran down from the bridge and along the bank. Aboetta and Gottlieb clambered into Fitz's boat, and Fitz pulled away, heading for the open gate. The Doctor slid into Anji's boat, causing it to rock alarmingly. Anji held on to the oars, fearing to let them slip into the black water. The Doctor's face was like a hard, stony mask. Anji could tell that he was thinking about what Gottlieb had done to the Watchkeeper. She grabbed the oars and began to row. Wordlessly, the Doctor leaned forwards and took the oars from her. He pulled strongly on them, making the boat slide smoothly through the water, straight for the river-gate.

It had been raised just enough to allow them to pass. Weeds hung down from the bottom section like slimy fingers. Anji ducked, but couldn't prevent some of the dripping tendrils from caressing her face.

Then they were through the river-gate, and out of Totterdown.

The Doctor kept on rowing, head down, intent on keeping going. They overtook Fitz's boat. Anji caught a glimpse of Fitz's face, grimacing with the effort of rowing. She looked ahead. The river ran straight for a hundred yards or so, then curved to the left. The banks were overgrown with great spiders of bramble and overhanging branches, and the Doctor kept as close to these as possible, to hide themselves from view. This was tricky – he sometimes had to manoeuvre around great clumps of bramble or a dense knot of dangling foliage, venturing dangerously far out from the bank.

Anji turned and looked back. The torches on the winch-towers burned brightly, and she could see other beacons, ranged along the wall which surrounded the settlement.

She was glad to be out of it.

But what lay ahead filled her with fear. More dangers – these Wildren, whatever they were, for one. Anji shivered in the cold night air.

Fitz's arms felt like they were made of lead. 'Faster!' hissed Gottlieb from behind him.

'I'm going as fast as I can!' groaned Fitz. 'How about taking over for a bit?'

'When we're out of sight of the Watchtowers, I will.'

But Aboetta suddenly lunged forwards, making the boat wobble alarmingly, and put her hands over Fitz's, preventing him from rowing.

'We can't leave the gate open!' she gasped. 'That would endanger the settlement. I can't let that happen!'

Fitz looked over his shoulder. The river-gate stood open, leaving a sizeable gap above the water. They *could* go back, close it and climb over the gate, he supposed – but then he noticed that at the top of the gate, between the winch-towers, was a formidable row of spikes, gleaming in the firelight.

'We haven't got any choice,' said Fitz, gently taking Aboetta's hands from his and starting out towards the Doctor and Anji.

Aboetta knelt before Fitz, eyes wide, staring forlornly at the open gate. 'I can never return now.' Her face creased as if in pain. 'What have I done?'

'Shut up, girl!' hissed Gottlieb from behind Fitz.

Aboetta glared at him and then at Fitz, anger in her dark eyes. Fitz got the impression that she was the sort of girl who hated people to see her cry. Great. Borderline psycho chick with a gun in front, nasty rude violent priest in back.

'I really do pick my friends,' muttered Fitz.

Keeping his eyes fixed on the Doctor and Anji in the other boat, Fitz concentrated on rowing. Soon the river began to curve left. Fitz didn't allow himself to relax until they had passed underneath the bridge they had crossed earlier. Beyond this, the river widened, the banks grew taller and more overgrown, the sky a star-speckled strip overhead.

'Rest,' called the Doctor, just as Fitz's arms were beginning to feel as if they were about to pop out of their sockets. He brought his boat in as close to the other as possible.

He smiled at Anji and she smiled back.

The Doctor rounded on Gottlieb. 'That was unnecessary. You didn't need to kill that guard. You could have just rendered him unconscious.'

Gottlieb glared at the Doctor. 'And how do you do that? A blow to the head can be fatal – or just knock someone out for a minute or so. And I couldn't risk that. Killing him was the only choice, under the circumstances.'

'Well, I don't agree,' said the Doctor.

'It's too late to argue about it now,' said Fitz. 'It's done, and that's it.'

'No more killing,' said the Doctor.

'Very well,' said Gottlieb. 'Except for in self-defence, of course.'

The Doctor glared at Gottlieb, but said nothing.

Aboetta seemed to have recovered herself a bit. 'They will be upon us as soon as it gets light. When they find the boats gone, the river-gate open...' She shook her head. 'We must put as much distance as possible between us and Totterdown.'

Fitz groaned. 'I don't think I can row this thing any more, Doctor.'

'Then I will take over,' said Father Gottlieb.

They shifted positions, taking care not to capsize the small boat. Soon they were under way, Gottlieb's strong strokes keeping their boat level with the Doctor and Anji's.

Fitz leaned back. His arms felt stretched, and he knew they would ache in the morning.

'Now we're out of Totterdown,' said the Doctor, 'I trust we can talk freely about the Cleansing?'

Gottlieb laughed. 'We can! As long as Aboetta does not object?'

Aboetta, who was crammed at the back of the boat next to Fitz, shook her head.

From the other boat, Anji spoke up. 'Well, don't keep us in suspense. What *is* this Cleansing?'

Gottlieb spoke as he rowed. 'A hundred and sixty years ago, at Year Nought, there was a cataclysm, a worldwide disaster. Over ninety-five per cent of the population of the world was killed. Some say it was God's punishment on the human race. "Born again in all innocence." That's what Cluny and his ilk believe.'

'But you don't,' said the Doctor. 'What do you believe?'

'What do I believe?' said Gottlieb between strokes. 'Not that it was God's will.'

'Seems a bit of a pointless thing for a God to do, kill off most of his creation,' put in Fitz.

Gottlieb shook his head. 'No, that's not the problem. If God wants to destroy, then God can.' Gottlieb smiled. 'But I don't believe that it was God. The Cleansing was indiscriminate – if you were over a certain age, saint or sinner, you died. Whatever caused this alleged "Cleansing", it was no deity. A freak of nature, an accident. Or something caused it deliberately. But not God.'

'Over a certain age, you say.' The Doctor stopped rowing. 'What happened? What could have killed so many people?'

Gottlieb also stopped rowing. 'Time.'

The Doctor stared at the priest.

Fitz exchanged a worried glance with Anji.

'It took the survivors years to work it out, and some still dispute it,' Gottlieb went on, 'but in 1843, time accelerated. Forty years passed in just as many seconds. Almost everyone on the planet aged to death.'

Chapter 7
The Cleansing

There was a silence over the river.

'Time speeded up?' said the Doctor. 'How do you know?'

'Some of the survivors worked it out,' said Gottlieb. 'Most people over the age of puberty died instantly – their bodies couldn't handle the shock of ageing so rapidly. But children of ten or so suddenly found themselves in bodies aged fifty or more. Many were killed. But some survived, grouped together. It took time, but some of them worked out what had happened. And prevailed.'

'And went on to establish settlements like Totterdown,' said Fitz.

'They called themselves the Citizen Elders,' said Aboetta. 'Morgan Foster's great-great-grandfather Henry founded Totterdown in Year Three. He built the Wall to keep out the Wildren and outlaws.'

'Outlaws?' said Fitz.

'There are some who survived the Cleansing, of the same age as the Citizen Elders, who decided or happened not to join the settlements,' said Father Gottlieb. 'They and their descendants became known as outlaws.'

'Killed?' said the Doctor suddenly. 'By whom – or what?'

Gottlieb smiled without humour. 'By their younger brothers and sisters. Babies who suddenly found themselves in adult bodies, and did what came naturally in order to survive.'

'That's grotesque,' said Anji.

'Imagine if you were a newborn babe,' Gottlieb said slowly. 'Barely two days old. Suddenly, you find yourself in the body of a forty-year-old, fully-functioning adult. You'd be a shambling imbecile. You either starve or die of fright. Now imagine if you were an older child, say, four or five years old, in the same situation. You'd know enough, instinctively, to survive. You'd revert to a primitive, feral state. Most would die. But some would learn how to reproduce, almost by accident. It is the descendants of these unfortunates we call *Wilde Kinder*, the Wildren. Children of the Cleansing. Over the generations, they have regressed into little more than animals.'

'Fascinating,' said the Doctor. 'Yes, that makes sense. Society has stratified. There are people like you and Aboetta, civilised descendants of the survivors of the Cleansing. And then there are the Wildren.'

The things that had attacked Aboetta, thought Fitz. They weren't aliens, or monsters, but human beings. Fitz shuddered – but at the same time, he felt a pang of pity for them. After all, the Cleansing wasn't their fault.

'Animals,' said Fitz slowly. 'If forty years passed so quickly no animals would survive.' He struggled to remember his biology lessons at school. How long did cattle live? Horses? Certainly not more than ten or at most twenty years.

An uncomfortable thought occurred to Fitz. 'These Wildren – they're cannibals.'

Gottlieb turned his face towards Fitz. 'Yes. They eat each other. And us, if they can catch us.'

'So, you're all vegetarians then.'

Gottlieb smiled. 'Choices are limited.'

'There are some, not Wildren, who eat human flesh. Supposedly civilised people,' said Aboetta. Her voice was a hiss of anger. 'We do not count them as Citizens.'

That explained the bad teeth and thin, malnourished-looking limbs, Fitz thought. But what about time speeding up? He looked at Anji. 'It's like that time when we met those people who were turning into clocks – people ageing to death in seconds.'

'Only this time it's affected a whole planet, all at once,' said Anji. 'Our planet.'

74

'One version of it. The wrong one,' muttered the Doctor.

Gottlieb looked at him sharply. 'What was that?'

The Doctor looked startled. 'Nothing! Nothing at all.'

'What could have caused it?' asked Anji. 'The same thing that happened to the clock people?'

The Doctor shook his head. 'No. I have a theory, but it's not a nice one. It's year 160, correct?'

'Yes,' replied Gottlieb.

Fitz felt Aboetta stir next to him, but she didn't speak.

'And in 1843, forty years are supposed to have passed, practically instantly.'

'I see!' said Anji.

'Well, I don't,' said Fitz.

'Remember the yearometer. It's 2003, remember?'

'How do you know?' asked Gottlieb.

The Doctor waved a hand. 'I just do. Now, if the Cleansing made forty years pass in forty seconds, surely at the end of the process it would be 1883. And, a hundred and sixty years on, this should be 2043.'

'I think I'm getting a headache,' said Fitz.

'So what must have happened, instead of "time" speeding up, the *effect* of time speeding up must have happened! And at the end of it, it was still 1843. The Cleansing affected people's metabolisms, accelerating them to death.' He lapsed into silence.

'Well that explains why there are no animals, anyway,' said Fitz. He nudged Aboetta. 'And why you're so impressed with my jacket.'

Aboetta glared at him, her eyes shining in the moonlight.

'There's more than one dimension of time,' said the Doctor suddenly. 'It would appear that whatever this Cleansing was, it caused time to speed up only along a few of them. Those linked to the metabolism of the universe itself.' He shuddered. 'So total time stood still, whilst segments of time were accelerated. Rather like being pulled inside out. Almost as if whoever or whatever caused this, wanted people to suffer, wanted the universe to feel pain. But why?'

'Are we going to float here talking about the Cleansing all night?' said Aboetta.

'You're right,' said the Doctor. 'We'll find somewhere to hole up, get some sleep.'

'Sleep! After all this?' said Anji.

But Fitz could already feel his eyelids closing. The gentle motion of the boat was soothing.

The last thing he heard before he dropped off was the Doctor's voice, talking in low tones to Gottlieb.

Fitz stepped from the TARDIS, one hand clasping Anji's. The warmth, the closeness, felt good. He looked down at her smiling up at him, nothing but fondness in her beautiful brown eyes.

Above them, an endless vista of stars twinkled down. 'Oh no!' bellowed the Doctor, striding out into the field of black grass, waving his arms.

Leading Anji, Fitz went over, marvelling at the darkness all around, the thick black grass clinging at his boots.

The Doctor was staring down a gentle slope at a field spread with bright objects like glass candle globes.

'What is it, Doctor?' said Fitz.

'Yes, Doctor, what's wrong?' piped up Anji. Fitz gave her hand a reassuring squeeze.

The Doctor, face like thunder, made a sweeping gesture across the field. 'All these wrong realities!' he cried. 'We've got to stamp them out!'

So saying he ran over to the nearest one, raised his foot and stamped on it. It burst like an incandescent balloon, scattering sparkling dust into the air. The dust faded as it fell, until no trace of it was left. A cold wind blew up, and the blades of black grass stirred like the fur of a shivering animal.

Fitz thought he could hear the dying screams of uncountable souls.

'Come on, come on!' yelled the Doctor, turning to them. His eyes were blazing like idling blow-torches. 'There are *trillions* of them!'

With a cry of pleasure Anji shook herself free from Fitz and scampered over to the nearest reality. She bunny-hopped on to it, smashing it with both feet, and gave an excited squeal as the fairy-dust bloomed around her. She clapped her hands and smiled at the Doctor, who nodded approvingly.

Fitz turned away in disgust, only to feel the Doctor's hand on his arm. 'Come on, Fitz, we've got work to do.'

Fitz raised his eyes to the stars, only to see that they weren't stars – they were wrong realities. There were more than Fitz could stand.

Anji giggled.

'Come on, Fitz,' said the Doctor.

'Come on Fitz.' Something prodded him in the ribs. 'Fitz, wake up. We've got to get going.'

Fitz opened his eyes to see Anji looking down at him. He blinked, dispelling the last remnants of the dream, not wanting to think about what it was trying to tell him about his relationship with Anji, or the Doctor, or their current situation.

He sat up, wincing at a sharp pain in his neck. Must have been lying at a funny angle. Anji was leaning over him, using the end of an oar to prod him to wakefulness. He shoved back the rough blanket that someone – presumably Anji – must have thrown over him as he slept. As well as his neck, his arms ached too, just as he'd feared.

It was just starting to be morning. To his right, a mass of land arched its back, above which the sky was still too dark for Fitz to make out any details. He could hear the ocean-like sound of leaves rustling in the morning breeze. To his left, the city – crumbling docks and warehouses like collapsed packs of cards. It was a forlorn thing to see first thing on a cold grey morning.

Fitz shivered. 'Where are we?'

'Look over there.' Anji pointed downriver.

Fitz sat up and turned, trying not to rock the boat. Behind him, the ruined city climbed surprisingly steeply up the side of a hill, some of the shattered buildings perching almost on the edge. Fitz could still make out terraces leading back into the town. At the topmost point was a large hotel-like building, its façade of yellow stone crumbled away like broken biscuit. Where the buildings ended, trees began, and at the highest point – a couple of hundred feet at least above the river, at the top of a great grey face of rock – stood a tower. On the other, dark-wooded side, was a similar tower, and between them was a bridge. It looked at once delicate, as though it had been somehow drawn into the air, and yet enduring, graceful and powerful. Fitz recognised it at once from photographs. 'That's the Clifton Suspension Bridge, then.'

Anji nodded, and helped Fitz out of the boat. 'Malahyde's estate is on the other side.' She indicated the mass of trees beyond the bank.

'Great,' said Fitz. 'Any breakfast on the go?'

'You might be in luck,' said Anji with a smile.

She led him from the bank, which was basically just mud – Fitz sank up to his ankles in the stuff – and through some waist-high reedy grass. Behind this, a rutted path ran parallel to the river. The Doctor, Aboetta and Gottlieb were standing on this road, clearly waiting for them.

'Morning!' said Fitz as brightly as he could.

Aboetta nodded curtly at him, whilst the priest just stared, as if Fitz wasn't there.

'Ready?' said the Doctor, and without another word headed up the path in the direction of the bridge.

Miserable bunch, thought Fitz, yawning. He still hadn't woken up properly. 'What about that breakfast?'

Aboetta handed Fitz a wodge of something that looked like a flapjack. Fitz bit into it – it was hard, crumbly and dry and tasted of mushrooms. But it was better than nothing.

'So what's the plan?' he said through a mouthful of the stuff.

The Doctor gestured for Fitz and Anji to walk ahead with him.

'I don't want Aboetta or Gottlieb to hear this,' he said in a low voice. 'They seem to accept us, thankfully, and I don't want to jeopardise that.'

Fitz looked behind. Aboetta and the priest were walking on opposite sides of the path, obviously ignoring each other. Aboetta probably hadn't forgiven him, and would probably never forgive him, for leaving the river-gate open.

The Doctor spoke quickly. 'These alternative realities – however many of them there may be – are all vying for attention, trying to assert themselves as the prime reality. But they didn't all spring up just like that. Each must stem from a branching event, a catalyst, something that set history on a different course. Like this Cleansing. Once the correct reality has been restored, it should, er, "take", merely by dint of being longer established than all these aberrant versions.'

'So,' said Anji, 'all we need to do is go back and prevent the Cleansing. That will bring back the real reality?'

Talk of 'real realities' was beginning to annoy Fitz. The path under his feet, the trees, the river, it all seemed real enough to him. And was even more real to those who lived here.

'You're forgetting Aboetta,' said the Doctor. 'Something's amiss with time in this reality and I need to get to the bottom of it. So before we start going back and fixing things I need to have a chat with Aboetta's employer.'

Fixing things, thought Fitz. Jesus. He made it sound so casual, so mundane, like mending a puncture. Or – he remembered the dream – like making a puncture. Letting the air out of someone else's world.

'You think Malahyde's behind it?' said Anji.

The Doctor smiled knowingly. 'The man's a recluse. Aboetta told me there's something strange in the cellar.' His voice dropped to a whisper. 'Textbook stuff.'

Fitz laughed. 'So things could be worse than we thought?'

The Doctor sighed again. 'I don't know. I hope not.'

Fitz spread his arms wide and almost shouted. 'How can it be worse than the final end of everything ever?'

The Doctor turned to face him. 'Fitz, I need both of you to be calm and capable, whatever happens. As long as we keep our wits about us I'm sure we can deal with anything.'

Fitz stomped off up the path. 'Thanks for the pep talk.'

He hated to admit it to himself, but he was beginning to feel unsettled. He looked back. The Doctor had struck up a conversation with Aboetta. He pointed at the bridge, which they were almost underneath now, and Aboetta pointed in the other direction, into the woods.

'This way!' called the Doctor.

Fitz and Anji followed the Doctor, Gottlieb and Aboetta up a steep, narrow path which led through the woods. The going was tricky – big stones and tree-roots meant Fitz had to think about every footstep.

'Hope we don't bump into any Wildren,' panted Anji from ahead. 'Now I know what they are I really, really do not want to make their acquaintance.'

In a mercifully short time they broke out of the forest on to a rough, overgrown road crowded with squat, thorny bushes. The ground still sloped upwards at a wearying angle.

On the far side of the road was a wall.

Fitz stood and gazed at it. It was the same height as the Wall around Totterdown, and similarly forbidding. Or even more forbidding, as it was made of stone. A rough edifice of grey blocks, rising over twice a man's height from the ground. And at its top, supported on metal posts driven into the stone, a six-stranded fence of vicious-looking barbed wire, angled slightly outwards. Behind and above this forbidding barrier were trees, their leaves the rusty shades of autumn.

'Hmmm.' The Doctor walked up to the wall, swishing through the long grass. 'This must be the Ashton Court estate,' he said. 'Home of the Smythe family – or at least it was. Used to be a deer park, as far as I recall. Though thanks to the Cleansing there won't be any deer left.'

They began to walk beside the wall, up the steep uneven path. Fitz stumbled on a loose stone and grabbed on to Anji for support. She glared at him.

'How many people live on the estate?' asked the Doctor.

Aboetta shrugged. 'A couple of dozen guards, gardeners, general workers.'

'What does Malahyde do with all that land?'

'Farms it,' said Aboetta. 'He sends produce out to the settlements in times of need. Helped us through some bad winters, when I was a child.'

'A benefactor,' said the Doctor, nodding approvingly.

'Not such a philanthropist, Doctor,' said Gottlieb. 'He has power. Electricity!'

The Doctor turned to Gottlieb with a look of surprise. 'You know of such things?'

Gottlieb switched at the ground with a stout stick as he walked. 'I know of many things, Doctor. The researches of Faraday, Volta, Daniell – books survived the Cleansing, even if their authors did not.'

'And Malahyde's got a generator?' said the Doctor, excitedly. Then, with a quizzical look at Aboetta, 'in the cellar?'

Aboetta looked confused. 'I have never heard of the things Father Gottlieb speaks of.'

'Electricity,' said Father Gottlieb, with enthusiasm. 'It's a form of power. Power which could transform life for us all! And yet Malahyde keeps it all to himself.'

'Does that remind you of anything you've seen inside Malahyde's mansion?' asked the Doctor.

Aboetta shook her head. 'We have oil-lamps and a wood-burning fire. Just as everyone else.'

Gottlieb threw his stick into the trees. 'Malahyde's got something in there. I'm sure of it. And he should share it! Why should the rest of us cower in the dark and freeze in the winters, whilst he –'

'All right, all right,' said the Doctor, 'calm down. We're there now.' He pointed to a gatehouse set in the wall. Two castellated pillars of grey stone stood either side of a great archway framing an iron gate.

The Doctor turned to Aboetta. 'You're sure you want to go back?'

Aboetta nodded. 'There is nothing left for me in Totterdown.'

As they drew nearer, a smaller gate set into the larger one opened and two guards emerged, rifles levelled at the new arrivals.

'Halt! Who goes there?'

'Huh,' muttered Fitz. 'Haven't heard that one before.'

The Doctor moved forwards, hands raised – just as he had done in Totterdown the day before. But it didn't look as if they were going to be as lenient as Morgan Foster had been – well, initially at least.

'I'm the Doctor,' said the Doctor. 'These are my friends. We've brought Aboetta safely back across Bristol.'

The nearest guard – a blond-haired bear of a man – nodded curtly at Aboetta. 'Miss Cigetrais.'

'We'd like to see Mr Malahyde,' said the Doctor.

The blond guard gave a mirthless laugh. 'No chance.'

'Halt!' The other guard – thinner and darker than his companion – had caught Gottlieb edging round towards the open gate.

A shot rang out and something thwacked into the ground before Gottlieb's feet. The priest leaped back, startled.

Fitz looked. There were more guards, leaning from the windows of the gatehouse. They all had the same red uniforms. Fitz instinctively began to back away. Anji did the same.

But the Doctor stood his ground. 'Could you please tell your boss that we need to speak to him as a matter of urgency?'

The blond guard spat at the Doctor's feet.

Aboetta had started towards the gate, escorted by the other guard.

'Aboetta,' said the Doctor. 'Convince them of our good intentions? Please?'

But Aboetta didn't even look back.

'Aboetta!' cried the Doctor.

Another gunshot.

Then Aboetta was through the small gate. The blond guard locked it after her.

'Aboetta!' cried the Doctor. 'I thought you wanted to help us!'

But she had gone.

The Doctor was beside himself. 'Why did she do that?'

The burly blond guard raised his rifle. 'I'll count to ten. If you're still within sight at the end of it, I'll shoot. One... two...'

'Come on,' said Fitz. 'Let's run away, to not fight another day.'

'Three... four...'

They ran down the hill, keeping low. The road curved to the right, so they were out of the guard's sight well before he reached the end of his countdown.

The Doctor cast a frustrated look at the impassive stone wall. 'We need to get in there. But it isn't going to be easy. We need to create some sort of distraction.' He sighed.

Fitz noticed Gottlieb perk up at this. 'I have associates, who will be able to help us get inside.' He shook his head. 'I'd rather it hadn't come to this, as Malahyde's estate is well defended, but we really have no choice but to force our way in.'

'You know the more I get to know you, the less like a priest you seem to be,' said the Doctor.

Gottlieb scowled. 'In a sense you are right, I am nothing like Cluny and his cowardly kind.' He looked earnestly at the Doctor. 'Will you accept my help?'

'Well you've been helpful so far,' said the Doctor. 'Yes, yes, I accept.'

The Doctor and the priest shook hands.

Why did Fitz get the strangest feeling that the Doctor was making a pact with the Devil himself?

The Doctor shook his head and stared back up the hill. 'I feel like a knight on a nine-square chessboard. Never able to reach the centre square.'

Fitz got a fleeting impression that the Doctor was twenty times more dangerous than this mysterious priest. He shuddered.

The Doctor clapped Gottlieb on the back, his mood suddenly brightening. 'Come on, let's go and meet these friends of yours.'

Chapter 8
The Island of Time

They found the two rowing boats where they had left them, moored beside the bank of mud, with the Clifton Suspension Bridge framing the view down-river. Fitz stood on the bank in the long grass, enjoying his last cigarette until they got back to the TARDIS.

The crumbling remains of the buildings on the slopes of the Gorge made it impossible not to think about the Cleansing. Almost everyone in the world growing old and dying in less time than it took to light a cigarette and take the first grateful drag.

Fitz took a final grateful drag on his cigarette and flicked it into the long grass.

Say what you like about the alternative Edinburgh, at least there had been people there. Nasty people in the main, but it had still been recognisable as twenty-first century Earth. This, though, was living death. He thought of Aboetta with admiration now, and Totterdown didn't seem such a primitive, backwards place. It seemed like a crowning achievement, a triumph in the face of horrendously crippling adversity.

But was it really any worse than the world Fitz and Anji called their own? Fitz was a sixties cat – Anji a twenty-first century fully functional organised person, but their journeys with the Doctor had brought them so close together that they may as well be separated by months, not decades. They both knew the same world, the same

Earth, and this one was equally alien to both of them. No World Wars, no Industrial Revolution, no environmental pollution or large-scale terrorism. Fitz breathed in. The air tasted sweet, untainted. Perhaps a world with drastically fewer people in it had more chance than the over-populated world he and Anji knew.

He found himself hoping it had a future. Then he remembered that they were there to ensure that it didn't.

He felt in all his pockets, to make absolutely sure he didn't have any more cigarettes, then trudged back to the path. It was now mid-day and they were making the most of the rations they had – mostly rather sour apples and more of the mushroom-flavoured bars.

Fitz watched the Doctor munch a withered apple with far more enthusiasm than such a meal warranted, and something occurred to him.

'Doctor, I've just thought of something – if the Cleansing killed off most of the people and animals on the planet, what about plants? They're living things, they age. How come so many survived?'

The Doctor swallowed the last morsel of apple and wiped his lips. He started to speak, but Gottlieb got in first.

'My theory is that the effect of the Cleansing moved only across the surface of the Earth. Anything with its seeds buried deep enough underground survived.'

The Doctor nodded, clearly impressed at the way Gottlieb had thought things through. 'You may be right – temporal anomalies are funny like that. Or maybe certain species were hardy enough to weather the effects – trees can live for hundreds of years, for example.' He shrugged. 'I won't know until I've discovered what caused it.'

'But without insects, there would be no pollination,' put in Anji.

'Pollination can occur without insects,' said the Doctor. 'Pollen can be carried on the breeze, for example. Am I right in supposing that in the summer, there's a distinct lack of flowers?'

Gottlieb nodded. 'You are right. Though certain genera of insects did survive – ants and termites, for example. Which supports my theory of the Cleansing only affecting the surface.'

Anji pointed at the graceful span of the Clifton Suspension

Bridge. 'I've thought of something too. How come things like bridges and buildings survived, and haven't crumbled completely into dust?'

The Doctor rubbed his hands, then opened them in Gottlieb's direction.

Gottlieb returned the gesture. 'I'd like to hear your theory, Doctor.'

'Remember, the Cleansing was the effect of forty years passing in forty seconds. There wasn't forty years of weather in those forty seconds – there weren't forty summers and forty winters. The Cleansing affected only some of the dimensions of time, those linked to the metabolism of living things. And as buildings aren't living things...' He shrugged.

'What about all those crumbling buildings?' said Fitz, thinking he'd caught the Doctor out.

'That's all happened in the years since the Cleansing,' said the Doctor. 'At Year Nought they would have been intact, and would be today if they'd been properly maintained. Ditto for the suspension bridge,' he said, glancing up at the graceful span. 'Without maintenance it would have collapsed into the Gorge within a decade. Malahyde's obviously been looking after it.' He peered at it, shading his eyes against the pale mid-day sun. 'It shouldn't be there, of course.'

'What do you mean?' asked Fitz.

'Think about it. The Cleansing happened in 1843, but the Clifton Suspension Bridge was completed in the 1860s, after Brunel's death.'

Fitz looked uneasily at the bridge. It seemed to be smiling down at them.

'That means history must have changed *before* the Cleansing,' said Anji.

'Things aren't quite as straightforward as I thought,' said the Doctor glumly.

Straightforward? thought Fitz with astonishment. Since when was navigating a multitude of realities ever straightforward?

'This is fascinating,' said Father Gottlieb suddenly, a huge grin breaking over his swarthy face. 'You cannot believe how glorious it is to speak freely of the Cleansing without fear of imprisonment, or even execution!'

'Yes,' said the Doctor pensively. 'How did all that happen? Why has the human race become so superstitious?'

Gottlieb gazed out over the river. 'A rather otiose question, Doctor. It seems obvious that an event of such magnitude would stir up the fearful, credulous side of human nature.' He sighed. 'But it might not have been so. After the Cleansing, once the survivors – Citizen Elders, that is, those that had been elder children before Year Nought – had realised what had happened, they tried to rationalise it. But they couldn't. How can you rationalise such an event? So they looked to God for an answer, and saw that it was His way of removing evil from the world. Birthing the human race again, in full innocence. Only the children survived.'

'But you don't believe that,' said Fitz.

Gottlieb shook his head. 'Although I am a priest, I am a rational man. I believe in a rational God. No God would cause something as sweeping and unilateral as the Cleansing.'

'Bet that doesn't go down well with the other priests.'

Gottlieb stared at Fitz, then laughed. 'As you will appreciate, the Church was the only institution to survive the Cleansing. Once the Citizen Elders came to believe it was God's will, the Church took hold. They began to preach of a Cleansing, a Winnowing.' He kicked a pebble. 'But that later term was discarded; people felt uncomfortable being compared to wheat. There were various doctrinal squabbles over the decades, but now the Protestant Utilitarian faith is predominant. It preaches hard work, conservatism, and forbids discussion of the Cleansing.' His dark eyes flickered. 'I am not of that faith.'

'So what are you, then?' Anji was clearly interested.

'I have my own beliefs. They are in a minority. Call me a rational survivalist. If you like.'

The Doctor stood, brushing himself down. 'We'd better get moving. Where are these associates of yours?'

Gottlieb smiled grimly. 'There is a fortified inn, near the centre of Bristol. A haunt for outlaws such as myself.' He moved off to prepare the boats.

Anji glanced nervously at Fitz. 'Why can't we just use the TARDIS?'

The Doctor shook his head. 'We'd have to get back to it first. It's probably best we use whatever help we can get.' He walked gingerly over the mud to help Gottlieb untie the boats.

'A fortified inn,' mused Fitz. 'Sounds good to me!'

Anji hugged herself, frowning. 'Come on, let's get this over with,' she muttered.

Aboetta took the heavy key from her overcoat and unlocked the door. Though it had only been yesterday, it seemed like a lifetime since she had passed the other way. Or at least ten years, she thought humourlessly.

She heaved the door open just enough, slipped through and let it fall shut behind her. Something seemed to pass through her mind as she stepped under the arch, a stray thought or an elusive memory. Immediately she was aware of a sudden drop in temperature, and she looked up at the sky. It seemed greyer, somehow thinner. As she neared the house, the distant lonely notes of a violin being played slowly and thoughtfully reached her ears.

Aboetta felt a rush of conflicting emotions – joy mixed with fear, trepidation and anger. There was something about the tune, a subtle, knowing quality, as if Mr Malahyde had been invisibly watching Aboetta ever since she'd left the estate, and was now playing this lament just for her. A lament for her lost father, her lost love, her lost years.

But that was impossible – wasn't it?

Aboetta realised that she didn't know any more. Anything seemed possible now.

The main door was slightly ajar, which added to the feeling that Malahyde had been watching her. Then she remembered that she had left it that way – yesterday. Surely he would not have left it unlocked overnight? Something must be wrong.

Aboetta pushed the door open and stepped inside the hall. The empty square space, with its stone walls and suits of armour (which Aboetta had always thought rather comical) was comforting. A voice inside Aboetta sang: this your home now.

The music continued – he couldn't have heard her enter – and so she marched straight into the drawing room.

Mr Malahyde was standing in front of one of the windows, gazing out at the garden as he played. A ray of sunlight fell on his dark green jacket.

Aboetta deliberately made her footsteps as heavy as possible on the parquet floor.

When she was a short way into the room, he turned and looked at her, letting the violin fall in one hand to one side, the bow to the other.

They stared at each other for what seemed like a long time, in the sudden silence.

Then Malahyde took a step towards her. His eyes looked more alive than she had ever seen them before, lit with a kind of joy. But still there was the taint of sadness about every movement of his body, every cadence of his voice. 'You came back.'

Aboetta could do nothing but smile.

Then he said, 'Why?'

The simple question – the most simple question of all – sparked Aboetta's thoughts, reminded her of why she had left in the first place.

She turned away from Malahyde, turning her gaze to the ashes in the fireplace. Hadn't he bothered to light the fire, in the day and a half since she left him? 'My father is dead.'

Then she looked at him again.

He closed his eyes, his head nodding slowly. Then he put the violin and bow down carefully on a nearby chaise longue. His movements were deliberate, resigned, and Aboetta suddenly grasped another part of the mystery. 'You knew, didn't you?'

Malahyde looked down at his shoes. 'I – I didn't want you to go, but I couldn't explain. I had to let you go.'

His stuttering non-explanations reminded her oddly of Robin. She suddenly felt a stab of impatience at these men who were holding back information from her. 'Couldn't explain what?'

Malahyde threw himself on to the chaise longue. He put his head in his hands. 'Oh, Aboetta, I should never have summoned you here!

It's all my fault!'

She wondered what all the fuss was about. *What* was his fault? She felt a sudden urge to be cruel. 'You stole ten years away from me.'

Malahyde turned away.

Aboetta folded her arms. 'That's why I've come back. Because I've got nowhere else to go.'

Malahyde said, and did, absolutely nothing.

Aboetta took a step towards him, anger swelling in her. 'You haven't even asked about Collins and Bryant!'

At last he turned to her. His eyes were desolate. 'What happened to them?'

'Wildren. We were attacked the moment we entered Clifton. Collins and Bryant were killed. I got away.'

Malahyde slumped back into the chaise longue. 'So much death,' he muttered. 'Why go on?'

His words scared Aboetta. He sounded like he had lost all hope. Father Cluny had taught her that was the worst sin of all. To despair in yourself, in God – it was the ultimate blasphemy. The people of Totterdown worked hard, endured many hardships, but never gave up hope, never despaired. And here was Mr Jared Malahyde, secure in his well-guarded estate, muttering in his well-furnished drawing room about how he couldn't go on!

It didn't make sense.

But somehow Aboetta sensed that Malahyde wasn't just wallowing in self-regard. There was something about his manner which suggested that he had greater burdens to bear than the Citizens of Totterdown.

'Why do you say such a thing?' she whispered.

'Aboetta, I am so sorry for all this.' He sighed. 'I understand you're angry with me but when you know the truth you'll understand how difficult it is for me.'

'I'm not angry with you. I just want answers. Why is that so difficult?'

'I can't explain. Not just like that.'

'Try.'

He looked at her then, and his eyes were appraising. 'Are you ready for the truth?'

'I have never been more ready.'

'Very well.' Malahyde stood and walked to the long curtained windows at the far end of the drawing room. 'When you went back to Totterdown, did you find that maybe ten years had passed there, whilst you had only been here four months?'

Aboetta nodded.

So did Malahyde. 'I knew as much.'

'Then why didn't you warn me?'

His face creased in a grimace of anguish. He reached out and grasped her hands. 'What could I have said? I wish I had told you, but – anyway, let me proceed with my explanation.'

Aboetta looked down at their hands. It was the first time her flesh had met his flesh. The sensation was astonishing and distracting. It made her want to grasp him to her.

Blue boxes roaring out of nowhere and temporal anomalies and lost decades were as nothing against the surprise Aboetta felt at *this*.

She looked up into his eyes as he spoke, wondering if he felt the same. Wondering what he would say.

He said, 'Time moves more slowly in this house. How long have you been gone?'

Aboetta tried to collect her thoughts. 'A day and a night.'

Malahyde smiled. 'From my point of view, you've only been gone an hour and twenty minutes.' He let go of her hands – her palms still tingled – and pointed at the wooden instruments recumbent on the chaise longue. 'I've been playing, ever since you left. Playing and thinking about you and wishing I had explained everything before I let you go.'

He'd been thinking about her. And playing his music, the music that took her body and made it into a song.

For one and a half days.

For one hour and twenty minutes.

'How can this be so?'

'This may be difficult to understand,' he said slowly. 'Time moves differently within this house and its gardens – up to the perimeter wall.'

Aboetta remembered the change in the climate. 'So it is still February in here... Why have I never noticed?'

'The mind has a wonderful capacity for adapting the facts to fit what it can understand. You would never even think of time moving differently in different areas, so you would never come up with that explanation.'

Aboetta sat on the chaise longue next to Malahyde's discarded violin.

'It's an interesting phenomenon,' continued Malahyde. 'In one way, time moves more quickly within this house in the sense that, if you stay here four months, when you step outside the perimeter, ten years will have passed in the outside world.'

Aboetta looked out of the window at the grey wall. For her, it had always been just that – an old wall. Now she had to believe it was a barrier between areas of time.

'And then in another way,' he went on, 'time has slowed down – because from our point of view, ten years have passed in the outside world but we have only aged four months.' He smiled a sad little smile. 'It's an interesting anomaly. We're effectively living in our own island of time, cut off from the outside world.'

Aboetta stood and walked to the window. She felt a sense of dreadful excitement, as if she was on the brink of a terrible discovery.

'I have been living in this house since before Year Nought.'

His voice, barely a whisper, chilled Aboetta and she turned to face him. 'What – what do you mean?'

'I mean what I say. I was thirty-seven when the Cleansing occurred. Since then, whilst a hundred and sixty years have passed in the outside world, only five years have passed inside this house.' He smiled, without humour. 'It is still Year Five in here – or 1848, as I know it.'

Aboetta suddenly felt scared. His words made no sense – but then he never did speak of his family – so if Year Nought was only five years in the past for him – she felt overwhelmed by the whirl of her thoughts, her mind rebelling at what it was being asked to accept.

Malahyde was watching her carefully.

'I think I understand,' said Aboetta. 'But what has caused this? Is it something to do with the Cleansing?'

Malahyde blinked sharply, almost a wince of pain. Then he sighed. 'I almost hoped you wouldn't come back. But since you have, you are entitled to know the truth. Follow me.'

With that he turned and walked from the room.

Aboetta followed him.

Chapter 9
The Utopian Engine

It was the silence that got to Anji the most.

Cities were noisy places – the traffic, the bustle, the blare of horns and sirens, music blasting from bars and cars. And at night the distant whine of air-conditioning, the low rumble of a jet plane, the distant discordant singing of drunks roaming the streets. You never felt alone, except maybe if you happened to be awake in the deadest hours between three and four in the morning. Then you'd find that the psychic pressure of so many waking minds around you had eased, and you were to all intents and purposes totally alone in the soft orange-black night of the city.

Anji had always remembered Bristol as a particularly noisy place. Maybe it was the traffic system, which had grown around the old buildings like a boa constrictor slowly squeezing the breath out of the town. Or maybe it was because the hotel she'd stayed in had backed on to a supermarket, where delivery vans had rolled in with an ungodly clamour at the equally ungodly hour of five o'clock in the morning.

But in this reality, Bristol had never got the chance to grow from a small yet important town surrounded by a loose collection of villages, into a city in its own right. Its ambition had been curtailed by the Cleansing, by time itself jumping a groove.

It was like walking through a tomb.

Or rowing. Or, more precisely, being rowed by Fitz.

There was no sound apart from the slap of oar on water. For some reason, the desolate silence was hard to break. The faces of the ruined buildings looked down from the hillside like onlookers at a wake.

Post-apocalyptic, she thought. This is a typical post-apocalyptic scenario. Only the extinction-level event had not been nuclear, biological, or chemical. It had been temporal. A silent apocalypse, leaving behind an etiolated shell, a fading echo.

And it was their job to restore the proper reality, bring back the clangour and hustle and life of the twenty-first century. Anji suddenly felt a strong surge of longing for home. 'Maybe we should just go straight back to the TARDIS,' she said, continuing her thoughts aloud. 'Go back to 1843 and do our temporal editing.'

Fitz stopped rowing and stared at her, holding the oars out of the water and letting the boat drift slowly to a halt. 'I don't know how you can talk about it so casually!'

'You know the situation,' Anji replied with irritation. 'If we don't go back and fix –'

'You mean wipe out.'

'I mean, *fix* these wrong realities, then everything's going to come to an end. You know that.'

Fitz frowned. He was obviously having problems with this. Surprising – he'd travelled with the Doctor for much longer than Anji had. Would have thought he'd be used to such things by now.

Then he said, 'Well, maybe that's how things are. Maybe everything's meant to end. Maybe we'll be unable to prevent it.' He leaned forwards, the boat rocking gently against the slight movement, and spoke in a whisper. 'And what if *this* is the right reality, and *we're* from the wrong one?'

'You know it isn't,' Anji said scornfully. But his words unnerved her. She hadn't even thought of that. No wonder Fitz was feeling freaked.

'I *hope* it isn't,' muttered Fitz. 'But I don't *know* it isn't.' He then concentrated on following the Doctor and Father Gottlieb in the other boat. Their course became very tricky – as, in order to reach Gottlieb's fortified inn, they had to pass through what had once been the city's Floating Harbour.

On their flight from Totterdown the Doctor had given Anji a quick history lesson. The section of river they were traversing was artificial; in the early nineteenth century, a Floating Harbour had been created, at vast expense, in an attempt to improve Bristol's standing as a port. This harbour, unaffected by tides, was controlled by locks at either end, and made to run parallel to the south of the river proper along an artificial channel running from Totterdown to an outlet just below the Suspension Bridge. But in this reality, trade and commerce had been made irrelevant by the Cleansing, and the lock gates, neglected for decades on end, had long since rotted away. And so the waters of the Floating Harbour had merged once more with its parent river.

So Fitz was able to steer their little boat through the inlet of the Floating Harbour, between the sheer walls which had once held the lock gates. Anji felt a sense of oppression as they passed through, as if the walls of the lock were about to slam shut on them. But once through the derelict lock the way opened out into a wide open oval of water and her sense of dread passed away.

To either side, piles of rotting timber showed where wharves and warehouses had once stood. Dry docks held the remains of what may once have been ships. It was hard to tell. There were no vessels on the water itself – they would have rotted away and sunk decades ago. It was incredible to think that this solemn stretch of water had once been part of the second busiest port in the country. There seemed to be nothing left in this world to represent human endeavour and ingenuity, besides the Suspension Bridge. Anji was overcome by a sense of sadness. The silence and desolation really brought home to her how the Cleansing had stopped the human race's progress in one savage swoop.

But as they drew farther in to the harbour, they saw several iron-clad ships, moored as if ready for a voyage.

The Doctor had stopped rowing and they drew alongside.

'That's odd,' he said. 'Without maintenance those ships should have rusted through and sunk *years* ago.'

'Perhaps someone's been looking after them – like Malahyde and the bridge,' suggested Fitz.

The Doctor regarded him thoughtfully. 'Yes. Or perhaps there's another explanation.' He gazed at the ships again.

Their hulls were crusted and grimed with decades of weathering, but Anji couldn't see any rust. As well as masts each vessel had a funnel amidships, just in front of an impressively large cowling for the paddle-wheel.

'Steam-ships,' said the Doctor. 'Wonder if they're still seaworthy.' The enthusiasm in his voice was clear.

'I have heard of plans to get the steam-ships going again,' said Gottlieb. 'But the people of Bristol are too timid. They would rather remain safe behind their walls, than venture out to the wider world.'

The Doctor shook his head. 'I can't believe that the human race's spirit of adventure has died away, just like that.'

'It still persists, in people like you and I.'

The Doctor frowned, as if he was going to mention that he wasn't a member of the human race, but obviously decided against it. Instead he picked up the oars and began to angle his boat in towards the left-hand bank. There was a gap, a rectangular inlet, clearly man-made. A dock, Anji realised. They were going in to dock. Once a daily activity amidst all the bustle and commerce of nineteenth-century Bristol – but now, a once-in-a-blue-moon occurrence.

The dock receded for about ten metres, and at the end of it chains hung from a stone wall and steps ran up to dry land.

The Doctor had shipped oars and was waiting for them. Fitz took their boat in close, groaning with relief as he too stopped rowing. Beads of sweat were standing out on his forehead and Anji realised he must be exhausted. Their little argument now seemed pointless and she smiled at him.

To her relief he smiled back. 'Knackered,' was all he could gasp.

The Doctor, of course, looked as if he'd just leaped up refreshed from a long and deep sleep, showered, shaved, breakfasted heartily and nutritiously, dressed, and brushed his hair.

'Father Gottlieb says we have to cross an area called Queen Square,' he said. 'The pub's on the other side of it.'

'The river's blocked by a collapsed bridge,' muttered Gottlieb. 'If it wasn't for that we'd have been able to row almost right up to the front door.'

The Doctor took up the oars again and moved the boat in close to the wall of the dock. Fitz followed and Anji tied the mooring rope to a rusting metal ring set into the stone, feeling, as she did so, that it was futile – not as if they'd be needing the boats again. Or would they? Maybe they'd be part of Gottlieb's plan.

Steps set into the dockside led upwards to the shore. To get to them Anji and Fitz had to step into the other boat and walk along it. Anji was glad when the Doctor helped her on to the stone steps – the water looked dark and very, very deep.

Stepping over coils of rusted chains, the small party crossed a derelict street, then slipped up a narrow alley to emerge into a wide, open square. To Anji's surprise the buildings lining the square looked almost unspoiled – if you ignored the odd smashed window and the collapsed roofs caused by rotting timber-beams. There was a statue in the centre of the square, an iron figure on horseback staring at the derelict houses. If it wasn't for the overgrown grass the scene could almost be said to be verging on the genteel.

Just then rain began to drift slowly down from the overcast sky in soft gentle clouds. Soon the chalky smell of wet stone filled the air.

The Doctor paused at the edge of the square, motioning for all to be silent.

'What is it?' said Fitz in a stage whisper.

'I thought I saw movement,' said the Doctor, pointing at the other side of the square. He shrugged. 'I may have been wrong. Let's hope so.'

They moved quickly across the square, keeping close together. Gottlieb was leading them towards another alley almost exactly opposite the one they'd emerged from. They were halfway across the square, about level with the statue on the stone plinth, when Anji caught sight of a movement off to her left. Something running.

She grabbed Fitz's sleeve.

'What?' he said, half turning.

'I thought –' she began.

'Shit,' interrupted Fitz, eyes widening, staring past her.

Anji turned to look in the direction of his stare, and, through the veil of slow-falling rain, thought she saw a grey flapping object at a second-storey window. Could have been anything. A pigeon maybe.

But there weren't any pigeons in this reality.

Then an inhuman howl rang out, echoing around the square so that it was hard to tell exactly where it was coming from.

The Doctor stood in the long grass, hair caught in a slight breeze as he looked this way and that.

Father Gottlieb, fists bunched, stood in a fighting crouch. 'Wildren!'

Fitz stood as immobile as the statue, mouth and eyes open wide.

And Anji, soft rain falling on her face, watched with horror as skinny, rag-clothed, grey-skinned creatures – dozens, maybe even hundreds of them – came pouring, running and scampering from the doorways and alleyways on every side of the square.

Malahyde led Aboetta through the hall and along a corridor through the south wing. At the end of the passage was the door Aboetta knew led to the cellar. She had tried the handle a few times out of curiosity, in her first few weeks, but it had always been locked solid. As the months passed, she more or less forgot about it – or more precisely, accepted it as part of her new life.

Now Malahyde stood before this door, fishing in his waistcoat pocket for a key. Aboetta could see a sheen of sweat on his forehead, though it was far from warm, and his fingers fumbled as he slid the key into the lock.

A nervous glance in her direction. 'Follow me, and for the sake of the Lord do not touch anything, other than the floor with the soles of your boots.'

He opened the door to reveal stone steps leading down, bathed in a strange pale green glow. Aboetta leaned round the door-jamb and peered down; at the bottom, the glow seemed to intensify. Like sunlight strained through green glass.

Malahyde started down the steps. He paused half-way down and looked back. 'Come along!'

She walked down after him. For some reason her legs were trembling, as if she had run herself breathless. But her breathing was slow and sure, filling her chest with a heaviness as though there was something wrong with the air.

Or perhaps it was because she was terrified about what she'd find down there.

The steps led down quite a distance, and opened out into a vaulted cellar with a surprisingly high ceiling, at least twenty or maybe even thirty feet. Around its outside edge, fluted columns bordered alcoves, lending the subterranean room a Classical atmosphere.

But Aboetta didn't immediately take in these things.

What seized her attention was the thing in the centre of the cellar.

It was a column, as thick as a tree-trunk, which ran from floor to ceiling, supported on a circular metal platform. Against the far wall was a bank of machines which hummed and throbbed with power. In one corner was a squat black furnace, with a flue going up into the ceiling. Before the central column was a chair and a wooden desk. There was something on the desk, a metal box with buttons and little circular windows. Black snaking ropes ran from the back of this to the circular platform.

The column glowed with a soft green light unlike anything Aboetta had ever seen.

Eventually she found her voice. 'What – what *is* it?'

Malahyde walked up to it, gazing at it with a look of reverence and fear, his hands clasped tightly over his chest.

Then he turned to Aboetta. 'It is the Utopian Engine, and it is – I am – responsible for the dystopia in which we now exist.'

Chapter 10
The Outlaws

Anji ran, feet slipping on the wet grass, following Father Gottlieb as he made for a gap in the closing circle of Wildren. They wouldn't make it, that much was obvious. But what else was there to do, other than run?

She watched as Gottlieb smashed one of the creatures with his fist, sending it sprawling into its fellows. He kicked another in the stomach, jackknifing it. The thin, malnourished things were clearly not too strong individually, and gave him a wide berth, heading for easier prey – Anji.

She put an extra spurt on, twisting past an outstretched grey hand, leaping over a lunging body, once almost slipping on the damp grass. To her amazement, she found herself running across open ground, no Wildren in sight, following Father Gottlieb towards a narrow alley in the east side of the square.

She allowed herself a look back as she left the grass and her boots skidded on cobblestones. A host of bent grey backs, thin legs, black ragged hair, converging on the centre of the square.

The Doctor and Fitz –

They'd got away? They'd got away. Had to believe it.

Then she turned and ran after Father Gottlieb.

The alley opened out on to another cobbled street, on the far side of which was a derelict shipyard and another stretch of the Floating Harbour. Gottlieb was running towards this.

Anji's heart jumped as three Wildren emerged from behind a crumbling building and scampered towards her. Gottlieb, who had reached the edge of the dock, turned, arms akimbo, and shouted.

The three Wildren crept closer to Anji, slowly, sure now of catching her. Two were tall and thin, but the middle one lagged behind, shuffling along on its knees. Anji circled around, trying to get between the Wildren and the edge. But the two taller ones anticipated her move. They darted round to cut off her escape.

It was the first time Anji had seen the creatures up close. They were clearly human, but thin, horribly thin, and they walked with hunched backs and gangling, spindly arms. They wore stinking rags, and their feet were bare. Their faces were masks of grey skin, pinched with malnutrition and malice. Their gaping, drooling mouths held pointed shards of yellow-brown teeth. But it was their eyes that upset Anji the most. They weren't what she'd been expecting – egglike zombie-eyes, or even feral slitted cat-eyes. They were human eyes.

The third one was circling round on its knees, making a pathetic mewling cry, its sticklike arms stretched out towards the other two. Its *parents*? Anji couldn't tell the difference between the two advancing Wildren, facially at least, but then she caught a glimpse of flaccid, swinging breasts beneath the filthy rags of the creature to her left.

The other one – the male, the father – began to laugh, a low, throaty, idiot chuckle.

Father. A word so loaded with connotations of family and protection and safety and love had no connection with the dribbling, leering thing creeping towards her.

Suddenly, the Wildren lunged.

Anji threw herself to one side, slipping on the damp cobblestones, sprawling on the ground. A hand grabbed at her hair, ragged nails dug into her scalp. Another hand closed around her throat. She screamed, until a dirty palm closed over her mouth. She gagged at the fetid odour of the creatures. The giggling of the father changed into a savage, hungry snarling. She could hear the child – it seemed to be crying 'feed me! feed me!' like a hungry seagull chick. Then the grunting of the male turned into an oddly human cry of alarm, and the female – the *mother* – emitted a piercing shriek which made Anji's ears ring. Then suddenly the hands let go of her hair, neck and face and she scrambled free. She twisted into a crouch, pulling her rain-dampened hair away from her face, tenderly feeling the area above her left ear where the Wildren had scratched her.

She watched as Gottlieb, having already snapped the neck of one of the adult Wildren, grappled with the other, hands around its neck. Then in one swift movement he drew his right hand back, formed his fingers into points and jabbed forwards into the creature's eyes.

It shrieked and dropped to the cobbles, hands covering its face.

Anji turned away whilst Gottlieb finished the creature off by stamping on its neck.

Then he was by her side, pulling her to her feet. His black hair was plastered to his forehead with rain and sweat, he was panting, and his teeth were bared. To Anji he looked almost as terrifying as creatures he had killed.

Anji made to follow Gottlieb towards the water's edge, then stopped as she felt something tugging at her leg.

She looked down, and shuddered. *The child*. It was pointing to the bodies of its parents. Its mouth was open, and it was making little mewing noises. She could see the spittle strung between its teeth like a cobweb. Its eyes were round and baby blue and they were looking straight at her. It – she could not tell if the creature was male or female – looked no older than four or five.

It was only a child. The Wildren were the idiot children of the Cleansing, and this shuffling thing terrified Anji far more than its taller brethren. It was innocent. It was not evil. It just wanted to survive.

Father Gottlieb bent down and picked up the small creature by its legs. Anji stepped back, wondering what he was going to with him – her – it.

Without a word, Gottlieb walked towards the water's edge, raised the child above his head, and dashed its brains out against an iron mooring-post.

'Wilde Kinder,' he spat, wiping his hands on his trousers as he walked back towards Anji. 'Can you swim?'

Anji made an inarticulate noise and stepped towards him.

'Come on, then!' he snarled, grabbing her arm. 'It won't be long before this place is crawling with Wildren. The water's our only chance.'

He all but dragged her to the edge of the dock, past the remains of the Wildren child. Shrieks and howls were coming from the square behind them. Anji turned to see Wildren running through the alley into the shipyard.

She looked down at the water's surface, stippled with the drifting rain. Every instinct in her shouted out against jumping in.

But it was preferable to being eaten alive.

Anji shuffled to the very edge.

'Ready?' said Father Gottlieb.

Without answering, Anji jumped.

There was a strange interlude as Anji felt as though she were floating. Then, before her body and brain could register the sensation of falling, she hit the water in a crashing explosion of light and sank beneath the surface. She clawed her way back upwards, treading water, spitting and choking.

A glance at the harbour side. Wildren, crouching on the stone like ragged grey monkeys, their faces distorted with hate.

Father Gottlieb was treading water next to her. 'Can you swim underwater?' he shouted.

Anji just nodded.

'Then follow me.'

He took a deep breath, and was gone.

Anji filled her lungs, ducked under the water and kicked out, arrowing into the depths of the river.

She could see Gottlieb already some distance away, heading for the harbour wall. Rippling sunlight reflected through the surface on to the stone. The water around her was clear, ice cold, and clean. She'd been expecting to be choked and blinded by pollutants, but then, of course, in this reality there was nothing to produce pollution.

Trying not to think of how long she could hold her breath, she swam after Gottlieb. He was keeping close to the wall, swimming along in a frantic doggy-paddle, his hair floating like weed around his head.

Anji could feel the blood vessels pounding in her temples, her heart machining away in her chest. Breath escaped from her mouth, bubbles blurring her vision. She groped about in the silver storm around her, and her fingers brushed the harbour wall. Underwater it was smooth and slippery, like soapstone. She felt her way along it, kicking out her legs behind her. She could feel her denim jacket clinging to her, sucking like a mouth. As she swam, she twisted over on to her back. Above her the wall vanished where it met the water, and above that she could see nothing but a shimmering distorted picture of the wall and the white sky.

It was getting farther and farther away.

She was sinking.

Lungs bursting with the effort, she twisted round and kicked out again, propelling herself along parallel to the wall, outstretched fingers brushing its slimy surface. Purple blotches began exploding all over her field of vision and a sudden, sharp pain sliced in behind her eyes. She wanted to open her mouth to scream but if she did she'd suck in water and drown.

She felt almost calm about it.

Then she must have blacked out for a second, because the next thing she knew a strong arm was hooked round her neck, hauling her upwards towards the shimmering white. Then she was bursting through the mirror, coughing out spouts of water, then breathing in great gulps of air. The arm round her neck loosened, she felt herself slip again, but hands moved over hers, guiding them forwards until her palms hit something rough which flaked against her grasping fingers. She still couldn't see – her eyes stung – but she instinctively grasped what it was, and hauled herself up the ladder, her boots slipping on the rungs which were below water.

Once completely out of the water, Anji was seized by a swoon of nausea. She suddenly felt so heavy that she almost dropped back down into the river.

A voice from below her: 'Climb, girl! Before they see us!'

Mention of 'they' reminded Anji of the shuffling thing with baby blue eyes, and with renewed determination she hauled herself up the ladder, ignoring the sharp pains in the palms of her hands as the rusted rungs cut in. *Won't be able to get tetanus jabs in this reality.* Then suddenly her fingers touched stone and Anji hauled herself painfully up on to the dockside. She lay on her back, gasping for breath, her vision at last clearing. Above – white sky. She shivered and sat up, sloughing off her jacket.

Father Gottlieb grabbed her and hauled her to her feet. Jacket half on, half off, Anji let herself be dragged squelching across a cobbled courtyard towards a half-timbered building. The lower ten feet of it were boarded up with great plates of rusting iron. At one of the upper windows, a face looked down, a pale smudge against the darkness within.

As they approached, a hatchway opened in one of these plates – it looked to Anji like it had once been the hull of a ship – and Gottlieb propelled her inside.

The hatchway slammed behind them. Anji heard the clunk of a heavy lock.

Then a figure lurched round a corner to face them, a rifle in one hand, an oil-lamp in the other. A man in a shapeless white shirt open at the neck, wearing breeches and boots. His ferret-like face was emaciated, and below his ragged yellow beard Anji noticed with repugnance a weeping sore on his chin.

He was looking at Anji with undisguised lust.

To her surprise Gottlieb gave the man a shove, sending him staggering backwards. 'Forget it, Conro, she's too good for the likes of you. Just take us up.'

Conro sneered, revealing a mouth of yellowing teeth that looked oddly sharp – or maybe it was a trick of the guttering yellow light from the lamp.

'We bin waitin' for you,' said Conro, in a surprisingly deep voice. He smiled and snorted, an odd, sniffing sound like a rooting pig. 'Got a good feast ready.' His narrow eyes shifted to Anji again.

'Good,' said Gottlieb thoughtfully. Then he turned to Anji. 'Don't worry, you are perfectly safe. This is the inn I told you about, and these, sad to say, are my present associates.'

Conro tutted and stomped away. His lamp revealed varnished wood panelling and a staircase.

'Come along,' said Gottlieb, offering his hand to Anji. He frowned in concern, obviously noticing that she was shivering. 'There'll be a fire upstairs.' He turned to look at her, eyes narrowing. 'And I expect you're hungry.'

Anji stood there, dripping and shivering in the darkness. 'What about the Doctor and Fitz?'

Gottlieb sighed and looked away. 'There is no hope for them now,' he said curtly. He looked at her again. 'Believe me. Unless they followed us into the water, the *Wilde Kinder* will have caught them.'

Anji closed her eyes. The thought of being alone in this world was too much to bear. She had to believe the Doctor and Fitz had escaped, for her sanity's sake if nothing else. 'OK, lead on.' Her stomach rumbled. 'You are right – I am hungry.'

Gottlieb nodded and looked away quickly. His next words did nothing to comfort her. 'Try not to be upset by my associates.'

'What do you mean?' Alarm rose as she squelched up the stairs after him.

'You are clearly a woman of some refinement – a Citizen, as you say, from the north of this country. They – we – are outlaws. Our ways are different from yours.'

He led her up the stairs, along a corridor, through a door.

And into bedlam.

It was the stench that hit Anji first. Unwashed bodies and rotting food. Tables and chairs were strewn around the large room, and in the farthest wall, a fire blazed. Everything was picked out in orange and black. People were sitting or lying around. A murmur of comment burst out as they saw Gottlieb and Anji.

Gottlieb held up a hand. 'Yes, I have returned. And I have some work for you, you lucky rats!'

Groans and howls, but some cheers.

'I thought there was a feast to hand, Mary?'

He was addressing a thin woman in a filthy dress, which, despite its decrepitude, clearly counted as finery in this company.

'It's comin',' the woman said in a broad Bristolian accent. Her upper teeth protruded alarmingly, and her chin was lost in folds of leathery skin. 'Who's this?'

'Her name's Anji, and she's to be left alone.' The warning was clear, but still they gathered around her.

'Look at her skin!' came a gasp from behind her.

'Look at her clothes!' cooed Mary, reaching out to fondle the lapel of Anji's jacket. Her eyes narrowed in a frown. 'Bin swimmin'?'

'Yes,' said Anji. Somehow, the way Gottlieb was protecting her gave her confidence. 'I've been swimming.'

This prompted laughs and even applause.

'Where did you get *her*, Father Gottlieb?' cried Mary.

'Never you mind!' shouted Gottlieb irritably. He stepped forward, the silver cross bright orange in the firelight. 'Now listen, all of you. Soon we must be on the move – to Ashton Court.'

There was silence for a few seconds, then someone cursed. 'We ain't ever gonna get in there,' came a mutter from the shadows.

'I have a plan,' said Gottlieb, smiling and folding his arms across his chest. 'You still want to get hold of Malahyde's treasures, don't you? All the food and wine, all the weapons.' The last word was almost a hiss. 'All his secrets! All his power! You could rule Bristol – take over every settlement!'

They seemed to perk up at this.

'Or would you rather skulk here, taking whatever measly scraps you can find?'

'There's always her,' said Conro, leering in Anji's direction.

'I warned you!' snarled Gottlieb.

Flattered though she was, Anji was beginning to wonder why she merited this special treatment.

'Of course we don't want to stay here,' said Mary. The smile was gone. She slumped down into a chair and looked up at Gottlieb. 'You know we want a better life, but the settlements won't 'ave the likes of us.'

'So you're with me, then?'

There was a general grumble of assent.

'Very well. Now, we'll eat.'

Gottlieb took Anji to a table in front of the fire. She sat opposite him.

They looked at each other for a few moments. Anji felt the heat of the fire begin to dry out her clothes. 'Thanks,' she said, uncertainly.

'For what?'

'For keeping your mob off me.' She imagined that she could feel their stares as an itch at the back of her neck. 'I've got to ask why.'

Gottlieb leaned back. 'Because you interest me. You just don't fit in, and neither did the Doctor or that fellow Fitz.' He smiled.

Anji sensed something in the way he was looking at her. 'Is that the only reason?'

Father Gottlieb's features softened slightly. 'Ah. You think that I have a romantic interest in you.' His mouth hardened into a tight line, and he closed his eyes briefly. 'Would that I could know what that meant, enjoy "love", whatever that means. Every woman I have had, I have taken by force. I could take you by force, now, in one of the rooms upstairs.'

Anji met his gaze. Let him try, she thought, let him try. I'm not going down without a fight. Then immediately after this, a qualm of sheer panic: there are too many of them, I won't have a chance.

'But I will not,' he said at last. He kept staring at her, and she somehow knew that he didn't want her gratitude.

'You are unlike any woman I have ever met. More beautiful, more intelligent, more refined. It is almost as if you have dropped down from another world.'

Anji shifted uncomfortably. Her stomach rumbled. When was this food going to arrive?

Father Gottlieb was still struggling with his words – it was like being on a date, but a date straight from bizzaro-world. 'And I cannot treat you like – those others.'

'Right,' said Anji. 'OK. So you don't fancy me, you're just "interested" in me.'

Father Gottlieb nodded. His eyes narrowed as he grasped her meaning. 'Of course, you could leave here at any time. But I wouldn't advise it. The Wildren will be milling around for days.'

'So we're stuck with each other, then.'

Father Gottlieb smiled. 'Yes.'

Anji smiled, resolving that the first chance she got, she'd high-tail it as far away from this bloke as she could. 'So what is your plan, then?'

He leaned back and put his arms behind his head. 'I came to Bristol a month ago, with the sole intention of getting into Ashton Court. Everyone – that is, anyone who is interested – knows about Malahyde and his servant Aboetta. When news of her father's illness spread, I reasoned that Aboetta would have to return to Totterdown. So I went there and made myself useful, hoping to ingratiate myself with the girl.' He frowned. 'But things didn't go quite as I planned. The arrival of you and your friends, for one.' He leaned back in the chair, a calculating look in those feral eyes. 'I suspect there is more to you than you are letting on. More to the Doctor as well. He knows more about the Cleansing than he's telling me – I've picked up on certain things he's said.'

'Really,' said Anji.

'Yes. It is a pity he's dead.'

He said this too casually for Anji's liking.

A commotion behind them.

Gottlieb's head jerked towards the doorway. He grinned. 'Ah! Dinner is served!'

The door opened and the woman Mary came through, wheeling something on a wooden trolley. Enthusiastic cries from all within the room.

Father Gottlieb stood, looking down at her. It seemed as if he was about to speak, but he turned away.

Anji also stood, craning her head to get a view of the meal over the heads of the outlaws crowding round the trolley.

It smelt like meat. Cooked meat, like pork.

Then Anji saw what it was.

It was a roasted human torso.

Anji's hand flew to her mouth.

Father Gottlieb glared at her, his expression impassive,

challenging. The horrible thought occurred to her that, despite all he'd said, perhaps she was next on the menu.

Then came the worst thing. At the scent of the cooked human flesh, Anji's stomach began to rumble with hunger.

Chapter 11
Fighting Back

The Doctor – to Fitz's utter amazement – was walking slowly towards the encroaching horde, hands raised.

Fitz gazed in anguish after Anji, then darted forwards, grabbing the Doctor's arm. 'What the bloody hell are you doing?'

'They're human,' said the Doctor. 'Or at least, their ancestors were. Maybe it's possible to reason with them.'

'Bollocks to that!' said Fitz. 'Look at them! How can you reason with *things* like *that*?'

The Doctor stopped in his tracks. 'You're right. *Run!*'

Fitz didn't need to be told. He ran.

'Head that way,' cried the Doctor. 'Towards the river!'

Oh yes, Wildren couldn't swim. Looked like an early bath then. As he ran he realised that they were going the opposite way from Anji and Gottlieb. He tried to shout to the Doctor but couldn't see him through the mass of scampering bodies.

Somehow, he made it across the grass, across the cobbled road at the edge of the square and down a narrow alley. Wildren grabbed at him as he ran, but he managed to shake them off – even one that leaped on his back, clawlike hands clutching at his face.

At the end of the alley he rounded a corner – dead end. Blocked with rubble. He turned back the other way and collided with something which said 'oof' and grabbed his elbows.

Fitz screamed – but it was the Doctor. The Doctor's face, inches from his own. This close his blue eyes looked as wide as oceans. Fitz briefly wondered what the Doctor could see in his, Fitz's, eyes. Streaks of yellow, he wouldn't wonder.

The Doctor's hands moved to Fitz's chest, palms against the brown leather of his coat. The Doctor shoved Fitz away from him and yelled. 'Run!'

They hared out of the dead end, dived down a narrow alley, splashed and skidded through puddles of silty water, and emerged into an open area which looked a cross between a building site and a bomb site. Iron girders lolled together in rusty recumbence. Wooden crates piled up against the side of a long, low building whose roof had partly collapsed. Something about the scene made Fitz think that people had been here since Year Nought, maybe trying to recolonise Bristol. There was a vague order to things. Much of the rubble had been cleared away and someone had obviously tried to make sense of the decay which had befallen the city. A brace of carriages, wheels still intact, stood in a line and Fitz made a run for these, vaguely believing in that mad instant that he could leap in, crack a whip and away.

He sprawled against the wheel of the nearest carriage and grasped its spokes. They crumbled in his hands like breakfast cereal. Of course – unmaintained, they'd perished.

The Doctor was close behind him, Wildren right on his heels. He bent to pick up a length of rusted pipe and turned to face the Wildren, who were almost upon him now.

Fitz winced as the Doctor swung the pipe with deadly accuracy, saw it connect with a Wildren's skull with a sharp crack. Saw the Wildren tumble to the ground, a jet of blood staining the cobbles. Its fellows stumbled over the body, seemingly unconcerned, and made straight for the Doctor.

The Doctor swung again, roaring in anger and horror. Another Wildren fell. And still more came running.

The Doctor didn't stand a chance.

Before Fitz, on the rain-dampened ground, lay a long metal lever, about the size of a cricket bat.

Now was the chance to redeem himself.

Fitz snatched up the length of metal and launched into the fray, staggering forwards and swinging the thing before him. The Wildren scrambled backwards, stumbling over the dead bodies of the creatures the Doctor had killed. Soon he was shoulder to shoulder with the Doctor.

Fitz was quite glad he hadn't actually had to kill one of the things yet. Then he remembered Anji, and what they would do if they caught her, and yelled, striking out at the nearest Wildren. The blow caught the creature on the side of the head and it staggered for a while, then fell to the ground twitching.

Fitz felt sick, and from the look in his eyes, so did the Doctor.

'There are too many of them,' said the Doctor. 'They'll bear us down with sheer weight of numbers.'

This was true. Fitz's arms – already strained from the rowing – ached painfully. 'Then what do you suggest?'

The Doctor gestured behind him with his thumb. 'There's another stretch of the Floating Harbour that way.'

Fitz gasped. 'I can't swim!'

'I thought Anji had been teaching you!'

'Two lessons, Doctor, and all I could manage was to stay afloat – just about!'

'You'll make it. Survival instinct.' The Doctor grabbed his arm and pulled him away from the Wildren, who had formed a wary, swaying circle around them. They're bound to make a jump for us sooner or later, thought Fitz. The Doctor was right. The water was their only chance.

He supposed drowning was better than being eaten alive. But not much better – the end result was the same: finito Fitz.

But when the Doctor cried, 'Now!' Fitz hurled the metal lever at the Wildren and ran. He didn't dare look behind. He just pelted across the open area in front of the river, yelling his guts out. The edge came up horrifyingly quickly and Fitz half fell, half dived into the water. A huge confusing splash enveloped him, and the water was so cold the breath was driven from his lungs. Flailing, gasping, he surfaced in time to see the Doctor dive head first into the water and begin swimming across. By the time Fitz had recovered, the

Doctor had already passed him, swimming with powerful strokes.

Fitz dragged himself across in an awkward doggy-paddle, his jacket slowing him down. He couldn't quite believe it, but he was actually making headway! Even though he'd been told that the Wildren couldn't swim he was terrified that they were in the water beneath him, clutching hands reaching up to drag him down. So it was with a huge sense of relief that he reached the far side and hauled himself up a set of stone steps cut into the harbour wall.

The Doctor was waiting for him, and, apart from the fact that he was dripping wet, he seemed completely unfazed. 'I knew you'd make it.'

'Well, I didn't. What now?' said Fitz, shaking water from the sleeves of his jacket.

'Look.' The Doctor pointed, fascinated.

Wildren stood on the opposite bank, pacing up and down, snarling and hooting. Fitz glanced along the length of the harbour, anxiously looking for any way the creatures could get across. But the wide artificial river stretched in either direction, safely separating Fitz from the Wildren.

Fitz grinned and waved to the creatures.

Then he thought of Anji and his smile vanished.

The Doctor strode past him, making for the buildings lining the dockside. 'Back to the TARDIS.'

Fitz raised his eyebrows and stared at the Doctor's retreating back. 'What about Anji?'

The Doctor didn't answer.

With a final glance at the Wildren, Fitz caught up with the Doctor. 'What about Anji?' he repeated.

The Doctor turned to face him. 'I don't want to think about what may have happened to her. I just hope she managed to get away.'

'Is that it?' cried Fitz. 'Can't we go back and look for her?' Even as he said it, Fitz realised it was impossible. They'd barely managed to escape this time.

The Doctor shook his head. 'You know we can't.'

Fitz was shivering after his swim. He was drenched to the bone. He thought guiltily of the TARDIS, a hot bath and a change of clothes. 'I suppose you're right. Our only option is the TARDIS.'

The Doctor looked over at the Wildren. 'There's bound to be a way across, somewhere. Come on – let's get out of here before they find it.'

The Doctor and Fitz picked their way through the ruined city. As well as regaining his second heart, the Doctor also seemed to have regained his homing instinct for the TARDIS. He led Fitz unerringly through the eerie, empty streets, constantly on the look-out for Wildren.

Soon they emerged from the town into an area Fitz recognised. The open countryside just outside Bristol and below Clifton, through which they had passed on their journey to Totterdown with Aboetta the day before. The bushes glistened with the recent rainfall. It had stopped raining now, and a baleful sun had emerged from behind the clouds. By its position in the sky, a hand's width from the horizon, Fitz judged it to be some time in the afternoon.

Suddenly, there was a sound from behind him. The faintest of metallic clicks.

Fitz whirled round – to be faced with a man pointing a rifle straight at him. 'Bloody hell!'

The man stepped closer. He was smiling, but not in a friendly way.

The Doctor walked back to stand next to Fitz. The barrel of the rifle swung to cover him.

The Doctor put his hands up. 'Hello, Robin,' he said. 'What are you doing so far from home?'

'I should shoot you,' said Robin Larkspar slowly, ignoring the question. 'You took Aboetta away. You left the river-gate open.' He swung the rifle back towards Fitz.

Fitz closed his eyes.

'But I ain't going to.'

Fitz opened his eyes to see that Robin had lowered the rifle.

'I'm glad to hear that,' said the Doctor. 'Now would you care to tell us why?'

'Doctor,' said Fitz warningly. 'Isn't it enough that he's not going to shoot us?'

'No,' said the Doctor. 'After all, he has every reason to.'

The rifle was brought back to bear on the Doctor. 'I don't like you or trust you,' he said, a harsh edge creeping into his soft West Country accent. 'But I have to thank you, oddly enough.'

'Why?' said Fitz.

'Not here,' said Robin. 'Too open. Follow me.'

He led them into a copse of trees in the centre of which was a bramble bush the size of a small house. Robin, or someone, had hacked their way into the centre of this. Fitz squeezed through after the Doctor. Inside, on the dry dusty ground, Robin had made camp. There was a blanket, a bottle of beer and a loaf of bread. Robin sat on the blanket, inviting them to follow suit. There was just enough room for them all, knees touching.

'Very cosy,' said the Doctor.

'Where's Aboetta?' said Robin, the harsh tone once more evident.

The Doctor regarded Robin levelly. 'She's with Malahyde.'

Robin grunted. 'Thought so.' His eyes narrowed. 'You helped her.'

'It was her choice,' said Fitz. 'And anyway, *she* helped *us* escape.'

'Which one of you killed Billy?'

The Doctor frowned. 'Billy? Oh, I see, the Watchkeeper at the river-gate. You probably won't believe me, but it was Father Gottlieb.'

'I do believe you,' said Robin. 'Always thought there was something odd about him. Outlaw written all over him. Where's *he* now?'

'Missing. With Anji – our other friend.'

Robin nodded sadly. 'Wildren.'

The Doctor sighed. 'I'm afraid so.'

Fitz was trying not to think about Anji. 'What about you? You said you had reason to thank us.'

'Have some bread,' said Robin, breaking off a chunk. Fitz accepted but the Doctor waved Robin away.

'Well, it was because of what you did – taking Aboetta away – that I've left Totterdown. Probably for good.' He smiled, and seemed to look amazed at himself. 'Ten years I waited for Aboetta. Ten years as Watchkeeper, keeping everything safe for everyone. And you know what happened when I said we should go and get Aboetta back?'

'I can guess,' said the Doctor.

'Nobody wanted to help. So I'm going to do it on my own. I'm going to Malahyde's estate, and I'm going to get Aboetta back.'

'You know that you haven't got the slightest chance of getting into Ashton Court,' said the Doctor. 'It's too well defended, and even if you did manage to get over the wall, you'd be shot on sight.'

Robin's expression was bleak – he clearly accepted the risk.

The Doctor leaned forwards. 'But I can get you in.'

Robin stared at the Doctor.

So did Fitz.

The journey back to the TARDIS passed without incident or sight of Wildren. Fitz managed to conduct a hissed, terse conversation with the Doctor about letting Robin come with them, but the Doctor had shrugged and said that he might come in useful.

The TARDIS was where they had left it, in the crumbling cul-de-sac where Aboetta had been attacked by the creatures. But there were no signs of them – perhaps they were nomadic, moving from place to place in search of food.

Once inside the TARDIS, the Doctor went immediately to the console, not seeming to be bothered about his wet clothes.

Fitz sat Robin down in a comfortable armchair and went to his room to get changed. Brown leather jacket – ruined. Trousers, shirt – soaked. Shoes, also ruined. Forsaking a bath, Fitz clambered into black jeans, a white shirt and a stand-by black leather jacket, hoping that he wouldn't have to do any more swimming. On his way out, he paused, turned back and picked up his guitar. Time enough for a quick strum, surely? Would help calm him down. He fingered a chord and strummed – and the top E string snapped with a *twang*.

Not a good sign, thought Fitz as he gazed at the shimmering silver length dangling from the headstock. The crippled chord hung in the air. Fitz waited until it had faded right away, then leaned the guitar against the wall, making a mental promise to re-string it later.

When he returned to the console room, Robin had left the armchair – his rifle propped up against it, Fitz noted with relief – and was wandering around, clearly gobsmacked.

The Doctor was on his back beneath the TARDIS console, busy rewiring a spaghetti-like cluster of cables. His jacket was hanging from a lever. Somehow, it was dry. Fitz looked down at the Doctor's trousers and shoes. They were dry, too. How the hell?

Fitz shrugged. *What* the hell.

He went up to Robin. The man looked dazed. Fitz snapped his fingers in his face. 'Now. Look. If you're coming with us, you have to cope with this pretty damn quickly. You think leaving Totterdown was a big step – you haven't seen anything yet.'

Robin seemed to return somewhat to his senses. 'What is this place?'

'It's called the TARDIS. It's our ship, and our home. It takes us from place to place, and time to time. Don't ask me to explain how.'

'And it's going to take us inside Ashton Court? To Aboetta?'

Fitz gave a double thumbs-up. 'Yes! Well, hopefully. Hang on.'

He walked over to the console and crouched down beside the Doctor.

'Doctor. I'm rather worried about this. Surely, if we dematerialise, won't we end up in yet another alternative reality? And everything will be even more mucked up than it already is?'

The Doctor continued to work. 'I know, it's immensely, terribly, insanely dangerous and I was leaving it as a last resort. But there isn't a way into Ashton Court without getting ourselves shot, and I've been turning the problem over in my mind and I think there's a way, if I disconnect the time element, that I can bounce us a few miles across space into the Estate without even entering the Time Vortex.'

'Bounce?' said Fitz. 'Sounds dodgy.'

'It is,' said the Doctor. 'But it's the only way. Short cut to the centre square.'

'Cheating, you mean.'

'Ah, but I bet the other fellow's cheating harder.'

At least this plan, dangerous though it sounded, wasn't to do with going back and erasing realities. Perhaps, when they met this Malahyde bloke, everything could be sorted out without wiping out a hundred and sixty years of civilisation – rudimentary, yes, but still civilisation.

The Doctor emerged from beneath the console, stood and hunched over the controls. 'Right. Here goes,' he said.

He started flicking switches and pulling levers.

Robin looked questioningly at Fitz. 'What happens now?'

Fitz looked warily at the Doctor. 'You tell me.'

Chapter 12
Encounter on the Downs

'What do you mean?'

Malahyde, his face bathed in green light from the glowing column, just stared at Aboetta.

'Mr Malahyde,' said Aboetta. 'How can *you* be responsible for the Cleansing?'

'I know it sounds impossible. But it's true.'

'But how? And what is this machine?'

He didn't reply, just began to bustle her towards the steps.

Aboetta resisted. 'You can't do this! You can't show me this, say what you said, and not explain any further!'

'I am going to explain!' he shouted, his voice echoing from the alcoves. 'But not down here.'

Aboetta followed Malahyde out of the cellar, noticing that the walls of the cellar were blighted with what looked like burn-marks. She watched him lock the door, his movements jerky. She was bursting with questions, but could see that Malahyde was having some sort of crisis.

They returned to the drawing room, where Malahyde told her to sit.

'I knew that if I took on a housekeeper, one day I would have to let them in – let *you* in on my secret. What I am about to tell you may sound like the ravings of a madman. All I ask is that you hear me out.'

Aboetta nodded. 'Go on.'

Malahyde sat in a chair beside the fire and folded his arms, clearly making an effort to compose himself.

'You have read about the world before the Cleansing, Aboetta. You therefore have some idea what it was like. But you cannot imagine how different it was. Bristol was full of people, full of business, full of life.' He sighed. 'I never cared for commerce or industry, but I would give anything to have things back the way they were then. I was a poet, Aboetta, or at least I had pretensions towards becoming a poet. My father, you see, was a prominent cutler - a steel-maker - in Sheffield, a large industrial town in the north of the country. He wanted me to follow on from him, take over his business, but I was never interested. I stuck out my apprenticeship, but at the age of twenty-one I left, against my father's wishes. I worked as a clerk for a firm of solicitors in Sheffield for four years, working on my poems in the evenings. Those were good years, serene and productive.' He grew silent, staring into the fire.

'Why have you never shown me any of your poems?' said Aboetta.

Malahyde looked at her. 'I destroyed them when I realised how useless they were. But I sometimes wish I had kept the best of them.' He gazed into the fire again, as if the ashes were the remains of his works.

'I moved to Bristol when I was twenty-five,' he went on. 'I was beginning to find Sheffield oppressive, and father kept petitioning me to take over his business. A fellow clerk had a relative who ran a boarding-house in Bedminster. And so in the summer of 1831, I left Sheffield forever. I spent the first weeks acquainting myself with my new home, taking walks about the city, finding coffee-houses and inns where I could sit and observe, make notes, compose. I had saved enough money from my time as a clerk, and had inherited a small fund on my majority, so I had no immediate financial worries.'

He smiled at her. 'You see in those days I was confident of my success. Confident that my work would bring me fame and renown.' The smile faded. 'I saw it as a way only to increase my standing in society. I was hot-headed, arrogant, certain of success.' He paused. 'I never stopped to consider whether my work was of any worth.'

'Now, no one will ever know,' said Aboetta.

Malahyde snorted. 'Now, it doesn't matter.' He walked over to the windows and stared out at the gardens and the surrounding wall. 'Doesn't matter at all.' He stood for a moment, then returned to his seat. 'That's the last I will talk about poetry – I don't write it any more, never will again. All you need to know is that it was the reason why I moved down to Bristol. That's all. I have nothing to do with art.'

'You play the violin very well. Though as I have never heard any one else play, I can't be the best judge.'

He laughed. 'The violin! I learned that when I was a boy. Now, I find that playing – helps me forget.'

'And my dancing?'

He looked at her gravely. 'Is as good as any I have seen. Even before Year Nought.'

This was getting interesting. 'Was there anyone special in those days?'

Malahyde shook his head. 'No! I was far too shy. And in my mind, I reasoned that I wanted to keep myself pure for my art. With hindsight, however, maybe a little experience of life would have improved my poetry.'

'I thought you weren't going to mention that again.'

Malahyde blinked. 'Yes.' He sighed and slumped back in his chair. 'Though I grant you it would be far easier to talk on in this manner, Aboetta, than to tell of what happened to me in Bristol.'

It was pleasant to talk so openly to Mr Malahyde. 'You did promise to tell me.'

Malahyde sat up, clasped his hands in his lap, and for a moment Aboetta was sure he was about to leap up and flee from the room.

Then he began to speak again. 'In the evenings, I took to walking upon the Downs. You know them now only as the wasteland on the far side of the Gorge, thick with brambles and weeds and Wildren nests. But back in 1831, the area was common land. Some of it was maintained as parkland, but most of it was rough untended heath. It was a haven for loners, lovers, poets – and engineers, as I was to find out one night in October.

'This night was particularly clear and calm. I had spent the day composing an epic poem I cringe to think of now, but as dusk fell I found myself beset with problems. The poem began to fail, to fall apart before my eyes. So I went for my customary walk upon the Downs. I had traversed the length of Ladies Mile – a long road which bisects the area – and was approaching the point which overlooked the Avon Gorge. I dimly realised that I could be accosted by vagabonds and I was minded to turn back, when a figure blundered from the cover of some bushes and lurched towards me.

'I had time to shout, "Evening, Sir!" and dodge to one side – not in enough time, for the fellow collided with me, hard enough to wind me. But luckily this was no vagabond, the stranger was most solicitous and waited until I'd regained my breath. Then he introduced himself as Isambard Kingdom Brunel.'

Malahyde paused and looked at Aboetta expectantly.

'Brunel – the man who built the Suspension Bridge.' She had read about him: a great engineer, with ideas to change the world. Ideas which had come to nought, erased by the Cleansing.

Malahyde nodded. 'I had heard of him, and his father, during my apprenticeship. Bumping into him that night was a rude reminder of the world I had come to Bristol to escape. However, we struck up conversation, and he asked me what I was doing on the Downs. I said I was a poet seeking inspiration. "Inspiration!" I remember Brunel shouting this word up to the stars. For some reason he seemed eager to take me into his confidence. "It is not inspiration I lack," he told me, "but something more mundane."

'He began to talk of his frustrations. During a recent convalescence in Bristol, he had formulated a plan to bridge the Avon Gorge. A legacy had been in operation since 1754, set up by a wealthy Bristol merchant, in order to bridge the Gorge from Clifton to Leigh Woods. Brunel had submitted a number of designs for such a bridge and with his persuasion one of the designs had won: a type of suspension bridge – though this meant little to me at the time. Work had indeed begun on the bridge in the summer of 1831 but the Bridge Committee, set up to administer the legacy, had proved rather incompetent and therefore funds were not sufficient to carry on work. That was the mundane matter Brunel spoke of – funding.

The Committee were about to launch a fresh appeal for funds – and that was why Brunel had come out to the Downs tonight, to look over the Gorge, stare wistfully at the foundations stones and hope.

'I listened whilst he railed and ranted and began to feel that here was a man who only liked to talk of himself and his exploits. He was not interested in my poetry at all and asked no questions about it. Despite my unfavourable impression of him, I remained polite, and we parted, cordially, at about eight o'clock in the evening. He made his way back down towards Clifton, whilst I lingered for a while, somehow reluctant to make for home.

'If only we had not parted! If only I had accepted his offer of brandy! But I cannot change anything, and it is useless to wish. I walked back across the moorland, the hems of my trousers dampened by the long grass. I could see for quite a distance around me, the starlight and moonlight making the Downs into an arena in which I was the only moving thing.

'And then it happened.

'I became aware firstly of difficulty breathing, of a weight on my chest. Every time I inhaled, a pain sliced down through me, right to my stomach. I immediately thought I was having a heart attack, then I thought of the injustice of this at the age of twenty-five, then I fell to my knees. Then there was the most intense pressure in my head, behind my eyes, as though my brain was swelling in my skull. And all around me there was a glowing fog, of the most unearthly green. I heard a scream – of course, it was me – then there was a flash of light indistinguishable from pain and then I must have blacked out.

'When I woke, I was lying down, on something hard which felt like granite or marble – smooth rock, cold and almost frictionless against my fingertips. My head ached, and my limbs were heavy, as if I had a dose of the influenza. I remember just lying there idly wondering if this were a dream, and if so what a tedious one – all I could see was the swirling green fog.

'Then the mists cleared, and I sat up, still thinking I was inside a dream, and gazed around in wonderment.

'I was in a chamber of immense size, conical in shape as if a mountain had been hollowed out and made into a cathedral. The sheer scale of it was dizzying, and for a while I could make no sense of it. The walls had been smoothed and moulded into shapes at once wonderful and grotesque – great sweeping buttresses, archways, protuberances, bridges – but there was no overall pattern to it, no discernible purpose. There was no sound – indeed, any movement I made produced no noise, as if my ears were clogged with wax. Clouds of vapour drifted here and there, some on a level with where I sat, but most at the apex of the chamber. A dim, greenish light came through sinuous apertures in the walls, as if whoever had built this place had decided that the best way to illuminate it would be simply to slice through the outer wall to let the daylight in – such as it was. There were other points of light scattered around – bright, bluish-white spheres, countless in number, which hurt to look at. Some were travelling quite fast high above, others were drifting more slowly and seemed to be converging upon me. Their combined brightness was such that to avert my eyes I glanced down, past the edge of the block upon which I sat – and saw that this chamber continued for miles and miles beneath me. Though I had thought I was at its floor I was in fact drifting on this granite block through the vast green space of the chamber! And it wasn't the spheres of light converging on me – I was travelling towards them! This came as such a shock that I scrambled back from the edge, only to slide across the smooth surface, and fall off the other side.

'I did not fall, not exactly. I floated. At the time, I screamed aloud, my voice sounding dully in my own head, and flailed my arms uselessly. Then suddenly I was before three of the glowing spheres. I twisted in pain and shaded my eyes. Then I felt something slide over my forehead. Opening my eyes I saw that a hoop of some smooth semi-opaque material had been fitted snugly around my head, and I could look at the glowing spheres without pain. Perplexed, rather than scared, I floated there, still wondering if this were a dream. Then I remembered what had happened on the Downs – meeting Brunel, my "heart attack"', the green fog. And then the spheres spoke to me.

'At first I didn't realise what was happening. I suddenly remembered something someone had once said to me – a very strange statement. It was, "You are disoriented – can you understand us?" Where had I heard this? And then I remembered something else: "We repeat – can you understand us?" I dwelt on the memory, and realised I had never heard these words spoken aloud by anyone. But they were there in my mind! I became afraid and shouted out, hoping to wake from this nightmare. And still the memories came: "Do not be afraid. You are safe. We do not intend to harm you." Then came a memory which seemed to make sense of it all: "You are not accustomed to this method of communication. It is called telepathy. You are disoriented – but do not be afraid."

'And so it was that I came to realise that these three globes of light floating around me in the green twilight were alive. Alive, and sentient. As soon as I grasped the truth of this I asked questions, speaking out loud: 'Where am I? Why have you brought me here?' – the questions one would naturally ask. My voice sounded awfully muted as if my ears were plugged with cotton wool.

'As insane as this sounds, the beings had names. I learned that the three before me were called Amaroth, Watchlar and Thune. They answered my questions – in fact they filled my mind with so many "memories" that I feel that I know the Eternium as much as they.

'The Eternium – that was what they called their home – was not merely a world like Earth, but an entire Universe. *Our* universe! For these beings, these Eternines, told me that they were the ultimate stage in the evolution of the human race. And that they had brought me forwards through billions and billions of years to meet them.'

Malahyde paused. A look of doubt passed across his face. 'You don't believe me, do you?'

'I believe you,' said Aboetta emphatically. 'I've learned so much these last few days.' She leaned forwards. 'You must go on!'

Malahyde took a deep breath and continued. 'I remember panicking when they told me this, and trying to "swim" away from them. I could not take in the scale of time, could not relate to these blue-white spheres who spoke in memories. It went against everything I have ever learned, and ever believed. To know that the human race would evolve beyond the need for God – would virtually *become* God – seemed like heresy. I must have blacked out again, because when I came round I was sitting in a chair – quite a normal chair, though fashioned from some strange light metal – in a room, with four walls, a floor and a ceiling. The Eternines told me that they had provided this environment for me, so that I would not feel so disoriented. They manifested themselves before me as roughly humanoid shapes, tall and thin, still glowing but not quite as intensely, and with no faces.

'Then they told me what they wanted me to do, those three manlike shapes in the pale green room billions of years in the future. At the time from which the Eternines plucked me, Mankind was on the verge of a great Revolution, after which came a great Enlightenment, the first step on humanity's evolution to the Eternines. But this is not certain. The outcome of this Revolution could be darkness. Mankind could be heading for a Fall, a second Dark Age of ignorance. The early 1900s were – and I don't profess to fully understand this – a nexus point, where the fate of Mankind could go either way. Onward to the Eternium, the pinnacle of our evolution, or downwards, through war and disaster, into extinction.

'There is only one way to ensure that Mankind succeeds, and the Age of Enlightenment dawns. And that is for the Eternines to travel backwards through time and guide the human race through the nexus point.

'I argued that, as the Eternines were before me telling me this, then surely Mankind must have escaped the Fall? But Amaroth replied, quite vehemently (if a memory can be vehement – but that is what I remember) that time doesn't work like that. At every point, there are infinite branchings of probability. My head filled with memories I could not understand, which, thankfully, quickly passed away.

'They then told me that though they could pluck me through time, they could not travel back themselves. A time engine would need to be constructed first. And that is what they wanted me to do – go back to my time, and build this engine for them!

'I remember babbling that I wasn't an engineer, that they'd got the wrong man – Brunel was the one they needed! But they assured me that I would be able to complete the task. The one named Watchlar drifted towards me, his form resuming its habitual sphere-shape, and glowing brighter.

'I somehow grasped what was about to happen, and I screamed.'

Chapter 13
Uneasy Alliances

Anji sat on a rickety chair in a back room of the fortified inn. She was wearing a borrowed dress, one of Mary's, a sorry and badly stained rag fit only for the bin. A small fire was crackling merrily away, Anji's sodden clothes draped over a line in front the grate. Her denim jacket – £129.99 from Donna Karan, irreplaceable in this reality – was beginning to steam gently, making the room smell of home. In one of the pockets she'd found a small bottle of mineral water, half empty (she wasn't feeling optimistic) and its clean, fresh taste made her yearn even more for home.

In one wall there was a tiny window, still miraculously glazed. From this, Anji could see the dark channel of the river, the ruined buildings on the far side, and the star-strewn sky above the city. Occasionally, a dark shape would scuttle from shadow to shadow, eyes gleaming in the moonlight.

Anji stopped looking out of the window after a while.

Suddenly there was a knock at the door.

Anji held the bottle in front of her like a protective talisman. 'Come in.'

It was Gottlieb (she'd long since stopped thinking of him as 'Father' Gottlieb).

Anji stood with her back to the fire. 'Well?'

He was carrying a plate. 'I've brought you some food.'

Anji's stomach rumbled again. 'Thank you.'

She took the plate from him. It bore a rough hunk of bread, and a beaker of water. That was it.

He must have noticed her grimace, because he said, 'I'm afraid that's all I have to offer. Unless you care to partake of the main course?'

'This will do fine,' said Anji firmly. She picked up the bread and bit into it. It was dry and rough, but not too bad to taste. She took a sip of mineral water to wash it down.

'You know, I knew someone like you once. Enjoyed eating people's livers with fava beans and a nice bottle of wine.'

Gottlieb frowned. 'What are fava beans?'

Anji laughed, spraying crumbs over his black robes. Once she started, she couldn't stop, and sank down to the floor, overcome with the giggles.

When she came to, she looked up at Gottlieb. He was standing over her, arms folded.

'Sorry,' she said. 'And thanks for the food.'

Gottlieb bowed, and smiled at her. He watched whilst she ate the rest of the bread, and she watched him. He was a cannibal, a fiend like Hannibal Lecter. But that thought immediately turned itself on its head. He was a cannibal, yes, but not a fiend. It was clearly a matter of survival for him, the word 'cannibal' and all its connotations didn't adequately describe the man. Perhaps *predator* was better – but that was even less comforting. And whilst Gottlieb shared some characteristics with Lecter – they were both calm, sophisticated, even perversely likeable – Gottlieb was no monster. He was plainly, prosaically, and infinitely more tragically, a man, a man made by this world for this world. And a man is infinitely more complicated than a monster.

Anji felt a burning need to understand him. 'Why do you eat people? Is it just because there's no other source of meat? The Citizens seem to manage.'

'And suffer as a result. Malnutrition. Weak, wasted muscles. No protein in their diet.'

'But still,' said Anji. 'Cannibalism is, well, wrong.'

'Why?'

'You just don't eat other people! It's not –'

'Civilised?' He grinned. 'You forget, I am an outlaw. I was a Citizen once – or the equivalent of one. I lived in a settlement similar to Totterdown. Perhaps you'll understand why I am this way, why I do this thing you consider so wrong, when I tell you my story.'

Strangely, Anji wanted him to stay. She didn't want to be left alone in this attic room with its desolate view. 'I'd like that.'

Gottlieb sat in a chair next to the fireplace, whilst Anji sat cross-legged on the floor.

'My family lived in Germany, in a town called Koblenz, on the banks of the Rhine. Like the people of Totterdown, the people of Koblenz shut out the wider world, and never spoke of the Cleansing. Our main problems were outlaws, Wildren, and flooding. Several times a year the Rhine would flood, and the settlement would be awash with muddy water. But the Elders refused to move, proximity to the river was good for trade with other settlements up and down the Rhine. And it offered a means of escape should we come under mass attack.

'As I grew up, I naturally became curious about the world outside. My parents did not like this. They wanted me to follow in their footsteps, work in the mill. But despite them I journeyed outside the settlement to the old town, found buildings still standing, and in them, books and documents which spoke of a world before the Cleansing. When I challenged my parents about this they told me never to speak of it again. I argued, and left the settlement, wanting to rebuild the world as it had been before. I wanted to hear the music of Beethoven, wanted to live in a house in a big city, not a wooden shack on the banks of a temperamental river. Naive dreams of a young boy of only ten.'

His next words were clipped, terse, as if he wanted to get through what they described quickly and efficiently. 'I was captured and tortured by a gang of outlaws, escaping after three weeks when they were attacked by another gang. Traumatised, I went home, only to find my settlement burned down. There were no survivors. Wildren had attacked, and taken everyone. Eaten everyone. Including my parents. I wandered starving for days, until found by another group of outlaws, city-dwellers. One of them, a woman called Freya van Steiner, took me in. It was Freya and her band who taught me how to survive, how to take from others. And how to eat human flesh.'

He looked at Anji then, a distant look in his eyes. 'I resisted at first, but soon came to realise the logic of this. The wild ones preyed on the settlements, the settlements tried to defend themselves, raised their measly crops, and largely starved. And so we culled the Wildren, ate them. We were doing the settlements a service! Freya's group were highly organised. There was even a breeding programme, so we would always have a fresh supply of meat.'

Anji shuddered. The life he was describing sounded hellish and alien. But she realised then that had she been born into this world, had she lived a life like Gottlieb's, then there was every chance she would have turned out the same. Become a cannibal, and not even worry about it. She suddenly felt intensely homesick for her own world – sushi bars, cable TV and e-mail, the whole crowded, busy lot of it.

'But I wanted more,' Gottlieb continued. 'By the time I was sixteen, after many years with Freya's gang, I left them. Like the Citizens of Koblenz, they were content with their lot. They didn't want to find out what had caused the Cleansing, didn't care about rebuilding the world Before. So I left and joined a religious order for a few years.' He uttered a short, wheezing laugh. 'I found God. I saw him not as the vengeful deity who had caused the Cleansing, but as a guiding light. I knew that as long as I had faith, I would find answers. Maybe even begin to build the world as it had once been.

'I travelled around Germany for ten years, talking to people, piecing together evidence. A year ago I heard of this Jared Malahyde, of how he lived in seclusion in a mansion house in England, jealously guarding – something. I worked out that he could be the descendant of the Jared Malahyde who had invented the Malahyde Process – something I had read about, a new process for manufacturing steel. Shortly before the Cleansing, this Malahyde had revolutionised the industry of the world!'

Anji frowned. That didn't sound right – she'd never even heard of Jared Malahyde. She wished the Doctor was here – he'd know.

'So I came to England to find this descendant of Malahyde's. Find out his secret. In a few days, I might.' Gottlieb stopped speaking and sighed. 'You're the first person to whom I've told my story.'

His words seemed to suggest a new intimacy between them, an intimacy Anji did not want. So she changed the subject. 'So we're off to Ashton Court tomorrow?'

Gottlieb shook his head. 'We must stay here tonight, and most of tomorrow. Wait for the Wildren to move on.'

Anji stood. 'What?'

'They are nomadic creatures,' said Gottlieb. 'They will mill around for at least a day after the recent excitement. We cannot risk leaving yet.' He turned to leave. 'You will be comfortable. There is a bed, a ewer of water, other facilities. And do not fear – I will not let anything happen to you.'

With that, he was gone.

Anji looked at the thin, miserable bed.

Thought of Gottlieb's associates. The way they had looked at her. Even with his protection, what could she do if they rushed her?

Anji lay down on the bed, looking forward to a night of jittery insomnia.

Mr Malahyde continued.

'I tried to leap up from the chair and flee, but somehow I couldn't move. Then Watchlar grew brighter, until the glare seemed to burn into my very mind. The next thing I knew I was lying on a bench, on the Downs, not far from where I had met Brunel. I lay there for a while, staring up at the clear blue sky, with the worst headache I had ever experienced.

'In a trance, I walked back to my lodgings, not sure of what had happened, and though it was morning, went immediately to bed and fell just as immediately to sleep. I did not dream.

'The next day I walked around the town, trying to work out what had happened to me. Was it a delusion? A ridiculous thought – perhaps it was my Muse speaking to me, and this was a great poem I was meant to write!

'Then, as I sat in Woodes coffee-shop, I suddenly remembered that

I had something extremely urgent to do. Panic seized me – how could I have neglected this most pressing of tasks? I leapt up and ran outside. As soon as the chill autumn air hit my face I began remembering other things: plans for a machine, specifications, materials, so much detail that I sank to my knees.

'It was then that Watchlar completely took over. It felt as if I was shoved to the back of my own mind. I tried to scream, tried to run, but I could not move. And then Watchlar spoke to me in my own voice, using my own lips and tongue. I – he – spoke in an urgent mutter, covering his – my – lips with my hand. What he said was this:

> I find this as unpleasant as you and desire to keep
> such occurrences to a minimum. But if I have to, I can
> and will possess you. I am Watchlar of the Eternium.
> We have a task to do – which I am sure you must
> remember. Now I am going to return control of this
> body to you. I assume your co-operation.

And then suddenly I was back in my own mind.'

He paused again.

Aboetta realised that her hands were trembling, so she clasped them together. 'This being, this Watchlar, is it in your mind now?'

Malahyde smiled. 'You'll see what happened when I get to the end of the story.

'It was a strange experience, sharing mind and body with another being. I could feel Watchlar's presence there the whole time, at the back of my mind – not as a physical sensation, but as a kind of persistent memory. Say, one is in debt, and one's creditors are beginning to threaten one's life. You spend an evening at the theatre – you have read about the theatre, Aboetta? – so you become wrapped up in the experience, forget your woes. But the moment the curtain falls for the interval, the moment the distraction ends, the memory comes slamming back and with it the feeling of helplessness and panic. That it what it was like. Watchlar and I were together – for better or for worse – closer than any man or wife.

'When I got home, he filled my head with details of this machine.

And I began to realise the impossibility of the task. It wasn't so much the complexity – Watchlar would guide me – but the cost. Materials I had never heard of, processes not yet devised by man – it was beyond my means. But was the human race to fall because of a lack of funds?

'And then the riots began.'

Malahyde fell silent once more.

'Riots?' prompted Aboetta.

'Something to do with political reform.' Malahyde waved a hand dismissively. 'I didn't care about the cause then, and now it is less than irrelevant. But at the time, those riots seemed to endorse the Eternines' warning about the fall of humanity. If I wasn't convinced before, I certainly was then. Convinced – and terrified. What a burden to shoulder – saving the entire future of Mankind! I must confess I lost control for a while. I tried to escape from Watchlar – but how do you escape from something that lives within your own head? I even tried to kill myself, by leaping from bridges, wading into the river with my pockets weighted with stones, but at the crucial moment, Watchlar would always seize control and remove me – us – to safety.

'But as the riots died down, I began to reason. And I came up with a plan. The day after the riots ended, I put it into action.

'I walked down to Queen Square, and saw the devastation at first hand. Two sides of the square had been burned down. I hadn't imagined the damage to be so severe. Of course, this got my mind running on the warning of the Eternines once more, and so I hurried up from the town to Clifton, bearing with me the plans Watchlar and I had drawn up. Obtaining Brunel's address had been easy enough, and I thanked the stars that I had encountered him upon the downs that fateful night, for at least I wouldn't be approaching him as a total stranger.

'He answered the door in his shirt-sleeves, and failed to recognise me at first. I piqued his interest at once by immediately telling him that I had a business proposal, and – a little reluctantly – he invited me in.

'Soon I was sitting in a leather chair in a wood-panelled room. It was chilly; there was ash in the fireplace – an uncomfortable reminder of the devastation – and the pale autumn sunlight streaming through the windows did nothing to warm me up. Above the fireplace was a large framed sketch, caught in a ray of sunlight.' Malahyde smiled. 'It was a drawing of the Suspension Bridge.

'Brunel looked exhausted, and despite the earliness of the hour, had a glass of brandy to hand. He had only that morning got back from his duties as Special Constable, trying to restore order, rescuing valuable paintings and suchlike from the burned-out mansion house. I marshalled my thoughts, wondering if Watchlar was observing – I could feel his presence as always, like a continually dawning realisation in the back of my mind, a sense of impending doom.

'I put forward my proposal. Watchlar's scientific knowledge being far in advance of mine, and even of Brunel's, made it possible for the being to devise a new process for the manufacture of steel. Lighter, completely rust-proof, less brittle and able to withstand decades of weathering.' Malahyde gestured in the direction of Bristol. 'You see, I remembered Brunel talking of his financial troubles. If I could help him overcome these, win his confidence, together we could make the money I needed to save the human race!

'I sat whilst Brunel looked over the plans which I, under Watchlar's guidance, had sketched out. Despite myself, I had retained some knowledge of the steel-making process from my apprenticeship and it was upon this that Watchlar had drawn.

'Brunel didn't seem enthusiastic. I remember him saying, "I'm an engineer, not a metallurgist. I will need to have someone look these over. Have you a business card?"

'I hadn't, so I scrawled my address on the corner of the plans, and then Brunel abruptly showed me out.'

Malahyde sat back and sighed. He looked tired, as if the effort of telling his story was draining him.

Then he continued. 'A week later, a letter arrived from the offices of I. K. Brunel, suggesting a partnership to develop what he referred to as the "Malahyde Process". Well, from then on, things moved extremely swiftly. I entered into partnership with Brunel, yes, rejoined that world of commerce and industry from which I had fled. But it was a means to an end – a means to the greatest end. The Malahyde Process was a spectacular success – used in all types of industry, shipping, railways, and of course the Suspension Bridge. It brought in fortunes. In 1832, I purchased this estate from its previous owners, the Smythes – you know them from the portraits in the entrance hall. I was initially reluctant to oust them from their family home, but Watchlar insisted, telling me that we needed somewhere large, relatively remote, and defensible.

'By this time Watchlar and I had been together over six months, and our relationship had settled. He trusted me with the business side of things, concerning himself only in the construction of what I came to call the Utopian Engine. Sometimes it was necessary for him to possess me totally, and this was unpleasant, but most of the time I could work under his bidding. He was like an invisible foreman in the back of my mind, communicating in memories. So strange to relate now, but I was used to it by then.

'And so we began to construct the Utopian Engine. A task which took twelve years to complete. During that time I had the wall around the estate fortified – made twenty feet high and topped with a barbed wire fence, constructed of metal made with the Malahyde process. I became a recluse, leaving the business side of things to Brunel, signing the occasional contract for a new application of the Process.'

'Twelve *years*?' said Aboetta. 'Why did it take so long?'

Malahyde closed his eyes. 'Twelve long years of toil. I had to work from scratch, under Watchlar's guidance. Had to travel across the world to fetch strange crystals from deep within the rainforests. Had to persuade metallurgists to forge their materials in the way Watchlar required, which often didn't turn out right. Had to build an electricity generator – an entirely new process – to provide the Engine with its initial source of energy.' He opened his eyes. 'There were setbacks, of course. Interminable setbacks, requiring months of work to put right. And interruptions – from Brunel, representatives from my father's business, and others, demanding to know what I was doing. I put them off as best I could. And, over the years, I had doubts. What if Watchlar was lying to me? What if, instead of saving the human race, the Utopian Engine would destroy it?

'But in the summer of 1843 – which you know as Year Nought – the Utopian Engine was ready. Ready to bring the Eternines back through time.'

Malahyde leaned back in his chair and let out a long, sighing breath.

Aboetta was on the edge of her chair. 'So what happened?'

Malahyde smiled sadly. 'When the machine was ready, Watchlar informed me that he had to take over my mind completely. I, of course, had no choice in the matter. So Watchlar took over my mind, and I knew no more.

'When I came round, I was lying in the cellar next to the Utopian Engine. Its central column was glowing with eerie green light, exactly as it is now. Of Watchlar, there was no sign of his presence in my mind. He had gone.'

Malahyde's eyes widened. 'I didn't know it then, but the Cleansing had happened. Something must have gone wrong with the Engine – instead of bringing the Eternines back, it had accelerated time.'

Aboetta closed her eyes. She could picture all too well people ageing to death – babies growing to adults in the space of less than a minute – the human race 'born again in all innocence' – but the Cleansing hadn't been an act of God.

Malahyde's voice was hollow. 'Don't you see, Aboetta, it's all my fault? The fall of Mankind that I was chosen to prevent – I have instead *caused*!'

Chapter 14
The Assault

Anji crouched in the ditch, waiting for the signal. Night was falling fast, shadows seeming to seep from the forest behind her. The wall rose to Anji's left, cool and depressingly solid to the touch. Uphill from Anji, Gottlieb stood silhouetted against the gathering darkness, staring up towards Clifton Lodge.

Conro had hitched a rope-ladder to the barbed wire fence. He stood at the top, cutting through the wire. The sound of the saw was a dry rasp, the action of Conro's arm transmitting through his body, making the wooden rungs clack gently against the stone.

Anji looked up. The barbs stood out against the dark blue evening sky like transfixed spiders. Why was it taking him so long? It was only wire.

Not for the first time Anji thought of making a break for it and returning to the city to search for the Doctor and Fitz. But soon it would be night again, and she shrank from the idea of going back into the ruins, with Wildren eyes peering from the dark windows. Like it or not, she was stuck with Gottlieb and his ragged band. If she was lucky, she might get shot by one of Malahyde's Estate Guards. If she was unlucky, well, there was no mistaking what was behind the furtive glances that Conro, Mary and the others had been sending her way. How long could Gottlieb protect her from them? And what if he changed his mind? Got hungry?

Anji shrank down in the ditch, hoping that maybe, in the heat of the battle, they would forget about her and she'd be able to slip away.

Gottlieb turned to look at her, as if he could read her thoughts. His face was invisible in the gloom. The silver cross caught the fading light and glinted like a winking eye.

There was a twang from up above, which brought to Anji an image of Fitz slouched morosely over his guitar. Two more twangs and they'd be able to climb through the gap.

At least she was out in the open. She'd spent a mostly sleepless night at the inn, and the next day alone in the attic room, except for mealtimes when Gottlieb would bring her more of the bread. She'd passed the time trying not to think of what had happened to the Doctor and Fitz, and in conversation with Gottlieb. As dusk fell she had helped with the preparations for the attack. Aside from herself, Gottlieb and Conro, there were a dozen outlaws crammed into two boats, making them run dangerously low in the water. They were well armed, Anji was surprised to see, with pistols, crossbows – even swords. She began to wonder why they hadn't attacked Malahyde's estate before, but she read from the grim looks on their wasted faces that this was no off-the-cuff jaunt. This had been planned as a last resort, anticipated for weeks. Some of the outlaws had a hypnotised look as if they knew they weren't coming back alive.

As for herself, Anji was going along with Gottlieb's plan because there really wasn't much choice. Stay in the inn? End up as the main course. Leave on her own to search for the Doctor and Fitz? Ditto.

Gottlieb's plan. It was insanely, suicidally simple. Whilst Gottlieb, Conro and Anji waited, the other outlaws would attack Clifton Lodge. Once they heard the signal – the sounds of gunshots, of battle being joined – then they would scale the wall under cover of this distraction. The wall around the estate was five miles in circumference – and unless Malahyde had hundreds of men under his command, there was no way that he could keep watch on every inch of it. As far as anyone knew Malahyde's Estate Guards numbered perhaps thirty, maybe even as many as fifty – but no more. All it would take was one major distraction and if they were quick they could be in and running towards the mansion house under cover of darkness before anyone realised what was happening.

What Gottlieb planned to do once they were inside the house, he was keeping to himself.

It was almost full night now. Anji shifted uncomfortably.

Another twang from above.

And then came the sound of a gunshot from up ahead.

Gottlieb sprang into life, leaping into the ditch and running along towards the ladder.

Anji stood, wondering if she'd been forgotten already, but Gottlieb hurried along the ditch and grabbed her wrist.

'You first,' he said, shoving her towards the ladder.

'But he's only cut through two – there won't be room.' Anji began to protest, but Gottlieb wasn't listening.

He dragged her to the foot of the rope-ladder. Before she had time to think, Anji began to climb.

Conro couldn't fit through the gap, so in order to let Anji past he was hanging braced against the wall, one foot on a rung, one hand gripping the fence-post to which the rope-ladder was lashed. This meant that Anji had to slide uncomfortably close to him, squirming her body past his. The smell was giddying, almost overpowering. He couldn't have bathed, well, ever. Aware that his left arm was swinging free somewhere behind her, she fixed his pallid, unshaven face with the most steely glare she could muster under the circumstances. His lips parted and his yellowing teeth gleamed with a nauseating lustre in the fading light. His lust wasn't carnal, it was culinary. She almost wished he *would* grope her bum. At least that was normal, something she knew how to respond to. But *this*!

Fingers hooking the opposite edge of the wall, one heave and Anji was under the wire. Barbs snagged her jacket but she wriggled free.

Then her feet slipped off the rung and kicked into space, and she felt a hand on her left calf. She flexed her legs and swung them round and through the gap, hoping but failing to catch Conro with the heel of her boot in the process.

She lay flat on the wall, trying to ignore the pains in her elbows and knees, trying not to think of the drop on the other side. But the wall was a good two feet thick, so once under the wire fence Anji could stretch herself out on the bumpy stone surface. The stars were just beginning to come out and Anji could see the familiar angular shape of the Plough. It reassured her, because she'd often stared up at the constellation from her reality, and somehow it gave her hope that she would be doing so again.

Trees blocked the view into the estate, their branches in places tangling with the barbed wire, as if they were trying to escape. Anji could smell the sweet musk of decaying leaves, and a gentle-giant breeze whispered through the treetops. She tried to peer past the trunks, but couldn't make out anything except more trees. This meant that they couldn't be seen from inside the estate – good, they needed all the cover they could get.

In the distance she could hear gunshots. Shouts. Screams.

Gottlieb scrambled under the wire and lay facing her.

'What was the problem with the wire?' he hissed at Conro.

Conro stared at the barbs. He shrugged. 'Not like any wire I've seen – too strong for wire-cutters, had to saw through the stuff.'

'Wait here,' said Gottlieb, uncoiling a length of rope from around his waist and fixing it to the post. 'I'll send someone for you when we've taken the estate.'

There was a slight flicker of suspicion in Conro's eyes, as if he realised that he was being used. Then he nodded, folded his arms and leaned through the gap.

Anji peered over the edge. Below, bare dirt, leaves, a few twigs. Not a soft landing.

Gottlieb was first down, gripping the rope with both hands and bracing his feet against the stone. He looked up sharply once, as if checking on Anji.

Like there's anywhere I could go, she thought.

There was a rustle as Gottlieb touched down and then Anji followed, swinging out from the wall and letting herself down slowly, not wanting to get rope burn or fall or anything stupid like that.

She landed beside Gottlieb who immediately began to strike out through the woods.

Soon they were in open ground, under the stars which were now brighter against the darkening sky. In the distance, down a long gentle slope, she could see what must be Ashton Court's mansion house. A big, sprawling stately home. In the gloom it looked full of secrets. Full of danger.

'There don't seem to be any Estate Guards in the vicinity,' said Gottlieb. 'The plan must be working.'

Anji could make out a circular wall around the house. More security? This Malahyde certainly liked his solitude. She pointed to it. 'So we climb over that, too?'

Gottlieb shook his head. 'There must be a door.' He drew a flintlock rifle from a holster hidden beneath his cloak. 'Here's the key.'

Aboetta and Mr Malahyde were walking in the garden that was February, whilst outside in the rest of the world it was October. Malahyde had calmed down after his outburst, and relapsed into a resigned melancholy. Nothing Aboetta could say would dissuade him of his view that the fall of Mankind rested entirely on his shoulders, but she felt that her presence went some way towards improving his mood.

He had told her of the years after the Cleansing, how he established links with the Citizen Elders of the settlements around Bristol, how he recruited his Estate Guards, the gardeners and workers who came to live within the Estate in exchange for produce sent out to their home settlements. How he learned to manage them from within the house so that their descendants never caught on that the Malahyde who had recruited their great-grandparents was really the same person for whom they now worked.

And how throughout all this he had contemplated suicide.

'I would have ended my life long ago, once I realised what I had done,' he told her as they strolled between the barren flower-beds.

'But for one hope, which I have never abandoned.' He looked up at the clouds. 'Maybe the Eternines will come back somehow, or – despite everything – Watchlar will re-appear, help me activate the Utopian Engine, help me restore the human race to what it was before the Cleansing.' He sighed. 'Or – maybe I can get the Utopian Engine working in another way, roll time back, to before.'

'Then I would never have been born,' Aboetta chided.

He smiled. 'Yes. Yes, you would.' He stopped walking, took her hands in his. 'You would have been born, twenty years ago, into a better world.'

'A world full of people.' Aboetta tried to imagine it, but couldn't. 'But would I have been me?'

He let go of her hands and shook his head. 'Oh, Aboetta, I have almost driven myself mad with paradoxes and what-ifs.'

'There's something you haven't told me,' said Aboetta. 'Why does time move differently here?'

'I'm not entirely sure.' He glanced back meaningfully at the looming south wing of the house. 'I think it's a side effect of the Utopian Engine.' He indicated the wall around the house and its gardens, a grey curve running between the ground and the sky. 'I was able to map the perimeter of the time distortion, and had the wall built along that perimeter. You may have noticed that the stone on the outside of the wall is much more weathered than within.'

'Why do you need the wall?'

'It keeps the time distortion a secret,' said Malahyde. 'Without it, you would be able to see out into the estate – but contemporaneous with our island of time. That is, you would see October, Year 5 – for as I have explained, from my point of view, it has only been five years since the Cleansing. But step through the edge of the time field, and you'd be in October 160.' He smiled and pointed at the outer door – for now they had walked round to the front of the house. 'Each time you leave, you travel through time without knowing it.'

That explained the strange feeling she got when she went through the door, thought Aboetta. She felt awed by this new knowledge, and frightened at the unknown power it implied.

Malahyde went on, seemingly oblivious to her fear. 'And it works the other way – from beyond the wall, looking in, you can see this house as it will be in Year 160.' He smiled. 'So it's possible to see into our future. The house is still here, a hundred and fifty-odd years on from now. If it had burned down at some point after now and before Year 160, we'd be able to know, just by going outside and looking back in.'

Aboetta shivered. Were there corpses inside that future mansion, skeletons gathering the dust of decades? Aboetta looked for somewhere to sit down, but there was nowhere between the wide impassive stone face of the house and the curving wall.

'I would say that all this was reason for leaving rather than staying. Why do you stay here? Why don't you come and join us in Totterdown?'

'I cannot leave, Aboetta. I must wait for Watchlar to return.' He smiled strangely. 'Think of me as the caretaker for the Utopian Engine.'

'But what if it doesn't return?'

Malahyde shrugged. 'I cannot risk it. I must believe that, one day, the Eternines will find a way. We are their past, remember. Without us, they cannot exist. They have to save us.'

Aboetta wasn't too sure. From what Malahyde had told her about Watchlar, the being seemed evil, cruel.

Malahyde stopped walking, turned and put his hands on her shoulders. 'But you can leave, Aboetta, at any time. I would understand. Now is the time for you to decide – will you stay, or will you leave?'

Aboetta looked beyond him to the grey stone wall with its patches of moss. To the featureless sky above it. And then to Malahyde's face, the thin sensitive nose, the deep-set blue eyes, the receding yellow-white hair.

'Will you stay with me, Aboetta?'

Aboetta opened her mouth to speak – but just at that very moment, there was a sudden sound behind her, like a muffled gunshot.

She whirled round in time to see the door swing open and two figures burst through.

Chapter 15
The Reunion

The smell of gunpowder catching in her throat, Anji stepped through after Gottlieb. As she did so she staggered slightly. Something had just occurred to her – something important. She tried to remember, but once through the door forgot all about it.

Because suddenly, it was day.

The door closed with a thunk behind her and Anji gaped at the scene: the mansion house, Gottlieb stalking up the stone path towards Aboetta and a thin man in a long coat and waistcoat (was this Malahyde?) – the grey sky above…

She turned and opened the door, looked outside. Yes, it was daytime outside too! The hill she'd run down just seconds ago was bathed in a watery, baleful autumn light.

She stepped back through the door – a moment of disorientation – and outside it was dark. Looking back in – it was also dark, and she couldn't see Gottlieb.

She slipped back through, again feeling that there was something she should be remembering, then closed the door gently behind her.

Weird.

She ran to catch up with Gottlieb, slowing down when she realised that he'd drawn his flintlock and was pointing the weapon at Aboetta. The girl had bravely – strike that, stupidly – interposed herself between Gottlieb and the chap who must be Malahyde.

She was expecting someone a bit more imposing. Not a gaunt-looking chap of medium height with thinning blond hair and an expression somewhere between panic and fear. Hiding behind a woman.

Aboetta had her hands on her hips, her eyebrows lowered in a contemptuous frown. 'Leave us in peace. There's nothing for you here.'

'You know that's not true, girl.' Gottlieb must have noticed the change from dusk to daylight but it didn't seem to be worrying him.

Aboetta noticed Anji for the first time. 'You! What are you doing, associating with this outlaw?'

She spoke the last word as if it was the worst insult she could think of.

'I wasn't given much choice,' said Anji, with a significant glance at the gun.

Now Malahyde had come forward to stand beside Aboetta. He seemed to be drawing strength from the girl. 'Who are you and what do you want?'

'I am Father Franz Gottlieb. True, I am an outlaw, but I am also a freethinker. I have followed a trail which has led me here.'

Aboetta spoke, not taking her eyes from the priest. 'He came to Totterdown. Asked questions about you, Mr Malahyde.'

'I am sorry it has come to this,' said Gottlieb, indicating the gun with a slight nod. 'But I have come so far, suffered so much. It's about time you shared your secrets with the rest of us.'

Who exactly did he mean by *us*? thought Anji. The band of outlaws he'd used for his own ends?

'How did you get past the Estate Guards?' asked Malahyde.

Gottlieb shook his head. 'Not important. All that matters is I am here and I want answers.'

Malahyde sighed. His blond hair made him look youthful, but up close Anji could see the lines on the pale skin, the bags under the eyes. 'Answers.' His voice had a hollow, cynical ring.

'Well?' said Gottlieb.

Malahyde sneered. 'There's nothing you can do to me!' he hissed suddenly and with surprising vehemence. 'If you shoot me, then that's the end of it!'

'No!' cried Aboetta. 'You can't throw your life away like that! What does it matter if one more person knows?'

'I don't *want* to shoot you!' said Gottlieb. 'You're better than – the others, the Wildren. You're like me,' he indicated Anji. 'Like us. Civilised.'

Anji drew away from him, shaking her head, not wanting to be lumped in with him.

'But I *will* shoot, if you do not comply.'

'And what about you?' said Malahyde. 'Do you seek answers as well?'

Anji realised that she did want answers, almost as much as she wanted to see the Doctor and Fitz again. 'Yes.'

Malahyde looked uncertainly at them both, and then at Aboetta. 'Very well. Come with me. There is an alarming amount to tell you.'

Inside the house Anji was caught off guard again. It was like a well-preserved stately home: massive fireplace flanked with evil-looking pikes, stone walls hung with faded tapestries. There were even some wonky-looking suits of armour.

Malahyde led them along a long gloomy corridor, and stopped outside a nondescript door. Producing a key from his waistcoat pocket, he opened the door and ushered them through, Gottlieb first, then Anji, with himself and Aboetta bringing up the rear.

Anji had enough time to take in the eerie greenish glow, like a faulty fluorescent light, and to think, hey! this has all the classic makings of a trap! as she descended, footsteps echoing off the stone walls.

And then she got to the bottom, where Gottlieb was standing staring at the thing which dominated the cellar.

The central column was opaque, reinforcing the resemblance to a fluorescent light. You could only look at it for a few seconds, any more and the backs of your eyes started to throb. At its top was a circular cowling inset with vents. Metal struts ran out from this cowling to the ceiling. Around the base of the column were half-a-dozen doughnut-like tubes of steel inset with dials, switches and meters. Their surfaces shone dully, like lead. From these tubes, cables wormed their way out towards further machines which lurked in alcoves between the columns lining the walls.

Prominent in front of the central apparatus was a mahogany desk and chair. On the desk was a bank of instruments which looked oddly like a cross between a synthesiser and an ancient valve amplifier.

Was this a TARDIS? She wasn't sure. There was no reassuring soporific hum. And around the walls, no roundels, but instead columns topped with dusty arches. It all looked like it had been cobbled together over a number of years, and it all looked strangely amateurish, as if the person who had built it hadn't quite known what they were doing. And it was all bathed in the sick spectral neon of that central column.

Malahyde and Aboetta had joined them. All stood still in the green glow like figures in a silent film.

Gottlieb's eyes were wide, his lips bared in a sneer. 'This?' he said. 'This is the source of your power?'

'What power?' Malahyde shrugged. 'It is the Utopian Engine.'

As if that explained everything. One of the machines – a bulbous thing hunched in a corner – looked familiar to Anji. 'Isn't that some sort of electricity generator?'

'Electricity!' cried Gottlieb. 'I knew it!' Then he frowned. 'But this house is lit by oil-lamps. Why don't you use this power?'

Malahyde shrugged. 'I don't know how it works, any of it.'

Gottlieb laughed harshly. 'You don't know? Yet presumably you built all this! What's it for?'

Anji had been piecing things together, and had come to a conclusion – the only conclusion. 'It's causing the time distortion around the house, isn't it?' She looked pointedly at Aboetta. Then she advanced on Malahyde. 'But that's not all! It caused the Cleansing, didn't it?'

Malahyde looked sick. He nodded.

'But why?' said Anji. 'What was the point?'

Gottlieb bore down on Malahyde. He was almost trembling with excitement. 'Is this true? Did this "Engine" cause the Cleansing?'

Malahyde nodded dumbly.

Gottlieb smiled. 'Then I was right – it was not an act of God.' He sat at the desk.

Malahyde strode up to him. 'Get away from those controls!'

Gottlieb swung round in the chair, gripping the arms, almost snarling at Malahyde. 'It is *your* fault the world is like this! Your fault almost everyone in the world died! Your fault those who survived had to grub for existence, starved of meat, of civilisation, of progress!'

For a moment Anji saw all the pain of this world in Gottlieb's tortured expression, all the hardships and the deprivations. For a moment Gottlieb seemed like the embodiment of humanity's thwarted spirit, raging in full torrent against its destroyer.

Then Gottlieb leapt up from the chair, swung out and cuffed Malahyde around the head.

Malahyde staggered backwards, and dropped to his knees.

Aboetta rushed to him, helping him to his feet.

'It was an accident!' cried Malahyde. 'I was chosen, it was not my intention!' He began to sob. 'It was meant to *save* the human race.'

And then there was the sound, horribly powerful and threatening in the confines of the cellar, of time and space being torn apart, and then the TARDIS materialised before Anji's eyes.

Fitz held on to the console as the TARDIS rocked and juddered around him like a boat in a storm. The TARDIS engines, somewhere below, were roaring like beasts in pain.

'What's happening?'

'We're caught in some sort of temporal barrier!' yelled the Doctor.

Robin was gripping on to the console for grim death. Suddenly he fell.

'We're being dragged back through time,' gasped the Doctor.

Suddenly the shuddering and roaring stopped, and Fitz slumped over the console. 'Are we there yet?'

The Doctor was poring over the TARDIS instruments. 'Fascinating! Somehow, within this temporal barrier, time has been slowed through *all* its dimensions. It is 1848 here, five years after the Cleansing.'

'Well, that explains Aboetta's problem,' said Fitz, helping Robin to his feet.

'What could have caused such a thing?' said the Watchkeeper.

The Doctor operated the scanner, to reveal a vaulted cellar lit with eerie green light. 'At a guess, that.'

He indicated a pale green pillar in the centre of the cellar. It made a striking contrast with the blue of the TARDIS's central column.

Then Fitz saw –

'Anji!' cried Fitz.

'Aboetta,' breathed Robin.

'Oh, look. There's our friend Father Gottlieb,' said the Doctor. 'Must thank him for rescuing Anji – unless it was the other way round.' He flicked the door control and Robin, who had been waiting by the doors, slipped outside.

Spurred on by a meaningful glance from the Doctor, Fitz stepped out after the former Watchkeeper.

As well as Anji and Father Gottlieb, Aboetta was there, supporting a thin, drab-looking chap with thinning blond hair.

Everyone was staring at him – everyone except Robin, who was advancing on Aboetta.

'Hi, everyone,' breezed Fitz. 'Hi Aboetta, Father G, Anji, and you just have to be this Malahyde chap.'

A hand in his back shoved him gently aside. The Doctor walked past him, staring up at the green column. 'What have we here?'

'This is the Utopian Engine,' said the blond-haired guy.

'Is it really?' said the Doctor, walking up to the desk which sat rather incongruously in front of the column.

Fitz went up to Anji and hugged her. Tears sprang to his eyes as he realised how pleased he was to see her.

'How have you been?' he said, through a laugh he couldn't hold back.

'Almost drowned, almost eaten by cannibals – oh by the way Father Gottlieb's one – otherwise OK,' she said briskly. She saw Robin and frowned. 'What's *he* doing here?'

'Guess,' said Fitz, rolling his eyes.

Aboetta had the advantage over the others, except the girl Anji, in that she'd seen the blue box appear before, so she was able to get over the shock of its appearance and regain her composure more quickly. As she expected, Robin walked straight up to her. Was she never to be free of him? Then she felt immediately guilty – not so long ago, from her point of view, they had been lovers.

But now he was just a nuisance.

'Aboetta!'

'Robin.' She folded her arms. 'Before you ask, I've made my decision. I'm staying here.'

'What, with him?' Robin glared at Malahyde, who was standing with the Doctor and Father Gottlieb by the desk.

'Yes,' she said, vowing to tell Mr Malahyde at the earliest opportunity.

Robin stared at her, his gaze hostile. She was obviously meant to be impressed that he'd come for her. She glanced at the blue box. Had he bullied the Doctor and Fitz into bringing him here?

'You've made your decision,' said Robin, his voice trembling with feeling. 'Or was it made for you?'

Aboetta frowned. 'I made it myself.'

'What about love?' His voice echoed round the cellar, making the Doctor look round briefly from where he was standing.

Aboetta just stared at him.

The dark-skinned woman Anji strode up to them, gesturing at the glowing column of the Engine, the men gathered around it. 'Can't you see that there's something else going on here beyond your selfish obsession?'

Robin said nothing, merely turned away and walked off towards the TARDIS.

'Thanks,' said Aboetta, gazing uncertainly after Robin.

Anji sighed and fixed her gaze on the Doctor's back. 'I hope he knows what he's doing.'

Aboetta clenched her fists. 'He should not interfere!'

'Well, this is clearly the source of the time anomaly *and* the Cleansing,' said the Doctor. 'Which is odd because it's not a time machine, not in the strictest sense.'

'What is it then?' asked Fitz, wandering over.

'Some sort of time manipulator,' said the Doctor. 'It's operating on standby at the moment, but we can soon fix that.'

The Doctor flexed his fingers and reached out towards the banks of switches on top of the desk, but Malahyde grabbed his arm.

'You must be Jared Malahyde,' said the Doctor, his voice heavy with irony. 'Pleased to meet you at last.'

'Don't interfere with the Engine!' spluttered Malahyde.

'Why not?' said the Doctor. 'It must be de-activated.'

'If you do that, time inside this house will catch up with time *outside* and –'

'– and you'll age to death. Or at least that's what you fear.' The Doctor held his hands up, away from the controls. 'Fine, I've no wish to kill you, even if you are responsible for all this.' He leaned towards Malahyde. 'Are you responsible for all this?'

Malahyde nodded.

The Doctor glanced round at the glowing green column, the lurking hulks of cobbled-together machinery. 'I'm impressed. This technology, whilst composed of contemporaneous materials, uses processes far, far in advance of the early nineteenth century.' He smiled at Malahyde, but his eyes were dark. 'How?'

Malahyde looked sick and scared in the green light. 'I had some help.'

'From?' prompted the Doctor, coaxing Malahyde with outstretched hands.

'A being – it called itself Watchlar, it was from the future. It told me to build this machine, to aid humanity.'

'Aid humanity?' growled Gottlieb. 'You destroyed humanity!'

The Doctor shushed him and asked Malahyde to explain.

'This creature is – will be – us. It's from our future. Our ultimate evolved form. It wanted me to build this machine so they could come back through time, help the human race, prevent its fall.'

'And how would they do that, these homo superior?'

Malahyde looked embarrassed. 'Watchlar never fully explained. They would help us progress, conquer disease, wipe out famine, avert wars.' He looked at the Doctor, enthusiasm creeping into his voice. 'Ensure Mankind's survival – thus ensuring their own existence!'

The Doctor groaned and put his head in his hands. 'Oh Malahyde, you *believed* this? Have you never heard the word paradox?'

Malahyde was suddenly angry. 'What else was I to believe? I have visited the future! I have seen it!'

The Doctor snorted. 'Visited the future? First of all this isn't a time machine and second – where is this creature now?'

Malahyde shook his head.

The Doctor was striding around now, his voice sharpening with anger. 'Well maybe this "Watchlar" was lying to you! Maybe you were meant to cause the Cleansing after all.'

'Be silent!' shouted Gottlieb.

Everyone turned to look at him.

Oh shit, thought Fitz.

He had hold of Anji and was pointing a gun at her head.

'If this machine caused the Cleansing then it can be made to undo it,' he said. 'Step away from the desk, Doctor.'

The Doctor complied, eyes fixed on Gottlieb.

Gottlieb stepped awkwardly up to the control panel. 'Tell me how it works! Tell me!' he bellowed.

'I told you, I don't know!' cried Malahyde.

'Gottlieb! Stop!' roared the Doctor.

Gottlieb twisted a control.

There was no sound, but the central column glowed brighter, phasing from green through to yellow to white. Fitz put his hands in front of his eyes. He could hear voices shouting – the Doctor, roaring at Gottlieb, Anji swearing, someone screaming – a thump as someone tripped over –

And then, suddenly, the light was gone.

Fitz opened his eyes, but all he could see for ten seconds or so was a lava-lamp of swimming purple blobs.

Then the Doctor came into focus, hunched over the controls of the Utopian Engine. His head was bowed.

Aboetta and Malahyde were clutching each other.

Robin was standing by the TARDIS, mouth open in astonishment.

As for Anji and Father Gottlieb – they were nowhere to be seen.

Chapter 16
Fitz's Choice

Fitz stumbled towards where Anji had been. 'What the *hell* just happened? Where is she?'

The Doctor didn't move for a second or so, then straightened up and turned to Fitz. He had that look on his face – his mouth set in a tight, straight line, chin jutting out, the muscles in his temples rippling as though he was grinding his teeth.

The look in his eyes scared Fitz. 'Is she dead?'

'I did all I could.'

'What do you mean?' Fitz felt like grabbing the Doctor and shaking him. He hated it when the Doctor got like this, acting like the weight of the universe or the multiverse or whatever passed for reality these days rested on his back and his alone.

What the hell.

Fitz reached out and grabbed the Doctor. 'Don't spare my feelings!' he shouted. 'Tell me what's happened to Anji!'

The Doctor put his hands on Fitz's shoulders, but he didn't squeeze, he just rested them there. His stern expression softened, lines creasing around his eyes. 'Gottlieb's interference opened a gate into the Vortex. I managed to shut it off, but I was too late to save Anji.'

The Time Vortex.

Fitz let go and stumbled away from the Doctor. He felt faint. Anji – gone, just like that? 'Is there any chance she's alive?'

'If she's in the Vortex, no.'

If. But where else could she be?

Malahyde approached. 'What's happened?'

The Doctor ignored him. 'Fitz. We're leaving.'

'Leaving?' Fitz didn't want to go just yet, he couldn't shake the feeling that Anji might reappear at any moment. But he didn't tell the Doctor this; instead, he gestured at the Utopian Engine. 'But haven't we got to, well, sort all this out?'

'That's exactly what we're going to do,' muttered the Doctor, and without another word, he walked away.

Malahyde and Aboetta were holding on to each other, scared looks on their faces. 'Can one of you please tell us what has happened?' said Malahyde.

The Doctor merely looked at him, his face blank and dispassionate, and then stepped into the TARDIS.

Malahyde rushed over to the desk and leaned over the controls, rubbing his bottom lip.

'Come on, Fitz!' came the Doctor's voice from inside the TARDIS.

Fitz hesitated. Robin was bearing down on Aboetta. As Fitz watched he grabbed Aboetta's hand. 'You're coming with me!'

Aboetta tried to shake him loose. 'No!'

Fitz went up to Robin. 'Look, mate, she doesn't want to go with you.'

'I'm staying here,' said Aboetta. 'With Mr Malahyde. I've made my decision.'

Malahyde looked up from the controls, and walked over, blinking, looking as if he didn't quite believe what he'd just heard.

'You've made your decision?' he said, hands clasped in front of him as if he didn't know what to do with them.

'Yes. I was going to tell you before we were interrupted. I want to stay here with you.'

Malahyde stood gazing at Aboetta with an unmistakable doe-eyed look.

Blimey, thought Fitz – in the midst of all this, a love triangle. Well at least this time I'm not one of the corners.

'Let her go, Robin,' said Fitz as gently as he could. 'You can't force someone to love you.'

'Stay out of this!' hissed Robin. He yanked at Aboetta, making her stumble towards him and cry out.

Without hesitation Fitz stepped forward and cracked Robin on the jaw with a straight punch which probably hurt him more than its victim.

Robin staggered backwards, looking shocked.

Fitz rubbed his aching knuckles. 'If there's one thing I can stand it's bullies. Especially people who bully women.'

Robin's look of surprise switched in an instant to one of anger, and he lunged at Fitz, fists bunched.

Shit, thought Fitz – there's no way I can beat this guy. That was my sole moment of bravery this year. He looked around – the cellar steps were beyond the TARDIS – there was no escape. He backed against the desk as Robin advanced.

'Leave him alone!' cried Aboetta scornfully.

There was a swift blur of movement behind Robin – a hand, chopping down, connecting with his neck – and he fell.

The Doctor caught Robin under the shoulders and began to drag him back towards the TARDIS. 'Will you come *on*, Fitz?' he said as Robin's booted feet bounced on the dusty flagstones of the cellar.

'Nice work, Doctor,' said Fitz, flooded with relief at the removal of the threat of immediate physical violence.

But before he entered the TARDIS, he turned and looked at the green column of the Utopian Engine, and his relief faded, to be replaced by a sense of frustration that there was nothing they could do for Anji. His gaze wandered to Malahyde and Aboetta, who were stood clasping each other like shipwreck survivors.

He remembered the Doctor's words – *that's exactly what we're going to do* – and suddenly had a horrible premonition of what the Doctor was planning.

He felt that he should say a proper goodbye.

'Er, goodbye, Aboetta, Malahyde. Hope things work out for you chaps.'

The words sounded hollow and insincere, but Aboetta smiled and said goodbye, whilst all he got from Malahyde was a bewildered stare.

'Hope things work out,' Fitz repeated, more to himself than to Malahyde and Aboetta. Then he turned back and stepped into the TARDIS.

Aboetta watched with mixed feelings as the blue box faded away to nothing, accompanied by the now-familiar roaring sound. She was relieved that Robin was gone, but couldn't help feeling some of his pain. Still, it wasn't her fault that he couldn't understand. And she'd probably – hopefully – seen the last of him.

As for the others, the Doctor and Fitz – well, she'd probably seen the last of them as well. She'd certainly seen the last of the girl Anji and Father Gottlieb. She didn't quite understand where they'd gone, but from what the Doctor had said it seemed certain they wouldn't be coming back. Now the blue box was gone with no indication that it had ever been there, and Aboetta was alone with Malahyde in complete silence.

They stood facing each other for a moment.

Then Aboetta stepped up to Malahyde and kissed him lightly on the lips.

From the look on his face, you would have thought she'd slapped him. 'Sorry,' she said, feeling the colour rush to her cheeks.

'Sorry?' he gasped, and then he smiled – the most carefree, genuine smile she'd ever seen on him. 'There's no need to apologise for *that*, Aboetta!'

Still feeling slightly embarrassed, she reached out a hand and he took hold of it, looking down as if he didn't know what to do next.

'Oh, Aboetta,' he murmured. 'So much has happened.'

Aboetta withdrew her hand, not wanting to rush things. After all, they existed in their own island of time.

They had all the time in their world.

'I'd better check the Utopian Engine,' said Malahyde, nodding decisively. He walked over to the desk and gingerly adjusted a few controls.

'It seems to be all right,' he said uncertainly. 'But then how can I know?'

Aboetta was thinking of Father Gottlieb and Anji, of how they had got in. 'Hadn't we better check that everything's all right, you know – outside?'

Malahyde blinked, and then realised. 'The guards!'

He ran across the cellar to the stairs, Aboetta close behind him.

Fitz stood in the console room, not knowing what to do or say.

'Can't we at least *try* to rescue her?'

The Doctor was busying himself at the console, and didn't look up. 'Humans can't survive in the Vortex. The Time Winds would tear them apart. And with the Vortex in the state it is at the moment...' He left the sentence unfinished.

Fitz looked glumly around the console room, suddenly acutely aware of the impotence of all this technology in the face of mortality. He belatedly realised they were in flight. 'Hey – where are we going?'

'Back to Totterdown,' said the Doctor. 'We can't take Robin with us. Not where we're going.'

Robin was slumped in an armchair, head in hands, the loss of Aboetta clearly rendering him insensible to the wonders of the TARDIS.

'So where are we going after Totterdown?' asked Fitz, fearing the worst.

'More a question of when, actually,' The Doctor turned away from the console and approached Robin. 'Can you tell me exactly when the Cleansing happened?' he said gently.

Robin looked up. His face was streaked with the traces of tears. 'Year Nought. The nineteenth of July.'

The Doctor stared into the distance. '1843. The very same date as the launch of the *SS Great Britain*. Ah! We've landed.'

The scanner showed a dark room cramped with stacks of barrels. The Doctor operated the door control. 'Robin, we're back in Totterdown. Your home. It's time for you to leave.'

Robin stood. His gaze was defiant. 'I've got nothing to go back for. Can't I stay in here? Think things through?'

'No,' said the Doctor. 'It really is time for you to go.'

'Come on,' said Fitz, gently propelling Robin towards the doors.

'Looks like a fine autumn night and I could do with a walk.'

Ignoring the Doctor he stepped out of the TARDIS into the sawdust-floored barn, or storehouse, or whatever it was. Outside it was mild, though a cool wind occasionally blew up.

They were on top of a steep hill, almost directly above a Watchtower upon which torches blazed. The sight seemed familiar and strangely reassuring to Fitz. To his left a strange, conical building rose into the sky – a windmill, he realised, its sails almost reaching the ground.

The sky was cloudless, star-speckled, a yellow-gold harvest moon low down above the black hills surrounding Bristol. In this version of Earth man had never set foot on its surface, thought Fitz suddenly. And somehow that didn't seem a bad thing. The moon was still a mystery, home to the Man In The Moon, still potentially made of cheese.

There was still so much to discover.

Surely, thought Fitz, the human race still had a chance? The Cleansing had killed so many but here he was, standing in a settlement that was a testament to humanity's endurance and ingenuity. Civilisation prevailed, and so what if there hadn't been an Industrial Revolution? Perhaps that was a good thing – without the internal combustion engine, without the pollutants and effluents of industry, without man's gradual enslavement to the machine, maybe the human race would retain its dignity.

He looked at Robin, who was staring morosely down at the Watchtower. *His* biggest problem was girl trouble. Wasn't that a ringing endorsement of these people? They'd coped with their basic needs – food, shelter, survival – got all that sorted out, thank you very much, and so had time to be bothered by the pangs of unrequited love.

He suddenly felt a strange kinship with Robin Larkspar, despite the guy's obvious flaws. He shuffled closer to him, a question forming on his lips – what was he going to do now?

'Fitz.' The Doctor had emerged from the storehouse.

Fitz turned round. 'Yes?'

The Doctor's features were hidden in shadow. 'Come on. We're leaving.'

Fitz folded his arms. 'Are we?'

The Doctor also folded his arms. 'We are.'

Fitz heard Robin's footsteps swish through the long grass, and glimpsed the back of his jacket as he ran off down the hillside.

'I shouldn't worry about him,' said the Doctor.

Fitz felt a rush of anger. 'Oh, of course not, because you're going to go back and erase this reality, so he won't ever exist!'

The Doctor walked past Fitz and stared down at the blazing torches on the Watchtower below. A sudden breeze blew up and stirred the Doctor's hair. Above them, the sails of the windmill – a huge black cross against the vista of stars – creaked and groaned like the masts of a ship.

The Doctor spoke quickly and softly, keeping his eyes fixed on the flames. 'Yes. I am going to go back to 1843, to Year Nought. I am going to prevent Malahyde from operating the Utopian Engine.'

'What good will that do?' said Fitz. 'You've already pointed out that history diverged before 1843. The bridge, remember?'

'I know!' snapped the Doctor. 'But I don't know when the initial divergence was, or what caused it. If I go back and prevent the Cleansing, that should put history more or less back on its tracks. Then I can do a bit of research, find out what happened.'

'You don't sound convinced.'

'What if I'm doomed to go back through history, forever looking for the branching event, forever altering and – worse – maybe even causing these changes? What if these alternative realities are all my fault?'

'Exactly!' said Fitz triumphantly. 'You can't risk it.'

'But I must try,' said the Doctor. 'The Vortex can't sustain all these alternative realities.'

Fitz's heart sank to his boots. The Doctor's moment of self-doubt had passed in a beat. He gazed out over the settlement, the houses on the opposite slope. How many people lived in Totterdown? A thousand? Two thousand? How many settlements were there in Bristol? In England? Or the world? How many people would cease to exist – would never even exist – if the Doctor carried out his plan? 'What right do you have to wipe out a whole reality?'

'Fitz.' The Doctor's voice was resigned, but resolute. 'I probably have no right. But I have a responsibility. If I don't do this, you know the consequences. Total collapse – the end of everything.'

Fitz turned away. He'd thought he could cope with this. 'You'll be killing all these people,' he said, almost to himself. 'Even worse, they will never have existed. Aboetta, Robin, Gottlieb – all these people!'

'They won't know a thing about it, Fitz.'

The casual tone of his voice made Fitz want to hit him. 'Oh well, that makes it all right then!'

The Doctor turned to Fitz, his voice carrying down the hill so that the Watchkeeper in the tower looked up. 'Fitz, because of the Cleansing, millions died. And look what's left over – sad remnants of humanity roaming the ruined cities, feeding on what they can get, feeding on each other. A few settlements, just about clinging to civilisation. It'll take time, but the human race's seed will wither and die. Humanity will never reach the stars, never make contact with other races, never achieve their full potential, not in this reality.'

'But don't you see, all this' – Fitz gestured to the settlement around them – 'represents the triumph of the human spirit? In the face of adversity, and so on? Come on, Doctor, that sounds exactly like the sort of thing you would say!'

'It is,' said the Doctor. 'I admire the people of Totterdown. But they're in a minority, and besides it's irrelevant. This reality is endangering all others. Endangering your reality.'

'My reality.' Fitz shrugged. 'What good was that? In this reality, the atrocities of the Twentieth Century never happened,' said Fitz. 'No World Wars, no holocaust, no nuclear accidents, no over-population, no ethnic cleansing –'

'Isn't the Cleansing an atrocity to rival those?' the Doctor interrupted. 'And, to bring things home to you – if you hadn't been travelling with me, if you had stayed in your own time, you wouldn't exist because of the Cleansing!'

Fitz was immediately on his guard. 'Don't try to get round me by talking temporal bollocks like that.'

'Fitz, don't you see what the Cleansing is? Whatever caused it – this Watchlar creature Malahyde spoke of – it was a deliberate act. An evil act. Don't you think it's worth trying to stop it?'

Fitz closed his eyes. 'Doctor, what if *this* is the right reality?' He swept an arm round in a gesture which included the windmills, the Watchtower and the houses of Totterdown. 'Just because it's not ours, doesn't mean it's the wrong one! *We* could be from the "wrong reality"!'

The Doctor looked at him strangely. 'Fitz, this isn't a parallel universe. This is the one universe, the quantum universe – *our* universe. There can be only one true history within it – and you *know* that history, you're part *of* it.' He was speaking passionately now. 'You *know* this is wrong!'

Fitz shook his head. 'I'm not sure I do, Doctor. I know what you're saying makes sense, but…' He sighed. 'It's not how I feel.'

'I don't like it any more than you, Fitz.' The Doctor sighed and shoved his hands in his pockets. 'But I have to do what I think is right.'

They stood on the hillside together as an uncomfortable silence developed between them.

Then at length the Doctor said quietly, nodding his head in the direction of the storehouse beside the windmill, 'Are you coming with me?'

Fitz took a step towards the Doctor, and then hesitated. So the Doctor had spelled out the consequences of inaction. All well and good. But what were the consequences of *action*?

'Doctor. Say you go back, restore history. What happens then? Will the "real" 2003 snap into place, like a picture in a slide show?'

'Not exactly,' said the Doctor. 'If I succeed, then this reality will never come into existence. I would then travel forwards to 2003 to hopefully find the real one in place.'

'I meant,' said Fitz carefully, 'if I stayed behind, what would happen to me, if you succeeded?'

The Doctor stared at Fitz. 'You're seriously thinking of staying?'

'Yes,' said Fitz through gritted teeth – as if he didn't have a mind of his own! 'So what would happen to me?'

The Doctor stared at him as if he were mad. 'Fitz,' he said

warningly. 'If you stay here I can't guarantee your survival.'

'What, I'd cease to exist along with the rest of them?'

The Doctor shook his head. 'No. Like myself and Anji and the TARDIS, you're from outside this reality. Therefore, if you remained here whilst I went back and altered history – well, look at it this way. Time is like a river, in some cases – certainly this one. It's flowing round this islet of reality. Now if I go upriver and alter the course of the flow so that it runs around another islet – well, you'll be left high and dry.'

'And what does that mean, in practical terms?'

The Doctor's next words chilled Fitz. 'You'll be dragged into the Vortex.'

'Like Anji...'

'Yes. Now, are you coming with me?'

'Wait a minute,' said Fitz, seized by a sudden idea. 'It's a paradox, isn't it? If you go back, change history, this reality will never happen. But it was only by coming to this reality that you were aware that something was wrong, and that you had to go back and correct history. Right?'

'Yes,' said the Doctor, his voice a knot of exasperation. 'But –'

'So,' interrupted Fitz, his brain doing cartwheels as he tried to follow the thought to its conclusion, 'you can't go back and change things, because if you did, then the circumstances would never arise in which you *had* to go back and change things!'

'Fitz, it doesn't work like that and you know it!' shouted the Doctor.

'I'm not sure,' said Fitz, backing away. 'Go back and try it. But I've got a feeling you won't succeed.'

'Fitz,' implored the Doctor. 'Why are you being like this? I don't understand.'

'Just go.'

'Fitz, you're not yourself, and I think it's something to do with what's going on.'

'That's just your excuse.'

The Doctor shook his head. His expression was pleading – his voice commanding. 'Fitz, I'm going to get to the bottom of this, whatever it takes. Come with me! Please!'

Fitz turned away.

He heard the Doctor walk back over towards the storehouse. Moments later came the sound of the TARDIS dematerialising. Fitz realised he was shuddering, sweating with fear. 'Oh mother of God,' he whispered to himself. 'What have I done?'

He turned and scrambled towards the storehouse, slipping on the damp grass. He hurled himself through the doorway, already knowing he was too late, swearing at himself.

Of course, the TARDIS wasn't there.

Fitz sank to his knees, tears squeezing from his eyes, images flickering through his mind: Anji with Gottlieb's gun against her head, Robin's scowling face as he grabbed Aboetta's arm, the Doctor's face in the yellow moonlight.

He recovered himself with an effort and staggered from the storehouse. The cool air soothed him and he stared out over the settlement.

He'd made his choice.

He'd prove the Doctor wrong, or die in the screaming wastes of the Time Vortex.

Chapter 17
The Apparition

Robin ran down the steep side of Windmill Hill to the road which ran between that and the main hill of Totterdown settlement. To his left, torches blazed on the Watchtowers, reminding him of the position he'd forfeited the moment he'd fled Totterdown. It was stupid of him to come back here, but he hadn't really had much chance to consider his options. He reached his cottage, to see a light blazing at the window. Clear what had happened – they'd appointed a new Head Watchkeeper. Had to be Thomas Cope – Robin had faced down many challenges to his authority these last years, many from young Cope. Well now the lad had got what he'd been coveting all this time.

And then he ran into Morgan Foster.

The Chief Elder didn't show much surprise upon seeing his former Head Watchkeeper wandering about the settlement. He greeted Robin without enthusiasm. 'You're back, then.'

Robin stood before him, his mind full of the things he'd seen – the TARDIS, this strange Utopian Engine that seemed to have caused the Cleansing, the vanishing of the priest and the dark-skinned girl – and realised that there was no way he could explain any of it to Morgan Foster. The man simply didn't have the capacity to take in anything beyond the running and defence of Totterdown settlement.

In that moment, Robin felt bigger in every way than the Chief Elder. 'Yes. I am back. And I ask nothing of you, Morgan Foster.' An idea hit him. 'I am leaving tomorrow, for another settlement.

Bedminster, or maybe farther. Whoever will have me. I'll trouble you for this night only.'

And so he shoved past Morgan Foster, with no plans beyond getting drunk.

Aboetta followed Malahyde up the cellar steps at a run. She waited as he fumbled with the key, thinking that there wasn't much point, the secret of the Utopian Engine was out – how much longer before others came to know the truth? And a locked door was pretty useless against the Doctor's blue box. But she didn't say anything, not wishing to upset Malahyde.

He moved as if to run along the corridor back towards the Hall, then turned and grabbed Aboetta's arm. 'How long has it been since that priest and the girl arrived?'

Aboetta had no idea. 'An hour, maybe more?'

'That means over a day will have passed in the world outside. Come on!'

He led her along the corridor, through the hall and out of the front door into the garden. Dusk was just starting to fall in their private island of time. The circular wall cast a long shadow across the thin, pale grass, almost as far as the barren flowerbeds. Above, the sky was a mass of low grey cloud like the underbelly of some vast beast. And the house loomed behind them, its windows seeming to bear an oddly defensive expression, now she knew its secret.

They strode along the path to the door, their boots crunching on the gravel.

Then Malahyde stopped dead. 'Of course – the lock!'

Aboetta remembered the gunshot. She ran up to the door, to find it loose on its hinges. She stepped outside, into another time. Here it wasn't dusk, it was morning, the sun low in the sky above the wood on the hillside, mist still clinging to the grassy slopes, the air crisp and fresh in her throat.

Aboetta shielded her eyes from the sun's orange glare and scanned the grounds. No sign of Estate Guards or anyone. Sudden fear gripped her – what if they had been invaded, what if all the Guards had been killed?

She retreated inside, staggering slightly as the strange sense of mental turbulence she now knew to be the result of the time-distortion swept briefly through her mind. Then she closed the gate and turned to see Malahyde talking agitatedly to one of the Estate Guards.

Aboetta ran up to them. The Guard – one of the captains, Wilson she thought – looked disoriented, confused.

'You should never enter the house!' Malahyde looked terrified – and with good reason. What would happen if people found out about the Utopian Engine and its strange effects?

'I'm sorry, sir,' Wilson said, staring up at the sky. 'But I rang the bell – no one came.'

'We were otherwise engaged,' said Malahyde, with a glance at Aboetta.

'That may be so, sir,' said Wilson. He was a stocky man in his forties with close-cropped red hair and a way of turning his whole upper body when talking to you. 'Sir, may I ask –'

'No, you may not,' said Malahyde. 'You may tell me why you rang the bell.'

'We came under attack,' said Wilson. 'Bunch of outlaws. We managed to polish most of 'em off, the rest of 'em legged it into the woods.'

Except for two of them, thought Aboetta, but she kept quiet.

'How many men did we lose?'

'One, sir. Young Peters.'

'Ah.' Malahyde looked uneasy, as if he couldn't recall who this Peters was. 'Well done on repulsing the attack. Now what I'd like you to do is increase vigilance around the perimeter of the Estate…'

Malahyde began to lead the soldier gently up the garden path towards the broken door.

Aboetta hovered nervously behind. Now that Wilson had seen inside the garden, seen the difference in the sky, what would happen? She had the uneasy feeling that their isolation was going to end soon, one way or another, what with these visitors, and now *this*.

* * *

Robin drained the last of his pint, rose from his seat and half walked, half lurched over to the bar.

'Another,' he belched.

Blaney took the tankard from Robin's hand and held it under the tap. Robin watched the foamy liquid spurt and splutter into the pot.

Already too drunk to walk straight, but Robin didn't care. Wanted to get drunk, more drunk than ever. If he fell into the river and drowned, then it would be for the best.

He had nothing to live for now. No woman, and now no occupation. This didn't depress him, didn't force inebriated sobs from his chest, or drunken tears from his eyes. On the contrary, the thought of his death produced in him a strange sense of elation. Soon it would all be over, and the more drunk he got the less he'd know about it.

Blaney slid the frothing tankard across the rough wooden bar. 'Putting it away a bit aren't you?' he said, without much conviction.

'What if I am?' said Robin, taking the pint and returning to his table, in the darkest corner he could find. He'd worry about paying Blaney back later – if there was a later. The bubble of doomy elation burst within him and he laughed through the head of the pint as he brought it to his lips. The ale tasted good – warm and fruity, with a real kick to it – and Robin drank deeply.

Laughter from a table across the inn. People he knew, or used to know, their faces lit by the dancing flames in the wall-brackets. There was Adam Rebouteux, relaxing after a hard day's work. At another table were a trio of off-shift Watchkeepers. Thomas Cope was there, probably celebrating his promotion. Robin caught his eye for a brief moment, hoping against himself for a glimmer of recognition, but he might as well be exchanging hostile stares with a total stranger.

Robin looked away and ground his knuckles against the underside of the table as more laughter reached his ears. He stared at his pint-pot as though it was salvation. But it was too late. It was as if their laughter had punctured his mood. All sense of elation seemed to whistle out of him in one great sigh.

He knew that he wouldn't die tonight – he was too scared to

commit suicide, however drunk he got. No, his life would go on – a life of disgrace, a life of humiliation.

A life without Aboetta.

A shadow fell over his table. The sound of a chair scraping against the flagstones, a grunt as someone sat down.

Robin looked up to see Fitz looking back at him, his eyes red-rimmed, face pale under the beard which covered his chin.

Could almost be a reflection, mused Robin.

'I need beer,' said Fitz.

Robin laughed. Almost as if his own need to get drunk had somehow communicated itself to the newcomer.

Fitz leaned across the table, his expression earnest. 'Look. You might have every reason to hate me but you're the only person I know in this whole settlement.'

'I don't hate you, mate,' said Robin, buoyed up with a sense of beery bonhomie. 'In fact...' He frowned. What *did* he feel about Fitz? He'd hit him – the punch hadn't hurt. Nor had the Doctor's – whatever it was he'd done. They'd brought him back here, the bastards! But they had rescued Aboetta from Wildren. And had helped him get into Malahyde's estate in the TARDIS (best not think about that: bad enough whilst sober) – much good that had done.

No – Fitz hadn't done him any great evil.

Robin gripped his tankard with both hands. 'It's Malahyde I hate,' he hissed. 'For taking Aboetta away from me.'

'Oh, and not because he wiped out almost the whole human race?' said Fitz, sitting back and folding his arms.

Robin didn't want to think of that either. 'Have a drink.'

Mention of drink made Fitz hunch over the table again. 'Well, I would, and God knows I need one – at least – but I haven't got any money.'

Robin frowned. Where exactly did this chap say he was from again? He gestured with his thumb over his shoulder. 'Blaney there will keep a tally of how much we drink, and then decide what work we'll need to do to pay it off.' His spirits sunk slightly again. 'Up until not long ago, I was allowed a quota of two pints a day.'

'Got the sack, have we?' said Fitz.

Robin nodded, not wanting to speak about it. Not wanting to do anything except drink.

'Right,' said Fitz, standing up with a determined gleam in his eyes. 'I am off to get the first of many, many beers.'

'Get us another one while you're at it,' called Robin at Fitz's retreating back.

Malahyde had replaced the shattered lock with a makeshift bar across the door. Once he and Aboetta had searched the house and satisfied themselves that it was empty, they drew the curtains and prepared dinner.

They usually ate in the dining-hall, a long rectangular room in the South Wing, with a view over the gardens, and, of course, the wall. Sometimes Aboetta ate alone in the kitchens, when Malahyde was busy in his study or in the cellar (she now knew why).

Tonight they ate in the dining-hall as they had done many times, but there was something different about this meal. Before, they had dined as master and servant, but now, it seemed, as equals. There was nothing physically different – Malahyde took his place at the end of the long white-clothed table, Aboetta to his left, facing the windows – but there was a subtle change in the atmosphere, a narrowing of the distance between them. They talked more easily, more casually, about the events of the day and what the future might hold for them. Though concerned about the intruders, Malahyde seemed more relaxed than usual, more open, more able to share his feelings. Aboetta was pleased to see him like this, glad to see his brow for once free from worried creases.

It was a simple meal: a thick, nourishing soup, bread, and for the main course boiled potatoes and steamed vegetables. To Aboetta's delight, Malahyde brought out a bottle of wine.

'Somehow, this survived the Cleansing,' he said as he poured the golden liquid into the crystal glasses. 'I found it in the cellars of a merchant's house in one of my forays shortly after the Cleansing.' He sipped and raised his eyebrows appreciatively. 'So its vintage is rather open to question. Did the effects of the Cleansing allow it to mature? Or has it spoiled the flavour?' He sipped and smiled sadly.

'Even something as horrendous as the Cleansing has its good side.'

Aboetta sipped the wine. Mr Malahyde was right – whatever its vintage, it was glorious. She had tasted wine before, back in Totterdown, but it was sickly, cloying stuff, nothing like this golden liquid which seemed to dance on her tongue.

Thoughts of Totterdown subdued her, made her think of the people she'd left.

Malahyde must have noticed this. 'What's the matter?'

'I was thinking of home.'

Malahyde looked uneasy. 'You miss Totterdown?'

Aboetta nodded.

Now it was his turn to look despondent. 'I understand if you wish to return.'

Aboetta frowned, irritation sweeping aside her gloom. Did he really have such a low opinion of himself, to think that she'd up and leave each time she missed the place where she had grown up? Did he really think her so shallow? Didn't she realise how she felt about him?

She looked at Malahyde as he stared down at his empty plate, fingers fiddling with the silver cutlery. A sense of helplessness swept over her. She had never been good at communicating her feelings. In her experience, words only made things worse, they got in the way, muddying waters which before were crystal clear.

So she chose her words very carefully. 'I've made my decision. But even if I did want to go back, I couldn't. The place were I grew up doesn't exist any more – it's ten years in my past.'

He began to speak, but she held up a hand to silence him. 'I know that you think it is your fault, but it was my choice to come here, and it is my choice to stay. Even if I could go back in time, I wouldn't. My place is here – with you.' She took another sip of wine, hoping that these words were enough to seal the matter.

'It wouldn't be so hard to go back. People would accept you, even welcome you.' He was clearly thinking of Robin. 'Why have you decided to stay with me?'

The direct question caught Aboetta off guard. It hung in the air like a challenge. But in a sense Aboetta welcomed it. It meant that she had to spell it out to him. Well, if that was what it took, so be it.

'Because I love you.'

Malahyde stopped fiddling with his fork and stared at Aboetta. 'I never dreamed…'

Malahyde was the opposite of her when it came to words – he liked to discuss things from every angle, leaving nothing unsaid. Before he could speak, she reached out for his hands, clasped them in hers, leaned across the table and kissed him.

He seemed to wilt in her arms, and when she disengaged and sat back, he looked stunned.

'Aboetta,' he said at last. 'I – well, if I talk too much, I could ruin this moment. I never imagined that when I asked for someone to come and live as my servant, that it could lead to this.'

There was no need to ask him to return her declaration. She could see it in the light in his eyes. And she knew that she would never have to repeat the declaration, because she had said it, said those words to a suitor for only the second time in her life, and they were true until she told him otherwise – though she could never imagine that happening.

Malahyde remained seated, Aboetta standing.

'Would you like me to play for you?' he said.

Aboetta smiled. 'No. Not now.' She held out a hand to him. 'Come with me.'

Slowly, he rose from his seat, his napkin falling on to his empty plate, and allowed Aboetta to lead him upstairs. Halfway up the stairs with their faded maroon carpet, he stopped and said, 'I have never, ever even kissed…' The words descended into a sigh of embarrassment.

Aboetta squeezed his hand. 'Don't worry.'

They went into his room. Aboetta went round and lit the candles on the dresser, watching Malahyde undress in the big mirror.

Soon they were together in the big four-poster bed, holding each other gently. Though older than Robin, his skin was smoother, his body more boyish. He was trembling slightly, so she kissed him. At first, he was shy, awkward, but soon he began to respond, and with a passion to match her own.

Aboetta looked down at his face, beginning to abandon herself to the sensations building inside her. She seemed to be entering a timeless state of being, her mind floating far above her body, the rhythm of the act pushing her further than she had ever been before, until –

Aboetta gasped, feeling herself falling as if from a great height. A memory formed in her mind, and there was a name attached to it. She screamed, tumbling from Malahyde and sprawling in the bed beside him, staring up at the canopy.

For a moment she saw something – a figure, shaped like a man, but with no face. It sparkled like raindrops in the sun.

It began to move towards her.

Aboetta screamed again – and the apparition vanished.

'What's wrong?' gasped Malahyde. 'Oh God, what have I done to you?'

'It's not you,' said Aboetta. 'I – I sensed something.'

'What do you mean?'

'I had this feeling.' Aboetta turned to look at him. 'A memory I didn't realise I had.'

Malahyde's face was coated in a sheen of sweat, and in the candlelight, his eyes widened. 'A *memory*?'

'It had a name,' said Aboetta.

Malahyde drew back from her. 'Watchlar.'

Aboetta nodded. 'What does this mean?'

'I don't know,' said Malahyde. 'It could be that somehow the idea of Watchlar has got hold of you, and during, whilst –'

'Shh…' said Aboetta.

They kissed and clung to each other, and soon, Malahyde was asleep.

Aboetta stayed awake for a while longer, eyes searching the dark corners of the room, but soon she too was sleeping.

Chapter 18
Time's Prisoners

One minute Anji was trying to wrestle herself free from Gottlieb, the next she was falling, accelerating through a whirling, spinning tunnel of light –

And then she slapped face-down chest-first on to something unyielding. The impact knocked the breath from her body and kicked her chin sharply back, cricking her neck painfully. Her outstretched fingers curled, digging into – was that sand?

She could hardly breathe. Each indrawn breath seemed to die in her throat, her lungs a starving ache in her chest. Her head pounded and throbbed, there was a sharp pain at the backs of her eyes. She opened them – and could see nothing. Was she blind? Was she dead? What had happened?

Her hands clutched at her throat and she sat up, her breath now coming in a strangled wheeze. Lights flashed in her head and she felt as if she were going to pass out at any moment. Telling herself to stay calm, she took slow, deep breaths, and after a few minutes her lungs began to fill with thin, cold air and the throbbing in her head subsided. Her hands smoothed the surface she was sitting on, and she realised that it *was* sand – stone cold and dry.

Now her vision had adapted to the darkness, she could see that it wasn't complete. To her left was a ribbon of water, lapping gently on the sand. It glowed very faintly with a green phosphorescence. The same green as the Utopian Engine.

A voice moaned close to her, making her jump. In the near-complete darkness, she could just make out a humped shape which could have been a rock, or someone on their hands and knees.

'Gottlieb?'

The voice moaned again, and then rasped. 'Can't – breathe!'

Anji slid over the sand towards him. After what he'd done, she'd be perfectly justified if she let him die. But she couldn't do that. 'Breathe deeply, and slowly,' she advised. 'Try to stay calm.'

As Gottlieb's breath sawed in and out of him, Anji looked around. Beyond Gottlieb, something vast and dark seemed to rise into the – sky? Anji looked up. Above, the blackness was even more profound.

She looked again at the ribbon of phosphorescent water. It faded into the distance in either direction, a line of bright lime-green foam at its edge. It was a sea, Anji realised, and they were on the shore. Looking out to where the horizon should be, Anji saw only blackness – the green glow of the water diminished with distance, giving the illusion that the ocean faded into nothing after a few dozen yards. This made it seem as though they were floating in space next to a rippling green band of wavelets surging on to an invisible shore.

Where *was* this place?

Her teeth were chattering. It was so cold here, but nothing like the chill of winter. More a metallic cold, dental injection cold. She hugged her jacket more closely around her.

She heard Gottlieb scrambling about on the sand. 'Are you all right now?'

'Yes,' gasped Gottlieb.

'Good.' Anji took a deep breath. 'You bloody idiot!' The exhortation made her gasp for breath. 'What – have you done – sent us into the – future or something?'

Actually, this could be the future, she thought. Billions of years on from the twenty-first century, when the sun had gone out, the human race had been dead for almost ever and the atmosphere had thinned away to virtually nothing. Didn't explain the eerie green ocean though. So maybe this was an alien planet on the other side of the universe. Not even the Doctor seemed to know what the

Utopian Engine was capable of. Whatever it was for, and wherever they were, there was one thing for certain. They were stranded.

'You bloody idiot,' she repeated.

Unexpectedly, Gottlieb began to sob.

She suddenly remembered the gun, started feeling around on the sand for the weapon. Gottlieb must be nuts, trying to operate a machine he couldn't possibly hope to understand. But then, how little she really knew about him. If the whole purpose of his life had been discovering the truth behind the Cleansing, then it was understandable that he would go to pieces on completion of that purpose.

Her search for the gun turning up nothing except more sand, Anji stood and walked to the shore. Any exertion made her heart pound and her breath drag in her throat, so she moved slowly and carefully, crouching down at the water's edge. Tiny wavelets surged and receded with a gentle lapping motion. There was no seaweed or other detritus. She took a tissue from her jeans pocket and dropped it in the water. It floated there, apparently unharmed. She touched the water with her fingers. It was lukewarm, and felt slightly soapy between her fingers, like bathwater. She brought her fingers up to her nose – it had a faint chemical smell.

This close the foam cast a light bright enough for her to be able to see her boots, her hands, the fine black sand beneath her feet. She looked over her shoulder. Perhaps that black mass was a cliff-face, perhaps there were caves.

She began exploring her jacket pockets for something in which to capture the luminous substance and her fingers closed around the mineral water bottle. There was a mouthful of water left, which Anji quickly drank. Then she dipped the bottle into the water, filling it right up. She screwed the lid back on, satisfied with the results. The luminous bottle cast enough light for her to be able to see for a few metres around her. There was Gottlieb's flintlock – it had been right under her nose the whole time.

She picked it up, wondering how it worked, if it was loaded, and then sought out Gottlieb, who was sitting with his head in his hands.

'Stand up,' she said, pointing the gun at him.

Gottlieb looked up, saw what she was carrying, and obeyed. 'What is that?' he said, pointing at the strange lantern.

'Improvisation,' she said.

'Wh– where are we?' he said, shivering and hugging himself.

'That's what I intend to find out,' she said. She indicated the cliff-face with the gun. 'Now get moving.'

Gottlieb stumbled away. Anji followed, keeping the gun trained on him. The pool of light cast by the mineral water bottle was barely enough to illuminate them both.

Soon they came to the end of the beach. A smooth face of black rock reared up before them. It looked man-made, like a wall, though Anji could see no joins in the stone.

'There must be a way up,' she gasped, tired from the effort of the walk.

Gottlieb slumped against the rock, his face crumpled and weary. 'I'm sorry,' he said. 'Sorry for bringing us here.'

Anji was about to shout – or rather, gasp – at him, but he sounded genuine, so she didn't.

'Look, there's no point in apologising,' she said. 'We're here, wherever here is. We've got no food, there's water but I don't know if we can drink it, it's freezing cold and pitch dark. Our chances for survival don't look good. Our only chance is to find our way to civilisation – if there is one here. So come on – help me look for a way up.'

Gottlieb sighed, but heaved himself upright and began to walk with Anji through the blackness.

'Get up!'

The words jolted Fitz from a dream he forgot immediately. Reality asserted itself – a reality of a throbbing head, a desert-dry mouth, and churning guts.

'I said, get up, lads! You've got work to do.'

Fitz groaned, threw back the blanket and heaved himself out of bed.

Blaney stood in the doorway, arms folded, pinched face bright yellow in a ray of morning sun which slanted from the attic window.

The landlord shook his head. 'What a sorry state to be in.' He laughed. 'But who am I to complain at such good customers?'

The lump in the other bed moved and groaned, a pale arm and a white black-stubbled face appeared.

'Leave us alone, Blaney,' said Robin.

Fitz grinned but his amusement was short-lived. Blaney walked across the bedroom and dragged Robin from the bed. 'Listen, you may once have been Head Watchkeeper but you ain't nothing any more! You're working for me now, until your debt's paid off.'

'All right, all right!' yelled Robin, kicking off the blankets and struggling free of the landlord.

Blaney thrust his red, perspiring face at Fitz. 'And the same goes for you, lad.'

'Yes, Blaney.' Fitz knew better than to argue with the landlord when roused. He had a terrible temper that was nothing to do with drink, and all to do with temperament.

'Now there's a delivery in today, barrels of ale from Gloucester. It's due at ten so you've got an hour to ready yourselves.'

Fitz groaned. Why had he drunk so much last night? Now lugging the cart up the hill from the river would feel like ten times more work than it actually was.

Grumbling to himself, he rose, thrust his legs into his trousers and went downstairs for a breakfast of water – he couldn't face food, not just yet. In the daytime, the empty inn always looked barren and unfriendly.

Fitz went outside and gazed down the hill. People were moving about, the sun was up – a nice, warm autumn day.

A groan from behind him.

'You bastard,' said Fitz. 'Making me drink so much.'

Robin groaned again. 'Sorry, mate. But I had reason to drink.'

'Well, I didn't, other than to keep you company.' Fitz frowned, remembering how desolate his friend had been last night. 'Are you still thinking of leaving?'

Robin yawned and rubbed his eyes. 'I dunno. I might have to – this place reminds me of *her* too much.'

Fitz groaned. 'Forget her, mate – plenty more round here.'

Robin managed a smile.

'Come on then,' said Fitz, heaving himself up from the table, doing his best to ignore the creaks of protest from his joints. 'That beer ain't gonna deliver itself.'

The Doctor waited for a minute or so, in case Fitz changed his mind, and then closed the TARDIS doors.

He stood for a while, alone in the console room, listening to the surging cadences of the TARDIS's engines, allowing the rhythms to soothe him. Then he busied himself at the controls, projecting a temporal map on to the scanner, plotting the course to Year Nought – or 1843, as it was known then. And if he succeeded, would remain so.

Another part of the scanner showed a churning pattern of undulating blue and gold tunnels, like mouths competing to devour the TARDIS. Or whirlpools, vying to be the first to claim it for who-knew-what depths. The Time Vortex. The TARDIS's natural habitat. Only it wasn't any more. There was something different: darkness was spreading from the whirlpool-mouths, and flashes of lightning streaked across the screen. Like a fish in a polluted ocean, the TARDIS was in danger in its home environment. The Vortex was sick, deformed, dying, unable to cope with the strain of the multiple realities.

The Doctor closed his eyes. Anji would have suffered a horrible death, her body torn apart by the energies in the Vortex – aged to death and then back to birth in the space of a nanosecond, her life eaten up and spat out and then eaten up and spat out again.

Trying not to dwell upon Anji's fate, the Doctor tripped the dematerialisation switch, noting the sudden rise in pitch of the sound of the engines. He checked the yearometer: the TARDIS was moving back through time, its course slow and deliberate. Nothing he could do now but wait. He wandered over to the library, intending to brush up on a few historical details. He hadn't attended the launch of the *SS Great Britain*, Brunel's famous steam-ship. Now then: Rolt's book on Brunel would be a good place to start.

But as he entered the library, he paused. Something was wrong.

There were gaps.

The Doctor ran up to the nearest shelf. Nothing but dust. He went to the section of the library devoted to twentieth-century Earth history – all the shelves were bare. He ran a finger along a shelf. Dust.

Almost half the books had vanished.

He rubbed the dust between his thumb and forefinger, the implications beginning to dawn on him. A quick scrutiny of the library confirmed that everything published after the middle of the nineteenth century had vanished. His first editions of Shakespeare were intact, as were his collections of metaphysical poetry, the Mahabarata, Chaucer, Beowulf, Virgil, Homer, Plato, the Mabinogion, the Bible, the Koran. All were still there. But of later works – his collection of Wyndham novels, Hobsbawm's *Industry and Empire*, his shelf of Proust – there was no sign.

The explanation was uncomfortable, and worrying. The reality of Year 160 had somehow affected the TARDIS. It was beginning to 'naturalise' itself to Year 160 – and, beginning with its library, was beginning to adapt to fit in with the reality.

'But that shouldn't happen!' said the Doctor aloud, returning to the console. 'You should be able to resist outside influences,' he told it reproachfully. The Doctor realised he'd probably left just at the right time – how much longer before the TARDIS had naturalised itself out of existence, turned itself into a potting shed or something?

It was fascinating – but terrifying. Somehow, the Vortex was attempting to right itself by removing all the inconsistencies in the multiple realities it was fighting to sustain. That way, it would survive intact. That way, the reality he'd just come from would end up being the dominant reality.

Perhaps that's why Fitz had been acting so strangely, unable to see the flimsiness of his own arguments, asserting that the wrong reality was the right one. Perhaps he, like the TARDIS, was beginning to 'naturalise', the diseased Time Vortex acting on his biodata, twisting it to fit into the wrong reality in a desperate attempt to ensure its own survival.

The Doctor moved to the console, fully intending to return for Fitz, and drag him into the TARDIS by force if need be. But he hesitated, fingertips brushing the controls. Wait – if he went back to Year 160, went out into that reality, there was a danger that not only would the TARDIS become naturalised, but he himself too – then all would really be lost.

The Doctor stepped back from the console, swamped by a feeling of impotence: he couldn't help Anji, he couldn't help Fitz...

Restoring their reality was the very least he could do.

Chapter 19
Year Nought

It was a hazy, hot morning. The sun glared down from a cloudless blue sky, and not a whisper of wind moved the sails of the ships docked in the Floating Harbour. The water of the artificial river sparkled like diamonds, and on the dockside, people went about their work, cursing in the heat, some working bare-chested. The other side of the harbour was under shadow from the tall buildings set back from the quayside.

The Doctor stood on the quay, in the shadow of the hull of a great iron steam-ship. Its five masts reared up into the sky in dizzying perspective, the single black funnel seeming squat in comparison. Its sails were furled, and there was no sign of activity on deck.

He called to a passing docker, who stopped reluctantly.

'This ship,' said the Doctor, pointing. 'Could you tell me its name?'

'She'll be the *SS Great Britain*.'

The Doctor smiled, shaded his eyes against the sun. 'I see. And – when was she launched?'

'Five year ago,' said the docker. He looked the Doctor up and down, his sun-burned face twisting in a scowl 'Thought everyone knew that.'

'What's she doing here?'

'In dock for repairs – engine trouble you see. Problems with the water-heater. Blew up. Flooded the engine room.'

'Yes, yes,' said the Doctor irritably. 'Now this may sound like an

185

odd question, but could you please tell me the date?'

The worker shook his head slowly. 'Well… it's July the nineteenth, eighteen hundred and forty-three.'

The Doctor looked thoughtfully at the man. 'Yes. Of course it is. Sorry for troubling you, and thank you for your time.'

The docker slouched on without a backwards look at the Doctor.

The Doctor stared up again at the ship, the iron hull, painted jet black, stretching away in front of him.

The *SS Great Britain*.

It was the date of her launch – and yet, it wasn't.

There were no cheering crowds, no flags, no church bells ringing. It was business as usual. What he'd discovered in Year 160 on seeing the Clifton Suspension Bridge – that the path of history had changed before the Cleansing – was confirmed resoundingly in the shape of the vast iron leviathan that was the *SS Great Britain*.

But what had caused this initial divergence?

The Doctor stood for a while, and then left the docks and walked into the town. He hailed a cab and asked for Ashton Court, the obvious destination. But instead of the driver taking them along beside the river through Bedminster and thence up to Ashton Court, he took a route through the centre of the town and up towards Clifton.

'Excuse me,' said the Doctor. 'I asked to be taken to Ashton Court, not Clifton.'

'That's where we goin',' shouted the driver. 'Cross the bridge!'

Of course. The Doctor wondered how it was that Brunel had managed to complete his bridge, and his great ship, before time. Had to have something to do with the initial divergence. Alien interference? Or – a dark thought – Sabbath?

As they crossed the bridge, the Doctor looked out at the suspension rods and cables of the construction. He frowned. It looked different somehow, but the difference was so subtle that he couldn't put his finger on it. Something about the material, the engineering. It looked too advanced for the mid-nineteenth century.

More clues, nothing conclusive.

He gazed out at the shining curve of the River Avon far below, the neat buildings of the town and the hills beyond. His foot tapped impatiently on the floor of the cab. He had no idea at what time of day the Cleansing had happened – it could be in one hour, or one minute. And if it did happen now, could he survive it? He knew he wasn't quite human, but could he survive the passing of forty years in forty seconds?

He leaned out of the window and shouted for the driver to go faster. A curse, a crack of the whip and a clatter of hooves as the horse picked up the pace. The Doctor leaned back, trying to relax.

Soon they were over the bridge and on the road which ran up to Clifton Lodge. As they approached the Doctor was surprised to see that the surrounding wall had already been extended, and the barbed-wire fence already installed.

The Doctor hopped down from the cab, turned to the driver and paid him with some coins he'd scraped together in the TARDIS. Then he walked up to the Lodge.

Someone was standing in front of the closed gates, loudly remonstrating with a grey-haired figure leaning from one of the upper windows. Their conversation was drowned out in the receding clatter of the cab – to which neither of them seemed to have paid any attention.

Despite everything, the Doctor couldn't help himself breaking into a huge grin when he realised who the younger man was.

The short, erect figure, the commanding posture – hands tucked into waistcoat – the fine yet crumpled dark tail-coat, but above all the hat. The reinforced top hat favoured by engineers of the period.

The Doctor walked up to the man, still smiling, and extended a hand. 'Isambard Kingdom Brunel, I presume!'

At this point in his life Brunel was in his late thirties, hale and healthy, at the peak of his career. He fixed the Doctor with a glassy stare. His hands remained in his waistcoat pockets, elbows cocked.

'Who the devil are you?'

The Doctor withdrew his hand. 'I, sir, am the Doctor.'

Mixed feelings passed through the Doctor's hearts. He had always wanted to meet Brunel, a man he much admired, but the shadow of the Cleansing was cast over this moment.

'Doctor?' said Brunel, looking him up and down. 'What's your business here?'

The Doctor glanced up at the old man leaning from the window. 'I've come to see Mr Jared Malahyde.'

'No visitors, as I been tryin' to explain!'

'And as I have been trying to explain to you,' said Brunel, 'I have contracts that require your employer's signature. Would you cause expensive delay to vital engineering projects?'

'Mr Malahyde has given orders. He's not to be disturbed.'

'Fool!' thundered Brunel.

No wonder, thought the Doctor. 'Why do these contracts need Malahyde's signature?'

Brunel frowned, and then looked calculatingly at the Doctor. 'I should have thought that was obvious. He's the inventor of the Malahyde Process, therefore any new project requiring its application, also requires his signature.' He pointed through the gates. 'Several months ago I sent him the contracts for the trans-Atlantic tunnel. The Committee won't proceed without his signature, whatever I say! Damned bureaucrats!'

A trans-Atlantic tunnel? Oh dear. 'This Malahyde Process,' said the Doctor. 'Pardon my ignorance, I am a man of medicine, not an engineer. What does it involve?'

'A process for the manufacture of steel, ten times stronger than tempered steel but lighter than wood,' said Brunel brusquely. 'What, don't you even read the papers, man?'

'Oh, now and then,' said the Doctor. His hearts were racing. This Process was surely the initial catalyst! Now it was even more important that he got to Malahyde.

Brunel looked up at the servant. 'Will you let me in!'

'Listen to me, I am a doctor,' called the Doctor. 'When was the last time you saw Mr Malahyde?'

The old servant shrugged. 'Few days ago. Week, perhaps?'

'A week?' cried the Doctor. 'A week and you've called no doctor! What kind of a retainer are you?'

Doubt began to dawn on the old face – but it was a false dawn. 'Not unusual for me not to see Mr Malahyde for weeks on end.'

'But he usually signs any contracts he's sent!' said the Doctor, pointing triumphantly up at the old man.

Doubt returned. He obviously hadn't thought of that.

The Doctor seized his chance. 'So he could be ill, or worse!'

Now the old chap looked worried sick and the Doctor felt sorry for him.

'Best let you in then.' He began to move inside, a shaking arm closing the window, but then poked his head sharply over the sill again. 'You say you're a doctor of medicine? What's your name?'

'Dr John Smith.'

The servant looked doubtful, then nodded.

All this time Brunel had been watching the Doctor with a faint smile on his lips. 'You have a way with people, Doctor Smith.'

The Doctor smiled, mentally urging the old servant down the stairs. 'I've often been complimented on my bedside manner.'

At last the gate opened, slowly, with a rusty creak of complaint, and the worried-faced old servant ushered them through.

As they walked along the tree-lined gravel drive towards the mansion house the servant, whose name was George, told them about Malahyde's conduct these past years.

'I'm the only one,' he grumbled. 'All the others left for other positions years ago. Didn't like what Mr Malahyde was up to. Strange noises, lights.' He shrugged. 'Doesn't bother me, as long as I stay away from the cellar.'

Brunel took out a cotton bag from an inside pocket, loosened the draw-string and extracted a cigar. He spoke as he lit it with a match produced from a box in his waistcoat pocket. 'I've always wondered... what exactly it is that Malahyde's working on.'

'Apart from his Process?' prompted the Doctor.

Brunel coughed, and sent pungent smoke drifting into the warm summer afternoon. 'He's been obsessed with a single project for over ten years, but won't tell anyone what it is.'

'Maybe we're about to find out.' The Doctor felt a pang of sympathy for Malahyde. How could he explain, even to a mind as open and as forward-thinking as Brunel's, about the Utopian Engine?

They soon came to the mansion house. Its gardens were long neglected and gone to seed, weeds running wild in the grass. They waited as George fumbled for a key and let them in.

Inside, the hall was silent, the air dead and musty as if the house were uninhabited. The air was as cold as stone.

'Mr Malahyde!' called George.

No answer came.

'He's most probably in the cellar,' said George, beginning to shuffle towards a door in the far side of the hall. The Doctor and Brunel followed, side by side. At the end of a long wood-panelled corridor, a door stood open, and from somewhere below came a powerful whining drone.

The Doctor started towards the door.

George hung back. 'I'm not going down there.'

'Coming?' the Doctor asked Brunel.

'Nothing could possibly stop me,' said the Great Engineer, eyes gleaming in the dim light of the corridor, cigar smoke wreathed around his reinforced top hat.

The Doctor insisted on going first, and so led Brunel down the stone steps. The green light of the central column of the Utopian Engine was dazzlingly bright, and Brunel shielded his eyes.

'What the devil is that?' he cried. Such was the noise of the Utopian Engine that the Doctor could barely hear him.

'Malahyde's secret project,' the Doctor called back. 'And it looks like we're just in time to stop it.'

The Doctor could see a figure, outlined in green light, standing before the Utopian Engine.

As the Doctor and Brunel watched, the central column spasmed and expanded into a luminescent ovoid pulsing like a grotesque abdomen. Tendrils of energy sparked from its surface to the stone walls of the cellar, leaving scorch-marks the size of dinner plates. An ominous crackling ripped through the air. The Doctor could feel energy prickling the skin of his face, lifting his hair like fingers of bone.

Brunel had dropped his cigar and was holding on to his top hat, eyes screwed up against the glare, face contorted as if weathering a storm.

Malahyde walked casually over to the control desk, disappearing behind the horizon of the expanding energy-sphere which now completely engulfed the central apparatus of the Utopian Engine. 'We've got to stop him!' cried the Doctor.

'Stop him doing what?' yelled Brunel.

The Doctor seized Brunel's arm and dragged him down the remaining steps, ducking under the crackling arcs. Waves of energy-loaded air pressed against the Doctor's face. A smell of ozone and overheated components reached down his throat. Such was the noise, so absorbed was the possessed Malahyde on monitoring the Utopian Engine, that the Doctor was able to walk right up behind him, grab his shoulders and wrench him away from the desk.

Malahyde twisted away from the Doctor with a snarl, and turned to face them.

Brunel stared at his former business colleague. 'Jared! What's happened to you?'

Malahyde's eyes were glowing with the same green light as the Utopian Engine.

'That's not Jared Malahyde,' said the Doctor. 'It's – Watchlar, isn't it?'

'Watch what?' cried Brunel in confusion.

Watchlar/Malahyde stepped towards Brunel and the Doctor. His face was contorted into a grimace of anger.

'Stop this now!' cried the Doctor. 'I am not going to let this happen!'

Watchlar/Malahyde lunged at him, hands reaching for his throat. The Doctor side-stepped neatly, deftly tripping the possessed man. Then he dived at the control desk – but paused above the rows of switches and glass-fronted dials with their quivering needles. He had no idea what this machine was for. What if he only made things worse?

Hands gripped his neck, yanking him backwards. The Doctor allowed himself to fall and pulled Watchlar/Malahyde down on top of him, bringing a knee up into his stomach. It made no difference. The Doctor gasped for breath as hands tightened around his throat.

But suddenly the Doctor was free, and Watchlar/Malahyde fell away. The Doctor sat up – to see Brunel locked in combat with the possessed man.

The Doctor scrambled back towards the machine, wincing as several lightning streaks seared the air inches above his head. A howling, oscillating whine had broken out, like something straining to get free.

The Doctor dragged himself to his knees, determined now to press every button, pull every lever, but Watchlar/Malahyde was upon him again, this time grasping him around the chest. The Doctor heaved backwards again, but there was no shaking the man/thing off. They tottered away from the desk, moving dangerously close to the billowing energy sphere. The Doctor saw Brunel sprawled on the floor, top hat beside him rocking back and forth on its brim. Brunel – *dead*?

With a roar, the Doctor twisted free, taking Watchlar/Malahyde by surprise, shoving him towards the energy sphere. He threw himself in the opposite direction.

The possessed man vanished with a high-pitched scream, and a flash of energy which sent the Doctor spinning into the control desk. He sprawled over it, and flailed blindly at every switch, every button within his reach.

Nothing happened.

The Doctor slid to the floor, unable to see anything but the spherical mass of the transformed Utopian Engine. He rolled under the desk, hands over his ears, trying to blot out the shrieking whine of the Engine. And there before his eyes was –

A cable, running down from the back of the desk.

Could it be that simple?

He looked out towards the Utopian Engine. A cable snaked across the floor from the desk into the billowing sphere of light.

The Doctor grabbed the cable and pulled. It didn't give an inch, it felt like it was cemented into rock. He pulled again, putting his whole weight into it.

And suddenly, with a shower of sparks, it came free.

The howling whine stopped.

The energy-sphere collapsed in on itself with an implosion of air which made the Doctor's ears ring.

After the chaos, all was silent. Terraces of smoke drifted in the air, and there were burn marks all over the walls, but everything else seemed normal.

His ears still ringing, the Doctor crawled over to Brunel. To his relief, the man was breathing, and as the Doctor watched, his eyes opened.

'What – what's happened?'

The Doctor looked over at the Utopian Engine. Its central cylinder had now reverted to its original state, though the green glow was paler than before. It obviously ran off its own energy, the cable he'd broken must have been some sort of command link. When he'd severed it the machine had shut down, gone into stand-by. Had he prevented the Cleansing? 'I don't know,' muttered the Doctor. He helped Brunel to his feet.

'Malahyde!'

The Doctor followed Brunel's pointing finger. Malahyde lay on the floor next to the base of the Utopian Engine. The Doctor ran over, crouched down beside him. There was a pulse, and he was breathing, though shallowly.

'He's all right,' said the Doctor. 'As for Watchlar, well, Malahyde didn't recognise me in the future, so just now he must have been possessed totally by the creature. And as Malahyde wasn't possessed by Watchlar in the future, then somehow the possession must have been broken.' He stared up at the Utopian Engine, then looked down at Malahyde.

Malahyde's eyelids began to flicker.

'He's coming round,' said the Doctor. 'Come on, we'd better get out of here.'

He led the dazed Brunel up the steps and back along the corridor.

There was a body lying in the hall.

The Doctor ran up to it. It was a desiccated husk – the skin paper-thin over the skull, flesh withered away from the hands.

'It's George!' The Doctor slumped to the floor, put his head in his hands. 'I've failed.'

He heard Brunel's footsteps approach. 'Failed? What do you mean, man? I think you'd better tell me what happened down there!' Brunel gasped as he caught sight of the corpse. 'What – what's happened to him?'

The Doctor looked up at the great engineer. 'The Cleansing,' he said bleakly.

Brunel stared down at him in incomprehension.

The Doctor smiled grimly. 'Welcome to Year Nought.'

Chapter 20
Victims

Anji was cold, tired and hungry. She huddled closer to Gottlieb for warmth, not caring any more what he was. The only light came from the luminescent water in the mineral water bottle. But it had grown very faint, illuminating nothing but itself, as though once cut off from the ocean, whatever made the water glow was dying.

As slowly and as surely as Anji and Gottlieb were.

They had walked for an uncountable time along the base of the cliff, looking for a way in, a way up. Stopping ever more frequently to catch their breath. Growing ever colder, ever hungrier, ever more afraid. At last they had found a crack in the sheer wall, quite by accident. Anji was walking along, peering into the gloom beyond the poor light cast by her makeshift lantern, trying to stop her teeth from chattering, outstretched hand maintaining contact with the wall of rock, when suddenly her fingers slipped into empty air. She stumbled, almost dropping the bottle, and Gottlieb – who was right behind – bumped into her. And so they found their cave – an elongated V-shaped slit in the rock. Anji hoped that it would lead somewhere, but it tapered back into a passage too narrow for them to squeeze through. Obviously a fault in the rock. Exhausted, disheartened, they had decided to rest for a while, settling down on the smooth, dry sandy floor of the cave.

Now, Anji thought that they'd never move again, and this would be their final rest.

She couldn't shake off the horrifying prospect that this world was totally uninhabited. There was no civilisation for them to stumble across, no rescuing helicopters would come chattering down out of the black sky. They'd die here as surely as two day-old babies abandoned in a coal mine.

She had one hope, one she dare not voice. The Doctor would be looking for them – looking for *her*. She could picture all too clearly the TARDIS materialising on the sunless beach, its arrival tearing away the darkness and silence. It was a painful, taunting image. But the only light came from the bottle, the only noise was their own breathing. Not even the ocean made a sound, the lapping of the tiny waves too far off to reach their ears.

Anji let out a long, shuddering breath. She had to break this silence, had to make conversation, do that final human thing before she froze or starved to death.

She was leaning against Gottlieb's chest, her legs curled under her, his arms protectively around her. She could feel his chin against the top of her head. A lovers' embrace, though this was borne out of necessity rather than any romantic inclinations.

Gottlieb squeezed her more tightly, his arms shuddering with the cold.

Other inclinations occurred to Anji. 'Hey, you're not planning to, er, eat me, are you?' she wheezed.

He relaxed his grip slightly. 'No.'

'Thank you.'

She felt his arms move as he shrugged. 'There's nothing here in which to roast you.'

'Otherwise you would?' Anji twisted round to look at him, then realised that he was joking.

'You, Anji, are far too good for the pot.' He paused to regain his breath. 'I think it is time, Anji, that you told me *your* story.'

Anji stared at the bottle of fading phosphorescent water. 'Well, to start with, I'm from another universe...'

Fitz lay on the grassy slopes of the riverbank, exhausted after a hard morning's work. Above him the sun beat down, a heavy heat drying the perspiration that soaked his shirt. It was a glorious day, balmy and clear-skied, with no hint of the winter to come. When the sun set, halfway between Six and Seven Bells, the evening would be chilly and the illusion of summer would be gone. But for the moment, Fitz basked.

'Bloody hell!' gasped a voice from somewhere beyond Fitz's outstretched legs. He lifted his head – it felt as heavy as the beer barrels they'd spent most of the morning hauling up the hill to the Henry – to see Robin lurching up the slope.

Robin collapsed beside him, letting out a mixed groan and sigh of relief. Two Bells rang out clearly across the arc of blue sky. Fitz caught himself wondering what lay beyond that perfect canopy. The moon, the sun and stars, he knew that. But what of the planets orbiting those distant suns? Were there people working and drinking and sleeping on their surfaces? An image of a landscape bloomed in Fitz's mind. A heat-hazed plain baking under two suns, one tiny and bright, the other like a giant bloodshot eye.

What was this? A dream? Or somewhere he'd been?

'Thank God that's over!' cried Robin. 'Nothing like working with a hangover, is there? Hell at first, but by lunchtime you've sweated out all the beer and are ready for some more!'

Fitz groaned. 'First the man takes a drink. Then the drink takes a drink. Then the drink takes the man.'

Robin ripped up a clod of grass and lobbed it on to Fitz's chest. 'You said that last week.'

Fitz brushed it off. 'Did I?'

'You're always saying it.'

Fitz sat up. He couldn't remember ever saying it. But perhaps it was something he said without realising. He leaned on one elbow and looked down at Robin. 'What are you going to do now we've paid off our debt? Still going to leave?'

Robin stirred restlessly. 'I don't know. I can't forget Aboetta. No amount of drinking's going to erase her from my mind.' His mouth twisted in a sneer. 'I can't stand the thought of her with him – with *Malahyde*.'

Fitz frowned. That name had a face. Timid eyes under a broad forehead and thinning blond hair. Hadn't there been some business recently about a cellar and a strange machine? 'My heart's still hammering away,' sighed Robin. 'Think I need to see a doctor.'

Doctor. That name had a face too. A long, serious face, brown hair flecked with grey. Piercing blue eyes which could switch from terrifying to terrified, from serious to quizzical in a blink.

Fitz sat up. His heart was hammering too now. 'Robin. Who's the Doctor?'

Robin shaded his eyes against the sun and peered at Fitz. 'What?'

'The Doctor. I know him! Long brown hair, fine clothes – he was here a few days ago, maybe even yesterday.' He put his head in his hands and groaned. 'Christ! Did I really drink that much last night?'

He heard Robin laugh. 'Don't worry Fitz, there's plenty more. Remember those barrels we spent all morning lugging up the hill? Well – they were full of beer!'

'No shit,' mumbled Fitz. He wasn't in the mood for jokes. 'I'm serious, Robin – this "Doctor" guy's important, I know it. And Malahyde.' He was beginning to remember more. 'He lives in that big mansion, on the other side of the Gorge.' He shook his head. 'I've got the strangest feeling that I've been there recently.' Another realisation. '*You* were there as well.'

Robin sat up too, facing Fitz. 'Course I was there!'

'Well, what the freaking hell were we doing there?'

Robin stared. 'You don't remember?'

'No!' Suddenly the sunny October day looked sinister, and somehow unreal. 'This is scary.'

'We went to get Aboetta back – remember? We got over the wall, past the guards, right into the mansion house!' He frowned. 'We found them together – Aboetta and Malahyde. Then he called the guards and had us chucked out.'

Fitz pressed his palms against his temples. 'No! That's not how it happened! The Doctor was there too – we – we went in the TARDIS!'

'What the bloody hell's a TARDIS?'

Fitz stared at Robin. 'I don't know.'

Robin shook his head. 'I think you've got a spot of sunstroke, mate.'

Fitz stood, gazing down at Robin. Another memory was forming. Another face, this time female. Looking at him in disapproval, shaking her head, but with a smile playing about her lips, just about to transform her expression into a friendly one.

'Anji!' cried Fitz.

He turned and ran up the hill.

In Year Nought, the Doctor and Isambard Kingdom Brunel were walking across Clifton Suspension Bridge.

'You're telling me that Jared Malahyde was possessed by an alien intelligence which forced him to construct an engine to accelerate time? Except – only a *part* of time was accelerated, for reasons which you cannot yet construe? And the reason that this alien intelligence gave Malahyde was just a ruse to gain his co-operation?'

'That's more or less it,' said the Doctor, gazing through the suspension rods at the river below, the city beyond. How many of its people had died because of the Cleansing?

'And the Malahyde process – which helped construct the very bridge we're walking across – was just a means to raise funding to build this engine?'

'That seems to be the case.'

'I've never heard such preposterous poppycock!' spluttered Brunel. 'Ridiculous!'

'You saw what was left of George,' said the Doctor. 'However ridiculous it sounds, it's the truth.'

Brunel puffed on a cigar. 'Then how is it that *we* haven't aged to death?'

'There must have been a safety zone around the Utopian Engine,' said the Doctor. 'Would be pretty useless if its operator got caught up in the effect, wouldn't it? That would be pretty shoddy engineering.'

Brunel stopped walking. 'I still don't believe it. Despite the evidence of my own eyes.'

'Try. Please try,' said the Doctor.

Brunel stared at him. 'And what is your part in this, Dr Smith?'

'My part?' The Doctor indicated himself. 'My part is to fix things.

Think of me as an engineer. A temporal engineer.'

Brunel's brows furrowed as he grappled with the concept. The nineteenth-century mind – even one such as Brunel's – was just not open to the idea of time as something that could be manipulated, perverted.

'If you are what you say you are, and this isn't some sort of protracted vivid dream, then this changes everything,' said Brunel softly. 'Everything I've understood about the way things work – it's just been scratching the surface.'

He looked desolate, so the Doctor patted him on the shoulder. 'Oh rather more than that, Isambard. Rather more than that. I can tell you now that your great ships and railways will change the world.'

'They were constructed using the Malahyde Process.' Brunel looked disgusted. 'Which you now tell me is a product of this alien intelligence.'

'But the design, the application, was yours!'

Brunel didn't answer.

They walked on in silence, crossing the bridge and going down into the town. There they began to see more evidence of the Cleansing. Carriages and carts lay overturned in the streets, horses lay like sacks of bones. The grass on the parkland below the Downs had withered to nothing, and the trees were barren of leaves, gnarled and grotesque. Human corpses were everywhere, in the same state as poor George. Brunel exclaimed in horror at the sight of the first, but then grew more and more withdrawn, silently puffing on his cigar, eyes wide as he took in the devastation.

As they passed a row of town houses, the Doctor heard a moan coming from the garden of a basement flat.

'What is that?' whispered Brunel.

The Doctor felt a cold sense of dread envelop him. 'Stay here.'

He walked down the steps. Crouching at the bottom was a naked woman who appeared to be in her forties. She looked up at the Doctor, her face distorted with terror.

The Doctor crouched down. 'Don't worry. I won't hurt you.'

The woman scrambled away from him, uttering hoarse, unintelligible gasps.

Brunel had walked down the steps and was staring at the woman. When he saw she was naked he looked away and coughed.

The Doctor took off his jacket and put it around her shoulders. 'Shh. What's your name?'

'Em – Emily,' said the woman, in a hoarse, slow voice, accenting every syllable.

The Doctor helped her up, noticing that her fingernails – those that hadn't broken off – were long and twisted, like bizarre seashells. And her hair was long, falling in black tresses almost to her feet.

'How old are you, Emily?'

The girl began to cry. 'My legs and arms – they *hurt*.'

The Doctor felt helpless. What could he do? There must be hundreds – thousands – of children like this, forced into adult bodies, their minds still young, innocent, untutored.

'Mr Brunel!' said Emily suddenly, her eyes widening.

'Emily?' said Brunel, bending to look at the child-woman.

'You know this girl?'

Brunel shook his head. 'No, I – Yes! Emily Riverston, the daughter of one of my associates, Charles, treasurer of the Great Western Steamship Company.' He stood up straight and gazed at the Doctor. 'But she's only four!'

The Doctor shook his head. 'Not any more.'

'I'm five in a week!' said Emily suddenly. Her voice was hoarse, the childish tones grotesque to hear. Then she began to cry again, sobbing into the sleeve of the Doctor's jacket.

Brunel looked down at her, ashen-faced. 'What can we do for her?'

'Nothing,' said the Doctor. 'You have to prepare yourself. This has happened all over the world – perhaps many worlds.'

But Brunel was having none of it. 'We must do *something*!'

'All right,' said the Doctor. 'We'll take her up into the house.'

Together they helped Emily up the steps. She could barely walk, and cried out at the cramps in her legs. Whilst Brunel supported her the Doctor broke open the door of the house.

Shielding her from the sight of the remains of its occupants, they took Emily to an upstairs bedroom. As Brunel talked soothingly to her, the Doctor found some clothes, dressed her, fetched her water. All the time she watched them both with wide brown eyes.

The Doctor made sure she drank some water, then she lay down on the bed.

The Doctor drew Brunel to the window. 'That's all we can do for her.'

Brunel stared at the recumbent child-woman. Tears were in his eyes. 'Mary.' He turned to the Doctor, his face contorted in agony. 'My wife... children...'

The Doctor didn't know what to say. 'I'm sorry,' he said, turning away and looking out of the window. He could hear Brunel trying to master his sobs. Emily woke and began to cry, so the Doctor went to her.

He took her hand in his. 'Shh. Shh.'

Brunel sat on the bed beside him. 'Henry-Marc is barely a year old.'

'There is something we can do,' said the Doctor gently.

Brunel appeared not to have heard him.

The Doctor cradled Emily's head in his lap. 'We can go back. Make sure Malahyde never builds the Engine in the first place.'

Still Brunel stared blankly at the wall.

'Will it save my family?' Brunel's voice had regained some of its edge.

The Doctor considered. 'Yes,' he said emphatically.

'And how do you propose we do this?'

'Travel back through time,' said the Doctor warily.

Brunel turned his head and glared at the Doctor. Then he lowered his gaze and sighed. 'I believe you, I suppose.' He sounded surprised at himself. He stood and gazed out of the window. 'The things I have seen today, preposterous though they are...'

The Doctor grinned. Despite everything, he felt a boyish excitement at the idea of showing Isambard Kingdom Brunel around the TARDIS. 'You're not through with preposterous sights yet, believe me.'

He turned back to Emily. 'We have to leave now.'

She began to whine and clutch at the Doctor's sleeve.

'Shhh, don't worry. Just wait here.' He didn't know what to say.

What would happen to her? Older children, who had worked out what happened, might find her. Or she might starve to death.

'Don't leave me, Mr Brunel!'

Brunel stared imploringly at the Doctor. 'Can't we take her with us?'

'No, we can't,' said the Doctor. 'Please, wait outside.'

Brunel looked as though he was going to argue, but then with an anguished glance at Emily he left the room.

The Doctor stood, Emily's fingers clinging to the lapels of his jacket.

'I'm going now,' he said.

Emily's eyes were unbearable to look at. 'Please,' she moaned.

Fighting down tears, the Doctor gently prised her hands away. 'Don't be afraid. You're going to be all right.' He sat her down on the bed. 'You're going to be fine. What were you doing just before – before it happened?'

'Pigeons,' sobbed Emily. 'I was with Nana and there were pigeons – they flew up.' Her face crumpled into a sob. 'Daddy won't – Nana said –'

The Doctor shushed her. 'Emily, will you do something for me?'

She nodded and sniffed.

'Lie down on the bed, now, and try to sleep. When you wake up you'll be chasing those silly pigeons again.'

To the Doctor's joy Emily smiled, very briefly.

Then she lay down on the bed, grabbing a pillow and hugging it to herself. She looked up at him one last time. 'Will I? You promise?'

The innocence of her manner touched the Doctor's hearts. Tears sprang into his eyes and he wiped them away, not wanting her to see them, wanting to give her strength. 'I promise.'

The Doctor walked over to her and smoothed her hair back from her face until she was fast asleep.

Then he crept slowly from the room.

When he looked back his face was impassive, but his eyes shone with determination.

'I'm going to make sure this *never* happens,' he whispered.

Chapter 21
Into The Eternium

Isambard Kingdom Brunel stood on the quayside, watching the Doctor with a shrewd, wary look. 'This is the "time engine" you spoke of?'

'Yes,' said the Doctor. 'This is the TARDIS.'

'Are you sure there's room for the both of us in there?'

From his tone the Doctor could tell that Brunel was humouring him. 'Humour me, and go inside.'

Brunel blew through his lips, shook his head, and stepped past the Doctor into the TARDIS.

The Doctor paused for a moment, just in time to hear Brunel's cry of astonishment, and then stepped in after him.

Brunel was walking slowly down the steps, head craning around to take everything in.

The Doctor stepped past him and walked to the console.

'This is – this is incredible!' spluttered Brunel. 'No, that's not the word,' he muttered. He lurched up to the Doctor, reached out and grabbed his arms. His eyes were wild, alight with curiosity, the burning need to know. 'The interior dimensions!' he shouted.

The Doctor gently disengaged himself, but couldn't help smiling. 'Impressed?'

'Impressed?' Brunel did a circuit of the console, and returned to where the Doctor was standing. He folded his arms. 'Now the shock has worn off, I am composed. I will prepare to be impressed when you tell me how it works.'

'Oh, I don't know,' said the Doctor with a casual shrug. 'It just does.'

'You don't *know*?' roared Brunel.

'Well, you see, I didn't build it.' He frowned. 'At least, I don't think so.'

Brunel stared at him. 'You mean to say you have no idea how it functions, or who constructed it?'

'I know how the tea-machine works.' The last thing the Doctor wanted right now was to get involved in a discussion of the workings of the TARDIS with Isambard Kingdom Brunel. Maybe when all this was over, but there were more pressing concerns. 'Would you like a cup of tea?'

'No I would not! I would like to examine this machine.' He turned to the console and began surveying the rows of switches and dials.

Pleased though the Doctor was that Brunel's mood had lifted, he wanted to get on with things. 'Believe me, if you studied the TARDIS for the rest of your life, you wouldn't begin to understand even the basic concepts. I mean no disrespect, but the TARDIS is simply beyond the scope of the nineteenth-century imagination.'

Brunel whirled round and drew himself up to his full height. 'I find your manner patronising – and insulting!'

The Doctor sighed. 'Listen, we have a job to do. Remember Emily?'

At once Brunel subsided. He took out a handkerchief and mopped his brow. 'Yes. Of course.'

'I need to know when you first met Malahyde. When did he come to you with his proposal for the Process?'

Brunel took out another cigar and lit it, deep in thought. 'It was over ten years ago, in 1831. After the riots. I can't remember the exact date, I was tired, I didn't pay much heed to the man. It was only when I had the proposals looked over that I began to take an interest.'

'We need to get to Malahyde before anyone saw those proposals. I'm pretty sure the Malahyde Process was the catalyst for the initial divergence of history...' He realised that Brunel was staring at him. 'What?'

'You're telling me that the past twelve years have been – the *wrong* history?'

'Ah.' The Doctor felt distinctly uncomfortable. 'In a manner of speaking.'

'And I am – an alternative?' Brunel's brow furrowed. 'What will happen to me if we stop this alternative history from coming into being?'

The Doctor was impressed with Brunel's grasp of the situation, and embarrassed about what he'd said about the nineteenth-century imagination. 'If we manage to restore the correct version of history, you won't know anything about it. You'll just return to 1843 and carry on as normal. Of course in the real history, things will be different. There will be no Malahyde Process. None of the innovations it facilitated will exist. The *SS Great Britain* will be launched today, not in 1838. The Suspension Bridge won't be built until after – er, a bit later. But you won't know a thing about it and you'll remember only the real history.'

Brunel frowned. 'Are you sure?'

'Isambard, you saw the Cleansing! That will cause a further, significant, devastating change in history! In fact you could say it's the end of the progress of the human race.' He pointed at the TARDIS console. 'I've seen the future, seen the people grubbing about for existence. Seen the twilight of humanity.'

Brunel raised his hands. 'Yes, yes, you've convinced me.'

'Good,' said the Doctor.

'So what do we do now?'

The Doctor moved to the console. 'We go back. To 1831.'

Brunel suddenly grabbed his arm. 'I've just remembered – I met him on the Downs one evening a week or so before the riots. Funnily enough, I can recall the exact date.'

The Doctor smiled grimly. 'A precise location, an exact date.' His fingers flew over the controls. 'Let's just hope we get to him before Watchlar does.'

It was a cold, clear evening on the Downs. Mist gathered in the bushes and trees lining Ladies' Mile. The sky stretched deep and blue-black above, peppered with stars. A few people were about: lovers, loners, poets. A solitary engineer, walking out his frustrations over his latest project. Hidden in the trees ten yards away was the TARDIS, in which another aspect of the same engineer brooded, trying to come to terms with the events of the last couple of relative hours.

It was the evening of 22 October 1831, and the Doctor was waiting for Malahyde. He'd ascertained from Brunel's recollections where on the Downs and what time in the evening his encounter with Malahyde had taken place, and had positioned himself by the low wall surmounted with railings which overlooked the Avon Gorge. He could just make out the river far below, between the dark forested shoulders of the Gorge. The bridge, at this point in time, had not been built, Brunel desperately trying to raise money for its construction.

This was the correct version of history. The real reality. And it would remain so, if the Doctor had anything to do with it.

Footsteps approached. The Doctor slipped into the shadows – there were plenty to choose from. Here came Malahyde, heading directly towards him. Almost looking straight at him. The Doctor tensed, ready to leap out and grab the unsuspecting poet. But there was a rustle in the bushes and a figure appeared. It was clearly Brunel, at this point in his life only twenty-five, the same age as Malahyde.

The Doctor heard Malahyde's cry of 'Evening, sir!' and Brunel's shout of alarm as he blundered into Malahyde. He heard them haltingly start up a conversation, and move nearer to the railings as Brunel indicated to Malahyde the expanse which he planned to bridge. They made an odd pair – though both short men, Brunel seemed taller on account of his top hat, which rose six inches clear of the crown of Malahyde's headwear.

Then they both walked off on to the Downs, Brunel pouring out his frustrations. The Doctor couldn't help smiling. Brunel didn't give a hoot who this chap Malahyde was – he just wanted a sounding-board.

Keeping far enough behind so they couldn't see or hear him, the

Doctor followed. He had to choose his moment carefully. If he interrupted too soon, and accidentally met Brunel, then the Brunel he met in 1843 (and who was now sipping tea in the TARDIS) might recognise him. And history was skewed enough already without introducing further paradoxes.

At last the two men parted, Brunel heading back towards the town, Malahyde loitering for a while, a thin, slight figure in his overcoat and hat, breath misting in the chill air.

The Doctor ran forward, just as Malahyde turned away and strode off into the night.

Now. It had to be now! 'Sir!' called the Doctor.

Malahyde stopped and turned round, alarmed.

The Doctor jogged up to him, assuming his most disarming grin. 'Jared Malahyde, I presume?'

Malahyde nodded. Even in the moonlight, the Doctor was struck by how much younger this Malahyde looked. His face was untouched by the lines of age, and he stood erect, not with the slight stooping posture of his older self.

'Who are you, sir?' he said. 'I came for a quiet walk, and find myself assailed by strangers!'

His voice went up and down. He was clearly afraid.

'Don't worry, I'm the Doctor, I'm here to help. You're in danger. You must come with me!'

Malahyde shook his head. 'I am off to my lodgings, sir, and I suggest you return to yours.' He turned and marched off, spinning round once more to shout, 'Don't follow me!'

The Doctor followed him. If he had to use force, he had to use force. Then Malahyde halted, as if struck, and collapsed to his knees. The Doctor ran to him. He was too late! It was already happening. A strange lenticular whorl was forming in the air above Malahyde, glowing green in the evening air.

Malahyde writhed on the damp grass. 'What's happening to me?'

'Trust me,' said the Doctor, and began to drag Malahyde away from the whorl. But he was immovable, as if pinned to the ground. The Doctor felt his arms stiffen and tense, as if being twisted by an unseen assailant.

He pulled away. He was too late – or was he?

He ran back towards the TARDIS.

The Doctor hurtled down the steps and dived on to the console.

Brunel was at his side in a trice. 'What's happening?'

'Malahyde's about to be abducted through a dimensional portal. To Watchlar's home dimension, I'd wager.'

'This is a time engine – why not simply go back a day, intercept him then?'

The Doctor locked the TARDIS on to the dimensional whorl. 'And so when Watchlar tries again, he'll latch on to someone else – maybe even the younger version of you that I just narrowly avoided meeting.'

Brunel stared at the Doctor. 'A younger version of me! Oh, the things I could tell him – me – if we met!'

'Don't even think about it, though clearly you already are,' said the Doctor. 'No, this is probably for the best – we can follow Malahyde through the whorl, deal with this Watchlar once and for all.' The Doctor hit the dematerialisation switch. Deep below, the TARDIS engines groaned, and the floor heaved beneath their feet. Brunel cried out and staggered backwards.

But in a surprisingly short time the TARDIS stabilised, and materialised. The Doctor operated the scanner. It showed a square room with glowing green walls – and Malahyde in a chair, looking back in amazement at the TARDIS.

'Malahyde!' said Brunel in hushed tones.

'I'm afraid I'm going to have to ask you to stay inside again,' said the Doctor. 'I'm not sure what's out there. It might be dangerous.'

'Then you'll need my help!'

'You can help by operating the door control,' said the Doctor.

Brunel looked truculent, but nodded assent.

The Doctor stepped from the TARDIS. Malahyde rose from the chair and stared at him. 'You!'

'Yes, me.' The Doctor went over to Malahyde, grabbed his arm and hauled him towards the TARDIS.

Just then three figures appeared. Three glowing humanoid figures with no faces. They looked like they were made of luminous glue, and the air crackled around them.

'Hello!' said the Doctor brightly, backing towards the open TARDIS doors. He ushered Malahyde inside. 'Which one of you calls itself Watchlar?'

The three figures raised their arms as one, and arcs of energy lanced into the Doctor.

The Doctor felt the energy pour through him, making his hearts stutter erratically in his chest, his skin prickle as if a million syringes were worrying their way into his skin.

An alien voice crackled in his mind.

You are not human. You have a time machine. You can help us. The Eternium is dying.

'All right! Stop hurting me and I'll help you!'

The pain stopped. The Doctor turned to face the three beings.

You will help us. We are dying. We need energy.

'Yes, well, death comes to us all. What exactly is the Eternium? And what are you? You're not the descendants of the human race, are you?'

The beings hovered before the Doctor, their forms melting and changing until they became three spheres.

We are Eternines.

'And what's an Eternine when it's at home?'

You ask too many questions. We have decided. It would be easier to possess YOU.

They surged as one towards him.

'Not today, thank you!' He twisted round and hurled himself inside the TARDIS.

'Door!' he yelled, dodging the blast of energy the Eternines hurled at him.

Brunel obeyed and the doors closed behind the Doctor. He stood, back against them, at the top of the short flight of steps which led down into the console room.

Malahyde was standing by the console, his hat in his hands, like a nervous dinner party guest.

He was staring at Brunel.

Brunel glared back at him. 'You! You caused – you killed –' He lunged at Malahyde.

The Doctor ran down the steps. 'Listen, he hasn't built it yet! This is the younger Malahyde, remember?'

Brunel's expression cleared, and he backed away.

Malahyde's eyes were wide with fear. 'I have just met you, on the Downs, before...' he shook his head. 'You look different somehow, older.'

Brunel blinked. 'And you look as I did when we first met.'

Malahyde frowned in confusion. 'What do you mean?'

The Doctor stepped quickly up to them. 'Ah. You two really, *really* shouldn't be here at the same time.' He turned to Malahyde, speaking soothingly. 'You'll have seen much that you can't understand. But don't worry, you're safe now.'

'And now that we have young Malahyde, presumably history is safe?' said Brunel, looking at the Doctor for confirmation.

'Theoretically,' said the Doctor. 'But I don't like to count my chickens before they're hatched.'

'I still remember my history,' asserted Brunel. 'The Malahyde Pro–'

'Tea!' cried the Doctor, with a warning glance at Brunel. 'Let's have some tea.'

Malahyde nodded towards the door. 'What about the Eternines?'

The Doctor waved a hand dismissively. 'Oh, they won't be able to break in here. But just to be on the safe side...' He moved to the console, flicked some switches. 'There. We're now moving forwards through time, destination 2003.'

Isambard Kingdom Brunel, engineer, and Jared Malahyde, poet, stared open-mouthed at the Doctor.

'Don't worry,' he said. 'I'll drop you off in your own times. Eventually. Now, how about that tea?'

Isambard Kingdom Brunel sipped his tea, and raised his eyebrows appreciatively.

'Chinese green tea,' said the Doctor. 'Yuan Dynasty. My favourite period.'

Brunel looked astonished, then recovered. 'Well, this is a time machine – I should try harder not to be surprised.'

Malahyde hadn't touched his cup. He was still in a state of shock, not taking things in his stride as Brunel had done. 'I can't shake the thought of what the Eternines told me, that I had to build a machine to save the human race from descending into savagery and ignorance.'

'That was just a cover story, to convince you to co-operate. The Eternium isn't in the future, neither are its occupants your distant descendants.'

'Then what and where is it?' asked Brunel.

'As far as the TARDIS instruments can tell, the Eternium is a pocket universe, contemporaneous with but much, much smaller than our own. And on the brink of death.'

'So what was it they really wanted? What was – would have been – the purpose of the machine I was meant to construct?'

'I don't know,' said the Doctor, taking a sip of tea, remembering his brief examination of the Utopian Engine. 'It appears to be some sort of time manipulator. But why the Eternines wanted it constructed in our universe, I don't know. Did they mean to cause the Cleansing? That can't be it.'

'If they did, they deserve to die,' said Brunel.

'Anyway, whatever it was the Eternines planned, we've stopped them,' said the Doctor. 'Saved the universe. Again.' He took another sip of tea.

'Again!' cried Brunel. 'This is not the first time?'

The Doctor shook his head. 'And probably not the last.'

Brunel stared at him incredulously. 'I should like to know who you are and where you are from, Doctor – only, if you are correct, when history is restored I won't remember!'

Then there came an insistent bleeping from the console.

The Doctor put down his cup. 'We've arrived.' He dashed over. His hearts skipped a beat when he saw that the yearometer read '2003'.

He operated the scanner.

'Oh, no,' he breathed, thumping the console. 'I should have realised!'

Brunel and Malahyde came over to the console.

'What's the matter?' asked Brunel.

The scanner showed a dark vista which was hard to make out. Was that glowing mass an ocean? Was that a shore?

'We can travel in time – but only in *this* universe!'

Malahyde blinked. 'But surely, how I got here...'

'The TARDIS followed you through a transient dimensional portal. It can't pass between universes on its own. Short of going back and asking the Eternines for help, we're stuck here. We're trapped in the Eternium – a universe on the point of death!'

Chapter 22
Between Universes

Fitz ran, despite his aching legs and burning throat. He ran past Totterdown Gate and the Three Lamps Tower, not caring if anyone saw him. He kept going, across the open ground before the gate, and through the lanes between the cottages on the other side. Here the ground fell away steeply, and was terraced with the houses of the citizens who worked on Windmill Hill. At the bottom, a wide road ran back up towards the church and the Henry. Fitz stumbled across the road, and began dragging himself up the grassy slope of Windmill Hill.

Children playing nearby jeered. Two members of the Watch, coming off shift, tried to accost him. He ignored them all.

Fitz stopped beside the nearest windmill, unable to draw breath He slumped down on to the grass. What was wrong with him? Had he drunk so much that it had totally wiped his memory? He stared down the hill, at the reassuring line of the Wall. A Watchkeeper was shouting to him. Fitz couldn't quite catch the words – something about reporting for duty.

He tried to remember. The first thing he could recall was waking up that morning with the mother of all hangovers. Other memories – of Malahyde, the cellar, the Doctor, Anji – were clear, but didn't connect to anything. And the TARDIS – Fitz could see it in his mind as clearly as the windmill. A tall, rectangular blue box, with little square windows and a flashing light on top.

What did it all mean?

He sat for some time pondering. Then he saw Morgan Foster approaching, puffing slowly but surely up the slope. Even from this distance, Fitz could tell that the Chief Elder meant business. He stood, brushing the grass from his rough canvas trousers, tucking in his sweat-stained shirt.

Morgan stopped before him, wheezing slightly. 'Watchkeeper Kreiner, I know all about your session with former Watchkeeper Larkspar. I don't approve. Nor do I approve of your aiding him in his sortie to Ashton Court.' He sighed. 'But I'm willing to give you one last chance.'

'Why?' said Fitz. He didn't relish the thought of being a Watchkeeper. In fact he'd forgotten he was one until reminded of the fact just now. 'Why not sack me as well? Drunkenness, dereliction of duty – you name it.'

Morgan shook his head sadly. 'You should know why I'm giving you this chance.' There was a slight edge of offence in the old man's tone.

'Should I?'

Morgan put his arm around him.

'I don't know what game you're playing, lad. You're obviously going through something. But you know you can always talk to me.'

'I – I feel I have no place here,' said Fitz. 'That I don't belong here.'

'I understand. But there's no reason to feel that.'

Why did he say that?

– He was an orphan. His mother came to Totterdown thirty-four years ago with baby Fitz in her arms. Both ill – fever. Mother died, baby lived. Brought up by Morgan and Anne Foster. Rough games with the other kids in the mud by the river. A best friend – Robin. Lessons in the school. Father Cluny teaching about the Cleansing and how not to speak of it. Robin and Fitz sniggering together, Robin and Fitz standing up to the bullies. Apprenticeship to George the Forge. His first foray outside the settlement – a boat trip to Gloucester, the excitement and wonder of seeing new places, new faces. Joining the Watch. The long hours on the Wall, alert for outlaws or Wildren. Getting drunk for the first time with

Robin. Rose, his first girl, who died of the fever just like his mother (and perhaps that was why he was so messed up) –

Fitz staggered as the memories hit him. He leaned on Morgan for support.

'Are you all right, lad?'

All Fitz could do was nod dumbly.

They began to walk down the hill. By the time they reached the bottom Fitz had remembered his whole life. Why had he run off like that? Something to do with – the Doctor? And An – Angela? And something called the Tar – tardy? Fitz shook his head, and even those fragments vanished.

'You'll be all right, lad. Best get along and report for duty.'

Fitz smiled. 'Thanks, Morgan.' He felt as though a weight had been lifted from him. Must have been all that beer last night after all. He knew who he was now.

Watchkeeper Kreiner set off to report for duty.

Anji was on an endless plain, a searing sun high in the sky above. She was only wearing a sari and her feet were bare. The sand beneath them was icy cold – which didn't seem to fit. Why was her body so warm, her feet so cold? She began to walk, then run, towards a wooden shack a hundred yards away, its planks bleached white in the heat. But however fast she ran, her feet wouldn't warm up. They were like little blocks of ice.

A man emerged from the shack, a man with a mane of dark hair and a pale face. He had his hands in the pockets of his coat – no, he had them tucked in the pockets of his waistcoat.

She came to a breathless halt in front of him. It was Fitz! Anji folded her arms across her chest, aware of how visible she must be under the sari. But no, it was the Doctor! And he wasn't paying any attention to her near-nakedness.

'Anji.' The Doctor's voice came from all around her. He laughed. He took her hands. 'Anji, Anji, Anji!' They danced around together, spinning on the sand, their feet – his in his brown shoes, hers *so cold* – kicking up a storm of orange dust.

The Doctor laughed again. 'You're going to die!' he shouted joyously.

Now the cold was creeping up her legs, as if she were sinking slowly into a barrel of ice-cold water. But the sun was so hot! And from somewhere a gale pounced, blasting the Doctor's hair back and hurling sand into Anji's eyes, so that she couldn't make out his face.

Anji let go of the Doctor's hand and wiped the sand from her eyes. When she looked at the man again, he was Fitz.

'What's going on?' cried Anji above the roaring wind. The sand was getting into her throat now and she could hardly breathe.

'You're going to die!' shouted Fitz in her ear. He wasn't laughing. He looked so serious. Then he held her tightly to him and said, 'I guess now is the time to tell you that I –'

Anji woke with a start, eyes opening to darkness, lungs gasping for air. It was dark and she was so cold – where was she?

Then she remembered – the phosphorescent sea, the cliff-face, the cave, this silent, dead world.

Silent?

She sat up, straining against Gottlieb – his arms were still around her – towards the entrance of the cave. A roaring sound was coming from somewhere outside, its cadences bouncing off the walls of the V-shaped cave, funnelling down to where she and Gottlieb lay. A bluish-white light flooded the black sand.

Anji squirmed away from Gottlieb – he was asleep, that or dead – and propelled herself on freezing, wobbling legs towards the cave entrance.

She couldn't believe what she saw, barely a stone's throw away. A tall, rectangular shape, illuminated by a bluish-white light on its top, which dimmed even as she looked at it.

Was she still dreaming? Anji staggered to her feet, praying for it not to dematerialise – if it did, she thought, she wouldn't be able to bear it, she would simply run into the ocean and drown.

But it remained there, its light extinguished now, its solid, reassuring shape merging into the darkness around it. Anji shoved herself forwards, the breath screaming in and out of her lungs, arms reaching out in front of her. She reached the TARDIS and hung on to it, gathering her breath. Then she began to beat on its doors. She couldn't yell, there wasn't enough breath in her body.

Exhausted, she slumped to her knees, against the TARDIS doors. They moved. Anji felt arms around her, lifting her up, and then she passed out.

When Anji came round she found herself sitting in one of the Doctor's Regency chairs, a pot of tea on a small table in front of her. Opposite her sat the Doctor, watching her with a look of grave concern.

The Doctor smiled. 'Welcome back, Anji.'

Anji put a hand to her chest. She was breathing normally, she was warm, she was safe. 'How did you find me?'

'I didn't,' said the Doctor. 'It must have been the TARDIS.'

He got up from his chair and came over to her, helping her to her feet. She stood, her legs feeling weak, letting the Doctor support her.

He looked into her eyes. 'Are you all right?'

Anji nodded. 'Fine. Ravenous, but fine.'

The Doctor hugged her. 'I thought you were dead.'

She hugged him back. It was so good to see him again.

'I'll get you something to eat,' said the Doctor, and let her go. She sat again as the Doctor went over to the TARDIS's refrigerator, a giant, bulky 1950s-type thing, sky-blue with enormous chrome handles.

'Pies and pasties, pasties and pies,' muttered the Doctor. 'Aha!' He took out a packet and thrust it at Anji. 'Scotch eggs.'

Anji grimaced. 'That all there is?'

The Doctor shrugged. 'Haven't had the chance to do any shopping of late.'

Anji took the plastic-wrapped snack, automatically looking for the sell-by date. She was amazed at how normal she was feeling, how quickly she'd recovered. The air seemed to tingle around her – perhaps the TARDIS had recuperative qualities. Then she remembered. 'Gottlieb!'

'He's here too?' said the Doctor.

'In a cave – not far away. If he's still alive.'

The Doctor grabbed a torch and headed out of the TARDIS.

Then Anji realised she wasn't alone. Standing by the console was a slim young man in a dark-brown suit that looked rather old fashioned. There was something familiar about him. Then she realised. 'Malahyde! What are you doing here?'

'Hardly believing any of this,' he said.

'Don't worry, it took me ages to get used to it. Scotch egg?'

He looked at the rust-coloured ball of sausage-meat and egg as if it was a dead rat.

'It's all there is.' Anji frowned. Malahyde looked so much younger – but how? Then it clicked. The Doctor must have been busy. Obviously time-snatched Malahyde before he could build the Utopian Engine. She let out a long, sighing breath. So reality – her reality – was safe. Hurrah for that.

Anji looked round the console room. There was something missing – or rather someone. 'Have you seen Fitz?'

Malahyde frowned. 'Fitz?'

'Tallish chap, looks like the Doctor's younger, scruffier, shiftier brother.'

Malahyde shook his head. 'There's no one here but the Doctor, myself and you, Miss Kapoor,' he said shyly. 'And Isambard Brunel.'

'What?' Anji looked round. 'Where?'

A man strutted out from the library. A short man in crumpled clothes, with a tall top hat, an imperious gaze and alert, intelligent eyes. He was smoking a cigar.

Anji suddenly felt faint. What the heck had the Doctor been up to?

'Here!' said Brunel. 'I must say, the Doctor keeps an incredibly well-stocked library.'

Anji glanced over to the shelves. That was odd – many of them looked empty. Perhaps the Doctor was having a spring clean.

Anji felt she had to be polite to such an important figure. 'Pleased to meet you,' she said, and extended a hand. 'Anji Kapoor.'

He took it and kissed it, his eyes fixed on hers. 'Pleasure to make your acquaintance, my dear.'

She took her hand away. On top of everything else, being chatted up by someone straight out of the history books would be too much.

Brunel seemed to remember himself, and coughed. 'And do you live here, inside this machine?'

Anji nodded. 'Yep. This is home.'

Brunel stared intently at her. 'Don't suppose *you* know how it works?'

'You'll have to ask the Doctor about that.'

Brunel frowned, and took a puff on his cigar. 'I already have, Miss Kapoor. I already have.' Then he wandered off, peering into the corners of the console room.

Then Anji remembered Fitz – or rather his absence. Perhaps he was in his room, sulking. He'd been unsure about the Doctor's plan to restore reality – perhaps they'd had an argument. Muttering an apology to Malahyde she ran from the console room.

But Fitz's room was empty. She picked up his guitar. One of the strings was broken. Perhaps he was dead. Perhaps the Doctor was sparing her the news for now. She ran back to the console room, in time to witness Brunel helping the Doctor carry the unconscious Gottlieb across the room and into one of the Regency chairs, whilst Malahyde hovered uselessly nearby.

'Where's Fitz?'

The Doctor was examining Gottlieb's eyeballs. 'I don't know. He stayed in Year 160 whilst I went back and restored the correct version of history.'

Anji sat down. 'Why did you let him stay?'

'It was his choice, or so I thought at the time. Anji, he was beginning to naturalise to the wrong reality. The Time Vortex was rewriting his biodata in an attempt to save itself. If I'd stayed any longer it would have happened to me – and the TARDIS.'

Gottlieb shifted and moaned.

Anji fought down the impulse to yell at the Doctor, to rail at him for not saving Fitz. But she knew that he would have tried everything to save his friend. She looked at the scanner – it showed the wiggling green line of the luminous shore receding into black oblivion.

'So where are we?'

It was Brunel who answered. 'A pocket universe. A dying pocket universe. Its inhabitants – Eternines, they call themselves – abducted young Malahyde, so they could use him to build their Engine in our universe! For purposes unknown as yet.'

'They told me they were going to save the human race,' said Malahyde. 'The Doctor tells me they were lying.' A smile writhed across his face. 'And this morning the worst of my problems was my poetry.'

'Believe me, that will still be your problem after all this is over. Aha!' cried the Doctor.

Gottlieb had opened his eyes. 'Where am I? Doctor? Anji!' A weary smile formed on his lips and faded just as quickly. The Doctor put a glass of water in his hand and the priest drank gratefully.

'He's going to want explanations soon,' muttered the Doctor. 'It's been quite a day for those.' He walked over to the console.

'Doctor, if you've restored the correct version of reality, why aren't we, well, *in* it?'

The Doctor sighed and leaned on the console. 'Because we're trapped here. I followed Malahyde through a trans-dimensional whorl created by the Eternines. And it's unlikely that they'll have the slightest inclination to help us.'

'You could always ask.'

The Doctor shook his head. 'I barely managed to get away from them. If I go back, they'll most likely enslave me, use me in the way they used – intended to use – young Malahyde here.' The Doctor grimaced. 'They might even get control of the TARDIS.'

'They might even be able to tell you how it works,' said Brunel sarcastically.

The Doctor ignored him.

Anji folded her arms. They'd won, apparently, but at a heavy price. 'So Fitz is dead, and we're trapped here, but the Time Vortex is safe.'

'That depends on how many other alternative realities have sprung into existence,' said the Doctor darkly. 'How many other history-distorting events have occurred, how many other versions of Earth there are.'

Anji remembered Fitz's words about forever going around stamping out false realities. 'But we've got rid of this one?'

'The only way of finding out for sure is by returning to our universe.'

'And we can't.'

'Not without something to fix on. Ah!' He broke into a smile and grabbed Anji's shoulders. 'Anji, *you* are the answer!'

'What do you mean?'

'Your biodata – the TARDIS could track it!' He frowned. 'It'd mean linking you to the TARDIS, but I'm sure you'll come to no harm.' He darted off out of the console room.

Anji went over to Gottlieb, who was staring about himself with a look of wonder. 'What is this place?'

'The Doctor's TARDIS – I told you about it in the cave, remember?'

'So we are safe?'

Anji considered. 'Yes. For now.'

The Doctor returned, carrying with him a disturbingly surgical-looking device consisting of a series of grey tubes connected to a central brass hub about the size of a tennis ball. He plugged one of the tubes into an aperture on the TARDIS console. Anji noticed with a qualm that several of them ended in needles.

'Bring one of those chairs over,' he called.

Malahyde and Brunel began dragging one of the heavy chairs towards the console, the latter still managing to keep his cigar going. Then Brunel stood back, watching the proceedings with keen interest.

Anji felt uneasy. 'What are you going to do?'

'Anji, you want to get home?'

'Of course.'

'Well, our only chance is for the TARDIS to track your biodata. This means you have to become physically linked to the TARDIS through this device.'

Anji barely remembered the little that Fitz had told her about biodata, and wished she'd bothered to find out more. 'Won't a blood sample be enough?'

'Normally,' said the Doctor. 'If we were trying to locate you, a sample of your blood would be sufficient. But we're trying to trace your biodata across realities. The TARDIS is going to need something more to work on.'

Those needles looked terrifyingly sharp, and the prospect of being linked to the TARDIS was somewhere past terrifying. But Anji trusted the Doctor.

She sat in the chair, shrugged off her jacket and rolled up her sleeve. 'If it's our only chance?'

The Doctor nodded. 'It is.' He produced a bottle of surgical spirit and some cotton wool from a pocket and began to clean one of the needles. When he was done Anji laid her arm on the polished wooden edge of the console. The Doctor dabbed her forearm with surgical spirit. Anji closed her eyes and gritted her teeth, but it didn't hurt when the Doctor slid the needle into her flesh. When she opened them again, it was to see the hair-thin needle in her arm, and the grey tube snaking from it between the switches and dials of the console towards the device which squatted against the central column. She felt queasy, uneasy, but no more so than she would at the dentist's.

All was quiet, apart from the background hum of the TARDIS and the ticking of the brass device. The Doctor was beside her, intent on the console, his face in profile serious and absorbed. Brunel was standing next to him, closely watching his every movement. Beyond him, Anji could see Gottlieb and Malahyde in a huddle over by the tea-things, both wearing expressions of the utmost confusion. Of course: Gottlieb would be expecting Malahyde to recognise him, at the same time wondering why he looked so much younger. And Malahyde would have no idea who this guy was with the silver cross round his neck. Anji found herself smiling, despite the circumstances.

And that was odd. Here she was, linked with the TARDIS – which was a big, scary, alien machine that not even the Doctor pretended to understand. And all she could feel was a slight tingling in her arm. But suddenly came a sensation of falling, like that shuddering start you feel when you think you're about to fall asleep but jolt awake with a hammering heart.

She gasped and gripped the arm of the chair.

The Doctor glanced down at her. 'All right?'

The sensation faded. 'Yes,' breathed Anji.

A tense minute passed, but nothing seemed to happen. The central column revolved in its tubular glass casing like a hound questing for a scent. Suddenly it stopped with a halting electronic judder.

The Doctor stepped back from the console, as if stung. 'Oh, no,' he said softly.

'Doctor, what's happened? Has the experiment failed?' said Brunel.

The Doctor leaned over Anji and slid the needle from her arm.

'The TARDIS can't find your biodata, in all of time and space. Except here, in you.'

Anji stood and rubbed her arm. 'So what does that mean?' The look on his face scared her and she giggled nervously. 'I don't exist?'

The Doctor didn't answer. Instead he called for Gottlieb to come over.

Anji could tell from his eyes that there was a lot going on behind them.

Gottlieb looked apprehensive. 'Yes, Doctor?'

'Would you please take a seat?'

Gottlieb sat, looking at the needle the Doctor was cleaning. 'What are you going to do?'

The Doctor glanced at Anji, and at Malahyde, who had come to stand beside her. Anji could tell from the hunted look on his face that he was about to lie.

'A simple medical procedure. You may have been infected by alien bacteria – you saw Anji go through the process, and she's fine now.'

Brunel looked at the Doctor in surprise. The Doctor gave a minute shake of his head.

Gottlieb obediently rolled up his sleeve and the Doctor applied the needle.

'I think I understand what is happening,' said Gottlieb. 'You, Doctor, have erased the world that I know. Have prevented the Cleansing!'

A look of anguish passed briefly over the Doctor's face. 'Yes.'

'For that, I thank you,' said Gottlieb. 'I have read of the time before

Year Nought, and often dreamed of what the world would be like if the Cleansing had never happened. And now I am going to see it!'

'Well, I am from the world before Year Nought, as you call it,' said Brunel. 'You, sir, are in for quite an experience!'

'I hope,' muttered the Doctor, hunched over the console.

The central column began to spin round slowly.

'What – what is happening to me?' Gottlieb began to rise from his seat but the Doctor shoved him roughly back down.

'Stay there!'

Anji stepped towards the console, wanting to help Gottlieb. What was happening?

Suddenly Gottlieb's back arched and he screamed. The needle slipped from his arm. The Doctor pushed Gottlieb down in the chair and stabbed the needle back into place, drawing blood.

Brunel swore and dragged the Doctor away. The Doctor wrested himself free.

Gottlieb yelled.

Anji began to yell too.

Gottlieb's screams merged with the surging roar of the TARDIS engines. The floor began to shake.

Anji stumbled over to Gottlieb but the Doctor barred her way. 'No! This is the *only* way out of here!'

The engine noise rose to a crescendo, and then stopped. The TARDIS stopped shaking. Gottlieb slumped back in the chair, apparently unconscious.

Malahyde picked himself up from where he'd fallen.

The Doctor leaned over the console, his face pale. 'We've made it. Thanks to Gottlieb, we're back in our home universe. But why did it work with him and not you?'

Anji crouched down by Gottlieb's chair. It didn't look like he was breathing. She felt for a pulse, couldn't find one.

The Doctor operated the scanner.

Anji looked up. It showed a gate flanked by two Watchtowers. A familiar-looking wall under a white sky. Simple stone and wood buildings, thin people in rough clothes fleeing from the site of the TARDIS's materialisation.

Anji blinked. 'That's –'

'Totterdown, Year 160.' The Doctor's face crumpled. 'That's why it worked with Gottlieb. I've failed.'

Brunel was staring at the scanner. 'This is the future? Why, it looks like some outcrop of Bristol, in my day!'

Anji let go of Gottlieb's wrist. There was definitely no pulse. She put her fingers to his lips. No sign of a breath.

Anji stood up, and looked at the Doctor. 'He's dead, Doctor.'

The Doctor glanced down briefly at the dead man, and then looked away, closing his eyes. His voice was barely audible. 'I'm sorry.'

Anji looked at the screen, then back at the Doctor.

She didn't want to say this. But she had to. 'And he died for nothing.'

Chapter 23
A Matter of Memory

From his vantage point in the Three Lamps Tower, Watchkeeper Kreiner could see the ruins of Bristol spread out before him, a wasteland of crumbling buildings. On the nearest structures ivy had taken hold, as if wanting to haul the stone back into the ground. Beyond, a few church spires still stood, though no worship went on beneath them. From his lofty position Watchkeeper Kreiner could make out the contours of the hills beyond the ruined city.

The cold autumn wind blew through his hair and ruffled his clothes and he turned away from the stiff breeze, looking out westwards where the windmills turned serenely behind the safe confines of the Wall, which stretched in a rust-coloured line all around the settlement. Above everything, the sky was golden-white, a perfect October day.

His reverie was abruptly broken by a noise from the settlement behind him, from the open area in front of Totterdown Gate. A sound like a muted clap of thunder, followed by an immense roaring bellow, the like of which Watchkeeper Kreiner had never heard before.

He swung round, rifle at the ready.

People were shouting and scattering away from the centre of the square, in which a tall blue hut had appeared out of nowhere. It had panelled doors and square windows and was topped by a blue-white light which pulsed in time with the roaring sound. 'The TARDIS!' said Watchkeeper Kreiner. 'That's the TARDIS!' He didn't know how he knew this – he just did.

He also knew that he had to get to it. That meant leaving his post – but he didn't care. This TARDIS meant something – he had to find out what.

Watchkeeper Kreiner clambered down the spiral wooden steps of Three Lamps Tower and ran across the square, ignoring the shouts of his fellow Watchkeeper from the other tower.

'TARDIS!' he yelled, throwing his rifle into the grit and dust.

'Not for nothing. We've at least escaped from the Eternium.'

'So what?' Anji waved a hand at the screen. 'We're back here.'

The Doctor shook his head, but he wasn't denying Anji's words. She could see the disbelief in his eyes as he looked up at the screen.

Malahyde wandered over to join them, eyes wide as he took in the sight of Gottlieb's corpse, lolling in the chair like a forgotten toy.

The young poet's voice trembled and his fingers plucked nervously at his lapels. 'Would you mind telling me what's going on?'

The Doctor whirled round and put his hands to Malahyde's face, palms against his cheeks. 'You're *here*, you're *safe*, you never merged with Watchlar, never built the Utopian Engine! So why – that?' He shot a fist towards the screen.

'Could it be your fault, Doctor?' said Brunel threateningly. 'You told me you are a time-engineer. You also told me that you do not know how this "TARDIS" works. Even I have learned, with age, not to be so reckless!'

The Doctor said nothing. He stalked off to the library, where he stood with his back to them.

Anji had never seen him like this. She walked up behind him and touched his shoulder.

He jumped, then visibly relaxed.

Anji's mouth was dry. 'It's because Gottlieb's from this reality. Isn't it? His biodata exists here – that's why we've ended up back here.'

The Doctor didn't say anything.

'The real reality's out there somewhere,' she said. 'It has to be. We could try to locate my biodata again – you know what the TARDIS is like, perhaps it missed it the first time round.'

More silence.

'Doctor?'

He turned to face her. He looked calmer, more composed, but there was fear in his eyes. 'It's impossible. Impossible.' Then he walked away and began to tidy up the tea things.

How could he bother with such triviality at a time like this? Was there nothing they could do but tidy away what they could and wait meekly for the End?

She walked back to the console, where Malahyde was hovering.

'Where are we?'

'Somewhere we shouldn't be. Somewhere that shouldn't be.'

Her gaze roved from Malahyde's confused face to the screen. Someone was approaching – a Watchkeeper, judging by the chain-mail tunic and metal helmet. The figure marched up to the TARDIS, shouting and waving his arms.

Anji stared. 'Doctor! Doctor, it's Fitz!'

A clatter of crockery and the Doctor was at the console, operating the door control, hope in his eyes.

The TARDIS doors swung inwards and Fitz stepped inside.

Everyone turned to stare at him.

'It's bigger on the inside than it is on the... but I knew that already.' Fitz's face crumpled, as if he were about to cry. 'What's happening to me?'

The Doctor approached him. 'Welcome home, Fitz.'

Fitz backed away. 'This isn't home.'

'This *is* your home, try to remember!' implored the Doctor.

Fitz shook his head. 'Home's...' he caught sight of the image on the scanner. He pointed. 'There!'

Anji shivered. This looked like Fitz, but there was a stranger behind his eyes. And his clothes – chain-mail tunic, rough trousers, boots that looked as though they were made of a combination of tree-bark and reeds – weren't him at all. 'You remember me, don't you?'

Fitz stared at her. 'I remember you, and the Doctor. And this place. But I don't know *why* I remember.'

'What's wrong with him?' said Anji.

'Not now,' said the Doctor, glancing at the library.

Anji noticed again that most of its shelves were empty, and understood. Somehow both Fitz and the TARDIS were becoming part of this reality.

'Fitz,' said the Doctor. 'Try to remember who you are. You recognise this man, surely?' He pointed to Brunel.

Fitz shook his head. 'No. Should I?'

'Well, yes!' said the Doctor. 'He's Isambard Kingdom Brunel!'

Brunel frowned at the Doctor.

'So?' said Fitz. 'Who's he?'

'The man who built the modern world!' The Doctor grinned maniacally at Brunel.

Brunel stared back at him. 'I can't take all the credit, man! Most of it, maybe.'

'Who's the other chap?' Fitz nodded at Malahyde.

'The man who destroyed the modern world. Or at least, would destroy, if – well, never mind about that now! You must remember Brunel, Fitz? The Clifton Suspension Bridge, the *SS Great Britain*, the Thames Tunnel? The Tamar bridge, the Great Western Railway – Paddington Station! You must know Paddington Station?'

'Paddington...' murmured Fitz. 'I've heard that name before.' He put his hands over his face. 'What's happening to me?'

The Doctor swung round. 'Anji. Take him to his room.'

Anji was shocked at the harshness in his voice. 'What, shove him out of the way? He needs our help!'

'His room,' said the Doctor, pointing towards the residential quarters. 'It might help him remember.'

'That's a point.' She went up to Fitz, gently took his hand. 'Come with me.'

Fitz regarded her with wide eyes. 'I – I just want to be alone. Need time to work all this out.'

Anji smiled. 'Well, come on then.'

The Doctor stood aside to let them pass and Anji led Fitz out of the console room and along the roundelled corridor. He stared around in amazement. 'How big is this place?'

'Not sure,' said Anji, watching him carefully. 'Look, don't try to think about it. Just accept it.'

He stopped. 'I – I must get back to my post.'

Anji grabbed his arm. 'No, Fitz, your place is here, with us.'

He stared at her. 'Somehow I *know* it is.' He frowned deeply. 'But I am a Watchkeeper, I have duties.' He turned to look back along the corridor.

Anji squeezed his arm. 'Come with me. You'll be all right once you're in your room.'

They began walking again.

'If this is my home, though I don't remember it, were you my woman?'

'What?'

His face was serious. *He* was serious.

'If it will help you to remember, no.' Luckily they had reached his room by now. 'Well this is it, your room, your bed, your guitar. All your things.'

Fitz stepped over the threshold, nodding his head and murmuring. 'Yes, this is familiar.'

'Just stay here for now,' said Anji.

'You're going?'

'I've got to have a little chat with the Doctor.'

Anji found the Doctor deep in discussion with Brunel. They were both hunched over the console, the Doctor talking animatedly, gesturing at the central column. Malahyde looked up over a cup as she entered; a fresh pot of tea had been brewed. Good sign.

Or was it?

Gottlieb had been pushed, chair and all, back into the library.

'Doctor. We need to talk.'

'Not now, Anji.'

She interposed herself between Brunel and the Doctor.

Brunel sighed and muttered.

The Doctor glared at her. 'Anji! There's no need to be like this.'

'Like what? Angry?' She tried to force herself to be calm – couldn't. She pointed to Gottlieb. 'A man has just died. Fitz has gone nuts. And you don't seem to care!'

'Anji, there's too much at stake! We can't remain here for too long.'

'Why?'

'Because what happened to Fitz will happen to us. If we stay for much longer, we'll suffer the same fate. Even the TARDIS.'

Anji couldn't imagine it happening to her. More than her biodata would have to change for her to fit in to this reality.

'And then there's our engineer friend,' said the Doctor, indicating Brunel, who had wandered a little way around the console. 'He's not of this time. Things are getting out of hand and I have to do something about it.'

The Doctor began flicking switches, setting co-ordinates.

Anji grabbed his arm. 'Wait – we can't go, not yet!'

The Doctor sighed, ran a hand through his hair. 'You heard what I just said.'

She pointed to Gottlieb. 'We've got to make sure he gets a decent burial.'

'Anji, there isn't time!'

'He saved us from being trapped in a dying universe!' said Anji hotly. 'We owe him.'

The Doctor shook his head. 'We owe our responsibilities more.'

'I can't believe you're saying this! What happened to the man who used to care about people, whoever they are?' Anji shouted. 'You used Gottlieb and now you can't even be bothered to do the decent thing!'

'It's got nothing to do with being "bothered"!'

They glared at each other.

'The girl's right.'

Brunel walked up to them, hands tucked in his waistcoat pockets. 'We can't leave him. Not like that. Whatever's going wrong, however much danger we're all in, we're still human.' He went over to Gottlieb's corpse. His voice became hushed, almost reverent. 'The man got – caught in the machinery.'

'All right, all right,' said the Doctor. 'But we must be quick. The more time we spend in this reality, the more likely we'll naturalise to it.'

The Doctor walked over to Gottlieb.

Anji followed. 'How did he die?'

'He had a heart attack.'

Anji felt sick. 'Would that have happened to me?'

The Doctor shook his head and said softly, 'Maybe he had a weak heart. You're younger, the TARDIS knows you, the shock of being linked wouldn't have killed you.'

It sounded like a very unconvincing list of reasons.

'But it could have?'

'Anji, I have never done anything like this before – I had no idea Gottlieb would die.'

But Anji took little comfort from his words. She suddenly realised that she was expendable. They all were. What mattered to the Doctor was saving their universe, their reality. He would sacrifice himself if that's what it took.

But would he sacrifice her? Fitz?

She looked down at Gottlieb, at his closed eyes, at the silver cross lying on the creases in the black cloak across his unmoving chest.

Was he only the first to go?

Robin Larkspar stared at the blue box. It meant something to him, he knew it did. But what?

Robin had watched Fitz run up to the box, seen its doors open, seen Fitz step inside only for the doors to shut immediately behind him. Robin had ran up to the box – fighting his way past most of his fellow citizens who were running *away* from it – and pulled at the doors, but to no avail. They were locked firmly shut.

Now a crowd had gathered, kept at bay by a cordon of Watchkeepers. People were shouting out, calling for the strange box to be burnt down.

'It's full of Wildren!' someone cried.

'We're being invaded!' shouted another.

TARDIS, Fitz had yelled. He'd said that word the other day as they lay in the welcome October sunshine. So Fitz knew what it was.

Robin remembered – remembered – a swoon of nausea passed through him, and he staggered, clutching his head. Brief glimpses seemed to flash across his vision: a dark-skinned girl, a man in fine clothes, sharing bread with Fitz in a bramble bush –

The sensation passed, the memories folded themselves away.

Coming rapidly to his senses, Robin shouldered his way past the Watchkeepers, only to bump into Morgan Foster.

'Steady, lad,' said Morgan.

'Watchkeeper Kreiner's in there,' said Robin, gesticulating at the box.

Morgan Foster turned to look at the box just as its doors swung open. A strange procession emerged.

First came a citizen in fine clothes, walking backwards, carrying the body of a man in black robes. Supporting the (dead?) man was another citizen also in fine clothes, wearing a strange, tall hat.

Memories began to unfold. Somehow Robin knew that the dark-haired man was called the Doctor. And the man in black –

'Father Gottlieb!'

Morgan Foster put a finger to his lips. 'Yes.'

The Doctor, stooped as he carried Gottlieb's body, craned up at Morgan Foster. 'Ah, hello! You remember me, don't you?'

Morgan made a grumbling sound in his throat.

'I do,' said Robin. 'You're the Doctor. Fitz spoke of you!'

'That's right!' The Doctor seemed surprised.

Morgan Foster looked utterly confused. 'You are familiar to me too, stranger – but I cannot place you.'

'I wouldn't worry about that for now,' said the Doctor, gently setting Father Gottlieb down on the ground.

The stranger in the tall hat stood defiantly, hands on hips, meeting the suspicious gazes of the citizens of Totterdown with an imperious frown.

Morgan Foster folded his arms and drew himself up to his full height. 'I am Morgan Foster, Chief Elder of Totterdown Settlement. Explain this intrusion!'

'I know who you are,' said the Doctor. 'You really don't remember, do you? The Vortex must be acting on your biodata too.' He pointed down at the body of the priest. 'You remember Father Franz Gottlieb?'

Morgan frowned down at the dead man, and shifted from foot to foot. 'Father Gottlieb – he visited when Pierre Cigetrais died.'

Mention of Aboetta's father jogged another memory. Suddenly Robin seemed to know what the inside of this TARDIS looked like – big, impossibly big. Didn't the Doctor help him get inside Malahyde's estate, to look for Aboetta? When he tried to think about it, he felt sick. But he had to know!

As Morgan and the Doctor spoke, Robin, fighting down his nausea, began to edge around to the still-open door of the TARDIS.

Anji and Malahyde stood in front of the screen, watching the events outside unfold. Everyone had their backs to the TARDIS except a tall unshaven bloke with a tangle of thinning black hair – Robin, Anji realised. He was staring at the TARDIS, a thoughtful look on his face. It appeared – though it couldn't possibly be so – that he was looking straight at her.

And then he darted forwards, disappearing from the scanner screen and appearing in the doorway at the top of the steps which led down into the console room.

'Get out!' snapped Anji.

Malahyde rushed forwards, but Robin brushed him aside as easily as if he'd been made of straw. He stared around himself with the same look Fitz had worn – not wonder, but familiarity.

A brief glance at the screen. Gottlieb's body had been taken away and the Doctor and Brunel were surrounded by burly, hairy blokes with crossbows, swords and knives. Brunel was gesticulating defiantly, and the Doctor's hands were raised as if to ward off his assailants.

'I said, get out!' repeated Anji.

Robin came down the steps towards her. 'Where's Watchkeeper Kreiner?'

'You mean Fitz? None of your business.'

But he'd seen her glance towards the corridor which led to the residential quarters. Robin grinned and loped away, disappearing through the doorway.

Anji made to pursue him – but on the scanner, she could see that the Watchkeepers were beginning to lead the Doctor and Malahyde away.

With an anxious glance after Robin, Anji stepped up to the console.

Malahyde got to his feet, groaning.

'Much use you were,' snapped Anji.

Watchkeeper Kreiner sank down slowly on his – his? – bed, hearing the springs of the mattress go *ping!* and *pop!* beneath him. *Mattress* – there was no such thing! But here he was experimentally bouncing gently up and down on one. He took off his helmet, put it on the floor and shook his head, feeling strands of hair drift free. Somehow that felt better, more… Fitz.

This room was full of things he had never seen before, but somehow he knew what they were, and could even name them. That tall thing with the long mirror: *wardrobe*. That black box thing with metal grilles on each side like gates: *stereo*. A glossy corner poking out from underneath a rug: *jazzmag*. Leaning against the wall: *guitar*.

Guitar.

Fitz half stood to pick it up, but sat back down again, frowning. His chain-mail jerkin might scratch the polished wooden body of the instrument. He took it off, and slung it into a corner of the room where it fell with a heavy chinking clunk.

Then he picked up the guitar – but a string was broken, the top E, the thinnest and easiest to replace. Not questioning how he knew this, Fitz laid the guitar gently on the duvet. He removed the broken string, tied it carefully in a knot and tossed it in the bin. Then he took a shining silver loop of new string from a packet he found in a drawer, undid it and removed the bridge pin from the guitar. He slid the ball-end of the new string through the hole in the bridge, secured it with the pin and then threaded it through the tuning peg. Soon all the strings were in tune, and the guitar was ready to play.

Fitz cradled it in his lap, right hand poised over the strings, left hand resting on the fretboard.

And realised that he had no idea how to play the instrument. He strummed – an idiot discord, ugly and meaningless.

He thought of Anji. Had they been lovers? Her denial seemed

strange, as though she were hiding something. The Doctor – he was his friend, he was sure of it.

Where had he met them?

He began to recall –

'Fitz!'

He looked up. Robin was standing in the doorway.

'What are you doing here?

Robin swaggered into the room. 'I've come to take you home, mate!'

Fitz shook his head. What was it that he was beginning to remember? Something about a planet, ending – a woman who wasn't a woman – 'meet me in St Louis' – Anji – a cave of ice...

Fitz clutched the guitar protectively. 'No. No. *This* is my home!'

Anji twisted a knob on the console. A tremendous klaxon blare burst from somewhere above. Anji clasped her palms over her ears.

She looked at the scanner screen. Chaos. Citizens were running everywhere, and several of the Watchkeepers escorting the Doctor and Brunel had dropped their crossbows. The Doctor and Brunel – prepared for this – shoved them aside and ran to the TARDIS.

Anji hit the door control, and they all but fell down the steps.

The Doctor smiled at Anji. 'Well done. That's the last we'll see of Totterdown, hopefully.' He began dancing round the console, flicking switches. The engines hummed into life. 'How's Fitz?'

'I'd better go and see how he is,' she said.

'Take Malahyde with you,' said the Doctor, coming over to her and putting his arm round her. 'We're going to Ashton Court, and I don't want him to meet his older self.'

'Right,' she said. 'Doctor, there's –'

But he was in a huddle with Brunel over the console and wasn't listening to her any longer.

'Come with me,' said Anji. She was beginning to feel like a tour guide.

She took Malahyde to a room she judged to be a safe enough distance from the console room. Its walls were painted with a crude seaside scene, and it was empty apart from two deck chairs and a paddling pool in which a yellow rubber duck bobbed jauntily.

'Stay here,' she said, intent on getting to Fitz's room.

'Why? What's going on?'

'Just stay here. Don't move unless one of us comes and gets you.'

Malahyde's youthful face took on a sulky aspect. 'I'm tired of being treated like a child!'

'Look,' said Anji. 'There's a very good reason for this. Trust me. There isn't time to explain right now.'

Malahyde sank down into one of the deck chairs. He stared at the duck and shook his head. 'I've gone mad, that's the only explanation.'

'Quite probably,' said Anji. She darted out of the room, closing the door behind her. She couldn't see a lock - just had to hope Malahyde would do as he was told.

She thought she heard a movement, farther down the corridor. A faint click, like a door being closed carefully.

'Hello?' she called. 'Anyone there? Robin?'

Anji walked a little way down. The corridor stretched on in a straight line to a point which seemed miles and miles away. Hundreds of doors lined the walls on either side. She felt a qualm of guilt - she should have stopped Robin, or at least told the Doctor about him.

'Hello?' she called again. 'Come on, I know you're there!'

Perhaps Robin had found Fitz and they'd got themselves lost deep inside the TARDIS. Anji ran back along the corridor to Fitz's room. It was empty. Then she heard voices ahead, and ran to catch up with them.

Fitz and Robin were striding towards the console room. Fitz had taken off his chain mail and thankfully there was no sign of the helmet either.

'Hey!' she called.

They both turned.

'Oh, hello Anji,' said Fitz.

'Where are you going?'

'To sort all this out with the Doctor,' said Fitz. He had a look of childlike determination on his face. 'Robin says I live in Totterdown and have done since I was a baby, yet I remember otherwise.' His expression brightened. 'I remember – London! I – I used to work in something called a garden centre. My mother...' He frowned. 'Something bad. Don't want to remember. Then the Doctor came along and took me away.'

Robin shook his head and clapped Fitz on the shoulder, a little roughly, Anji thought.

'Hey!' cried Fitz.

'Come on,' said Anji.

They entered the console room. The Doctor and Brunel were still poring over the console.

The Doctor looked up at the sound of their approaching footsteps, and frowned as he caught sight of Robin. 'What are you doing here?'

Robin folded his arms. 'I've come to take Fitz back home.'

'Well, you're too late. Anji, make sure he doesn't get in the way.'

Fitz walked up to the console. 'I'm sure this is my home now,' he said. 'I remember...'

'I remember this as well,' said Robin, his brows furrowing. 'It's – a travel machine! Where are we going?'

'To Ashton Court,' said Brunel. 'Where all this began.'

'And where it will end,' said the Doctor.

Chapter 24
The Anomalies

Aboetta danced.

She let the see-sawing notes of the violin take control of her body. Let her feet skip and pirouette across the parquet floor, let her arms sway and rise with the melody. She loved the sensation of her dress whirling around her, loved the almost dizzying sensation that gripped her as she danced. She felt as though she was being taken to places she could only dream of. She knew that Malahyde was watching her, his eyes full of the new knowledge of her body.

She felt alive.

Suddenly the music stopped.

Aboetta whirled to a halt, facing Malahyde. His head was cocked towards the door.

'What is it?'

'I thought I heard something, beneath the music.'

Aboetta went to him and they held each other's hands. She'd been too wrapped up in her dancing to notice anything. 'What did you hear?'

Malahyde went to a small bureau and took out a gun. 'A vibration – from somewhere below.'

He left the room.

Aboetta followed, stopping to pick up her pistol and bag of shot on the way.

Malahyde had already unlocked the cellar door by the time she got there, and was halfway down the steps. She descended until she was just behind him, and looked into the cellar. There, beside the Utopian Engine, bathed in its green glow, stood the Doctor's blue box. The Doctor himself was standing at the control desk. He hadn't seen them.

Nearby stood Fitz and Anji, talking animatedly – they also hadn't noticed Malahyde and Aboetta.

Another man was there. A short man, in crumpled yet gentlemanly attire. He was wearing a tall top hat. Somehow, she knew him.

This stranger was staring at Malahyde as if he'd seen a ghost. 'Jared Malahyde,' he said slowly. There was menace in the tone of his voice. 'I have some contracts that require your signature. But unfortunately the projects set out in them have been rendered utterly irrelevant because of what you have done!'

'Brunel,' gasped Malahyde as he walked down the steps. 'Isambard Kingdom Brunel!'

The Doctor turned round from the control desk, looked at Brunel, then at Malahyde. 'Oh, no,' he groaned.

Then out of the blue box stepped Robin. He saw Aboetta and made straight for her.

Seeing him again was a nasty shock. She didn't know at first what to do. She remembered the night she'd spent with him, before her flight from Totterdown, remembered the things he'd said. She raised her pistol. 'Stay away from me!'

Malahyde had his gun aimed at the Doctor. 'Step away from the controls.'

The Doctor remained by the desk. 'There's no need for this.'

Brunel stepped forward. 'Jared, listen to me! You must let us help you.'

Malahyde swung his gun round to cover Brunel.

Malahyde got up from the deck chair and crouched beside the paddling pool. He pushed the rubber duck under the water, and watched morosely as it popped up again, bobbing merrily. Its comical expression seemed to mock him. He thought wistfully of his rooms in Bedminster, Woodes coffee-shop, his unfinished poetry. Would he ever see any of them again?

He didn't understand what was going on, but he understood that he had to get out of here. He left the room and walked along the corridor, staring at the strange roundelled pattern on the pale wooden walls. Somehow its uniformity disturbed him. How did he know that the Doctor was right? The Eternines had told him that he and he alone could save the human race. What if the Doctor was lying?

He realised that he didn't care. All he wanted to do was go home.

He came to the main chamber, and peered around the edge of the doorway. To his surprise there was no one there. Where had they all gone?

'Hello?' he said, stepping into the cavernous space.

Then he saw the image on the scanner. It showed a strange machine, its main body a candlestick of pale green. Beside it stood the Doctor and Brunel.

And before them stood a man who looked strangely familiar.

But Malahyde's attention was fixed on the girl. She was like no one he had ever seen. Tall, with dark hair, she looked wild and beautiful. Malahyde could well imagine himself loving such a woman. She was pointing a gun at the Doctor, as was –

Malahyde gasped.

The man – the oddly familiar man – was *him*!

It was a stand-off.

Aboetta kept her pistol trained on Robin. Malahyde was aiming his straight at Brunel.

Behind Brunel, the Doctor stood by the control desk. 'Everyone keep calm. We're all on the same side.'

'Huh!' grunted Fitz.

Anji nudged him to keep quiet. They were nearest to the TARDIS, and no one seemed to be paying them any attention. Which was fine with Anji.

Robin walked up to Aboetta. 'You wouldn't really shoot me, would you?'

Aboetta slowly lowered the weapon. 'No. I just wish you would go away.'

Brunel stepped towards Malahyde. 'And *you* wouldn't shoot *me*, surely, man?'

'Yes,' said Malahyde. 'If you interfere with the Engine, you could kill Aboetta and I.'

'I assure you that's the last thing we want to do,' said the Doctor.

Anji jumped as Fitz squeezed her arm. 'I remember now – remember what he was going to do!'

'Shh!' hissed Anji.

Malahyde was blinking rapidly. It didn't look like he'd be able to shoot anyone. 'What are you doing here?'

'We've come to sort all this out,' said the Doctor. 'Now will you please put the gun down?'

Malahyde shook his head. 'No. You must leave now, and never come here again.'

Brunel's face was turning slowly red. Anji watched him light a cigar with shaking hands, and glare at Malahyde through a pall of blue smoke.

'Come back to Totterdown with me, Aboetta,' implored Robin.

'For the *last* time, no!' cried Aboetta, her voice hoarse with anger. Then she turned to the Doctor. 'Do as Mr Malahyde says. Leave us in peace.'

'You fool, Malahyde!' roared Brunel suddenly. 'You reckless fool!' He stepped towards Malahyde and dashed the gun from his hand. 'You caused the Cleansing – you killed my wife, and left my children...' Brunel shuddered. 'Do not attempt to stand in our way, Malahyde. I curse the day we ever met!'

'So do I!' cried Malahyde, his voice breaking into a sob. 'Do you think I wanted any of this?'

'He was possessed by Watchlar,' said the Doctor evenly. 'He didn't have much choice.'

'He could have resisted,' snapped Brunel. 'God knows, I would have.'

'God knows, I wish it had been you, that night on the Downs,' said Malahyde, and there was a fiery gleam in his eyes. 'How I have suffered.'

'How *you* have suffered!' shouted Brunel, bearing down on Malahyde and shoving him to the floor.

Malahyde fell to his knees.

Aboetta moved towards him, distracted.

Robin sprang forward and snatched her gun away. 'Now the tables are turned.'

Aboetta folded her arms and gazed defiantly back at Robin.

'Look!' said Fitz suddenly.

The Doctor had seized Malahyde's pistol and was now pointing it at its owner.

Malahyde and Aboetta moved together and clung to each other.

The Doctor looked embarrassed. 'I'm not going to shoot you.' He threw the gun into the farthest corner of the cellar, where it clattered noisily against the stone. His voice hardened, gained authority. 'Robin – follow suit. Now.'

Robin shook his head and brandished the gun towards Malahyde, who backed away, eyes widening in terror.

'Obey him, fool!' shouted Brunel.

Fitz lunged forwards, grappled Robin around the neck and wrested the gun away. It followed its companion with another noisy clatter.

Robin shoved Fitz away. 'I thought you were my mate,' he said, his voice like that of a sulky child.

'So did I,' gasped Fitz, panting from the sudden exertion.

Anji smiled and said, 'Well done,' but Fitz just stared at her.

'Right!' said the Doctor, clapping his hands and making everyone jump – even Brunel. 'Now that's out of the way, I think I've worked out what the Utopian Engine is really for. Do you want us to go, or shall I explain first?'

'Go,' said Aboetta. 'We don't need or want to know.'

'Well, I do...' began Malahyde.

'After all our help!' Fitz said suddenly. 'I remember now. We rescued you from the Wildren! Took you safely to Totterdown, and helped you come back here! And this is the thanks we get?'

Aboetta shrugged. 'Things have moved on since then,' she said, with a glance at Malahyde. 'But I suppose we could hear you out.'

'Good,' said the Doctor. 'Now this is only a theory, but it seems to fit the facts.' He pointed to the Utopian Engine. 'This machine was meant to speed up time through only some of its dimensions, those linked to the metabolism of living things. The Cleansing wasn't an accident – it was only the beginning of the process. If I hadn't stopped it...' the Doctor shook his head.

'You?' interrupted Malahyde.

'Yes, me, and Isambard Brunel,' said the Doctor. 'You can't remember, can you? Watchlar possessed you totally, activated the Engine – fortunately I was able to stop it.'

'What happened to Watchlar?' asked Aboetta.

'Now, that I don't know. Malahyde, er, fell into the core of the Engine, I thought he had died.' He turned to Malahyde. 'But afterwards I found you unconscious beside the machine, and knew from meeting you yesterday that Watchlar had gone from your mind.'

It took Anji a few seconds to work out the tortuous logic of that sentence.

'It must have separated from you and died,' said the Doctor.

Anji noticed Aboetta and Malahyde exchange glances.

'I don't understand any of this,' said Robin, sitting down at the control desk.

'I do,' said Brunel. 'Mostly.'

'I'm beginning to,' said Fitz. 'But what's the point of a machine that speeds up time?'

'What happens when you speed up someone's metabolism?' asked the Doctor in reply.

Anji shrugged. 'They age. And die.'

'Yes!' said the Doctor. 'People age, they die, more quickly than is natural. And a body – a person, a planet, a star – produces a certain amount of energy during its lifetime. So if you speed that up, whilst keeping all the other dimensions of time in place, an enormous amount of energy is produced. Temporal friction – on a massive scale. And the Utopian Engine is designed to open up a trans-dimensional portal to the Eternium. That's what Gottlieb inadvertently activated, how you, Anji, ended up there.'

'So all this energy would end up in the Eternium?' said Brunel, staring up at the Utopian Engine.

'Yes,' said the Doctor. 'They must have constructed a similar machine at their end, or maybe used the ocean as a giant battery.'

'So the Cleansing was *meant* to happen?' asked Robin.

'Yes – only it was meant to go on for much longer, releasing vast amounts of energy into the Eternium. It would have destroyed all life in the universe.' He gazed up at the Utopian Engine. 'I never imagined that it was so powerful, so dangerous.'

'Watchlar lied to me,' said Malahyde. 'All this work, all my suffering, was just to save *them*, not us.'

'So what are you going to do, Doctor?' said Aboetta. 'Now you know what this machine is for, are you satisfied? You can't undo its effects, can't undo the Cleansing. You may as well go, leave us in peace.'

The Doctor opened his mouth to speak but was interrupted by Fitz.

'I know what he's going to do!' His voice was shaking and Anji didn't like the manic gleam in his eyes. 'He's going to go back in time and wipe out this timeline so you'll never build the machine!' He pointed at Malahyde, Aboetta and Robin in turn. 'He's going to make sure you never exist!'

'Fitz,' said the Doctor. 'I've tried that. I've already gone back in time, done something which should have prevented this reality from coming into existence. But it didn't work.'

Everyone was staring at the Doctor. He was back in the state Anji had seen him in earlier, when he'd realised that the wrong reality still prevailed.

It was Brunel who spoke first. 'Doctor, I think I know what you mean. But I must bow to your experience as a temporal engineer. Please explain.'

The Doctor stood silently beside the Utopian Engine. Anji could tell by the look on his face that this was bad news, the worst.

When he spoke again, his voice was a whisper. 'It didn't work, and won't work if I try again, because this is the dominant reality now. Fitz, Anji – *we're* the anomalies. Our reality no longer exists.'

Chapter 25
The Return

Anji stared at the Doctor. 'Are you *serious*?'

'I've never been more serious.'

'Are you *sure*?'

'That as well.' The Doctor turned away.

'What does that mean? What do we do now? Are we gonna just fade away?' Fitz was babbling. 'Or stay here, become Watchkeepers and washer-women!'

'Be quiet, man!' snapped Brunel suddenly. 'Doctor, what can this mean for me? The time you took me away from –'

'– is continuous with this time. You're from Year Nought, just after the Cleansing. Though you're out of time, you're part of this reality.'

'But the plan we discussed!' said Brunel urgently.

'What plan?' said Fitz.

The Doctor glared at him, and then looked at Anji. 'There is no plan.'

Brunel opened his mouth as if to speak, but a look from the Doctor silenced him.

Anji knew the Doctor was lying, and was suddenly afraid. What could he possibly be planning that he wouldn't – couldn't – share with them?

'Will you leave now?' said Aboetta. Anji noticed that she'd retrieved her pistol. It was tucked into her belt.

She was just about to point this out when the Doctor swung

round to face Aboetta. 'No! Not just yet. I have to deactivate that.' He pointed at the Utopian Engine.

'You can't!' said Malahyde. 'We'll die.'

The Doctor waved a hand dismissively. 'Don't worry about the temporal effects – you'll be quite safe inside the TARDIS.'

'What's he on about?' said Fitz, frowning.

Anji ignored him. 'What about you? If you stay out here...' She made a face.

The Doctor grinned. 'I can link the TARDIS to the Utopian Engine via the telepathic circuits, shut it down from the console room.'

Anji gasped. 'Isn't that dangerous?'

'It's the only way,' he said, exchanging a dark look with Brunel.

Aboetta looked from the Utopian Engine to the TARDIS. 'Perhaps it is for the best.' She reached out and took Malahyde's hand. 'Watchlar is never coming back – and even if he were to, we now know his purpose was evil.'

Malahyde nodded. He looked old and tired – and Anji suddenly thought of his younger aspect, still hopefully sulking by the paddling pool in the TARDIS.

'So we're all agreed then?' said the Doctor, raising his voice so that it echoed around the stone cellar.

Malahyde mumbled agreement. Brunel said, 'Let's get on with it.'

'Right,' said the Doctor. 'Everyone into the TARDIS.'

Malahyde couldn't take his eyes of the screen, off the man who looked like him. He couldn't stop himself shaking, wishing he could wake from this nightmare. If the machine was the Utopian Engine, if the man who looked like him *was* him, then he'd somehow travelled into his own future, and was witnessing events he was never meant to witness.

Everyone began walking towards the open doors of the TARDIS. Fear gripped Malahyde – he'd read somewhere that if you met your doppelgänger you'd die – so he scurried into the shadows between the shelves of the library.

He heard footsteps descend the short staircase into the central chamber. Heard voices, people walking about. He peered out from behind the edge of the shelf. He could see the Doctor, working the instruments, his back to Malahyde. The strange, disturbed fellow Fitz was standing with his arms folded, talking quietly to Anji. They seemed to be arguing about something. Isambard Brunel stood nearby, watching the Doctor closely. Again Malahyde was struck by how much older the engineer looked since he'd met him earlier that evening on the Downs.

And the man who looked like him – *was* him, the older him – was sitting in the very same chair in which he had taken tea some hours earlier. The girl in white was sitting opposite the older Malahyde, her long dark hair spread out over her shoulders. Both the girl and his older self looked tense and watchful.

At the sight of his doppelgänger Malahyde began to tremble uncontrollably. He looked longingly at the door leading to the guest quarters. But there was no way he could make it without his double seeing him. He was trapped.

A powerful vibrating hum began to rise all around him. He returned his gaze to the Doctor, just at the moment when the Doctor stepped back from the console, rubbing his hands together.

'That's it – time has equalised. It's now Year 160 – or 2003 – inside the house, and without.'

These words meant nothing to Malahyde, but he saw Brunel nod in satisfaction.

'Now – the plan?' said the engineer.

The Doctor looked sharply at Brunel, then he sighed. 'It's the only way.'

'I thought you said there was no plan!' cried Anji.

The Doctor was about to reply – but then the central pillar of the strange machine began to glow with a blinding blue light.

And on the screen, the green column of the Utopian Engine pulsed in sympathy.

Malahyde felt himself drawn out of hiding – but then he caught sight of his other self, and darted back into cover.

A throbbing hum rent the air, over which Malahyde could hear shouted voices.

'What the devil is happening?' – Brunel.

'It's the TARDIS – it's linked to the Utopian Engine!' – the Doctor.

'Can't you stop it?' – Anji.

'Something's coming through!' – the Doctor again.

Something's coming through. Though dread turned his stomach to ice, Malahyde couldn't stop himself from peering around the edge of the shelf. The central pillar of the TARDIS was now a bloated sphere, crackling with arcs of blue energy.

There was something about it that was horribly familiar.

Malahyde saw the Doctor lunge for the console – but a lancing spark of energy threw him back.

And then it emerged.

Malahyde stepped from hiding. 'Watchlar!' he screamed.

No one could hear him, no one paid him any attention. They were all watching in horror as a glowing sphere detached itself from the central pillar and floated out into the chamber – floated towards –

Malahyde's older self.

He had stood up and was staring as the thing, the Eternine, approached. Malahyde saw his lips move, mouth the name he himself had just uttered.

The girl stood, interposing herself between Malahyde's older self and Watchlar. She stood right in the creature's path, gun drawn.

Her face was calm, composed.

But before she could fire, the energy-being surged forwards, enveloping her totally.

'Aboetta!' cried Malahyde's older self, stepping towards her.

Brunel also made a move towards the girl – but the Doctor held him back. 'Don't touch her!' he yelled hoarsely.

Anji and Fitz had both caught sight of the younger Malahyde, and were shouting at him to run.

But both he and his older self were transfixed on what was happening to the girl, to Aboetta. Somehow, hearing her name had provoked a pang of emotion in Malahyde's heart. His older self had loved this woman. And now she was dying.

No, worse than that. She was changing.

Watchlar was shrinking, its shining surface melting into a grotesque parody of the human frame. Inside, Malahyde could just make out Aboetta, like a figure glimpsed through torrential rain. She was screaming, but couldn't be heard over the tearing, crackling discharges of the energy-creature.

Then, with a flash, Watchlar disappeared. Aboetta stood, arms hanging limply by her side, head lolling on her chest.

No one dared move or speak.

'Aboetta?' said Malahyde's older self.

Aboetta raised her head. Her expression was terrifying – her mouth was pulled to one side, her cheek spasming. Her eyes were almost popping out of her head. She was making a spastic grunting, as if she were about to vomit.

Then with a shuddering convulsion, she returned to normal. Something like a smile writhed across her lips.

'Aboetta?' repeated the older Malahyde.

Aboetta raised her flintlock pistol.

'Watchlar, no!' cried the Doctor.

Aboetta – Watchlar – pulled the trigger. There was a sharp crack and a brief shower of sparks.

Malahyde watched his older self fall back into the chair, clutching his chest.

He realised he'd stumbled from the library, and was now standing in full view of everyone.

'Don't move!' cried the Doctor.

'I thought I told you to stay put!' shouted Anji.

'By all the – you're as stupid as your older self!' spluttered Brunel.

The possessed girl had also seen him. She began to re-load.

Malahyde turned and fled.

Anji watched stunned as the older Malahyde collapsed, a stain darkening his waistcoat. He stared up at Aboetta, grimacing in agony.

She saw the younger Malahyde turn and run into the depths of the TARDIS.

She watched Aboetta re-load the gun, slowly and deliberately.

'There was no need for that!' roared the Doctor.

Aboetta walked past the console, ignoring everyone, heading for the door.

Robin stepped up to her, his face ashen. 'Aboetta! What's happened to you?'

She raised the gun and smiled. Then she threw it to the floor.

'Aboetta?' Robin stepped towards her.

She raised a hand as if to ward him off – and a spark of energy crackled from her fingertips, slamming him back against the console.

Then she whirled round, advancing on Brunel.

He stood his ground, glaring defiantly at the possessed woman.

She spoke. It was Aboetta's voice, but hoarse and strained, as if something else had control of her vocal cords. 'Door!'

'Don't let it out, Doctor!' said Brunel.

Aboetta turned aside – and headed straight for Anji.

Sod bravery – Anji backed away, looking for somewhere to hide. Sparks of energy crackled around Watchlar/Aboetta's fingertips. Out of the corner of her eye Anji saw the Doctor go to the console and operate the door control.

'No!' she cried.

Aboetta swung away and darted through the door.

'*Now* what?' said Fitz.

The Doctor ran after Aboetta. 'Look after Robin and do what you can for Malahyde. And whatever you do don't come outside!'

On the screen Anji could see Aboetta at the control desk of the Utopian Engine.

'I'm coming with you!' cried Brunel. 'The creature must be stopped.'

'Stay here!' ordered the Doctor.

But Brunel shoved the Doctor through the TARDIS doors. 'Two of us will have more chance than one!'

Anji waited until they were out of the TARDIS, then closed the doors.

She turned to face Fitz. He looked freaked. She supposed she must look the same.

'What the hell do we do now?' said Fitz.

'What the Doctor said.'

She went over to Robin. He wasn't unconscious, just stunned and disoriented. She left him where he was, lying on the floor under the console, and went over to Malahyde.

He was sprawled in the chair, head tilted forwards on to his chest. His face was deathly pale, as were his hands, both clasped over the wound.

Aboetta – or rather the thing that had possessed her – had shot him in the chest. Maybe hit his heart. Anji didn't know. There was a lot of blood, the guy was taking great stretching gasps of air.

Anji looked up at Fitz. There was nothing they could do for him.

Malahyde was trying to say something. Anji leaned over him, her hands resting on his. They were cold and trembling.

'S… s…'

'Shh,' said Anji

'Save her… save Aboetta!'

The last word came out in a strangled gasp. Malahyde convulsed and was still.

Fitz turned away.

Anji stood. 'We'll try,' she whispered.

Jared Malahyde's dead blue eyes stared up at her.

Malahyde ran, fully expecting to be shot in the back at any moment, ignoring the cries of the Doctor and his friends. He ran, welcoming the burst of physical energy. It felt like he was doing something to get himself out of this nightmare. But however hard he pushed himself he could never get past the wood-panelled walls with their unchanging circular design.

He ran past the room with the pool and the rubber duck.

He ran until his chest hurt and he had to slow down for fear of injuring himself.

This was more than anyone could take – he had just seen *his own death*. He knew how he was going to die. Whatever he did, wherever he went, he'd somehow end up back here, in this impossible, confusing place.

He collapsed against the wall, fingers gripping the edge of an indented circle, and closed his eyes. 'Dear God,' he found himself saying. He rarely ever prayed, but now it seemed like the only thing he could do.'Dear God in Heaven, save me from this madness, return me home to write poetry extolling your glory, please Lord…'

'Hello.'

Malahyde gasped and opened his eyes. Standing before him was a slim girl of about his own age and height. She was wearing a plain, crisp-looking white shirt buttoned up to the neck, a skirt of indecent length which barely covered her knees, and strange shoes with enormous soles and heels. She had her arms folded and was looking at him with plain amusement.

He stumbled away from the wall.'Who are you?'

'I could well ask the same of you. Except I already know who you are.' She had high cheekbones and a rather pointed nose, a thin face and slanted green eyes.

'How – how do you know who I am?'

'Never mind about that.' Her eyes narrowed. 'Hey, are you all right?'

'I've just seen myself die.'

The strange girl smiled.'Aw. That must be terrible for you. Look, I wouldn't worry. I've been keeping tabs on things, and as the Doctor took you out of time before you could construct the Utopian Engine, then what you've just seen could never happen. It's an anomalous future.' The girl brushed a lock of mousy-coloured hair out of her eyes and her grin widened at Malahyde's confusion. 'Don't worry, the Doctor will sort you out, eh? Take you home. Your only problem will be trying to forget about all this.'

'If only I could.'

She looked him up and down appraisingly.'Look, I think the best thing you can do is stay with me until all this is over. Are you hungry?'

Malahyde realised that he was.'Yes.'

'I'll make you a tuna sandwich.'

She turned and walked briskly down the corridor, towards an open door ten yards or so away.

Malahyde hesitated. Should he trust this woman? So much had happened that he didn't know what to believe or who to trust. But he baulked at the idea of returning to the central chamber, seeing the body of his older self...

He set off after the girl. 'Excuse me!' he called.

She stopped and turned to him. She looked amused, as if he were there for her entertainment. 'Yes?

She was nothing like the few women and girls Malahyde had met. They carried themselves aloof, unapproachable, separate. But this girl – her very stare was indecently intimate. Malahyde couldn't help it. He blushed, he looked at his shoes, he wished he was elsewhere – anything rather than suffer that stare. 'What's your name?'

'Oh, you can call me Natasha.' Her green eyes widened. 'Can you keep a secret?'

The Doctor stepped from the TARDIS into the cellar, Isambard Kingdom Brunel by his side.

'How does this affect the plan?' said Brunel.

'I don't know,' said the Doctor. 'I wasn't expecting Watchlar to return.'

'Where did it come from?'

'At a guess, I would say it was trapped inside the core of the Engine. When I linked the telepathic circuits to it, Watchlar saw a way out – through the TARDIS.' The Doctor shook his head, keeping his eyes on the possessed Aboetta. 'I should have foreseen this!'

They sidled together towards the control desk. Already the central column of the Utopian Engine was beginning to glow more brightly, just as it had done back when 1843 had become Year Nought.

It was all happening again.

Watchlar/Aboetta was intent on the controls, and hadn't noticed the Doctor or Brunel, not yet.

The Doctor stepped forwards. 'Watchlar!'

Watchlar/Aboetta glanced up. Her – its – face was blank, impassive, indifferent, and the eyes had a green taint, reminding the Doctor forcefully of the possessed Malahyde he had battled at Year Nought. The Doctor braced himself, recalling what had happened to Robin.

But instead of blasting him back against the TARDIS doors, the creature smiled. And then the Doctor knew that it was no use reasoning or bargaining to try to save Aboetta. The survival of Watchlar's universe was at stake. What did the life of one mere human matter?

'Doctor. I remember you. You tried to stop me before.'

'I succeeded then – and I aim to do so now.'

Aboetta/Watchlar smiled. 'I do not think so. Both the Utopian Engine and myself are drawing on the energies of your time vessel. Nothing can stop me.'

'That's where I beg to differ,' began Brunel, stepping forwards.

A crackle of energy arced down towards him, scorching the floor between his feet. Aboetta/Watchlar didn't even need to look up.

Brunel backed away.

'Don't do that again,' said the Doctor to Brunel. 'Stay out of this.'

He turned back to the possessed girl. 'At least tell me how you came to be here. Last time we met, I pushed you into the core of that.' He pointed at the swelling green belly of the Utopian Engine.

Watchlar/Aboetta raised its head to regard him. 'When I entered the core of the Engine, I discorporated from Malahyde. My life-energy was combined with that of the Utopian Engine, and together we became the temporal barrier around this house. I tried to reach out, latch on to the minds within. And, at last, I recently gained a foothold in this girl's mind. Now I inhabit her totally.'

'And now I have freed you,' said the Doctor glumly.

'You could not have foreseen this,' said Brunel consolingly. 'Now, how do we stop it?'

'We might not have to.'

Brunel stared at him. 'The plan?'

The Doctor nodded.

Watchlar/Aboetta had turned its attention back to the billowing core of the Utopian Engine.

'But if we can stop Watchlar activating the Engine, things would be a lot easier. One last try,' said the Doctor, patting Brunel on his shoulder.

'Watchlar!' he called. 'I've been to the Eternium. It's contemporaneous with this universe, and it's a cold, dead, bleak place. There aren't any of your kind left! If you operate the Engine, restore power to the Eternium, you'll be its only occupant! You're the last of your kind, Watchlar. You'll be the loneliest being in existence!'

Watchlar/Aboetta's eyes gleamed. 'Dying, Doctor, but not dead! My fellow Eternines are waiting, stored in batteries deep below the crust of our refuge-world. Once energy is restored, they will live again.'

The Doctor stood back. 'Then, I've lost.'

Watchlar/Aboetta made no sign that it had heard.

The core of the Utopian Engine was now the shape of a rugby ball, and was slowly but surely growing. The air was crackling with energy.

'I said, I've lost!' shouted the Doctor.

Watchlar/Aboetta was now gazing up at the glowing core.

'Come on,' said the Doctor to Brunel. They began to back towards the TARDIS.

Suddenly an arc of energy lanced from the core of the engine, pinning the Doctor to the spot.

'I know what you are planning, Doctor,' cried Watchlar. 'And I cannot allow it!'

'Isn't there anything we can do?'

Anji was unable to take her eyes off the scene. The Utopian Engine was now a giant sphere, glowing with a green luminescence which reminded Anji of her makeshift lantern, of being in the cave with Gottlieb.

And the Doctor was writhing, caught in a crackling web of energy.

Anji moved towards the door control. 'We've got to go to him!'

'Don't be mad!' said Fitz, grabbing her by the arm. 'We'll be killed if we go out there!'

Anji twisted free. 'We've got to help him!'

'Open the door.'

Anji and Fitz sprang apart.

Robin was standing before them, holding Aboetta's pistol.

'Open the door,' he repeated.

'Look, mate,' said Fitz. 'Whatever that thing is out there, it's not Aboetta any more.'

Robin's face twisted in anguish. 'Open the door!'

The Doctor squirmed in agony, unable to free himself, unable even to cry out. Anger mixed with the pain – anger and frustration. All was lost if he couldn't get back to the TARDIS. Dimly he saw Brunel standing in front of him. Approaching him.

He tried to call out, yell at Brunel to save himself – but that was stupid, once the Engine was fully activated nowhere would be safe. The Eternium would drain off all the energy in the universe. The Doctor felt a transient moment of relief that it would all be over. Then his fight returned and he struggled against the energy-web.

Then something rammed into him, and he fell – he was free.

He rolled on to the dusty flagstones of the cellar floor.

Something – someone – stumbled against his legs, falling beside him.

It was Brunel. He must have forced himself into the energy-web, dragged the Doctor free. But Brunel was human. He would never be able to withstand such an onslaught of pure energy.

With a glance over at Aboetta/Watchlar – preoccupied with the Engine – the Doctor dragged Brunel towards the TARDIS.

But it was too late. The skin on his hands was blackened, there were scorch marks over his face. Brunel was dying.

'Doctor,' he gasped. 'You told me... that if you restored the correct history... then I would... not remember this.'

There was another burst of energy from the Utopian Engine.

An image of the young Brunel, suspended in a basket below a thousand-foot-long wrought-iron bar slung across the Avon Gorge, suddenly came to the Doctor. The basket – a temporary means of transporting men and materials across the Gorge, before the laying of the foundation stone for the suspension bridge – was stuck. Stuck in the middle of the bar, at its lowest point, a double victim of gravity and friction – for the roller it was suspended from couldn't be drawn up the other side. Not from within the basket, anyway.

Brunel, to the horror of the onlookers, climbing out, up one of the suspension ropes, freeing the stuck roller, climbing back in and continuing to safety on the other side of the Gorge. Brunel, having cheated death, going on to change the world.

But that was a different world. This reality, warped by the application of the Malahyde process, wrecked by the temporal savagery of the Cleansing, never knew of the benefits Brunel and others like him had brought to the human race. And *this* Brunel, in freeing the Doctor, in dying in the prime of his life, would ensure that his legacy would live on, in the real reality.

If the plan worked.

The Doctor knelt by Isambard Kingdom Brunel, to hear his final words, but he was already dead. The Doctor stood and looked down at him. 'I'll never be able to thank you,' he murmured. 'Because you won't remember who I am.'

Suddenly the core of the Engine burst into greater brightness. It was at critical mass.

It had to be now!

The Doctor turned and ran to the TARDIS.

As he reached it, the doors opened and a figure burst out, colliding with him.

'Robin!' cried the Doctor – then he stood aside and let him pass.

If the plan worked, there was nothing he could do for Robin, or anyone in this reality.

Anji saw the Doctor approach and throw himself down the steps. He fell on to the console, his hands a blur.

'What –' began Fitz, but Anji nudged him.

The Doctor threw a final switch and stepped back from the console. He was breathing hard. 'Look at the screen,' he gasped.

The glowing sphere was beginning to fluctuate in size, its glow strobing on/off, arcs of energy sparking from it to the walls of the cellar.

'It's happening,' said the Doctor. 'The Cleansing. And this time it won't be stopped.' He thumped the TARDIS console. 'Well, it's now or never.'

'Can't we do anything to save Aboetta?' asked Anji.

'Or Robin!' cried Fitz.

'No, and no!' said the Doctor, flicking switches. 'There just isn't time!'

'What are you going to do?' said Fitz, his voice low with suspicion.

'I'll tell you afterwards because you might try to stop me if you knew!' With that, he threw a switch and staggered back from the console, his eyes wide, staring at the yearometer.

Anji turned to look at it too.

The numerals were beginning to run backwards.

'What the *hell*?' cried Fitz.

Aboetta woke suddenly. Where was she? A light – bright, green, painful. A sound like fire, crackling, hissing. Underneath – a stone floor. Was she in the kitchen?

'Father?' she called out. Then she remembered more. 'Mr Malahyde? Jared?'

Someone at her side, lifting her up. Pain like fire along her back, down her legs. Hard to breathe. Head so heavy – couldn't lift to look –

Something in her head wanting out wanting her

A voice from outside.

'Aboetta.'

A shadow against the flickering green, the outline of a head. A man's head.

Aboetta tried hard to focus. 'Robin?'

'It's me, Aboetta.'

'Am I dying?'

'No! No.'

Aboetta cried out. Pain everywhere. '*Feels* like dying.'

Something wet hit her face, trickled down her cheek. Robin was crying.

Where was Malahyde? She wanted to die in his arms, not Robin's! But it looked like she didn't have any choice in the matter. Robin had hounded her right up to her death. The irony of it made her smile.

'Oh, Aboetta, don't die,' sobbed Robin.

She shook her head. 'Can't help it.' She wished she knew where Malahyde was.

Then came the oddest thing. She felt something crawling up her cheek.

She tried to reach up, but somehow she couldn't move. She couldn't move and everything had gone quiet.

Robin's face was still above her, stock-still against the green.

And then she saw the tears falling up, back into Robin's eyes.

And he started to look younger, just as he was when they first met.

She tried to cry out, to say something, but she couldn't move.

And then there was a terrifying sensation of falling, falling backwards, and Aboetta knew no more.

Chapter 26
Reality Check

The Doctor flicked another switch, and then leaned over the console. He sighed, long and heavily. Then he looked up at Fitz and Anji. His voice was hushed, but there was a gleam of triumph in his eyes. 'It's over.'

'What have you done?' said Fitz.

The Doctor pointed to the yearometer. It read *23 October 1831*.

'So we've gone back in time.' Anji was confused. 'What good will that do?'

'More than that, Anji. I've turned back time. It was the only way.'

Anji operated the scanner. It revealed the cellar of the mansion house of Ashton Court, but instead of the green column of the Utopian Engine, Anji could see a wall of wine-racks, a few dusty old chests, and bulky objects draped in sacking and cobwebs.

Fitz's face was contorted in anger. 'So you've just wiped out an entire reality? Killed all the people I know?'

'You have to realise they don't and will never exist – at least, not as you knew them.'

Fitz tapped a finger to his head. 'They exist – in here!'

Anji remembered Gottlieb. He was real – had been real – so how could the Doctor say that he didn't exist?

'How did you manage to turn back time?' she asked. 'I didn't know the TARDIS could do that.'

'It can't – usually. But linked to something like the Utopian Engine, it can.'

Fitz turned to the Doctor. 'There's something else. You said that our reality didn't exist! Said that the post-Cleansing one – the one I still remember – had replaced it!' He gestured at the scanner. 'So what the hell is this? Were you lying?'

The Doctor's face was as dark as a thundercloud. 'I didn't lie. It had become the prime reality. But in linking the TARDIS to the Utopian Engine, in reversing the effects, I was able to actually roll back time through all its dimensions to a point before history diverged. It's rather different than trying to go back and change history.'

'But just as bad,' Fitz kept on. 'You've still wiped out an entire reality.'

The Doctor sighed. 'It was the only way to stop Watchlar, Fitz.'

'You don't know what you've done,' said Fitz in disgust. 'You can't know how it feels!' He turned and walked from the console room.

The Doctor went up to Anji. 'Do you understand? I – I hope you understand.'

Anji remembered how the Doctor had used Gottlieb, and felt a cold seam of anger develop in her. She would never be able to forgive him for that. Or for the fact that it could have been her. But she nodded, if only to reassure the Doctor, and smiled, though it felt like a betrayal. 'Yes.'

'Thank you.' The Doctor's gaze roved over her face, then towards to the TARDIS library. Anji followed his gaze and saw that once more its shelves were full.

That meant history was safe. Presumably.

'What about Brunel?' said Anji. 'He died out there, I saw it. Won't that mess up history?'

'He's not dead, Anji. Not in this reality.' The Doctor frowned. 'There might be some temporal overspill…'

'Could someone please tell me what is going on?'

Anji whirled round. Malahyde! She'd forgotten all about him.

The Doctor beamed at the young man. 'Ah, Mr Malahyde! I've brought you home.'

Malahyde smiled. It was amazing how much younger and less troubled he looked than his older counterpart. Anji found herself glad to see that at least someone got out of this alive and unscathed. Physically, at least.

She heard the TARDIS engines start up, and then stop almost at once. A short hop.

The scanner screen showed a drizzly backstreet, a red-brick wall stretching off into the distance, punctuated by dingy entrance ways. A thin, bedraggled cat stood on top of the wall, outlined sharply against the grey clouds, staring right at the TARDIS. Thick smoke smudged the air, presumably from some factory or other.

'Please – let me stay with you!' said Malahyde plaintively.

But the Doctor was firm. He activated the door control. 'You must go, your place is here – not with us.'

The cat leaped down from the wall and began to prowl towards the TARDIS, its whiskers twitching.

'How can I go back to my old life, after all I have seen?'

'You'll manage.' They were at the top of the steps now, Malahyde on the very border of his life, his time.

Anji couldn't help but feel sorry for him. How could you get on with your normal life, after having seen the wonders of the TARDIS, of other worlds, other *universes*, without going mad?

'Stay away from the Downs for a couple of days, just to be sure.'

A shadow of fear passed over Malahyde's face. 'Don't worry, I will.'

'And keep up the poetry,' said the Doctor. He winked at Anji. 'I've a feeling that success isn't far away.'

And with that he stepped out of the TARDIS with Malahyde, and returned alone.

Malahyde appeared on the screen, stumbling backwards away from the TARDIS. The cat arched its back and hissed at him, and Malahyde jumped.

He stood staring at the TARDIS for a moment, the picture of dejection. Then he took a step towards the TARDIS, obviously thought better of it, turned and ran away into the drizzly distance.

The Doctor sighed. 'Another loose end tidied up.'

'Is that true? What you said about his poetry?' said Anji.

The Doctor looked at her. 'Have you ever heard of him?'

Anji shook her head.

'Neither have I,' said the Doctor, looking at the scanner screen. Malahyde had gone, vanished into obscurity. 'Neither have I.'

Fitz slumped down on his bed and closed his eyes. In his mind, he saw the world he remembered: those endless hours on the Watchtower. The occasional skirmish with the band of outlaws. Drinking with Robin. He opened his eyes, and saw his guitar. He reached over, picked it up, and without thinking, began to strum away, thrashing his fingers against the strings. To his surprise, he found himself playing a tune. Lyrics came into his head: 'I thought love was only true in fairy tales...' He sang, his voice wavering all round the notes. He bashed through the whole song, his voice growing louder, more confident, his fingers forming the chords without effort. He hit the final chord with a flourish and sat with his hand resting on the body of the guitar, staring down at the fretboard, until the notes had faded completely away.

'Where did *that* come from?' he muttered to himself. Now he thought about it he could remember more songs: 'Black Magic Woman' – 'Imagine' – 'Bad Moon Rising' – 'Wish You Were Here' – 'Ticket To Ride' – 'Railway Shoes' – 'Brand New Start' – they all came flooding back.

And with them memories – memories of sitting in this very room when times were bad, when playing his guitar had been his only solace.

He thought of Robin again, of his home in Totterdown. It seemed so real – but then he couldn't deny that this place was real too, that Anji and the Doctor were as much part of his life as the people of Totterdown.

His mouth was dry with fear. Was he losing his mind? What if he never fully remembered where he belonged? What if more memories came to him, of other Fitz Kreiners in other worlds? Was this what schizophrenia was like, in the beginning?

He remembered his mother, in a dim, dusty room in a big house – an institution –

But he had been an orphan – he had never known his mother –

Fitz strummed another chord, began another song, if only for something to do, if only to prevent himself thinking too much. 'I'm gonna clear out my head…'

Anji poked her head round the door.

He stopped playing immediately.

'No, don't stop,' she said. 'I like that song.'

Fitz hugged the guitar. Anji. Where did she fit in his life? His *lives*. 'What do you want?'

'Fitz, don't be like this.'

'Be like what?'

'A stranger.'

Fitz shrugged. 'That's how you seem to me.' He sighed. 'No, it isn't. I know I know you, but I can't remember all the details.'

She sat on the bed next to him. 'How much *do* you remember?'

He found himself strangely affected by her intimacy. Scared and excited at the same time, and something else – something he should remember but couldn't. How close had they been? 'Bits. It's like I've led two lives – one with you and the Doctor, one in Totterdown.'

'Only one of them is real,' said Anji. 'And please don't ask me to tell you which.'

'Robin was my friend. A lot like me – liked a pint, liked the ladies. And now he's gone forever. Never existed. Thanks to the Doctor.'

'Look. Fitz. Watchlar was about to destroy the whole universe – the Doctor had to stop it. At all costs.'

'Huh,' said Fitz. 'Seems to me like the "wrong" reality was on a hiding to nothing. Either Watchlar would have destroyed it – or the Doctor would have wiped it out to stop him. Her. It.' Fitz sniffed. 'Which is what's happened, actually.' He looked around. 'Anyway, how can we be sure that *this* is the "right" reality?'

Anji closed her eyes. 'How can anyone be sure of anything?' She opened them. 'The Doctor seems to think it is.'

'The Doctor's just wiped out the place I came from –' He held up a hand. 'Hear me out. OK, the place I remember I came from. I don't think I trust the guy any more – or put it this way, I don't even remember if I *used* to trust him.'

'You did, Fitz. I'm the distrustful one. Usually. And in this case.'

'So you don't trust him either?'

Anji looked into the distance. 'Not totally. Because of something he did. Something that made me realise…' She sighed, twisting her fingers together. When she spoke again, her voice was choked with emotion. 'We're expendable, Fitz. All of us. Even the Doctor. Oh, he still cares about us, but in the wider scheme of things that just doesn't matter.'

Fitz picked up his guitar again, gaining reassurance from the feel of its body against his. 'What *does* matter?'

'Saving the Time Vortex. And if we have to die to do it…'

'That's fine then,' Fitz muttered.

Anji stood. She nodded towards the door. 'Anyway. We'd better get back to the console room.'

'Why?'

'We're about to take off again. Go forward to 2003. See if the real reality has, er, stuck. The Doctor's got an uncomfortable feeling that now he's rescued Malahyde, the Eternines might manage to abduct someone else – and the whole thing might happen all over again.'

Fitz groaned. 'Trust the Doctor to think of that.'

'So you remember what he's like. Coming, then?'

Fitz shook his head. 'I'm staying here with my guitar for a bit.' He patted it. 'At least I know I can rely on that.'

Anji smiled at him. But her eyes looked scared. Then she was gone.

Fitz fingered another chord and strummed. A discord. The guitar was out of tune, the new top E-string must have stretched. He reached for the tuning peg, gave it a tentative turn – and the string snapped.

19 July 1843

Isambard Kingdom Brunel woke with a jolt. An anxious face peered down at him. From somewhere ahead came the sound of a powerful steam engine.

'Isambard? Are you all right?'

Brunel struggled to sit up. To his left, a window, green countryside flashing past under a cloudless blue sky.

Brunel immediately recognised the speaker. 'Gooch! Who's driving the train, man?'

Gooch waved a soot-blackened hand. 'Don't worry about that! Are you all right?'

Brunel struggled to stand, but his legs felt weak. Images flashed through his mind: the Doctor, his fantastic time engine, the strange dark other world, the girl Anji... and Jared Malahyde... the Process... but even as he tried to recall them, the memories began to melt away like ice in boiling water.

'Malahyde...'

Gooch frowned. 'Who? What's wrong with you?'

'Nothing, man!'

Gooch sighed, exasperated, but his eyes were worried. 'Out on the footplate, you fainted. Dead to the world! Had to carry you back here.'

'Fainted?' Brunel bridled. 'Never!' He tried to stand again, this time with success. 'Where are we going?' he mumbled as he stared out at the passing countryside.

Gooch was amazed. 'We're going to Bristol! For the launch of your ship, man!'

'What ship?'

'*The SS Great Britain!*'

'But she was launched in... is this 1838?'

'Is this some sort of joke?'

Brunel wasn't used to being spoken to in such a way, but Daniel Gooch, apart from being a worthy business associate, was also a close acquaintance.

Brunel marshalled his thoughts. 'Sorry old chap. I don't know what came over me out there. Of course!' he laughed. 'It is eighteen hundred and forty-three and we are on our way to Bristol.'

Gooch smiled but his gaze remained uncertain.

'Come on then man, I'm ready to go back to the footplate.'

Gooch led him up the train to the cab.

Brunel stood behind the controls, staring out at the shining rails leading off into the distance, the steam from the funnel rushing by. The familiar smell of burning coal filled his head. The sights and sounds reassured him more than usual, as if in some strange way all this – the speeding train, the English countryside – had been in some sort of peril.

He wished there was some way he could tell the Doctor that everything was safe now. Tell him that...

Isambard Kingdom Brunel frowned. The Doctor?

Who was he?

Acknowledgements

Thanks to:

Justin Richards and Jac Rayner. This was a long road, but one well worth travelling. Thank you for helping to make the destination something special.

The read-through squad: Peter Anghelides, Simon Guerrier, Paul Leonard, Mark Michalowski, Ian Potter, John Rivers, Paul Vearncombe.

Special thanks to Paul Leonard for his support and friendship during the writing of this book.

Special Mentions:

Bristol Fiction Writers: Paul Leonard, Mark Leyland, Christina Lake.

Bristol SF Group: (deep breath here goes): Ken, Clarrie, John and Phil (the Bristol Tav), Chris and Doug, Richard and Tina, Dave, Steve, Brian, Jane, Nathan, Tim (though I haven't seen him for ages), Sue and Graham.

Various Bristol public houses: The George in Totterdown (where some of this book was written - guess which bits), the Reckless Engineer (for obvious reasons), and the Scotchman And His Pack (where Bristol SF Group meet every Thursday).

Rodger Fowler for the loan of L.T.C. Rolt's excellent book on Brunel and other research help, Ben Woodhams for translation advice, and Ken Shinn for coming up with the idea for the cover. Last, but certainly not least, Paul McGann - Fall fan!

About the Author

Nick Walters lives in (the real) Totterdown in Bristol. It's nothing like the place described in this book (except on Saturday nights). This is his fourth Doctor Who novel.

BBC DOCTOR WHO BOOKS

THE ADVENTURESS OF HENRIETTA STREET by Lawrence Miles
ISBN 0 563 53842 2
MAD DOGS AND ENGLISHMEN by Paul Magrs
ISBN 0 563 53845 7
HOPE by Mark Clapham ISBN 0 563 53846 5
ANACHROPHOBIA by Jonathan Morris ISBN 0 563 53847 3
TRADING FUTURES by Lance Parkin ISBN 0 563 53848 1
HE BOOK OF THE STILL by Paul Ebbs ISBN 0 563 53851 1
THE CROOKED WORLD by Steve Lyons ISBN 0 563 53856 2
HISTORY 101 by Mags L. Halliday ISBN 0 563 53854 6
CAMERA OBSCURA by Lloyd Rose ISBN 0 563 53857 0
TIME ZERO by Justin Richards ISBN 0 563 53866 X
THE INFINITY RACE by Simon Messingham ISBN 0 563 53859 7
THE DOMINO EFFECT by David Bishop ISBN 0 563 53869 4

SHORT STORY COLLECTIONS

SHORT TRIPS ed. Stephen Cole ISBN 0 563 40560 0
MORE SHORT TRIPS ed. Stephen Cole ISBN 0 563 55565 3
SHORT TRIPS AND SIDE STEPS
ed. Stephen Cole and Jacqueline Rayner ISBN 0 563 55599 8

The Worlds of Doctor Who
April 2003 – Also this month

From BBC Video:

Meglos

by John Flanagan and Andrew McCulloch

Featuring the Fourth Doctor, Romana and K9

From BBC DVD:

The Talons of Weng-Chiang

by Robert Holmes

Featuring the Fourth Doctor and Leela

From Big Finish Productions:

Doctor Who and the Pirates

by Jacqueline Rayner

Featuring the Sixth Doctor and Evelyn

Doctor Who Books Telepress
covers, reviews, news & interviews
http://www.bbc.co.uk/cult/doctorwho/books/
telepress

Coming soon from
BBC *Doctor Who* books:

Loving the Alien
By Mike Tucker & Robert Perry
Published May 5th 2003
ISBN 0 563 48604 X
Featuring the Seventh Doctor and Ace

*Ace is dead. Or at least she will be - soon…. In a secret
room deep inside the TARDIS the Doctor has been
examining the body of Ace's future self. He knows how
she was killed, where she was killed and when she was
killed. What he doesn't know is why…*

*To find the truth the Doctor makes a dangerous
decision and takes the unsuspecting Ace to the very
time and place of her death, hoping to cheat Time and
find her killer before he can strike - but Time has other
ideas. With Ace missing and the clock ticking the Doctor
turns to old friends for help and finds that there is
unfinished business for him to deal with.*

*What is the secret experiment being conducted by the
British Rocket Group? Why are giant ants appearing in
the suburbs of 1950's London? Who is the mysterious
figure that is watching the Doctor's every move?*

*As events spiral out of control the Doctor realises that
someone is manipulating time with careless disregard
for the consequences to Ace - or the rest of the
universe…*